The Secr

The Scottish Highlands Series

Winter in the Scottish Highlands

The Secrets of the Glen

Return to the Lake House

AUTHOR'S NOTE

This series is best read sequentially to enjoy the story arc as it was intended.

The Secrets of the Glen is the second book

The Secrets of the Glen

The Scottish Highlands Series

Book II

ELISE DARCY

Penny Lane Press

ISBN 978-1-913147-28-0

"Your life does not get better by chance, it gets better by change."–*Jim Rohn*

1

Robyn fastened the buckle and looked up at David, who was holding out his hands. He helped her up. Her feet were unsteady. 'I really don't think this is a good idea.'

'There's nothing to it,' David assured her. 'Just glide …' He started moving backwards, pulling her along.

Robyn faced him, arms outstretched, holding both his hands, her legs motionless beneath her, her bum sticking out to cushion an inevitable fall. But to her surprise, she didn't fall. She stood up straighter, feeling more confident. She tentatively moved first her right foot, then her left, as she skated on the ice.

'There you go.' David spoke words of encouragement. 'Are you sure you haven't done this before?'

Robyn frowned at the question. She didn't know whether she had or not. Her memories since before the car accident on Christmas Day had not come back. Dr Jamieson at the hospital had told her she had something called selective amnesia, suggesting that although she'd suffered a blow to the head, and she was recovering from that, it was a combination of the physical and psychological trauma of the accident, and possibly of events preceding it, that had caused her memory loss to continue. It was the day after New Year's Day, and it had been playing on her mind since the car accident a week ago yesterday. What had happened before the accident that had been so terrible that she'd had to bury it deep in her subconscious, along with all her memories from her past? She hadn't even remembered her own name. Luckily for her, the police had run her number plate through the system and knew who the car belonged to.

Unfortunately, her purse with her driving licence and bank cards were missing, presumably lost in the accident. It was pitch dark, and her handbag must have been thrown from the car in the crash on the country road outside Aviemore. She had returned to the scene of the accident on New Year's Eve, passing by the spot where there were skid marks on the road. It was David who had saved her, pulling her free from the car.

She didn't know why she had been driving along that road alone on Christmas Day. She'd crashed into David's expensive sports car, writing it off. But, on returning to the scene, she'd also wondered what David had been doing there. He'd refused to answer that question, and when he'd asked *her*, she hadn't answered either – not because she didn't want to, but because she couldn't remember. She hadn't told him about her memory loss.

But questioning David further about the accident had precipitated their first row. They'd been getting on so well. David had been visiting her in hospital every day until she was discharged, and had then taken her to a New Year's Eve party. They'd even had their first kiss the previous day, New Year's Day, just after midnight.

Fortunately, their falling-out had all blown over, but it had raised questions about what secrets David was keeping. She'd assumed that she had lost control and ploughed into David's car, which had been coming from the other direction, but the skid marks suggested another story. Had she been trying to avoid him, and he was the one who'd lost control?

After that argument, when he'd been on the defensive over her questions, she hadn't brought it up again. But it had made her wonder for a time whether he'd been visiting her in hospital because he'd felt guilty. Even if that had been the case to begin with, though, those visits had quickly blossomed into the beginnings of a relationship. There was no denying they'd been instantly attracted to one another.

Still holding her hand, David came closer and turned to face forward so that he was skating beside her. 'That's it – glide …' he said again motioning at his own feet and encouraging her to take larger strides.

Fewer people were overtaking them now as Robyn started to match David's stride. She was beginning to skate more confidently. After a while, she took her eyes off her feet and smiled at David before casting her gaze about her. 'The scenery is just stunning.'

'I knew you'd love it here,' David replied.

The small frozen loch was surrounded by pine trees, the snow-capped Cairngorm mountains rising up in the distance. This place was just too wonderful to forget. 'I don't think I've been here before.'

'Oh, I know you've never been here before.'

'How would you know, for sure?' Robyn said. She felt defensive, as she couldn't be a hundred per cent sure herself.

'It's a closely guarded secret. Just us locals come to this place. Otherwise, there'd be a stampede. The frozen loch is too small to accommodate people in large numbers. And unsafe.'

Robyn looked at him sharply.

'Don't worry. I've been coming here in the New Year ever since I was a kid. It's like a tradition among us locals. Mind you, I wouldn't be surprised if some people who aren't in the know spot us from the road and venture down here. I mean, the place *is* lit up like a Christmas tree.'

Robyn could see what he meant; dotted around the circumference of the loch, placed a few metres apart, were a variety of large vehicles owned by the locals. On each one was mounted a large spotlight. It was like something out of a fugitive movie; they were the biggest and brightest lamps she had ever seen. The loch road wasn't far away. Anyone driving past was bound to spot the strange lights through the trees.

'But we do our best to keep it a secret.'

Robyn nodded, thinking, *more secrets.* Her gaze shifted to David's bad knee. She frowned. Unbeknown to him, she'd spied him using a walking stick to climb into his van. She guessed he had good days and bad days with the injury that had ended his promising ice hockey career.

'Look,' David whispered in her ear. He was holding up both hands.

'What?' Robyn asked, not sure what he was getting at.

'No hands. See?' David laughed.

'Oh.' Robyn felt her legs go all wobbly when she realised what David meant; he was no longer holding her hand.

'Whoa.' David caught her. 'Let's try again.'

David let go before Robyn could protest. He said, 'I think you *have* done this before.'

'Well, perhaps I have,' she said, trying to sound light-hearted, as though she was just having some fun with him. She felt guilty for not letting him into the secret that she'd lost her memory, even though he had secrets of his own. Although she knew he'd busted his knee and could no longer play professional ice hockey, and that he was back in his home town, where he'd invested in a house with his earnings from the game and was working at his father's general store, she still didn't know what exactly had happened when he had been landed in hospital with a shattered knee and a shattered career. He didn't want to talk about that. She'd assumed the injury had happened during a hockey game.

She looked at David, holding her hand, and said, 'Are you sure you should be on the ice?'

'What do you mean?'

Robyn looked ahead, concentrating on keeping her balance as she said, 'Don't you have to be careful with your knee? What if you fall?'

David grinned. 'I can assure you that I won't fall. I've had years and years of skating practice.'

That was one thing Robyn did know. David had told her all about his father putting a bat in his hand when he was very young. Then, all through school, it had been practice, practice, practice, fuelling David's resentment towards his younger brother, now a local police officer, who'd had a 'normal' childhood and adolescence. Robyn had pointed out to David that perhaps his brother, Joe, had some resentments of his own. After all, their dad had spent most of his time with David at ice hockey practice, which must have left little time for his other son.

'Hey!' someone shouted out. 'Hey – you guys!'

Across the frozen ice, Robyn could see a man waving at them. 'There's Joe!' Robyn exclaimed, recognising David's brother, who was standing with a group on the far side of the frozen loch. She'd met him at the party on New Year's Eve in the village of Granton-on-Spey. David had taken her there for a night out, which hadn't quite gone to plan. He had introduced her to his horrible dad – Mr Gillespie. The old man had barely acknowledged her presence. He had been so rude. David had clearly thought so too, because he and his father had got into an argument, which had ended with his dad punching him in the face. Luckily, Joe had intervened.

'I'm sorry.'

David took her hand, and they both skated to a stop at the edge of the loch. 'What for?'

'About that.' She turned to face him, pointing above his eye, where he'd been punched in the face by his father.

'It's not your fault, Robyn,' he paused. 'I have always had this way of provoking my father, bringing out the worst in both of us. I wish I hadn't introduced you to him. I don't know what I was thinking.'

Robyn decided to let it go at that. She had learnt that there were two sore points with David that were just not worth bringing up. One was his ice hockey, and the other was his father.

Robyn glanced across the loch at Joe. 'Why didn't you tell me your brother, Joe, is a police officer?'

'Why – are you in some kind of trouble or something?' David said, smiling at his own joke.

Robyn laughed nervously, 'Of course not.' The problem was that Robyn didn't know. Was she? What or who had she been fleeing from on Christmas Day?

Robyn didn't want to think about that. She changed the subject. 'I'm glad our matching bandages have come off.'

He'd had a cut from the fight, and a bandage, which had

matched Robyn's bandage from her car accident injuries. Their wounds had been checked and their bandages removed. Now, they couldn't be made fun of, in a good-natured way, by the occupants of Lark Lodge, the place where she was staying, thanks to her other hospital visitor, whom she'd met by chance: Gayle, a middle-aged, single, former nurse, who had returned home to Scotland to care for her elderly parents. Her father, a former local GP, had been in hospital over Christmas and had sadly passed away. The funeral would be at the end of the week.

Robyn thought it wasn't the best start to the New Year for Gayle, organising her father's funeral. But Gayle had been stoical, saying *such is life*. She had mentioned that at least her father had wished to be laid to rest in his beloved adopted country, Scotland, and she hadn't had to return with his ashes to Trinidad, a country she'd never been to. Gayle had been born in Scotland, unlike her older twin brothers and her sister, who had accompanied their parents to England on a boat in the sixties – part of the Windrush generation.

At least you'll get to meet my brothers and sister, Gayle had said.

Robyn wasn't sure she wanted to – not after what they'd discovered in the basement of Gayle's parents' house. Sadly, Gayle's mum, Doris, had dementia, which meant that the possibility the house would have to be sold to pay for her care was looming large. In the basement, it had become apparent that her brothers and sister were already anticipating the inevitable, along with the fact that she was quite elderly and might not have long to live. They'd packed up some of their mother's valuables, dividing them between themselves in boxes marked with their names.

Robyn thought it was despicable that they'd done that already, and worse, that they hadn't included Gayle, the baby of the family, in their decision. Gayle had only discovered them because Robyn had come across the boxes in search of family photos; Robyn had wanted to see how the house had looked before it became rather run down.

She wondered what Gayle's siblings would think of the plan to turn their childhood home into a guesthouse. It wasn't exactly official, and it hadn't started out as Gayle's idea. Robyn wanted to do up the house, redecorating a room at a time. It was a big old house, with plenty of spare bedrooms that could earn Gayle and her mum some extra money. She already had two houseguests – neither of them exactly planned.

Robyn, Gayle's first guest, didn't pay rent. Gayle had insisted that she was a friend, and could stay as long as she liked, even though she'd only met her just over a week earlier. Robyn had readily accepted going home with Gayle when she was discharged. She didn't want to return to her university, St Andrews, just yet. She'd discovered she was an undergraduate there – the police had found that her car was registered with an address at the university's halls of residence. Robyn had decided that redecorating the house would be her way of repaying Gayle's kindness, if Gayle would let her. She really liked Gayle.

Robyn also liked Joe. She smiled across at him as she skated. He was quite different to David in appearance – he was shorter, stockier, and blond. David said his brother took after his father's side, he after his mother. But Joe and his brother were both nice, kind, caring guys. They didn't get that from their father, in Robyn's opinion.

David waved at Joe and took Robyn's hand. He said, 'I think he'll probably come over. Let's stop a moment. He's a pretty good skater, but he does sometimes go a little too fast, and I'd rather he didn't plough into us.'

Robyn nodded. She got the impression that had happened to David in the past. Standing with him on the edge of the loch, out of the way of those skating in a wide circle, her eyes darted around the skaters to see if there was anyone else she recognised. She'd suddenly had a horrible thought: was Joe there with their dad?

She turned to David and just had to ask, 'Is your father here too?'

David furiously shook his head. 'This is the last place he'd come.'

Robyn wasn't surprised when David didn't elaborate on that comment. She imagined that the last thing his father would want to see was his once-famous ice hockey star son skating, reminding him what might have been if he hadn't been injured.

Robyn breathed a sigh of relief as she watched Joe turn to a young woman she hadn't seen before, who was dressed warmly in blue waterproof trousers, a blue-and-white ski jacket, and a red knitted bobble hat that didn't match her outfit. Robyn guessed, by the colour of the hat and the fact that it looked hand-knitted, that she might have been given it as a Christmas present.

The young woman waved back. Then they both left the group and skated across the ice.

'I didn't think you were going to make it,' said Joe, skidding to a controlled stop in front of them. He eyed Robyn.

She looked away, feeling her cheeks growing hot, despite the freezing temperature. David must have mentioned to his brother that he'd invited her, but that he'd had to convince her to come.

It wasn't just that, though, that had made her cheeks flush. She looked at Joe anxiously, wondering when he would learn the details of the accident on Christmas Day. Joe hadn't been at work over Christmas and New Year. She expected he might find out on his return. The police officer who'd interviewed her before she was discharged from hospital knew about her memory loss, and she realised that on Joe's return to work, he might hear about it too. She hoped not. At least not before she told David.

So far, she hadn't summoned the courage to tell him. She knew why. She didn't want David fussing over her or trying to come up with suggestions to get her memory back. She wasn't sure she wanted whatever she'd buried deep down in her subconscious to come back. If that meant all her memories before the accident wouldn't come back either, then so be it. She felt happy living in Gayle's family home, and she had a job lined up doing some interior design on a house belonging to a lovely old couple – Rose and George. She didn't want anything to jeopardise her new life; least of all someone from her past.

She tried to keep her expression neutral at the thought that there must be someone out there, someone she had been with. She only knew this because Dr Jamieson had told her that she had been pregnant, but that she'd lost the pregnancy in the accident. She hadn't been too far gone, but that wasn't the point. She must have had a partner, a boyfriend. Which begged the question – why hadn't he been with her in the car on the day of the accident? Had she been running away from him on Christmas Day? Was the fact that she'd even consider this possibility her subconscious telling her it was true?

She still couldn't remember his name or picture his face. Her mind was still keeping secrets. She felt strangely thankful. If something bad had happened, or had been about to, before she'd sped away in the car, she did not want to remember. Whatever or whoever she'd been running away from, she'd decided she didn't want to go back – ever.

'It took a bit of encouragement,' David said.

For a moment, Robyn was at a loss as to what David was talking about, until the young woman with Joe smiled and said, 'It took a bit of encouragement to get me out ice skating this evening too. To be honest, I was quite happy curled on the sofa with a novel in front of the fire, although now I'm here, I don't regret coming at all.'

Robyn returned her smile. She felt exactly the same.

2

She led me a merry dance, pretending she hadn't skated before. Either that, or she's taken remarkably well to ice skating if this is her first time.'

Now everybody's eyes were on Robyn. She felt her cheeks glowing red, and it wasn't because of the cold. She didn't want to be put on the spot if Joe or the lady with him asked if she had skated before. Robyn turned to the young lady and deflected the comment. She said, 'Hi, I don't think we've met.'

The young woman had wisps of jet-black hair escaping from the woolly hat, an angular face, a small button nose, pale complexion and dark brown eyes.

She hesitated. Then, glancing at Joe, she said, 'I'm Annie – Joe's wife.'

'Pleased to meet you, Annie. I'm Robyn – but then I guess you already knew that.'

'Yeah – shame my Joe clearly doesn't talk about me all the time like David does you.'

Robyn could feel her face flush with embarrassment again. This time, she was quite happy to hear it. She glanced at David, who looked embarrassed too. *Good. Now it's his turn*, she thought.

She smiled at Annie. 'So, how long have you two been together?'

'Oh, god. Like forever. Since high school, when we were fourteen.'

David sighed. 'Yeah – they're one of those annoying couples that met when they were young – and stayed together. Stop being so smug, you two,' he said light heartedly.

Joe replied, 'Well, until the accident, that was you and—' He stopped abruptly.

Robyn looked at him curiously before turning to David. His expression had clouded over. The conversation had clearly gone places David didn't want – that much was obvious. He was shaking his head at his brother; whoever he had been with before, the topic was clearly now off-limits.

Annie frowned at Joe and gave him a friendly punch in the arm.

'Ow! What was that for?' Joe said, nursing his arm.

For a moment, Robyn assumed it was for bringing up David's ex, but instead, Annie said, 'For not telling Robyn about me when you met her on New Year's Eve. And don't be such a baby. My little punch wasn't that hard!' She rolled her eyes. 'Honestly – men! Who'd have 'em?'

Robyn smiled. It was quite funny seeing this little skinny slip of a woman, who was five-foot-nothing, beating up her husband, although she wasn't really doing that. It was all just good-humoured fun.

'You're meant to introduce me, Joe.'

'But you introduced yourself, hon.'

She rolled her eyes again. Ignoring him, Annie turned to Robyn, 'Honestly.' She said again casting her eyes up as she linked her arm in Robyn's. 'So, tell me all about yourself.'

Robyn didn't like the way she dragged out the word *all* or the way she seemed to be just too friendly for a first meeting. Robyn couldn't put her finger on it, but something was making her feel uncomfortable. She turned to David to be rescued, but he was no longer beside her. David and Joe and had drifted in front of them, skating ahead together.

'You skate pretty well. For a first-timer,' Annie said, matching her stride.

'Thank you.' Robyn glanced at her, avoiding eye contact. She wished Annie would let go of her arm. She watched the other skaters and waited for the questions to begin; questions like *where are you from? What are you doing here?* Or more to the point, *what are you doing here with David?* Perhaps she shouldn't be surprised that Joe and Annie were protective of David – after all, she'd just found out that his last girlfriend had dumped him after the accident, once he was no longer a rising ice hockey star, with all the trappings – meaning money – that went with it.

But Robyn wasn't like that. She knew that David wasn't now earning whatever professional ice hockey players earned. All he had was his house, which she hadn't seen yet, and some money he'd squirrelled away in investments. She couldn't imagine he was working for his dad, doing grocery deliveries, out of the goodness of his heart, although he had said he wanted to help his father out. But even so, Robyn imagined he needed the money.

Robyn happened to glance over to her left at the people milling around on the shore of the loch. She thought she saw two familiar faces as she skated by. 'Hey, isn't that Rose and George Gordon?' she said.

Annie clearly knew them too. 'Oh yes! So it is.'

'Are they here to go ice skating too?' Robyn said in surprise. She hoped she wasn't being ageist, but they were getting on, and the majority of people skating were a lot younger: couples, young families, and those in middle-age.

She did notice that Rose and George weren't wearing skates. They were standing by a pop-up café – an old VW van that was selling hot chocolate and hot dogs in buns.

She waved at them. 'You know, I'd like a hot chocolate too.' Robyn had had enough of skating for one evening, and she wanted to escape any awkward questions Annie might have in store.

Annie waved at them too. 'All right, let's go and get a hot chocolate.'

Robyn frowned. She'd rather go by herself. Still, she was sure George and Rose would prove a distraction.

They skated to the edge of the loch and sat down on a log to remove their skates. Robyn had her shoes in a backpack on her back. So did Annie. They left the skates by the log.

'Will they be okay, left there?' Robyn asked. She'd borrowed the skates from David. She hadn't asked how come he had a pair that were not his size. They were definitely women's skates. She imagined they'd belonged to the girlfriend he didn't want Joe talking about.

Annie waved away her question with a flick of the hand. 'Yeah – they'll be fine.'

'I'd have thought Rose and George would be at home, snuggled in front of a fire, or, I don't know, tucked up in bed,' Robyn said, although she was happy to see them.

'Oh, don't be surprised.' Annie said in high spirits. 'This is always quite a big event. We get an extra bank holiday the day after New Year's Day here in Scotland, so there's an extra day to organise all this.' Her free arm flicked out, gesturing at the convoy of vehicles.

'Yes, I can see that,' Robyn agreed.

'My Joe organises it all, and of course, it all has to be pretty hush-hush around town. Isn't that right, Rose?'

'What was that?' Rose and George turned around simultaneously. 'Oh, Annie. We saw you skating with Robyn.'

Annie smiled. 'Then we spotted you guys with your steaming cups of hot chocolate, and we just had to have some too.'

Annie said to the lady serving the drinks, 'Two hot chocolates, please.'

The lady serving them was super-quick. Annie turned around with two takeaway cups, and handed one to Robyn.

Robyn took hers and sidled up to George, putting the couple between her and Annie, thereby avoiding further interrogation from Annie. At least she was right: the older couple were proving a welcome distraction.

Annie lowered her voice as they walked towards the loch with their drinks. 'I was saying, Rose,' Annie continued, 'that if word got out about this event, then we'd have the out-of-towners descending on this place like a swarm.'

'Oh dear, oh dear,' Rose said, shaking her head. 'We can't have that – can we, George?'

'No, my dear.'

'I can see why people would want to come,' Robyn said, taking a seat on a large log in front of the loch. She sat next to George, and Rose sat on his other side with Annie beside her. She sipped the delicious hot chocolate, watching the skaters glide past. 'It's so beautiful and atmospheric.'

'I'm glad you appreciate it,' Annie said, 'because Joe put up a real fight for you to come.'

'He did?' Robyn looked at Annie. 'How come?'

'Because you, young lady,' Rose intervened, 'must have caused quite a stir.'

'I have?'

'You're an out-of-towner, of course,' Annie said.

'It's that strict?' Robyn said to both of them.

'You have no idea,' Anne continued.

'It's the rules,' said Rose.

Next to Robyn, George was listening to the conversation and nodding his head.

Robyn hadn't realised she'd caused so much trouble. And to think that she'd nearly not bothered going at all.

'Still, Joe had a bit of leeway on his side,' Annie said. 'You *are* living with Gayle and her mum. Gayle's parents are really well known in these parts. As you know, her father was a local GP, served the community for years, working well into retirement.'

'That's right,' commented Rose. 'Such a lovely man. Shame, though, that he didn't have many years of retirement before he passed away.'

George said, 'I think his work was his life. I remember he was always so jovial. I just think he loved what he did, and probably couldn't imagine retiring.'

'Well, he's certainly retired now,' said Rose, 'permanently.'

They all fell silent.

'Are you going to his funeral?' Robyn asked, glancing at each one of them in turn.

They all nodded. Annie said, 'I think there's going to be a large turnout.'

'Are *you*?' George asked.

'Although I didn't know him, Gayle has asked if I will go. So, I will. I want to be there, for her.'

'Good girl,' said Rose, approvingly.

'It's the least I can do, given that Gayle is kindly letting me stay in her family home. But then, you all knew that already.' *Word spreads fast*, Robyn thought, looking at Rose, and narrowing her eyes. David, Rose and George had been the only ones who knew she lived at Gayle's house, along with the other lodger.

Rose was innocently humming a tune as she watched the skaters. Robyn had visited Rose's house with Gayle during Gayle's mobile hairdressing round. Although Gayle had been a nurse for years, and Robyn imagined she could have easily picked up some nursing work in the local community, the hours would not have been flexible enough for Gayle to work around caring for her mum. So she'd fallen back on hairdressing, a skill she'd learnt when she'd first moved to London years earlier, before she'd trained to be a nurse.

'And you're going out with a local,' said Rose. 'And none other than David Gillespie, a very well-known local.'

'Going out?' Robyn nearly spluttered into her hot chocolate. Did she mean *dating*? How did Rose know that? Besides, it had only been one date, if you could call it that – an invitation to a New Year's Eve party, and a kiss just past midnight. She couldn't have thought of a nicer way to see in the New Year than in David's arms, kissing.

She caught George winking at her. Did they know about that too?

'Yeah, the boyfriend/girlfriend thing really capped it, especially as it's David,' said Annie.

Rose chipped in, 'And hasn't poor David been through enough without some petty little rule to spoil things?'

'My Joe said he'd pull out of it otherwise,' Annie said, 'and then of course he'd want to ask someone to go in his place. You know, a gathering like this … you need permission. You can't just turn up, trucks parked on the edge of the loch like this.'

'Oh – Joe is on duty?' Robyn said, surprised.

'In an unofficial capacity, but it's nice to have someone from the department. We've also got an ambulance just a hundred yards away, parked in the car park in the woods on standby, in case there are any falls or cuts and grazes. It may appear quite impromptu, but it's anything but.'

Robyn had no idea. She was also taken aback by all the trouble she appeared to have caused. She wondered if Annie was exaggerating, but Rose seemed to back up what she was saying. In the silence, Robyn searched the faces of the strangers as they skated past, looking for any sign that people were throwing disapproving glances her way, making it plain they thought she shouldn't be there. But there wasn't any of that – just happy, friendly locals have a brilliant time together. No one was taking any notice of the four people sitting on the log and sipping their hot chocolates, chatting together.

Robyn was having a wonderful time too. She was so happy she'd come, even though she had a feeling, from David's past experience with girlfriends, that his family members were on their guard against him getting hurt again. She could understand that. Annie was friendly enough, but unlike Joe, Robyn imagined it might take a bit more time to win her over and become friends.

I'm not going to dump David, she wanted to say. Although at the back of her mind was the possibility that someone she'd been in a relationship with might be out there looking for her.

That wasn't all that was playing on her mind; what would happen if Annie and Joe found out she hadn't been honest with David from the beginning? And what would David think when he found out that she was keeping secrets from him about her memory loss?

'Oh look, George!' Rose spoke. 'There's the McKays.'

Robyn followed Rose's gaze to a couple standing a short distance away, holding takeaway cups as they watched the ice skating. She turned to George. 'Who are they?'

'They used to be my next-door neighbours.'

The older couple waved. They must have spotted Rose and George.

'We must go and say hello.' Rose stood up. 'Come on, George. Let's leave these two youngsters in peace.'

Robyn stood up too. 'Oh, please don't go.' She didn't want to be left alone with Annie and her potentially searching questions.

Rose smiled at Robyn. 'I'm sure you and Annie have interesting things to talk about, rather than making polite conversation with us old folks.'

'Oh no – we like your company,' Robyn protested, glancing at Annie.

'Of course we do,' Annie agreed.

'Well, that's as maybe, but I still want to say hello to my old neighbours. George!'

George was still sitting on the log. He rolled his eyes and grumbled under his breath, 'I was rather enjoying sitting here.' He reluctantly got to his feet.

Rose turned to Robyn. 'You'll be seeing us soon enough – remember?'

Robyn nodded. 'Yeah, tomorrow, as promised.' She was making a start on redecorating their bland new-build property on the new estate just outside Aviemore.

Rose smiled. 'I'm looking forward to it, Robyn, and to seeing all that lovely material for my curtains and upholstery.'

'Oh yes – I'm shopping around for those in the morning,' Robyn reassured her. She hadn't been out shopping yet to find swatches in materials and patterns Rose might like to have her curtains and matching cushions made from, so she wasn't sure where she was going to source them from.

'And we can have a nice long chat then, if you like.'

Robyn smiled knowingly. She knew what Rose meant by a nice long chat. Rose would be after any juicy gossip she had gleaned from Annie. Robyn vowed to herself that she would tell Rose every last juicy piece of gossip that came out of the interrogator's lips. 'Um … is it okay if I come to yours in the afternoon?'

'Of course, Robyn. Whatever time suits you.'

Robyn breathed a sigh of relief. 'Thank you, Rose.'

'No – thank *you* for sticking to the plan of coming over and working at our place.'

Robyn would have to spend the morning searching for a fabric shop.

Rose and George said their goodbyes. Robyn watched them walk over to join their friends. They appeared to be with a group whom Robyn assumed were the other couple's grown-up children, along with their grandchildren.

Seeing their old neighbours' extended family reminded Robyn what the site manager of their new estate, Nick, had said. Rose and George had moved out of their draughty old house into the modern four-bedroomed semi-detached property, thinking that their grandchildren would come to stay. Nick had told her that Rose and George had invited them, but that so far no visitors had turned up. He'd said that they were quite lonely. When he'd knocked on their door while she was visiting with Gayle, and she'd answered it, he'd assumed she was one of their grandchildren.

They'd got into conversation, and Robyn had discovered that Nick had had to leave the bed-and-breakfast where he was staying. He was desperate to find somewhere else close to the development where he worked. The company was paying for his food and accommodation as a business expense.

Robyn hadn't thought twice about offering a room at Gayle's family home – Lark Lodge. It had been extremely wrong of her to do that without Gayle's say-so. She really didn't know what had been going through her mind, other than the fact that when she'd needed a place to stay herself, Gayle had had no qualms about taking her in. She'd just thought that Gayle might take pity on Nick too, especially as he would be a paying guest.

And so, on New Year's Eve, Nick had turned up at Lark Lodge with his suitcase – and something else he'd failed to mention.

Fortunately, Gayle had a soft spot for dogs; puppies in particular. Nick had brought with him the reason he'd been kicked out of his B&B. They'd said they accepted pets, but Nick's pet had eventually become too much for the B&B owners. Olive was an Old English Sheepdog, and although she was still a puppy, she was nearly fully grown, and a very big, albeit soppy, dog. Luckily for Nick, and his big, soppy, affectionate dog, everyone at Lark Lodge loved her – Robyn included, even though she'd had no idea when she'd invited Nick to stay at Gayle's that he would turn up with a dog.

Robyn had a thought as she watched Rose and George talking to their old neighbours. They were lonely in their new house. New neighbours would be moving in soon, when more houses were completed, and hopefully they would make new friends. But in the meantime, Robyn had an idea. Olive was still a puppy and couldn't be left home alone for long. Nick had got away with it for a while at the B&B because the owners' son, who was unemployed and looking for work, had looked after Olive during the day – taking her for walks and being paid rather handsomely, Robyn gathered. Apparently, he'd got a job, starting soon after New Year, which meant doggy daycare would end. That was why Nick had been asked to leave.

They'd all spent New Year's Day together – Robyn, Gayle, Doris, Nick, and David. And Olive. They'd taken a picnic, and hot drinks in flasks, and had gone for a walk around the loch. But nobody had brought up what would happen with Olive when Nick returned to work the next day. Robyn had seen the state of the inside of Nick's car. Olive couldn't be left cooped up in his car for long periods. And she certainly couldn't be left home with Doris at Lark Lodge for extended periods of time. And Gayle couldn't take her along to her mobile hairdressing clients.

But I could take her with me to Rose and George's while I redecorate. Or better still, Nick could drop her off at their house. They had a lovely garden that Olive could play in. And although she was a bit boisterous at times, she was the sweetest, most affectionate dog to have around. She'd be lovely company for Rose and George. And Robyn expected they would be lovely company for

Olive. The dog would get lots of fusses and attention.

'Hey, share the joke.'

'Huh?' Robyn turned to look at Annie, who had moved along the log to sit next to her. Robyn was still grinning from ear to ear. 'Oh, I just had an amazing idea.' Robyn explained her plan.

Annie turned to look over at Rose and George. 'Oh, they're such a dear couple. I think that's a wonderful idea.' Annie paused. 'Do you think they'd manage a dog that size?'

Robyn had already thought of that. 'I'm going to ask Nick. I'm sure he'd walk Olive during his lunch break. All they'd have to do is give her lots of fusses, and let her lounge on their rug in front of the fire.'

'Sounds like what I wish I could do all day,' quipped Annie.

Robyn didn't know what Annie did for a living. She decided she'd ask David rather than getting into a conversation which might veer into her own past, and what she did, and where she'd lived before she'd found herself there. Instead, Robyn returned her attention to the faces of the strangers skating by, still anxious that she wasn't really welcome there. 'Do you think they're cross with me?' Robyn asked. 'Since my presence here forced them to break their golden rule?'

'Don't be silly,' Annie said kindly. 'Like I said before, you're practically one of the locals now.'

Robyn smiled. She liked the sound of that – one of the locals. Looking around at the locals gathered on the frozen loch, and all the work everyone had put in to make it an event for their local community, she couldn't think of anywhere she'd rather be than there, with the local community; her local community – if her past didn't catch up with her.

3

In town, Robyn walked up and down the high street in Aviemore but didn't enter a single shop.

Robyn got in the van and slammed the door shut. 'There isn't a single soft furnishing shop in this place where you can buy curtains, cushions, rugs – that sort of thing.'

'I could have told you that.'

'I know. I just had to see for myself.'

David started the engine. 'Where to?'

Robyn looked at her watch. She'd promised Rose that she'd be round in the afternoon with the swatches. She'd have to turn up empty-handed. 'I need to go to Rose's house, but only if you've got a delivery to make. I don't want you to have to go out of your way.'

'Robyn.' David smirked. 'I'm a long way out of my way already. Besides, how will you get to Rose and George's house otherwise?'

'There's a bus stop there now, so I could get a bus from Aviemore, I think.'

'You think?' David shook his head as he reversed the car out of the parking bay.

'Besides, this has been the best working day I've had in …' he lifted his hands off the steering wheel, 'so long.'

'How come?'

'Having your company, of course.'

Robyn didn't stop smiling all the way to Rose's house.

'How long will you be?' David asked as they drew up outside the house. He looked around. 'Wow, this estate is coming along in leaps and bounds, isn't it? It must be popular. Lots of *sold* boards.'

The *sold* boards didn't surprise Robyn. People were buying properties off-plan, so that the sales would complete by the time the houses were ready to move into. Very soon, Rose and her husband, the first occupants on the new-build development, would have lots of neighbours. Robyn wondered if any of their new neighbours would be interested in her interior design service.

Robyn opened the van door. 'I don't expect I'll be long. I just wanted to let her know that I have to go further afield to source some materials, so I'll go over some colour schemes with her before I do.'

David nodded. 'Sounds like a plan.'

Robyn glanced over her shoulder at the boxes in the back of the van, awaiting delivery. 'Look, I don't want you to get behind with your deliveries.'

'It's okay. I don't mind waiting.'

'Well, all right. I promise I won't be long.' Robyn left him sitting outside in the van.

When Rose opened the door, Robyn realised she must have been at the window and had spotted her arriving. 'I see there's a handsome young man waiting for you in the van. That's David, isn't it?'

Robyn's face flushed. 'Um, yes. He gave me a lift.'

'Well, invite him in. I didn't get a chance to speak with him at the loch the other night when you were ice skating.'

'Perhaps another time. I won't be staying long. I'm afraid I couldn't find what I was looking for in Aviemore, so I'm going to have to travel further afield.'

'Have you brought some swatches for me to be looking at?'

Robyn stood at the front door and bit her lower lip. It was the swatches she'd been talking about. Rose had mentioned there wasn't a fabric shop in Aviemore, but she'd wanted to look herself. 'I haven't got any yet.'

Rose shook her head. 'No matter. It was nice of you to stop by and let me know.' Rose glanced past her at the van. 'Are you sure David can't pop in too?'

'He's on his way to do some deliveries, so he hasn't really got time to stop and chat.' Robyn had intended for it just to be a quick stop. She imagined that if David went in too, Rose would insist on making a pot of tea, and interrogating David – in a nice way. Then the quick visit might go on into the afternoon if she wasn't careful.

'I'd recognise that van anywhere,' commented Rose.

Robyn wasn't surprised. Rose and her husband had lived in the area nearly all their lives. They'd probably seen the Gillespie van out on deliveries. David's father might have made grocery deliveries to their old street, or even to Rose and George themselves in the past.

'David is making deliveries at the moment for his father, Mr Gillespie.'

Rose nodded. 'Like I said, I'd recognise that van anywhere. Unfortunately, I have bumped into his father too on occasion when I've been shopping in Aviemore.'

What did she mean – unfortunately? Robyn wanted to ask. Although she didn't have to; David's father was a mean old man. At least, that had been her experience when she'd met Mr Gillespie on New Year's Eve.

Rose answered an unspoken question. 'He's a skinflint, a tightwad. He must make a lot of money with the extortionate prices he charges in his grocery store. Just because he's one of the few local grocery stores, and has a loyal customer base of people my generation – god knows why they're loyal, though.'

Robyn guessed that Rose didn't do her grocery shopping at Mr Gillespie's store.

She pointed at his van. 'It's men like him that you read in the papers about – they die extremely rich men.'

'Really?' Robyn glanced over her shoulder at the beaten-up old van and thought of the tattered, weather-beaten general store in town. She couldn't imagine David's father having money. If he'd had some once, it sounded as though he'd gambled it away, to the point where he'd lost his home. Now David had a house guest he didn't want – his father.

Robyn bit her lip and decided to keep that to herself.

'Never bought his kids much, you know.'

'What do you mean?'

'At Christmas, he'd go around delivering hampers and gifts with his boys. I recall I'd see him turn up where we used to live in his van, when his boys were young, and sit in the van while his two boys delivered hampers of Christmas food, and gifts, to my neighbours' doors. We had deliveries too, back then, before there were the supermarkets in Aviemore. I remember David being excited about Christmas when his mother was around. Theirs used to be happy Christmases, with a Christmas tree, and tinsel, and the best of all presents. But it all stopped when she disappeared.'

'She disappeared?'

'Just up and left – so the story goes. I remember thinking at the time that I just couldn't see her as the type to leave her little boys behind – not them, with that horrible man.'

❖

'What's got into you? You were really chatty before you spoke to Rose.'

Robyn just shrugged, avoiding eye contact.

When she didn't respond, he answered his own question. 'Some people will always have the capacity to cheese you off if you let them.'

'I like her.' Robyn went on the defensive.

'She speaks!' David attempted to lighten the mood.

'David?' Robyn turned to look at him as they drove back to Aviemore. 'What happened to your mother?'

He eyed her. 'Ah. I see that Rose has been stirring the pot again. She just loves to gossip.'

Robyn thought of the very first time she had seen Rose, her front curtain twitching as they drew up to her house in Gayle's car.

'She left us, to answer your question. Just walked out. Like me, she didn't have … how shall we say, a rapport with my father. But then I don't think many people do.'

'So, you never saw her again?'

David shook his head. 'My father said she wanted to take me with her.'

Robyn wondered what had happened that had made her go and leave her children behind.

'How old were you?'

'Eight – I guess.'

'I'm so sorry.'

'Don't be. If she didn't want to stick around – that was her prerogative.'

Robyn looked at him sharply. Was that bitterness in his voice? She wouldn't be surprised – David's mum had not only left him and Joe but had left them with that horrible man.

Robyn kept her thoughts to herself. Although she did ask, 'Do you remember what happened the day she left?'

David shook his head. 'I woke up one morning, and she was gone.'

'What, like, she packed her suitcases and left suddenly?'

'Oh yeah. I remember checking her wardrobe, not believing my dad, thinking perhaps she'd decided just to pop to the shops in Aviemore, and she'd be back. Except her wardrobe was empty, and all her clothes were gone. Even her favourite souvenirs and ornaments she'd collected over the years – she'd packed them all and taken them with her. All while we were sleeping. My brother and I didn't even get a chance to say goodbye.'

Robyn stared at him. How awful to wake up one morning and find that the life you knew was gone, changed forever. Robyn could empathise, in a way. 'Did she leave you a letter, a note?'

David shook his head.

'I'm sorry.'

'There's nothing to be sorry about.' He shrugged. 'It is what it is.'

'Did you ever try to find her?' Robyn ventured.

David shook his head. 'If she wants to get back in touch, we're still here. I did think that she might see me on TV – the sports news, or something – and maybe she'd get in touch or even return here. But that never happened.'

Robyn had to say it. 'Do you think she didn't come back because she was afraid of your father? Rose said he was mean, and never bothered with Christmas for you and Joe after your mum left.'

'Yeah, when I was younger, it occurred to me, but then as I grew older, all I saw was a man still grieving for the woman he loved. He was a changed man when she left. Before, he was so … different towards us. But once she was gone, it was like someone flicked a switch. All these years later, I think he is still grieving. He still goes for long drives in the evening.'

'Long drives?'

'Yeah. I didn't realise until we lived together again for the first time in years. He used to do that late at night when he thought we were asleep. I'd hear the car and see him go out.'

David fell silent as he started the engine and drove out of the development.

Robyn sighed. 'Your life sounds as though it really changed without your mum around.' She didn't know what else to say.

'Oh, yeah. Not just my life, but my dad's too, like I said.' He glanced at Robyn. 'I guess that's not surprising, losing the love of your life. And not only that, but he had a full-time business to run and two young boys to bring up all on his own. Who can blame him for not having the time to build a rapport with people?'

Robyn couldn't believe he was making excuses for his father.

'That didn't have to stop him building a rapport with his sons.'

David countered that comment. 'I think the life they had together wasn't easy – the general store involved long hours of work, and that was when it was open, even before the stock-taking, ordering, and balancing the books when the store was closed. I wouldn't be surprised if a part of him resented her just walking out and leaving her family – something I remember him saying to us, soon after she'd left. He said that he'd never leave us.'

That surprised Robyn.

'I think, in hindsight, maybe he wanted me to become this famous star, to prove he had been a success, you know, prove to the world that he had successfully raised his sons. And maybe as a message to my mother, wherever she was.'

Robyn thought about this. 'Or maybe he just wanted the money.'

'What money?'

'You know, from you being this big sports star.'

'I don't think so.'

'How can you be so sure?'

'Because I told him that I was going to make sure, whatever I earned, he never got a dime.' He smiled.

From what he'd told her about his childhood – his father forcing him to practise, practise, practise, to forego a normal childhood and adolescence for the sake of ice hockey – she wasn't surprised that he'd made sure his father never shared the financial gains.

Robyn thought of his flashy sports car that she'd driven into on Christmas Day. 'You spent it all, didn't you?'

'Yes, most of it, after I squirrelled away some money in long-term investments. Just to be sure I wouldn't be tempted if he ever asked.'

'And did he?' Robyn said, 'Ask – I mean?'

David didn't answer immediately. 'No.' He glanced at her again. I had pictured it so many times, the satisfaction I'd get from finally telling him to take a hike, actually just saying *no* to his face, if he asked.'

Robyn stared at him.

'That sounds pretty awful, doesn't it?'

'Actually, it sounded,' she giggled, 'I'm sorry,' she giggled some more, 'pretty funny.'

'Childish.'

'Yes.'

'Well, needless to say, he didn't get any money. I put it all into my house, and some stock market investments.'

'And your pretty sports car that I wrecked.'

'Yeah – that too.' He smiled. 'But seriously, I can't sit on my hands all day, doing nothing, so in the end I'm doing exactly what I vowed never to do, and that's help him out.'

Robyn sat reflecting on what she'd just heard. She knew that David wasn't just helping his father out at the store, but putting a roof over his head too. She could imagine the tensions at home.

She'd first found that out when he'd driven her home to Gayle's after their night out together on New Year's Eve. David had jokingly asked if there was a room free at Lark Lodge.

It hadn't been Gayle's intention to turn it into a guesthouse, but with demand in the area, and with Robyn and Nick staying there already, Gayle was coming round to the idea. She did love the company. And it was a lovely old house. It was little wonder that David found the thought of moving in appealing.

Even though it sounded as though David understood that his father was bitter because his wife had walked out, he still clearly didn't like the man. *Well, that makes two of us*, thought Robyn. She hoped she'd never have to meet Mr Gillespie again. The problem was that this was a small town.

4

'What was she like?' Robyn asked. 'Your mother? If you don't mind me asking.' She couldn't stop thinking about David's mother leaving her husband, leaving her boys. As she would never meet David's mother, she hoped David would share something about her.

'History.' He turned to her and smiled.

'History?' Robyn repeated.

'Oh, how she loved history.'

'She did?'

'Uh-huh. I think she particularly liked British history. And she also used to read me stories of legends like King Arthur and the Knights of the Round Table.' He was suddenly quiet, lost in his own thoughts.

He looked at her, his eyes glazed over. 'How I loved those stories.'

'Better than ice hockey?'

'Oh yes, no question,' he said quickly. Then he paused. 'That wasn't a question, was it?'

Robyn shook her head. 'You can tell when people talk about things they love …'

'Go on.'

'Oh I don't know.' Robyn looked out of the window. 'You can tell it's a passion.'

'Yes, I've always loved history.'

Robyn bit her lower lip. She had the makings of a brilliant idea. But first there was something she needed to know. She leaned forward in her seat. 'Isn't there something else you want to do with your life, besides driving that van around on deliveries?'

She couldn't imagine he'd want to spend the rest of his life working in his father's store. But he did seem stuck in a rut. Robyn knew it wasn't her call, or her business, but she still wanted him to turn his life around and do something meaningful for himself. She looked at David across the table. 'How about retraining in … in something?'

They were sitting in a booth in a café inside an out-of-town shopping centre. She would never have found the place if it hadn't been for David. It wasn't like a city centre shopping mall; it was more like a large farm shop and garden centre, with some pricey but very nice shopping outlets in the tastefully converted outbuildings. The buildings surrounded a central courtyard with seating outside where visitors could have a coffee or eat al fresco in nice weather, but they'd chosen to sit inside the café looking out on to the courtyard. Robyn had noticed the delicious array of home-cooked pastries, and cakes at the counter when they'd walked in.

She looked past David to the woman who was making her way towards them, carrying a tray.

'Here you go, folks.' The waitress set the tray down and put a cup of coffee on the table in front of David. She plonked

Robyn's cup down with barely a second glance and then hovered by the table, smiling at David, trying to catch his attention. Robyn thanked her. The waitress looked back at David, still smiling, and deposited the bill in front of him. He nodded briefly at her.

Robyn waited for the waitress to leave. Then she put both elbows on the table and leaned towards David. 'How about college?'

'College?' David was about to drink his coffee. He lowered the cup. 'I don't know where I'd get the money to go to college. Like I told you before, most of my money is tied up in the house and some investments.'

Robyn leaned against the plastic seat-back of the booth. She thought of Rose's parting words about the possibility of David's father really being wealthy. Of course, it was a ridiculous idea. Why would he have had to sell his own house, and move in with his son, if he had money? And even if he did have some money squirrelled away, would he pay for David to attend college? Would David even consider asking? As far as he was concerned, his father couldn't be trusted with money. Robyn knew that *no* was the short answer to both of those questions.

Robyn briefly considered whether she could ask David's father herself, but after the embarrassing brush-off at the New Year's street party, she wouldn't ask him for help if her life depended on it. Besides, she didn't even know him, and he scared her a bit too.

Robyn took a sip of coffee and looked at David as he asked, 'What would I do at college?'

'History,' she said simply as she brought the cup to her lips.

'Excuse me?'

Robyn put her cup down. 'You should go to college to study something you love, and you love history.'

'Okay. Suppose you're right, that I do love history.'

'Which you do,' Robyn said matter-of-factly.

'Alright, as you seem to have all the answers, tell me this …' He put his coffee cup down. 'When I've finished studying history, what exactly am I going to do, you know, as in a job, work, a career?'

Robyn placed her empty coffee cup on the table. Resting her chin in her hands, she stared into space.

'Well?'

'I'm thinking.'

After a brief moment, David breathed a heavy sigh. 'There, you see. It's pointless.'

To Robyn's surprise, he sounded genuinely disappointed that she hadn't come up with something.

She watched him sweep up the bill and go to pay.

But I will, she thought. Then lots of ideas came in quick succession.

David returned and immediately caught her expression. Searching her face, he said, 'You've thought of something – haven't you?' He sat down opposite her.

'You could be an archivist or a history teacher. What about a historian, or an academic researcher?'

David raised an eyebrow. 'I've got to be honest, Robyn. I don't really see myself as an academic. I wouldn't mind doing a bit of history as a hobby, but I think I'd be pretty useless in those jobs. The trouble with me is that the thought of going back to study at my age …'

'You can be anything you want, if you set your mind to it.'

David smiled at her. He reached across the table, and took her hand, giving it an affectionate squeeze, as he said, 'Nope, I think *you* can be anything you want if you put your mind to it, Robyn. You're creating your own business, your own money, out of nothing. You haven't even finished college, got a qualification.'

Robyn had told him she was at St Andrews University but didn't want to return after the Christmas break. He hadn't tried to persuade her to return, and had been quite honest when he'd said that for his own selfish reasons, he was glad she wanted to stay.

Robyn suddenly had a moment of self-doubt. She frowned. 'Do you think I'm crazy, not returning to university and getting a qualification before I launch my business?'

'Not at all. I think you know what you're good at, and you're just going with it.'

That gave Robyn an idea. 'What are *you* good at?'

'Ice hockey!'

Robyn sighed heavily and sat back in her chair. She should have known he'd say that.

They finished their coffee in silence. David stood up and held out his hand. 'Come on.' She took it as she got out of the booth. 'I believe you have some shopping to do.'

Robyn nodded and smiled, thinking about how thoughtful it was of him to bring her.

'I've got something I need to buy too that I can't get in Aviemore.' He glanced at his watch. 'I'll meet you back here in one hour?' He looked at her. 'Although it might take you longer if there is lots of choice. And if there isn't, at least there are plenty of shops to browse in.'

'That's fine.' Robyn looked at him. 'One hour.' She moved

off quickly. She wanted to make the most of the time and just hoped they had what she was looking for.

Although it was a cold day, the sun was shining, and people were sitting outside on the little al fresco tables and chairs, wrapped up in coats, scarfs and gloves, drinking tea and coffee, and eating fruit scones.

Robyn decided that the next time they went there, she'd like to sit outside and have some refreshments – even though there were some outside heaters, perhaps she'd prefer it in the spring, when it wasn't freezing cold.

Robyn stood for a moment, looking around the inner courtyard. There were shops fronting the courtyard with creative window displays enticing shoppers inside. Robyn wandered around the courtyard, looking in shop windows. There was a clothes shop selling woollen jumpers, hats, scarfs and gloves. Her mouth watered when she saw one shop with cakes, biscuits, homemade preserves, and savoury pasties and pies in the window display. She moved on to a shop selling fishing equipment, then several Highland souvenir shops, and one dedicated to all things tartan. She'd seen two coaches in the car park when they'd arrived, and guessed this was a popular place for daytrips and for stops on tours of Scotland. The café also served meals, all home-cooked from local produce.

Robyn was tempted to browse some of the shops, but first she needed to look for fabric. Across the courtyard, a shop displaying soft furnishings – a small armchair, with a throw, cushions, and a standard lamp, caught her attention. She walked into the shop and discovered that along with furniture items on the ground floor, there were stairs that rose to another floor which appeared to stock curtains and blinds. But did they sell fabric too? Robyn emerged at the top of the stairs into what looked like a haberdashery shop. There was a large counter selling buttons, ribbons, and lots of other small items for sewing and dressmaking. She sighed, disappointed. She was just turning on her heel to return down the stairs when a lady asked if she could help.

Robyn shook her head. 'I don't think so. I needed some fabric for curtains, cushions – that sort of thing. Some swatches would be good too.

'Come this way.'

Robyn looked at her, surprised. She followed her round a corner into another part of the shop where she found just what she was after – curtains, blinds, cushions, and rolls of fabrics by the metre.

She walked around, running her hands down the rolls of fabrics. She picked up large heavy, bound books containing different fabric swatches.

Robyn realised there was just too much choice – an hour wasn't going to be long enough.

❖

'Sorry,' Robyn said as they got back in the van. David had helped her back to the car, carrying a heavy book of swatches that the shop had been kind enough to lend her. She had some rolls of material too. She had been well over an hour.

David just shook his head. 'Hey, that's okay.'

She asked, 'Did you get what you needed?'

Robyn's eyes drifted to the brown paper bag in David's hand.

'Yep.'

He didn't say what was in the bag. She didn't ask.

'You?' he said, putting the book of swatches in the van.

'Yeah – kind of.'

"You call that kind of?' He gestured at the heap of multi-coloured material and fabric swatches she'd just deposited on the seat.

She gave a weak smile. He was right; the quantity was pretty impressive. But would Rose be happy with the quality of the fabric, or even the colours and patterns? She got the feeling that Rose would be a hard customer to please.

In Gayle's driveway, Robyn climbed out of the van and reached in for the fabric.

David put her hand on hers. 'Leave them.'

'But I need to take them to Rose's house tomorrow.'

'I know. So why load them out just to put them back again?'

David lifted his hand from hers.

'Do you have another delivery out there in the morning?'

David shrugged. 'Maybe.'

Robyn smiled. It was clearly a fib. She left them where they were. 'I guess I'll see you tomorrow then.'

'Morning or afternoon?'

'I'd like to go first thing – if that's okay with you.' She knew it would be. Robyn shut the van door. The window was still open on the driver's side. She walked around the van and paused by the open window. 'Now, are you sure I'm not being any trouble?'

David grinned. 'You've been trouble since the day we met.'

Robyn smiled knowingly. Of course, it was a joke, but then again, it wasn't far off the truth either. His sports car had been a write-off in the crash. And then he'd got into that fight with his father on New Year's Eve. Not that the fight had been her fault; it had been his dad's fault for being so rude to her.

She reached through the open window and tentatively touched the scar above his eye.

'I think Gayle might be right. You're going to be left with a scar.'

'Good.'

They exchanged another knowing smile. It had been in the early hours of New Year's Day, just the previous day, that Gayle, who had been cleaning the wound and applying a bandage, had mentioned he might be left with a scar.

David had come out with a silly comment that he wouldn't mind because women loved guys with scars. He'd read it in a women's magazine. Robyn and Gayle had burst out laughing. It was ridiculous. They'd said as much. Even so, David clearly didn't believe them.

He reached up and gently took Robyn's hand, surprising her by putting her hand to his lips and giving it a kiss. 'See you tomorrow, Robyn.'

She stepped away from the van and watched him reverse. She watched his van disappear down the drive and turn into the road, out of sight, then turned on her heel to face the house. She thought again of David's joke about moving in there, instead of going home, now that his father was living with him. Robyn wished he *would* move in. She was already counting down the hours until she saw him again in the morning.

'Why the glum face?' Gayle asked, catching her expression as she walked into the kitchen. 'Ah, you didn't find any fabrics or swatches for Rose.'

'No, I've got plenty of those.'

Gayle looked around.

'They're still in David's van.'

'You and David had another falling-out, then?'

Robyn looked at her hand, where he'd gently kissed her. 'No. I just miss him already.'

'How come? Is he going away?'

Robyn didn't understand the question. 'No, he'll be here in the morning to give me a lift to Rose's house.'

'Ah, I get it.'

'Get what?'

'Oh, Robyn. I'm not blind. Are you?'

Robyn took a seat at the kitchen table while Gayle put the kettle on. 'I'm sorry. I don't follow.'

Gayle shook her head and smiled. 'I remember feeling like you once, when I was a lot younger, years ago. I'd like to meet someone and feel that way again.'

Robyn looked at her blankly.

'Robyn, if you can't bear to be apart from him for one minute, let alone an entire night, then that means only one thing.'

Robyn frowned. 'What's that?'

'Oh, Robyn, you silly girl. Why, you're in love – of course.'

5

'Look over there.' Robyn pointed to where a group of boys were gathered. She glanced at David. His frown was unmistakable.

He'd collected her from Rose's, after she'd spent the day there, and had said he had a surprise. Then he'd driven to the loch again. He'd obviously assumed they'd be alone there this time.

She had noticed quite a few cars parked in the forestry car park near the loch. They were at the same place where they'd ice-skated the previous night. Before they'd spotted the boys, David had said he wanted her to see the beautiful frozen loch in daylight. Apparently, the temperature and weather conditions tended to change rapidly, which meant the loch might only be frozen over for a few days.

She'd noticed that the ice-skates were still in his van. The previous night, he'd told her that the thickness of the ice was carefully monitored before anyone was allowed to skate on it, which was the reason that the numbers on the ice had needed to be controlled and that various emergency services had been present. Robyn had noticed that not everyone at the gathering had been skating at the same time. It seemed that groups were taking it in turns, and avoiding the centre of the loch, where she guessed the ice was at its thinnest. And she imagined it was safest for everyone to remain close to the shore in case anyone got into trouble.

'What are they doing?' Robyn asked as she watched the boys from the shore. She turned to look at David, surprised, after what he'd said, that anyone was on the ice that day. 'Is that ice hockey?'

'Uh-huh.' David sounded uninterested.

There were a group of spectators – parents, Robyn guessed. Nobody in their right mind would let their kids skate on a frozen loch without supervision.

'Can we go and watch?' Robyn asked.

'I really don't want to—'

Robyn had already slipped on the skates that David had brought with them. Building on the confidence she had gained the previous evening, she skated along the edge of the loch, keeping close to the shore as she headed over to the far corner of the loch where the boys were playing. David had no choice but to follow.

She let her concentration wander for a second, taking in the scenery around her in the daylight, and slipped.

'Hey, careful.' David grabbed her arm just in time.

'No brakes.' Robyn laughed nervously, realising that thankfully David had been following close behind. 'I forgot how to stop.'

David stood behind her, holding both her elbows. She slid backwards ever so slightly and leaned into his warm body. She folded her arms to keep out the chill wind. His arms crept around her until they were folded over hers. They'd stopped on the ice a little way from the group of parents to watch the boys.

'So, what are the rules?' Robyn asked.

'You see that boy over there?' He lifted a gloved hand from hers and pointed at a small boy in a large, padded outfit. He was wearing a helmet with a grille pulled over his face. 'That guy is in the net to save the puck.'

'The poke?'

'No, puck – p.u.c.k.'

'Okay.' Robyn listened and asked questions, enjoying the closeness between them. She wanted to stay in that moment – that beautiful, peaceful, carefree moment, in these stunning surroundings, and not think about the future; not think about what would happen if – when – her memories returned. She still hoped they never would.

'Are they, like, a team or something?'

'No. I imagine they'd like to get into the Scottish Ice Hockey junior leagues, but I've seen them play before, and I've got to be honest …' He lowered his voice, and whispered in her ear. 'They haven't got a hope.'

'They're that bad?'

'I'm afraid so.'

They both watched one of the players race down the loch with the puck, aim, then swing, missing the net completely and falling flat on his face.

'That's why,' David said flatly.

'They seem quite dedicated.'

'Yeah, it's a pretty big thing around these parts.'

'Really?' Robyn was thinking. 'Since when?'

'Oh, I don't know. Always, I guess.'

The puck was on the move again.

'I bet it wasn't such a big thing until one of their own hit the big time?' Robyn said, turning to look at him. 'Maybe they're all trying to be the next David Gillespie.'

'Don't be ridiculous,' David scoffed.

They both looked back at the game. The players were now in a heap on the ice, including the goalie. And the puck was not in the net.

'Oh, this is embarrassing.' David spoke a little too loudly.

One of the players got up and skated over to them. 'I heard that. Why don't you come and show us how to do it better, then?'

'What's the matter Charlie?' An older boy called from the other side of the group. He skated over to join the younger child.

'He said we're embarrassing.'

Robyn looked at David. The situation was awkward. She cast a glance at the group of parents over to their left, who didn't seem to have heard what David had said, or to have noticed the two boys standing in front of them. The other boys were still getting up from the ice, proving a distraction.

The older boy said, 'You put me off my shot.'

David laughed. 'Oh, come on. I don't think so. It was just a lousy shot.'

'David!' Robyn looked at him wide-eyed, then turned to the two kids. 'I'm enjoying watching your game. I think you've got a lot of potential.' Robyn smiled at the boys, thinking that all they needed was some encouragement, not someone criticising them. She turned to David. 'Can't you give them some advice?'

'You're holding the stick all wrong.'

Robyn frowned at him. He was criticising them again. 'Don't just say that. Show them how to hold it properly.'

'May I?' David pointed at the stick.

They two players exchanged glances and shrugged. One handed over his stick.

'You want to hold it like this.' David's arms were dead straight as he tapped the ice with the stick.

'And when you want to hit the puck …' He paused as one of them slid the puck over to David with his foot. 'You want to move in slow, like this …' David started to skate with the puck.

'Hey, Cameron!' A boy called out from the group of players standing on the ice. 'What are you doing over there? Are we getting that puck or what?'

David turned his body to face the group of boys standing in a crowd, waving their hockey sticks in frustration.

'Do you want your puck back, lads?' David called out.

Robyn glanced at the parents. If they hadn't noticed her and David before, they certainly had now.

David had a wicked grin on his face as he tapped the puck, deftly moving the hockey stick, keeping the puck just in front of him as he skated. The two boys followed him. Robyn heard David say, 'So, you want to skate in, stick low, then, when you're in position …' With a great *thwack*, he sent the puck hurtling along the ice straight for the group of children.

'David!' Robyn shouted in surprise.

He glanced back at her. 'Just watch the puck.'

'Watch out!' Robyn called out.

The group scattered, skating in different directions to avoid the puck as it moved across the ice at full velocity towards the net.

'Bullseye!' David said when it hit the net dead centre.

'Wow!' Robyn heard Cameron exclaim. 'How did you do that?'

'Oh … beginner's luck, I guess,' David called over his shoulder as he skated back to rejoin Robyn at the edge of the loch. He winked at her.

'Hey, that's David Gillespie!' Robyn heard one of the parents comment.

'Is he going to coach our kids?'

David heard them too. 'Right, it's time to leave. I shouldn't have brought you here.'

'You weren't to know there was an amateur game going on.'

David took her hand. 'I think they are not going to be that pleased, having a puck hurled in their direction,' she said, looking past him. 'Look – they're headed this way.'

A moment later, the team had gathered by the side of the loch.

An older boy exclaimed, 'Hey, what did you do that for?'

'Guess some people were not impressed,' commented David handing the hockey stick back to the younger player.

'But didn't you see that?' The younger boy said. He was still looking in awe in the direction of the net. 'I can't get it in the net when I'm standing right next to it! None of us can.'

'Yes, I know,' David replied.

'What makes you such an authority?' The older boy spoke from the group. Taller than the others, Robyn assumed he was the eldest, and perhaps the team captain, if there was such a thing in ice hockey.

'Come on, David.' Robyn turned to go. 'Let's just let them play.' She was feeling cold, standing still on the ice. It was different to the previous night, when she'd warmed up with a hot chocolate, and she'd spent time ice skating, so she hadn't noticed the cold.

'David?' Cameron looked at him more closely. 'Are you David Gillespie?' he peered at David. He was getting excited. 'I saw you on TV once. My dad was such a fan.'

'Don't be stupid, Cam. He's just the guy who works at the general store in town.'

David looked at Robyn, 'That's right. I'm just the delivery guy,' he said sadly.

'No, he isn't. I'm telling you, he's David Gillespie. He's just working at his dad's store while his knee mends, stupid.'

'No, kid.' David said.

'You're not him?'

Robyn butted in. 'Of course he is.'

'What I meant was,' David continued, 'the knee injury means that I won't be able to return to professional ice hockey – ever.'

'No more professional hockey?' The kid sounded dismayed.

'No more hockey, kids.'

'That's sad,' said the younger boy.

They all looked at one another. Cameron said, 'Will you show us some more moves?'

David started to shake his head.

'Of course he will,' Robyn piped up, giving David a gentle push towards the group. 'Didn't I tell you?' Robyn said. 'All they need is a coach. I think it's a brilliant idea,' she said encouragingly.

David started to shake his head. 'I really don't think ...' but his voice was drowned out by the boys shouting 'Coach! Coach! Coach!' in unison, over and over.

Some of the parents had joined them, including Joe and Annie.

'Hey there,' Robyn said in surprise. She hadn't realised they were there watching the game too.

Joe said, 'What's going on? Are you coaching the team? I thought you said you wouldn't.'

So, David has been asked to coach in the past, Robyn thought.

The smallest boy caught his sleeve and said, 'We really aren't very good, are we?' He paused. 'Please be our coach.'

'How can you refuse?' Robyn said, smiling at the sweet little boy.

'Oh, jeez,' David said. He headed out onto the ice to the sound of cheering from the boys and the parents. 'But just this once.' He put up a gloved finger.

The boys pulled David forward. 'Come on.'

Robyn and the parents watched as David showed the other boys how to move the puck along the ice before scoring a goal. He positioned the goalie back in goal and talked to him for some time before leaving him standing in front of the net.

As David skated back along the ice, he waved his arms to warn the other boys out of his way. He pointed at one of the boys, held out his hand for a hockey stick, and with one deft movement, still skating, he slipped the puck in front and continued on his way to the far end of the loch. Then he stopped.

The kids watched.

Robyn watched.

All the parents, and the rest of the hockey team watched as a hushed silence fell.

With the stick in hand and puck on the ice, he started to skate. He took long strides, the hockey stick in his hand brushing the puck left, then right, left, then right. Then, suddenly, halfway to the goal, he came to an abrupt but perfect halt, slightly turning to his left.

'Watch the puck!' he shouted at the goalie as he hit it – *thwack*!

The goalie missed it.

The puck tore at the netting.

David raised his hockey stick high in the air to cheers from the boys and a cheer from Robyn, and a bravo from the parents. The cheers had brought other spectators, who had been walking around the loch. 'Who's that with the ice hockey team?' Robyn heard one of the walkers ask.

Robyn turned around to speak to one of the spectators standing on the shore. 'It's David Gillespie, from the store in ...'

'Oh, really? We didn't expect to see him here.'

'Let alone playing hockey.'

Robyn felt very pleased with herself because it was all her doing.

David was now doing a second circuit of the loch. This time, the boys were no longer standing and cheering but skating after him, trying to catch up, playing the game.

Robyn bounced up and down in her skates, the blades never leaving the ice, and clapped her hands. The boys were gaining, their sticks out in front of them, aiming for the puck.

Robyn clapped her hands excitedly. She'd never seen an ice hockey game before. She raised her eyebrows. *I've never seen ice hockey before*, she thought. *Oh god – does this mean my memory is coming back?* Next, she'd remember why she had been driving down that road all alone on Christmas Day, and what had happened before the accident.

Not now. Please not now. I don't want to remember yet. I just want things to stay as they are, here with David. She didn't want the past intruding on her future.

She thought the idea of coaching was better than the ideas she'd come up with the previous day in the café on their shopping trip.

'David!' she shouted at him., waving excitedly. 'You should definitely coach ice hockey!' It made sense. He might love history, but as he'd said, that wouldn't suit him as a job; it was more of a hobby. Ice hockey had been his life. It still could be. Not professional ice hockey, of course. But helping players achieve their potential, achieve their dreams.

David turned to look in her direction. He didn't see the younger boy skating towards him.

'Look out!' Robyn warned, but it was too late. The small boy, who she'd spoken to with the older boy, Cameron, didn't appear to be watching where he was going. He skated into David. Then a couple of the other boys also collided, landing in a heap on the ice.

The boys laughed in excitement and Robyn joined in. Everyone was having a good time, despite the collision.

One by one, the boys got up, but David continued to lie on the ice.

'David?' Robyn called out. The boys had gathered on the ice around him.

'What's going on?' Joe asked Robyn. He'd moved from the group of parents to stand beside her.

'Weren't you watching the game?' Robyn asked.

He shook his head. 'I was chatting to Annie, so I wasn't paying attention.' He cast his gaze over to where the team had been playing. 'I can't see David.'

Cameron and the small boy had left the group and were skating fast towards them.

'What's going on?' asked Annie, joining Joe and Robyn.

Cameron called out as he skated towards them, 'It's Mr Gillespie. He's hurt.'

Robyn said, 'David was skating when one of the boys careered into him. He fell on the ice.'

'He what?' Joe set off, skating toward David before she could say any more.

Robyn was about to follow when Annie caught her arm. 'This was your idea, wasn't it? Getting him back on the ice. I heard what you said about David coaching.'

Robyn pursed her lips. 'I thought it made sense.'

'Not everything in life makes sense, Robyn.'

'You're talking about the injury that ended his career.'

'Yes. So, I don't think coaching is going to do him any good. Besides, this lot are never going to make it to the junior leagues.'

Robyn disagreed. She didn't like Annie's negative attitude, but she kept her thoughts to herself.

'That is a case in point,' Annie said smugly, pointing at David, who was lying on the ice, clutching his knee.

'If it wasn't for you,' continued Annie, 'he wouldn't even be here.' She tugged Robyn's arm hard. 'Stay put! she ordered. 'We've already got one casualty.'

Annie skated off, leaving Robyn with the two boys.

'It's all your fault,' said Cameron.

For a moment, Robyn thought even the boys were blaming her. Cameron was staring hard at the younger boy. 'You're always ruining things. I just knew we shouldn't have let *girls* join in, especially *you*, Charlotte. You're always so clumsy.'

'Don't call me Charlotte,' Charlie wailed, 'you know how I hate it.'

'Good,' he said, and skated off.

Robyn stared at Charlie as she pulled off the protective helmet in a fit of temper to reveal a straggly blonde bob, with two red butterfly hairclips holding her fringe out of her eyes. Robyn eyed the little girl, whom she had assumed was a boy.

'What are you staring at?' said Charlie, her helmet dangling forlornly at her side. 'They're not going to let me play with them after this,' she said, staring at the crowd gathered around David.

Robyn felt sorry for the young girl. She said, 'It's not your fault.' After all, she had encouraged David to show them some ice hockey moves.

'Look,' Robyn said, 'these things happen.'

Charlie turned to look at her.

Robyn continued. 'Accidents – I mean. Look at the accident David had on the ice that ended his career.'

'What are you talking about?' Charlie was looking crosser than ever.

'Oh, you don't know anything about David's accident?'

'Of course I do!' Her little face twisted into a grimace. 'But he never had an accident on the ice, never! Not until today. And it's all my fault!'

'I don't understand … I thought he was playing a game of ice hockey when he had the knee injury.'

Charlie glared at her, then skated off.

6

Robyn watched Charlie skate off to join the others, probably to plead for a second chance. Charlie glided past the three figures on the ice, heading for the other side of the loch.

Joe and Annie were either side; David was in the centre with an arm wrapped around each of their shoulders; one foot on the ice, the other suspended awkwardly out in front of him. He cut a pathetic figure.

As they neared her, Joe spoke first, taking charge of the situation. 'Robyn, I'm going to take David to the hospital in my car.'

Robyn nodded.

'No hospital.' David spoke through gritted teeth.

Robyn quickly took off her skates at the edge of the loch. With David seated on a log, she helped Joe get the skate off David's good leg and a shoe on his foot so that he could hop along on it.

Once everyone was in their hiking boots, she fell in behind them, carrying their skates. They headed towards the car park.

'I'm not going to any damn hos—'

'Annie,' Joe cut in, still ignoring David, 'you take Robyn.'

'No, it's okay.' Robyn was quick to say. The last thing she needed was Annie's cold, disapproving stare all the way to the hospital, along with another lecture about whose fault it all was.

'I can't take her in our car,' said Annie.

Robyn was relieved. Obviously Annie didn't want her company either.

'I have to get back, home, Joe.'

Robyn noticed she was looking at her watch.

"Ah, the babysitter.' Joe slapped his forehead with his free hand. 'I forgot. She could only spare two hours this evening. One of us has to get back.'

Robyn blurted, 'I thought you were here to watch your child playing ice hockey.'

Joe shook his head. 'No. I heard about the game, and decided to tag along, check the depth of the ice, make sure it was still safe to skate on. Our little one isn't interested in the game.'

'Thank god,' said Annie. 'I don't want her on the ice.'

Robyn wondered what their little one's dad and uncle thought about that.

Joe said, 'Annie decided she wanted to come too, so she met me here. We'd had such a great time on the ice last night, we figured it would be a shame not to make the most of the frozen-over loch before it thawed.'

'Isn't anyone listening to me?' David shouted in exasperation. 'I said—'

'I know what you said, David.' Joe's voice was calm as he interrupted his brother. 'Your knee has given way again.' He pointed at David's outstretched leg. 'So if you don't let one of us take you to hospital, then we're leaving you right here.' Joe stopped abruptly in the middle of the forest car park. Robyn nearly walked into Joe's back. She caught herself just in time.

'You with me on this, Robyn?' Joe glanced over his shoulder at her.

Robyn gulped. There was no way she would leave him there, especially as this was all her fault. But something in Joe's demeanour had changed. He was no longer Annie's big-hearted husband, or David's little brother. That was just for appearances, or maybe that was just him on his day off. But when it was necessary, he came across as authoritative and decisive, able to quickly act, and make decisions. This was Joe, the local police officer.

She had no choice but to agree. She said, 'Yes, of course.'

David glanced over his shoulder and glared at her.

Robyn rolled her eyes, thinking how she had succeeded in getting on the wrong side of David's father, his sister-in-law, and now David himself.

She looked at Joe's back, thinking that at least someone was still her friend.

They slowly made their way to the car park, where they had arrived less than an hour earlier.

Robyn looked at the cluster of cars about a hundred yards distant. 'Shall I get the car?' Robyn offered as Joe eased David down onto a log. She could drive it down to the track where they were.

'No, we can make it.' Joe added, 'Robyn, can you give me a hand, please?'

Annie let go of David and gave her husband a peck on the cheek.

Annie placed a hand on David's shoulder. 'Are you going to be okay?'

Robyn watched David pat her hand reassuringly. 'Of course, I am. You know me – I've come through worse.'

Robyn wondered if he was referring to the accident that had busted his knee in the first place. It was something they hadn't talked about – exactly how it had happened. Robyn wasn't surprised. It was a tricky topic of conversation, raising the thing that had ended his career. But now she knew it had not happened while he was skating on the ice. It was quite a revelation to discover that her assumption had been wrong all along.

For some reason, this brought to mind the trip to the local library in Aviemore she had been intending to make – without David in tow, of course. She'd wanted to find old newspaper articles about his ice hockey career, hoping it would answer her questions, although Gayle had questioned her as to why she didn't just ask him herself. Robyn had never quite found the right time.

With Annie gone and Joe taking a moment to call the babysitter and tell them that Annie was on her way home, Robyn knelt down in front of David.

He was leaning back on his hands, which were spread out behind him, and he was panting, even though he wouldn't have expended that much energy crossing the ice and getting up to the car park. Joe and Annie had virtually been carrying him. Robyn guessed he was in more pain than he would have people believe.

She bent down and started to undo the other skate, not looking him in the eye, waiting for the inevitable ticking-off that she deserved.

'No. Don't touch it!' said David, as she reached for the skate. She drew her hand away fast and looked up at him. 'But the skate is quite heavy. It can't be doing you any good holding your leg out with that skate still on.'

'I'd much rather you do something else for me, if you don't mind.'

She couldn't believe he was being so nice to her after all this.

She stood up. 'What is it?'

'In the glove compartment of the van,' his voice was insistent. 'There's a bottle of pills. Get them, will you?'

Robyn looked from David to Joe. 'But I need to help you to the car, otherwise how will you get to the ...?'

'You go ahead, Robyn.' Joe came up and knelt beside David. 'We'll manage,' he said as he scooped David up in his arms. David grunted and reached for his leg.

Robyn went ahead to the van. She opened the heavy passenger door and climbed in. She pressed the button, and the glove compartment lid sprang open. Robyn tentatively put her hand inside, expecting to wade through all sorts of crap, but to her surprise, it seemed empty. She felt inside, and in the right-hand corner, her hand hit a small plastic container that rattled. She scooped it up in her hand and slammed the glove compartment shut before climbing out of the van. Robyn could see Joe heading to his car.

'Robyn!' Joe shouted at her from across the car park.

'Coming!' she shouted back.

She slammed the door shut. Then, clutching the pills to her chest, she ran.

Joe was already sitting in the driver's seat with the engine ticking over.

'Sorry.' She said as she opened the rear door and looked in on David who was propped up on a pile of coats.

'Did you get them?' David asked, his voice hoarse.

'Yes.' But Robyn looked at the pills, and hesitated. For some reason, she didn't want to give them to David.

'Give them to me!' he demanded.

Robyn's eyes went wide. Someone had spoken to her like that before. Some guy, she was sure of it. She froze. It was a memory – she was sure of it.

David sighed, 'They're painkillers – that's all.'

'Oh.' Robyn looked at the bottle in her hand before she handed them over. She watched him as he unscrewed the lid and tipped the bottle toward his mouth.

'Robyn, you ok?' Joe turned in her direction, his arm flung over the back of the front seat he was looking at her strangely.

'Oh, I'm fine.' She was trying to remain calm and keep her voice from betraying her. She wasn't fine – not at all. She'd had a memory – she was sure of it. She couldn't picture his face right now, but it was a guy, a young guy, demanding she hand over some pills. And she somehow knew they weren't just painkillers.

And she knew something else – if she didn't do as she was told by this mystery guy who'd popped into her consciousness, the repercussions were never good.

'Get in the car, Robyn,' said Joe.

Robyn looked at the police car and hesitated. 'Look, are you getting in the car – or what? I want to set off for the hospital now.'

Robyn looked at David, and said, 'I'm sorry. I'll follow in the van.'

Joe said, 'We'll swing by and pick up the van later.'

David misread her meaning too. 'Oh, Robyn, you don't have to worry about the van.'

Robyn wasn't worried about the van. She was worried about

getting into a police car, and she had no idea why.

Joe leaned across the front passenger seat, and opened the car door. 'Get in, Robyn.'

Robyn shook her head, and backed away. 'I'll meet you at the hospital.'

Robyn got in the van and glanced at the police car, wondering what she was so afraid of. She thought, *There must be a reason I don't want to get into a police car. Why do I feel like I've done something wrong?*

She switched on the ignition. Nothing happened. Robyn exclaimed, 'Please start!'

Joe pulled up alongside the van, wound his window down, and called out, 'Is there a problem?'

Robyn wound the window down. 'The van won't start.'

'Then you'd better come with us.'

7

On the journey to the hospital in Aviemore, she sat feeling subdued in the front of the car. David was in the back, sitting with his feet up on the back seat. He had insisted on taking off the skate.

She looked out of the passenger side window and stared at the familiar scenery along the forest road into Aviemore. Through the dense wood at the side of the road, she caught glimpses of the loch and the backdrop of the Cairngorm mountains. Robyn wished David hadn't taken her back to the loch. The sun was now setting. Gayle wouldn't be worried when she didn't return soon, though. She knew it was another date, and had said she wouldn't set a place at the dinner table for her – or wait up.

Do you know something I don't know? Robyn had said to her, partly in jest. But even so, she had wondered if David had said something to Gayle.

Gayle had said that he hadn't, although she had said that if David was taking her out on a date, she imagined it would involve dinner. Robyn had hoped so. Now, after what had happened on the frozen loch, all she wanted was for the day to be over. She felt guilty that she'd refused to accompany David in the car until she was forced to because the van wouldn't start. But if David had been bothered by that, he hadn't said anything; most likely because he was too preoccupied. She glanced back at him. The painkillers had kicked in, but she could tell by his expression that they weren't helping as much as she or he would have liked. He needed something stronger.

She glanced at Joe, who hadn't stopped talking since they'd set off for the hospital. She couldn't blame him for trying to lighten the atmosphere in the car. She sat with her hands clasped tightly in her lap. She couldn't wait to get out of the car. Every time the police radio went off, she had to try to remain calm and not flinch.

Every now and then, she nodded to show that she was listening to Joe's overly jovial attempts at conversation, although she wasn't really listening – her mind was elsewhere; on the thought of getting out of the car, and on hoping that David's injury wasn't too bad.

She thought that someone ought to tell Joe that his jokes were pretty awful, but seeing his worried frown, she guessed it was just his way of dealing with what was going on.

'Will you please stop with the bad jokes, Joe?'

David's voice from the back of the car made Robyn jump.

'I was only trying to pass the time.'

'I get that, and I get that you're worried. You always tell bad jokes when you're anxious about something – have done ever since you were a little kid.'

Robyn glanced at Joe and caught him looking her way, embarrassed. 'Sorry.' He asked, 'How are you feeling back there?'

'How do you think?'

At the hospital entrance, Joe pulled the handbrake on and jumped out of the car.

Robyn stared intently ahead, hoping that Joe would just deposit David on the nearest hospital trolley and come back to take her home. She knew it was very insensitive of her, but she didn't want to hang around at the hospital.

The car door clicked open. It made her jump.

The door opened wide, and Joe stood to one side.

Robyn looked dumbly up at Joe, who was standing there holding the door, and suddenly realised that he thought she was sitting in the car waiting for him to be the gentleman and open the car door for her. She didn't know what was worse; that he thought she wouldn't get out of the car unless he opened the door for her, or that under the circumstances he was actually standing there doing it.

Like a child reluctantly climbing out of the car for their first day at school, Robyn got out. She still just wanted someone to take her home.

'Joe?' David called from the back.

Robyn stared at the entrance to the hospital. She hadn't expected to see the place again this soon. It was only the previous Friday, the day before New Year's Eve, that she'd been discharged. David had been there, turning up in the van to see if she needed a lift anywhere, although it had been Gayle she'd gone home with that day.

She would never have thought she'd be back there, just five days later, with David being brought into A&E. *And it's all my fault,* she thought. She grimaced. Annie was right: she shouldn't have encouraged David when it came to ice skating. She should have stuck with encouraging him to study history.

Robyn silent cursed herself as she watched Joe help David out of the car.

'Robyn, we need some help here,' Joe said impatiently.

'Yes, of course.' She walked round the car to Joe.

'Can you go and get a wheelchair?'

'Oh – right.' Robyn ran to the entrance and plunged through the swing doors. A row of wheelchairs sat just inside the entrance. She took one back to the car and watched David eyeing it with a look of distaste on his face. He started to protest. 'I'm not—'

'Get in,' Joe said, cutting him off, 'or I'll drop you right here.' His tone was curt.

David and Joe glared at one another.

Robyn felt sorry for David. She wouldn't want to find herself back in this place either. 'Hey, look,' she said to David, tilting the wheelchair backwards, so the front wheels lifted from the floor. 'It's my turn to give you a ride.' She made *vroom vroom* noises and as she tilted the wheelchair.

She stopped abruptly. Joe was staring at her with his mouth open.

David shook his head, but she thought she discerned a wisp of a smile.

Robyn slowly let the wheelchair down until the front wheels clattered noisily on the floor. 'Not funny?' she asked David.

'You were on your way out of hospital, so we were raring to go,' David pointed out. 'But this is a bit different. I'm not exactly raring to go in there, am I?'

'Huh?' Joe said, looking from one to the other.

'Sorry,' Robyn mumbled, looking away, the colour rising in her cheeks. Then she noticed that Joe and David weren't the only ones staring at her in the car park. She turned back to David and said crossly, 'Well, are you going to get in the stupid chair or what?'

'Now you're talking my language,' Joe said.

Robyn stood, holding the back of the chair steady, tapping her fingers impatiently.

Once they had got David into the chair, Joe wheeled it into the reception area and left Robyn with David. He strode to the desk. Robyn watched him talking animatedly to the nurse, waving his arms theatrically in David's direction.

'Funny, huh?'

'Pardon?' Robyn was concentrating so hard on Joe that she hadn't realised David was speaking to her.

'I said it's funny. You. Me. Here. 'Except this time I'm the one in the goddamn wheelchair.'

'Yeah, I was thinking the same thing.' She shook her head. David turned his attention on Joe. 'What's he getting in a flap about?'

Robyn shrugged. They couldn't hear him from where they were, just by the entrance. The reception was busy, Robyn noticed, and noisy.

Finally, Joe stalked back. 'Right, come on.'

'What was all that about?' David said as Joe swivelled David around to face a corridor, then started down it at speed, passing a sign, which Robyn read.

Robyn stopped. 'A&E is that way.' She pointed down another corridor to their right.

'Exactly,' Joe said without stopping. 'They wanted me to take him there,' Joe's voice rose an octave, 'like this. I wasn't having that.'

'But isn't that what the A&E is for?' Robyn thought he'd had an accident, and this was an emergency. She continued after them and caught up, walking quickly to match Joe's pace.

'I threw my weight around,' he said, glancing back at Robyn, 'so to speak.'

Robyn stared at Joe. She was beginning to glean what the commotion in reception was all about. Joe was using his badge to get David special treatment.

'That's what big brothers are for.' David chirped. 'Literally speaking.'

'Hey, we'll have no jibes about my size, otherwise you will find yourself heading for casualty.' Joe threw back and winked at Robyn.

She was about to say that she'd thought David was the eldest, then realised he hadn't been talking about Joe's age when he'd said, *big* brother; he was referring to Joe's stocky build.

Robyn offered a weak smile. She wondered if this wasn't the first time David had benefited from Joe's position as a police officer, and how far Joe would go for his brother.

She still wished she wasn't there, back at the hospital. She wanted to phone Gayle, explain what had happened, and ask her to come and pick her up. Now, she wished she had her own mobile phone. She'd have to borrow Joe's or David's. She knew Joe would give her a lift home, but she didn't want another ride in a police car.

She had money, and lots of it, to buy a mobile phone. *I should have used some of that cash to buy one,* she silently berated herself. She knew why she wouldn't. Why she wanted to wait until Rose paid her for the work she was doing on her house.

She stole a glance at Joe. She'd found wads of bank notes at the bottom of the bag that she'd been told was hers, under some clothes. Why would a student have all that money? Until she remembered, she wouldn't touch it. She hadn't minded finding the savings book among her things. The deposits matched the cheques that she knew, from some letters, her mother had been sending her from abroad.

Her mother was travelling, and the letters Robyn had read from her had not triggered any memories from her past. The cheques that she'd apparently already deposited in her savings account matched the sums her mum had described sending, and were intended to cover air fares and expenses for Robyn to join her mum during her holidays from university. Robyn had apparently not withdrawn any of the money, and had concluded that she hadn't visited her mum once during her travels.

She knew she must have had her reasons, but until her memory returned, that would remain a mystery. Unless she contacted her mum. Robyn was still thinking about that. If anyone could tell her about her past, it would be her mum. So why did she feel hesitant to contact her? Just then, all Robyn had was her gut instinct. And her gut was telling her to leave things be – for now. And not to touch any of the money.

She couldn't touch the savings account just then even if she'd wanted to. Although she had the savings passbook, she imagined she'd need some form of ID to withdraw money from the account at a branch. Her driving licence and passport – if she had one – must be in another bag; one that had somehow been lost in the car crash.

Even if she'd had ID, she didn't feel inclined to walk into a bank and access her account. She was afraid a bank clerk might start asking questions when they saw the last deposit in her account. It hadn't been a cheque. It had been deposited straight into her account, presumably through another bank. If the wads of cash weren't worrying her enough, that six-figure deposit in her savings account certainly was. She thought there might be a simple explanation. She could just contact her mum, and ask. But if it was that simple, why was her gut instinct telling her not to?

'Are you okay?' David asked.

'Who – me?' Robyn looked at him, surprised he'd asked that question. He must have caught her expression. *I want to go home to Gayle's,* she wanted to say. But despite not wanting to be there, she did want to stay long enough to make sure David was going to be okay. She reached for his hand. They held hands as Joe pushed the wheelchair down the corridor.

8

Joe stopped outside a door with a small round portal window; he peered in. 'Right, this will do,' he said, pushing the door open. Robyn let go of David's hand so she could hold the door open for Joe. The small sign above the door read *Examination Room.*

Joe parked David beside the examining table in the centre of the room and walked back to the door.

'Where are you going?' Robyn asked.

'To see what's keeping the doctor.'

Robyn stared at the door. She hoped he wasn't long. She still wanted to get out of there as soon as she could. It was her memory issues that bothered her. Selective amnesia, the doctor had said. It was temporary, the doctor had said. And it wasn't a tumour. They'd done a CAT scan. But how temporary was her amnesia? It had been a little over a week, and still nothing.

Robyn frowned. That wasn't strictly true – and she knew it. Although she couldn't remember specifics, there were certain things, certain situations, that were triggering certain feelings, like being afraid to get in a police car. What was that about?

She hadn't anticipated that sort of thing. In some ways, it was worse than not remembering at all, because now she was left wondering what had happened in her past.

Her eyes drifted around the room. One wall was lined almost floor to ceiling with a glass-fronted cabinet housing various bottles and packets of drugs. Should they be in there without a medical professional present? She looked at the cabinet and imagined it must be locked.

'Shame you can't just help yourself, isn't it?' David commented.

Robyn glanced at him. His attention was riveted on the cabinet.

'I mean,' he continued, 'it's not as though I don't know what I need.' He reeled off some impossibly long name. Under different circumstances, Robyn would have laughed and accused him of making it up, but the seriousness of his tone made her think otherwise. He had been down this road before.

As if reading her mind, he added, 'This has happened before – my knee giving way. I know how this works.'

Robyn stared at him, thinking that it might not be like before. 'You've had a fall.'

David seemed to ignore that remark. 'In comes the doctor, questions, examinations, exclamations, second opinions even, then ...' he paused, 'after telling me what I already know, finally a prescription.' He raised his hands in exasperation.

Robyn sighed. *Poor David*, she thought. *It must be awful, living with an ongoing injury.* She just hoped the fall on the ice hadn't made it a lot worse. What if he needed another operation on his knee? She imagined he'd already had an op on it when he'd first got the injury.

'Oh, sod this,' David exclaimed, eyeing the cabinet. 'Robyn, see if there's some …' he repeated the impossibly long word.

Robyn shrugged. 'Why? They're bound to have some. If you need it, the doctor will give it to you.'

He turned his wheelchair to face her. 'Just go and look – please.'

Robyn stirred from her spot and walked over to the cabinet. What harm could it do? Besides, by the time she found it, Joe would be back with a doctor, and very soon she could go home.

'Well?' David said impatiently.

'Just a minute. Do you know how many boxes of medicine are in here, and how small the writing is?' She thought he was being very unreasonable to expect her to find it just like that.

'You don't have to read every single one. They must be in alphabetical order.'

Robyn felt foolish; he was right. 'Here we are.' She spelt it out; she wasn't even going to attempt to say it.

'That's the one.'

Robyn turned her back on the cabinet to face David. 'There, you see. I told you they'd have it. What is it, anyway?'

'Just a painkiller and anti-inflammatory, but it's really strong.' David moved his wheelchair just a tad closer to Robyn. 'Is it locked?'

'What?'

David's gaze shifted. 'The cabinet – is it locked?'

'I don't know.' Robyn shrugged. 'I imagine so.'

'Try it – will you?'

Robyn turned back and reached for the handle of the glass door. Then she suddenly pulled her hand back. What was she doing? If someone walked in, if Joe and the doctor returned, what on earth would they make of her standing there with her hand on the door of the drugs cabinet? Wasn't there some law against stealing hospital medicines? After all, that was exactly what it would look like she was doing.

'What's wrong?' David's voice sounded closer. She turned around to find him right next to her. 'Look, it doesn't matter whether it's locked or not,' she said, 'because I am not going to try to open the cabinet, if that's what you are asking.' David was really testing her patience. 'Besides, it must be locked. They're not going to leave a whole cabinet of drugs unlocked in an unattended room, are they?'

'Move over. I'll do it myself.' His voice was prickly.

'Be my guest.' Robyn held out her hand and moved aside, knowing very well that there was no way David could reach the handle. But she reckoned without his will power.

She stood aside and watched David manoeuvre his wheelchair into position and put the brake on. Then, gingerly putting his good leg on the floor and gripping the wheelchair with one hand, he slowly began the hoist himself out while reaching for the handle.

Robyn watched him until she could stand it no longer. 'Alright.' She breathed, pushing David back into his chair – none too gently. She grasped the handle of the door and pulled hard. 'You see, I told you—' It flew open.

David whooped.

Robyn's eyes flew to the door, expecting someone to thunder in as if an alarm had gone off.

Robyn slammed it shut.

'What are you doing?'

'OK, so you've proved a point – so what?'

'Open it, will you? Pass me the pills.'

Robyn stopped dead. 'You are joking, right?'

'Look, I need them. Just pass them out and then we can be out of here.'

Robyn moved away from the cabinet, away from David, shaking her head. 'Are you insane? I'm the one who would be out of here, in the back of Joe's police car, and he won't be taking me home, either.' She caught a breath. 'Besides you might need more than pills to fix that.' She glanced down at David's knee. 'You need someone to look at it first.'

'Oh yeah? And what makes you such an authority?'

'Someone who doesn't want to go to prison.'

David waved away her concerns. 'Who said anything about prison?' He raised voice. 'Just do what I tell you, and get them!'

Robyn flinched, and for just a moment she remembered an old caravan. She was sitting at a formica table inside, surrounded by other children – she had a feeling she was a child herself – and a young woman was screaming at her from the sofa, 'Just get my pills!'

'Do you think I want to stay here, in this hospital, for a moment longer?' said David.

The memory – if that's what it was – didn't give much away. Robyn was trying to remember who the young woman was. *Was that my mother?*

'Well, it's not my fault you're here,' Robyn retorted, even though that's what she'd thought on the way there. Now, with David's attitude towards her, she'd changed her mind.

'Oh, isn't it? Who wanted to see me play hockey on the ice?'

Robyn put her hands on her hips. 'Well, who wanted to show off on the ice?' Robyn knew this wasn't exactly true, but she was angry at David for blaming her. It wasn't *all* her fault. She hadn't forced him to play.

'All you have to do is hand me the bottle of pills – what's so difficult about that?'

'No.'

'No?' David started to move towards her.

She stood her ground. 'What are you going to do like that?' She felt cross and angry at his unreasonable demand. 'Hold a gun to my head?' she blurted.

He stared at her as if dumbstruck. 'What are you talking about?' he said slowly. 'Where did that come from?'

Robyn shuffled her feet and looked towards the door. 'I'm going to find a phone.' She didn't bother asking David to lend her his mobile phone.

'Wait!'

Robyn could hear the squeak of the wheelchair on the move behind her as she walked to the door.

'Robyn, please.' She felt a hand close around her forearm. Alarmed that he had moved towards her quicker than she'd anticipated, she whirled around. 'Let go of me!' she demanded as a wave of panic hit her. She tugged her arm to try and shake off his grip.

David held up his hands, releasing his grip immediately. 'God, sorry. What has got into you?'

'I don't know! Leave me alone!' She looked at David, and thought she could say the same about him. He'd never treated her like this before. But then she knew he was in pain, in a hospital, and she expected he was a little frightened too. She knew he didn't want to be admitted. He just wanted some pills, and for whatever was up with his knee to just resolve itself. Robyn had a feeling that things weren't going to turn out as simple as that.

'Are you leaving?'

'I just want to find a phone.' Robyn turned to the door once more. 'I want to go home.'

'But I don't want you to go home. I don't know where your home is.'

'Gayle's. I'm going home to Gayle's, of course.' Robyn didn't know where her home was either. She didn't know why a mobile home had come to mind when she knew she had been living in halls of residence. Nothing made sense.

When she turned to the door and attempted to push the door open, quite forcefully because she was in a temper, she heard a thud.

'Hey!' Joe's voice came from behind the door.

Robyn looked through the little portal window to see him standing just the other side of the door. He took a step back as she opened the door.

'I found out what was keeping the doctor,' he said brightly.

Robyn was relieved to see Joe. At least now she didn't have to feel guilty about leaving David.

'Everything okay?' he asked, looking at them both.

Robyn looked away. He must have sensed the atmosphere in the room immediately.

Joe was accompanied by a young doctor with a coffee cup in one hand. He had a tissue in his other hand and started dabbing a large brown stain on the front of his white coat. Joe must have stepped back into the doctor behind him when she'd attempted to open the door. Robyn gave him a brief apologetic look before heading out of the door.

She heard David call her name as she walked out of the room, but she didn't look back.

'Where are you going, Robyn?' Joe asked, but she didn't want to offer an explanation. She just wanted to get out.

'What happened between you two when I was gone?' she heard Joe say to David.

Robyn retraced her steps back to the reception, where she was sure she would find a phone.

In the reception area, she found a payphone. She picked it up and dialled Gayle's number, hoping she didn't mind accepting reverse charges. Robyn didn't have any money for the phone call.

'Come on,' Robyn repeated over and over, listening to the dialling tone. She hoped it was Gayle who answered the phone, because Gayle's mother was liable to put it back on the hook while she went looking for her daughter, and then by the time she found her, she had usually forgotten why she was looking for her in the first place.

'Pick up, pick up,' Robyn said impatiently.

She had been standing for what seemed like an eternity, but it was only five minutes. She had been keeping an eye on the clock above the receptionist's desk. A loud cough drew her attention away from the clock on the wall to an elderly gentleman standing behind her. 'My wife has just been admitted, and I need to ring my daughter.'

Robyn nodded at him. She listened for three more rings, then reluctantly put the phone down. She'd assumed she was the only person in the hospital without a mobile phone.

She watched him pick the receiver up. 'My wife fell down the stairs,' he said, still holding the receiver.

'Oh dear,' said Robyn. 'I'm so sorry to hear that. I hope she's going to be okay.'

'So do I.'

His hand fumbled in his coat pocket. Robyn could hear the jangle of change. 'They say she could have a broken hip.'

He dropped a coin in the slot, his index finger hovering over the buttons. 'She always was a clumsy oaf.' He smiled a weak smile and began to dial. A moment later, he was ready with another coin.

Robyn left the old guy on the phone and walked over to the reception desk. 'Is there another public phone?' She had a feeling he was going to be on the phone for quite some time.

'Take that corridor to the coffee machine at the end of the hall.' The receptionist pointed without looking up.

'Thanks.' Robyn started down the same corridor from where she had come. As she approached the examination room, she peeked through the oval window. She couldn't see anybody inside. She threw the swing door wide; the room was empty. Robyn stood for a moment, staring into the empty room. Surely, if David had been sent home, she would have noticed them leaving through the reception area, or they would have noticed her. She couldn't imagine that Joe would have left without asking her if she needed a lift.

Robyn let the door swing back and stood in the corridor. 'Payphone,' she reminded herself and continued up the corridor, trying not to let the possibility that they'd just left her there bother her.

9

Robyn eyed the vending machine across the hall. She looked at the money Joe had insisted on giving her before he'd left the hospital and gone home. He'd wanted to make sure she bought a drink and something to eat while she waited for David to wake up.

A couple of hours earlier, after she'd discovered that David and Joe were no longer in the examination room with the doctor, she'd been looking for another payphone when Joe had found her and told her that David had been rushed in for surgery. There had been a last-minute cancellation, and so they had carried out the operation he needed straight away.

At that moment, the phone call to Gayle had instantly been forgotten. She'd waited with Joe for David to come out of surgery. They'd been told it had gone well. They'd waited for the anaesthetic to wear off. Robyn had sat holding David's hand and had caught his surprised expression when he'd woken to find her sitting with Joe by his bedside. She'd thought, *how can I leave now?*

She'd finally stepped out of his room when he'd dozed off. The accident and then having an operation had clearly taken its toll; he was exhausted. She walked up to the vending machine.

There was also a café on site, but Robyn wasn't that hungry, and besides, she didn't want to leave David for too long in case he woke up again and thought she'd gone.

Robyn put some money in the slot. Her finger hovered uncertainly over the large square buttons. Each had a letter and number on it. She really didn't mind what she had, as long as it was hot. Coffee, tea, hot chocolate – anything would do. She closed her eyes as tiredness gripped her and randomly pressed a button. She opened her eyes – nothing. No cup had appeared. She banged the vending machine with her fist. Still nothing.

Robyn checked her purse. She had enough change for another go. She felt like she was playing a slot machine, and the lucky prize was a hot drink. She waited in anticipation as the machine whirred to life. The whirring sound ceased, a dull thud followed, and then all was silent. 'Where's my drink?' she muttered, staring at the machine with her arms folded, waiting.

'Are you going to get that?'

Robyn unfolded her arms and turned around to see a young man in jeans and a jumper pointing at the vending machine.

Robyn stared at him. What was there to get? Was he blind? There was no hot drink.

'Here.' He brushed past her knelt and lifted a heavy metal flap, squeezing his hand through, which to Robyn looked quite painful. Then he let it go with a snap, pulling his hand free just in time.

'Not my favourite chocolate, but my wife quite likes them.'

Robyn looked at him blankly.

'This place can get you like that sometimes.' He thrust the chocolate bar into Robyn's hand. 'When my wife had our first, I swear, I didn't know my ar—' He stopped abruptly and backpedalled. 'What I meant to say was I didn't know whether I was coming or going.'

Robyn stood back and watched him deposit some coins into the slot. 'But I feel like an old pro now.' He pressed A6. The machine gurgled. 'It's number four now, can you believe it?' he said proudly.

'Number four?'

'Yeah.'

Robyn had no clue what he was talking about as she watched a little paper cup appear in a slot between two pincers. It was filling with hot brown liquid.

'Longest labour she's ever had, though.' He shook his head as he carefully prised the cup from between the pincers. Thick brown liquid slopped down the sides. He turned to Robyn. 'Not to worry, eh?'

Robyn thought he did look quite worried. She smiled and said, 'I'm sure everything will be just fine.'

'Yes.' He nodded and his hot drink spilled some more, but he didn't seem to notice.

He turned to go.

'Is it a boy or girl?' Robyn asked.

'Oh, it's going to be a boy – I just know it.' He grinned. 'I'm aiming for a whole team.'

'Team?'

'Ice hockey. I'm going to have me a whole ice hockey team.'

She wondered what his wife thought about that, poor woman. 'How many is that?'

'Six.'

'What if it's a girl?' She was thinking of Charlie.

'You enjoy your chocolate now.' She watched him wander

down the hallway in the direction of the maternity unit. She was actually relieved that there would be no more talk of ice hockey.

Robyn stuffed the chocolate bar into her bag and turned back to the vending machine. A tinkle of coins and a gurgle later, she too had a hot drink, even though some of her luke-warm hot chocolate had spilled over her hand. Why did they make such flimsy cups to hold hot beverages?

Robyn slowly walked down the corridor towards David's room, holding her cup. She'd finished her drink before she reached his room. She paused by a seat in the corridor, deposited the small cup in a wastepaper bin, and opened her bag, looking for a tissue to wipe her hands. Instead, her hand closed around the chocolate bar. She looked at it for a moment before ripping off the wrapper and scoffing the lot. She was famished. She knew she could do with getting something proper to eat, like a sandwich, but she didn't want to be gone for long.

She looked at her sticky hands. Fortunately, she didn't have to trek down the hall to reception to find a public loo to wash her hands. David had an en suite room.

Robyn quietly opened the door to find David hadn't woken up yet. She walked over to his bedside and cast a glance at his leg, which was raised on a pillow, the knee wrapped in thick bandages. She felt guilty that she'd be leaving soon. Joe had offered her a lift home, but she'd declined. She'd wanted to be there when David came round from the anaesthetic – which she had been. But Joe had insisted on calling a taxi for her, otherwise she'd be there all night. He'd told her David wouldn't want that. She had a job to go to in the morning. David had mentioned to him that she was working for residents of the new housing estate.

Robyn checked the time. She had plenty of time to freshen

up and make it back to the hospital entrance with a few minutes to spare, just in case the taxi turned up early. She wanted David to wake again so that she could say goodbye and tell him she would back in the morning. She imagined that Rose and George would be understanding when she phoned them to let them know what had happened, and that she would make it over to them after she'd stopped by the hospital in the morning.

She glanced at David before she shut the bathroom door, disappointed that it looked as though he wouldn't wake up before she left.

The bathroom door swung closed behind her and she found herself in a small white bathroom with a small sink, a shower cubicle, loo, and vanity unit. She ran a sink of warm water and washed the chocolate streaks from her hands. She splashed some warm water on her face and felt instantly revived. As she unplugged the sink, she thought she heard something.

She turned to the freshly laundered towels and dried her hands on the smallest one. Her hand reached for the door handle. She heard someone come into David's room, then David's groggy voice. She realised he must have woken up. 'What are you doing here?'

She pulled the door handle, about to walk out of the bathroom, so happy that David had woken up. Then she heard him say, 'Dad – what are you doing here?'

Dad?

Oh no, thought Robyn, and closed her eyes.

10

'Joe told me about the accident.'

'He did *what?* I told him not to tell you.'

Robyn had heard David make his brother promise not to tell before he left, relieved that she wouldn't come face to face with that horrible man again.

And now here he was.

I still don't have to meet him again, thought Robyn. She slowly, carefully, quietly relaxed her grip on the door handle. *But what am I going to do, stuck in the bathroom? Well, it won't be for long. David will get rid of him,* thought Robyn. He didn't want his father there either.

She heard someone else walk into the room. 'Ah, you're awake. How are we feeling?'

'A bit groggy. Knee is sore, but the painkillers are working wonders.'

Robyn slowly nodded her head. David had finally been given the meds he'd wanted.

'Good god, woman!' Robyn heard his dad exclaim. 'Can't you see he can manage himself? He's not a goddam invalid!'

'Actually, I do need a hand. Thank you, nurse, you've been

very helpful. Sitting up is a bit of a struggle. Ignore my dad, he's just being he's usual recalcitrant self.'

There was a gruff response, which Robyn couldn't make out. Then she heard the door to the room closing.

Silence.

Robyn listened, wondering if they'd all left the room, and David was alone again. She was about to reach for the door handle once more when she heard David. 'What the hell did you treat her like that for? She was only doing her job.'

There was the brief sound of a chair scraping along the floor, and then a few short footsteps. She guessed that his dad had got out of the chair and walked over to his bedside.

Then she heard David say, 'Go on then, do it. I know you want to. What are you waiting for?'

Robyn stared at the door, frowning. She didn't know what to make of that remark. She listened intently, wishing she knew what was happening on the other side of the door. She really ought to announce her presence; the longer it went on, the worse it was going to look. Robyn really wasn't feeling very proud of herself, skulking behind doors, listening in on people's private conversations. If she discovered this was the type of person she really was when her memory returned, then she wasn't going to like herself very much at all.

Robyn looked down at the door handle and grasped it, taking a deep breath; whatever the outcome now, it could only get worse if she continued to skulk behind the door. What if one of them needed to use the bathroom? Robyn took a deep breath, intending to flush the loo before she opened the door. His dad hadn't been there all that long. If she did it now, it wouldn't look too odd when she emerged.

'That's right,' she heard David's voice again, 'take a swing at me – why don't you?'

Robyn took a sharp intake of breath. If she was hearing right, she expected that if she opened that door right then, she'd find David's father standing over his bed, his hand raised, about to strike. For what reason, she had no clue. Is that the way he had treated his boys while they were growing up?

She was about to launch out of the door in a fury when another altogether more frightening thought stopped her in her tracks. If that was how Mr Gillespie senior behaved to his own son, in a hospital bed, what would he do to her? And David wouldn't be able to protect her.

With that horrible thought, Robyn lost her nerve and started to back away from the door. What if he found out it was her fault David had been on the ice?

She looked about her for somewhere to hide. The shower had a blue shower curtain on a rail. All she had to do was step inside and pull the curtain. No one was going to come in for a shower.

She didn't step into the shower cubicle. She wanted to hear what was going on. She sighed in relief when she heard footsteps, guessing it was David's father retreating from the bed. 'I guess your knee is really shot now,' he said.

'I told you it was, before this accident, and you wouldn't believe me.'

'I thought you were on the mend.'

'Wait – you thought I'd be fit enough to return to professional hockey at some point down the road, didn't you?'

David's father didn't respond to that. Instead, he said, 'What in god's name were you doing mucking about on the ice with those kids?'

'I wasn't mucking about, as you put it. I was coaching.'

'Coaching?' he scoffed. 'Where did you get that stupid idea from?'

Robyn held her breath. *Please don't say it was me.*

'It's not a stupid idea. It's actually a great idea.'

Robyn smiled when she heard that. It wasn't what she'd expected to hear.

'But you busted your knee again.'

'Yeah – and it wasn't the first time, and no doubt it won't be the last. Although next time I'll have to pay for it.'

'What are you talking about?'

'I've just had knee surgery. I should have had it done in the first place, but …'

'You wouldn't have it done. I think just to spite me.'

David fell silent, until he said, 'You wanted me to get back in the game. It was never about my health, and what I wanted. Always the game. Well, I'm glad I had the accident on the ice while I was coaching. And you know what? I'm going to do it again – not the accident, obviously, but coaching. I can help others make their dreams come true. I'm never going to play professionally again. Even if I'd had the knee surgery. I've come to accept that. Why can't you?'

Robyn held her breath, wondering what his father was going to say to that.

She didn't hear him say anything. All she heard was what sounded like a chair scraping across the floor.

Robyn put her head to the door and listened intently. *What is he doing now?* she wondered.

'What are you doing?' David asked.

'I'm drawing up a chair to sit with you awhile.'

What – after you were about to go for him?

'What – after you were about to start a fight again? Which would have been pretty one-sided, with me in this bed. Now you're going to sit with me?'

Robyn nodded furiously, agreeing with David's sentiments. She was just as confused.

'You just drive me nuts, you know that?' David said, sounding exasperated. 'Always have.'

'Yeah, I know, son. I'm sorry.'

'You're apologising now? Is this for just now, or … or for everything?'

There was a long silence. Robyn quietly put the lid down on the loo, and sat down, staring at the door, wondering what was going to happen next.

'I'm like a walking reminder of her,' she heard David comment. 'Well, not a walking one, at the moment.'

She heard his father actually chuckle at that comment. But what Robyn wanted to know was what David was talking about.

'Every damn day,' said David's father.

Robyn remembered that when she'd first met Joe, she had thought how remarkably different the brothers were in appearance. When she'd met their father at the Hogmanay party, she'd noticed he had the same broad, heavy build as Joe. But David took after his mother – he'd said so himself.

'So, do you still want to punch my lights out?'

What are you doing? Robyn stood up anxiously. *Don't ask him that.*

'I never wanted to hurt you … but you're doing it now.'

'What are you talking about?' David asked.

'Looking at me just the way she used to.'

There was a long, drawn-out silence, during which Robyn wondered what was going on. She silently got up from the loo and put her ear right up against the door. She hoped to goodness neither of them needed the loo. Robyn looked at the knob on the door handle and wondered why she hadn't thought about it before. Slowly, she turned the knob. It clicked, locking the door. She winced at the sound before putting her ear to the door once more.

Was someone crying?

She couldn't hear great sobs; it was more subtle than that. But there was definitely someone crying on the other side of that door.

'Dad, Dad. Don't do that, please.'

Robyn stepped back from the door in surprise.

'I can't help it.'

'Look, you wouldn't want Joe to see you like that. I'm sure he'll be here any minute. He said he was coming back this evening.'

'Well, it would make a change, wouldn't it?' David's father said in between snuffles, 'to see me with a tear-streaked face for once.'

'That's all behind us now,' David said reassuringly.

'What about this?'

Robyn wondered what he was referring to.

'It's been fixed this time. You saw the X-ray. I may not be able to play professionally again – but having a knee replacement will make a vast improvement, and I will be in less pain. And it means I can get back on the ice and coach.'

'Are you really ready for that – being involved in ice hockey when you can't play professionally anymore?'

Robyn screwed up her face. *Why wouldn't he be?* What a strange question.

There was a pause.

'I think so. No, that's not right. I know so.'

'I just don't understand,' said David's father. 'All this time, you were adamant you didn't want anything to do with it.'

'Well, now I've seen the light.'

'But you wouldn't go through with the operation. It was as though you were punishing me, punishing yourself. So why now?'

'I told you. I was doing some coaching, and I fell. It made sense, when I'd talked to the doctor, to go through with the op, especially if I want to get back out on the ice and coach kids.'

'But what were you doing on the ice in the first place? I mean, I know for a fact you won't go near a pair of skates.'

When David didn't say anything, his father said, 'You went skating last night at the loch – didn't you? That's why you wouldn't tell me where you were going when you went out.'

'You live at *my* house, not the other way round. I don't have to tell you a thing.'

Good for you, thought Robyn, *standing up to your old man.*

'It's her, isn't it?'

'What do you mean?'

'The girl you were with at Hogmanay.'

Robyn heard Mr Gillespie sigh heavily. 'You think you're in love with her.'

Robyn listened intently, hanging on their every word.

'I know I am,' David said forcefully.

Robyn gasped. She clamped a hand over her mouth.

'But you don't even know her.'

That was true. Robyn nodded her head in agreement.

'What's there to know? I love her, and that's all that matters.'

'Is it now?' said Mr Gillespie, an edge to his voice.

'What's it to you, anyway?'

'I don't want to see you get hurt – again.'

'Alright,' David said slowly. 'She's not from around these parts.'

'Tell me something I don't know.'

'Her mother is abroad, travelling.'

Robyn frowned. *How does he know that?* she wondered.

'Yes – and?' Mr Gillespie prompted.

'Robyn is a student at St Andrews.'

'What's she studying?'

'Something to do with art and design. She's into interior design.'

'So, she's going back soon?'

Robyn caught the inflection in Mr Gillespie's voice. She imagined he'd be very pleased to hear that, if that were the case.

'No, I don't think so. Gayle said she's considering dropping out.'

So, David had asked Gayle a little about her. Robyn had been wondering how he knew all this. They didn't exactly speak about their past.

'Who is Gayle?'

'Gayle is a friend of mine, lives at Lark Lodge.'

'Ah Lark Lodge. I remember now, she's Dr Belafonte's youngest. How are the old couple doing these days? Are they still in the land of the living?'

'For your information, Dr Belafonte died recently. His funeral is on Friday.'

Robyn frowned. She did not want David's father at the funeral, and she was pretty sure Gayle wouldn't want that mean old man there either. She guessed David wasn't going to make it now. The doctor had said he'd be in for a few more days. The earliest he'd be discharged was over the weekend – if he was lucky.

David said, 'It's just her mother left now.'

'How is the old fruitcake?'

'I don't want to dignify that question with an answer, but for your information, Doris has dementia, poor woman.'

'So, Robyn is not going back to university?' Mr Gillespie asked.

'I hope not.'

'That's a shame.'

'Look, I know you don't like her, but you don't even know her.'

'I don't trust her, David. I think she's hiding something.'

'Aren't we all?' David commented.

Behind the bathroom door, Robyn frowned at that comment. What did David mean? What was he hiding? And how come his father thought *she* was hiding something? She could feel the colour rising in her cheeks. They'd only met once, and he'd barely said a word to her.

'I'm a good judge of character. You know that.'

There was another drawn-out silence. Then Mr Gillespie said, 'What about her father?'

'I don't know. Do you expect me to know her life story?' David said, exasperated. 'God knows, she doesn't know mine.'

'How much have you told her?'

'Nothing.'

'Good. Keep it that way.'

Robyn bit her lower lip, wondering what he meant.

'Why here?' Mr Gillespie asked.

'I'm sorry – now what are you talking about now?' David sounded exasperated again.

'Why is she here? It doesn't sound as though she has family in the area, otherwise she wouldn't be staying with Gayle at Lark Lodge.'

'I hadn't thought of that.'

'She was on her way out of town, must have been travelling at a speed to lose control and drive into you. Where was she going on Christmas Day?'

'I don't know. We haven't talked about the accident. Maybe she was just passing through on the way to family on Christmas Day.'

'Maybe? So you don't know what she was doing here, or where she was going?'

'She didn't say.'

'Why not?'

'I didn't ask.'

'Well, maybe you should.'

Robyn stood with her back to the door, listening to the conversation, listening to David talking about her, about what she barely knew herself, as though it was somebody else they were discussing.

She silently slid her back down the door until she was sitting on the floor. She drew her legs up to her chest, wrapped her arms around her legs, and rested her chin on her knees. Tears rolled down her cheeks.

David said, 'She must have been spending some of the

Christmas holiday in the area, and then she was on her way back to university.'

Robyn looked up. That was feasible.

'On Christmas Day?'

'Look, her mum's abroad. Perhaps that's all the family she's got.'

'So, if that's the case, why hasn't Robyn gone back to college by now?'

'How the hell do I know? I'm just glad she hasn't, and you know what? I don't know why I'm even having this conversation with you. I don't have to justify my choice of girlfriend. And why do you care?'

Robyn managed a smile. She hoped that marked the end of the conversation, and his father would just leave. The problem was that she would then have to walk out of the bathroom, and David would know she'd been there the whole time.

Was he leaving? She hoped so. Then she heard Mr Gillespie's voice again. 'What if she wakes up from this little holiday from her life and decides to go back, pick up where she left off?' He paused. 'Ah, I can tell by your expression that you haven't considered that. Well, maybe it's time you did.'

'I'll cross that bridge when I come to it. Who knows? Maybe I'll follow her.'

'What if she doesn't want to be followed?' He paused. 'What is she running away from, I wonder?'

Robyn stared at the door.

'What's wrong with a local girl – someone like Annie?'

'Look I'm really tired, so I think it's time you—'

'There's Mandy – remember her? You used to be in the same class at school. I'm sure she's still got a thing for you. I heard she and her husband split up. I see her checking you out whenever she comes into the store, always asking for you.'

'Dad, please.' David sounded mortified. 'I'm not having this conversation with you.' There was the sound of ruffling of covers. 'I'm really tired. I'd like to get some sleep before Joe arrives, if you don't mind.'

'It's not that late.'

'Yeah, well I've just had an op. It really takes it out of you.'

David's voice sounded muffled, as though he was speaking from under his covers. 'I know what this is really about, Dad. Just because mum left you, you think all women are bad news.'

A chair scraped on the floor. Robyn imagined Mr Gillespie standing up in a hurry.

'Don't talk to me about mine – just take a look at what happened with your fiancée. She didn't hang around, did she? As soon as you were out of professional hockey, and all the potential money that went with it, she was gone.'

'Well, gee.' David's voice was clearer. 'Thanks for reminding me. And what's that got to do with anything?'

'Maybe you need to be careful, in getting mixed up with Robyn, that it doesn't happen again. You know, you could be setting yourself up for a big fall, son, and none of us want to see you hurt again, in any way.'

'I want you to leave.'

'Fine.'

Robyn listened to the sound of footsteps and the door opening. She breathed a sigh of relief. She was just thinking that at least now she only had to explain herself to David. Then she heard Mr Gillespie again. She guessed he was standing by the door because his voice sounded further away.

'Just be careful, son. I've got a bad feeling about her.'

'I'd like you to leave.' David's voice was sombre. 'I'll call for the nurse, if you don't leave right now.'

'You always were a sissy, hiding behind your mother's skirts. I should have let her take you with her.'

'But you didn't, because it was the best way you could think of to hurt her – wasn't it?'

'Oh yes,' he said bitterly. 'And I hope she's suffered. I hope that was compounded by seeing your name in lights, seeing your face on television playing ice hockey.'

'My god!' David's voice sounded incredulous. 'Is that why—?'

'Do you really think I even liked ice hockey? When was the last time you saw me out on the ice?'

Never, thought Robyn thinking back to the conversation on with Annie.

'You know, it surprises me that you never figured it out for yourself,' he added.

'You *used* me.'

'Of course I did. It was just lucky that you were good at something that would garner such recognition. There was a while there that I was beginning to have my doubts.'

'That's why you pushed me.'

'Uh-huh. Little league, junior league – all in the paper for the world and your mother to see. Then you were heading for the big time. Now that's what I was waiting for – until you cocked it all up.'

'The accident wasn't my fault.'

'But you know what really surprises me?' David's father mused, appearing to ignore what David had just said. 'She must have known. It was in the newspapers. You could have died.'

Robyn hadn't realised the accident that had ended David's career had been that serious.

'But you know what?' Mr Gillespie continued.

David didn't say a word.

Robyn guessed what he was going to say next. She really wished she hadn't got herself into this predicament. She was already hearing too much for her own good. She thought about just covering up her ears with her hands, but she couldn't help herself, and besides, she wouldn't hear if anyone suddenly came in. But that was just an excuse. She really didn't want to hear Mr Gillespie voice what she'd thought herself.

'I thought she might come to see you. I was in that hospital with you day and night. I was expecting her. I was waiting for her ...'

David finally said something. 'Yes, of course she wouldn't come. She knew you'd be waiting for her. Do you think really she'd have risked it?' he said scornfully.

'For you, yes. I always expected her to come for you one day. Not Joe, though. You were always her favourite.'

'That why you never let me out of your sight.'

'She wasn't going to have you,' he said emphatically.

'You're a sick …'

Robyn put her hand over her mouth.

'Twisted …' David continued.

Robyn wondered what his father was going to do to him when he finished that sentence. Now she had to intervene. she put her hand on the door handle.

'Fu—'

Before he could finish the sentence, someone else rushed into the room. There was a flurry of footsteps before someone said, 'Excuse me, sir. We need you to step aside.' A young woman said, 'You pressed your emergency button!'

'Oh, did I?' David sounded genuinely surprised. Robyn guessed that perhaps if he was holding the buzzer, he had accidentally pressed the button in anger.

'Sorry. This man was just leaving.'

'Are you sure you don't need anything while I'm here?' the nurse's voice appeared to come from the other side of the room, near the door.

'No, thank you. Perhaps you could show him the way out.'

'Er, right.' The nurse sounded a bit confused. 'This way.'

Robyn heard footsteps.

'I'll swing by tomorrow,' David's father said, his voice distant.

'Why bother? She isn't going to turn up this time.'

His father must have left the room, as he didn't answer.

'Nurse, I'm quite tired, so no more visitors this evening, please. Can you do me a huge favour and ring my next of kin – that's my brother – let him know that I'm fine, but I need to rest. So perhaps he can visit tomorrow.'

'I'll see what I can do.'

'Thank you.'

The door to the room closed.

The room was silent.

Robyn stood by the bathroom door, listening to David moving his covers around.

'Son of a bitch,' he said. Then all was quiet.

11

Robyn stood on the other side of the door, wondering what she was going to say and how she was going to explain herself when she stepped out of the bathroom. If she'd known beforehand what type of conversation was going to take place on the other side of the door, she would have run out of that bathroom straight away and shouted her presence from the roof top.

Robyn twisted the handle of the door. She could feel her cheeks burning, her heart rate quickening. What she really wanted now was an invisible cloak to whisk her away.

Robyn took a deep breath, closed her eyes and opened the door. Keeping her eyes fixed firmly in front of her, she walked to the end of the bed and turned around, placing herself directly in front of him. He didn't say a word. She touched the bed post with one hand and forced her eyes upon his; they were closed.

Robyn realised she hadn't breathed since leaving the bathroom. She exhaled in relief. David was asleep. She glanced at the door, wondering if she should just leave. David had said to his father that he wanted no more visitors that evening.

Robyn took one step towards the door.

The bed creaked. 'Robyn!' David's eyes opened, and he was

struggling to sit up. His face beamed in delight. 'Where did you appear from? I didn't hear you come in.'

Actually I've been skulking behind your bathroom door, Robyn thought as she looked sheepishly in the direction of the bathroom, swallowing the urge to confess. 'You were sleeping.'

'I thought you were going home?' David was now sitting at an awkward angle, trying to make himself more comfortable but not succeeding.

So did I. Robyn remembered the taxi as she glanced at the clock on the wall. She'd missed it. It was lucky she didn't have a mobile phone, otherwise they might have called her number while she was hiding in the bathroom. Robyn glanced sheepishly past David at the bathroom door. It hadn't been very mature, hiding like that.

'Here – let me.' Robyn helped him sit up. She plumped a couple of pillows while David leaned forward, holding onto her arm. He leaned back into the pillows gently. Still holding her hand, he said, 'I see you missed me already.'

'No, I just missed my taxi.'

'Oh dear. How did that happen?'

Robyn smiled. 'I'm joking,' she said. Even though she *had* missed her taxi, she didn't want it to sound as though she would rather not be there with him. 'I know you're tired, and you don't want any more visitors, but would you like me to stay awhile?'

'How did you know I didn't want any more visitors?'

'Oh, er …' Robyn realised her gaffe too late. 'You look tired and um I just assumed …' she trailed off, avoiding eye contact.

'It's true. I didn't want any more visitors. Until you showed up. Will you stay a little longer?' He motioned at the chair by his bedside.

She hesitated. Robyn looked towards the door. What if Mr Gillespie returned?

'You're not leaving, are you?' David asked.

Robyn turned around. She knew why he didn't want her to leave. It was no fun staring at a blank wall. She could empathise, thinking back on her own stay in hospital. 'Don't worry. I'm not going anywhere. I don't know what I would have done if you hadn't come to visit me every day.'

Robyn sat down in the chair. 'I've got an ulterior motive for staying,' she said, smiling mischievously.

'Oh, yeah. What's that?'

Robyn took his hand. 'I want to make sure my ride gets better really quick, don't I?' she smiled at him. It wouldn't be the same, David not picking her up in the van and taking her places. She was going to miss his visits to Lark Lodge. When he was discharged home from hospital, she was sure Gayle wouldn't mind driving her over to David's house to see him while he recuperated. But there was a problem – it meant she'd most likely see Mr Gillespie too.

Robyn didn't want to think about that. She decided to stay until David fell asleep, which she guessed would be pretty soon because she found she was doing all the talking. He just nodded as she chatted. She avoided any prickly subjects like Joe and David's father. Instead, she talked about her new job; how things had gone that day at Rose and George's.

That morning, when he'd taken her over to their house with all the swatches and fabric she'd bought the day before and had left in his van, seemed like a lifetime ago.

'They loved the fabrics. I took measurements, and I've contacted a company who do made-to-measure curtains, blinds, and cushions. It's all going so well. I'm going to start decorating tomorrow. But I'll come and see you in the hospital first, I promise.' She squeezed his hand reassuringly.

'Did I tell you that it's Gayle's birthday soon? I'm not getting her a present to unwrap, though. I have something else in mind …'

David snuggled down under his covers, pulling them up to his chin as though he were a small child about to be told a bedtime story.

Robyn told him all about her plan for Gayle's birthday surprise. David nodded and blinked back sleep. When she had finished, Robyn excused herself to use the bathroom. Unfortunately, Mr Gillespie came to mind as soon as she stepped inside. She was thinking about visiting David when he was discharged. She could time her visits when his dad was out, working in his shop. But she had a job to do herself, and although Rose and George were understanding, she couldn't just flit in and out of their house, doing a bit here, a bit there when she felt like it. Besides, she imagined they'd want her to get on with the decorating, so the work would get done as soon as possible. That meant seeing David in the evening, after work, when his father was around.

Robyn had just thought of a way round that. She'd have to speak to Gayle. That didn't stop her sharing her idea. She opened the bathroom door, and said, 'David, I have the most amazing idea. Look, do you have to go home to yours after you're discharged? I'm sure you don't want your dad picking you up. Why don't you stay at Lark Lodge? There's a ground floor bedroom. And Gayle is – was – a nurse. She'll keep an eye on you.'

Robyn suddenly had a feeling of déjà vu. She recalled inviting Nick to stay at Lark Lodge. That was so cheeky of her, when she hadn't even discussed it with Gayle first. But Gayle had welcomed him, and the extra unexpected guest in the form of Olive.

But this was different. Unlike Nick, Gayle knew David. *And now I'm earning money, I can pay for both our room and board*, thought Robyn. She immediately could foresee a problem – she imagined David wouldn't let her pay for his stay. Robyn dismissed that thought – for now.

When she turned around at the foot of David's bed, wondering what David would say to her idea, he was sound asleep. Robyn looked at the clock, and decided that because it was so late anyway, she might as well sit for a few minutes more just to check he wasn't going to wake and find her gone at the first opportunity before she left to phone for a taxi.

Robyn sat back in her chair and looked around the room before focusing on David. She watched the covers rise and fall with his every breath. She rubbed her eyes, feeling exhausted. It was now getting on for ten in the evening – well past visiting hours, she imagined. Any minute, a nurse was going to walk in and tell her that she had to leave. She couldn't stay there all night.

12

Robyn thought she heard a whisper of voices; distant, then closer. She felt something heavy across her legs.

'Shh!'

Robyn's eyelids fluttered.

'She's stirring – look.'

The lights were too bright, hurting her eyes.

'Good morning, sleepy head.'

Robyn rubbed the sleep out of her eyes. 'Gayle! What are you doing here?' Robyn squinted at the bright sunlight streaming through the hospital window. 'Oh no! I've been here all night.' Robyn stretched stiffly in the chair, making the woollen blanket draped over her legs slip down her knees on to the floor.

'Yes – you have.' Robyn heard another voice she thought she recognised. She held up her hand to shield her eyes from the sunlight and saw Doris sitting in a chair by the window.

'When I got up this morning and knocked at your door with a cup of tea, imagine my surprise when there was no answer,' said Gayle. 'Then I popped my head inside and your bed was still made, so I knew you'd been out all night.' You can imagine what I thought.'

She paused, handing Robyn a takeaway cup. 'Here's a cuppa from the vending machine down the hall.'

Robyn took it gratefully.

'You can imagine what I thought,' Gayle said again.

Robyn didn't know what she meant. She looked at her, bemused.

'You and David have been getting along really well …' Gayle grinned.

Robyn eyed her. 'I still don't get what you … oh. Oh, I see.' She grinned too. 'This wasn't exactly how I thought we'd spend our first night together.'

'I'll bet,' said Gayle, still grinning.

Thinking of David, Robyn sat up with a start, nearly spilling her tea. David's bed was empty. 'Where—?'

Gayle rested a reassuring hand on her shoulder. 'Relax. David is with the physio.'

'He's up and about already?'

'The physio always gets them up and about, ensuring they start walking after knee replacement surgery as soon as possible. You'd be surprised how many people complain about that, but it's in their own interests to get mobile, obviously. They've taken him to a room down the hall where they have some physio equipment to practise stairs.'

'Well, that's great news. Did they say when he'd be discharged?'

'He'll be out in two or three days, so at the weekend, I expect.'

Robyn thought that was for the best, because she wanted to ask Gayle if he could stay at Lark Lodge. However, with Gayle's father's funeral the next day – Friday – she wasn't going to broach that idea until afterwards.

Preparations were already underway for the wake at Lark Lodge after the service. It sounded as though it was going to be quite a turnout from the local community – people wanting to pay their respects to the local GP who had served the community for decades. There was far too much going on with the funeral, and the wake, for Gayle to be expected to collect a new guest – David, no doubt on crutches – from the hospital before the weekend.

Robyn had no idea what David's house was like – whether it was a new-build, or an old property – but she thought Lark Lodge would be a wonderful place to recuperate; if David wanted to stay there, and obviously if Gayle and her mother were agreeable.

'How did you know I was here?' Robyn asked.

'David called me on his mobile. He told the nurse to let you sleep. I said I'd pop over, bring you home.'

Robyn's next concern was Rose and George. 'Oh, no. What's the time? Rose will be expecting me.'

'It's fine. I've let them know that David had an accident, and you're visiting him in hospital, but that you'll pop along later, if you can. They were very understanding.'

Robyn sighed in relief, until something occurred to her. 'I don't know how I'm going to get over to their house now that David can't drive me for the foreseeable.' She didn't know how long that would be.

'Don't you worry about that. I'll take you.'

'Oh, Gayle. I don't know what I'd do without you.'

Their conversation was interrupted by Gayle's mother. 'I want to see Horatio now. Where is he?'

'Who is Horatio?' Robyn asked Gayle.

Gayle sigh heavily. 'Horatio is my late father.'

'Oh.'

'What do you mean – late?' Doris said indignantly. 'He's never late for anything. My husband is always so punctual. Isn't that right, Gayle?'

Robyn looked at Gayle. Their eyes met. The funeral was tomorrow, and her poor mum had already forgotten he'd passed away.

Gayle whispered to Robyn, 'I had to bring her with me to pick you up. But I'm afraid that the hospital visit must have stirred up memories of when we visited Dad before Christmas.'

'I'm sorry.'

'It's not your fault, Robyn.' Gayle turned to Doris. 'We're leaving soon, going home.'

'Is Horatio coming with us?'

'No, Mum.'

Robyn gulped down her tea, anxious to leave, for Doris's sake. She wanted to see David, but as Gayle had said, he was in physio.

'Why didn't he wake me?'

'I told you. He wanted to let you sleep. It sounds as though it was a long night, what with David being rushed into theatre, and you spending the evening at his bedside.

'It was my fault,' Robyn admitted miserably. 'All my fault,' she said as they walked out of the room. She did take a long glance down the corridor, hoping that David was on his way back with the physio, but there was no sign of him.

'What are you talking about?' Gayle asked. 'How could it be your fault? David slipped on the ice.'

'Is that what he told you?'

'Yes.'

'But did he tell you he was playing ice hockey.'

'Really?'

That answered Robyn's question. 'Yes, well, he was coaching some kids who are hoping to get into the junior league.'

'Coaching? What a wonderful idea.'

Robyn frowned. She'd thought so too, until he'd fallen. She said as much. 'One of the kids skated into him, knocked him over.'

'These things happen, Robyn. I don't see how that was your fault.'

'Yes, but I encouraged him to coach the kids.'

'Well, I still think it's a brilliant idea. He does love ice hockey, even though it sounds as though he was forced into it, to begin with, by his father, who was pretty tough on him, I imagine. But that hasn't dampened his love of the game.'

'How do you know all this, Gayle?'

'My father was his GP.'

'Oh, I didn't know that.'

'Yeah, small town, small world. He saw him regularly afterwards.'

'Did your dad ever say anything about how it happened?'

'How what happened?'

'The original accident that ended his career?'

Gayle shook her head. 'Doctor/patient confidentiality. Although I imagine he was there to get regular prescriptions for pain medication. I overheard my father talking to himself once, saying, *Why won't that lad just have knee replacement surgery? It doesn't make sense.*'

Robyn knew why. She shared what she'd overheard. She couldn't help herself. 'I think that even though he knew that he still wouldn't be able to play ice hockey again professionally even if he had the surgery, he did it to get back at his dad for being so hard on him when he was younger.' Robyn thought of what she'd overheard when she'd locked herself in the bathroom, a fact she was not going to share with Gayle. 'I … um, get the impression that his dad thought if he had the surgery, he'd get back in the game. I think he'd pressure him to try, even though it would have been futile.'

Gayle nodded.

Robyn slowed as they reached the hospital entrance. She glanced over her shoulder.

'David is in good hands,' said Gayle. 'And so are you,' she added, placing an arm around Robyn's shoulders and steering her out the door. 'What you need is a hot shower, a change of clothes, and a good breakfast.'

Robyn had to admit that a hot shower and a change of clothes sounded really good, as did the breakfast. She was starving after only eating a chocolate bar for tea last night.

'Come on,' said Gayle, 'let's get you home.'

13

'Gayle, I don't know if I feel like going to work today.'

'Well, it's a bit late for that now. We're nearly there.'

Robyn looked out of the car window. She could see the flags up ahead marking the entrance to the new estate. She did feel much better after she'd showered and changed out of the clothes she'd slept in. Gayle had insisted on cooking her a full breakfast.

Gayle glanced her way. 'I think you're doing the right thing coming here today. It would take your mind off … things.'

Robyn knew what she meant by *things* – David's accident.

'After all, what are you going to do with yourself, hanging around Lark Lodge all day?'

If only you knew. Robyn smiled to herself.

'What are you smiling about, missy?'

'Oh nothing.' Robyn said innocently, avoiding her gaze. She was so looking forward to starting work on Lark Lodge, restoring the place to its former glory – Gayle just didn't know it yet.

'Besides, you won't be working at Rose and George's tomorrow.'

'Yes, I know,' Robyn said in a small voice. The next day was Friday, the day of the funeral.

They both fell into a sombre silence.

Gayle pulled the car up in front of Rose and George's house.

'Will you phone me straight away if you hear from David?' Robyn asked again for the hundredth time.

'You really ought to have a mobile phone, Robyn. We'll go shopping at the weekend, and you can buy one.'

Robyn could foresee a problem. She knew she had a savings account – which she couldn't access just yet because she had no ID. But what about a bank account? Wouldn't she have to set up some sort of monthly direct debit to pay for her new phone?

As if reading her mind, Gayle said, 'Why don't you start with a pay-as-you-go phone? That way you don't have to tie yourself into a contract.'

'I hadn't thought of that.'

'If your handbag and phone come to light – I assume you had a mobile phone, everyone does – then at least you haven't signed up for anything.'

Gayle looked at the houses opposite Rose and George. 'Well, this estate is coming on in leaps and bounds. Nick said it was. I'll be sad to see him, and Olive, go when the estate is finished.'

Robyn followed her gaze. 'It's going to be quite a large development. I think Nick will be staying at Lark Lodge a while yet.'

'I hope so.'

Robyn smiled some more. 'Nick and Olive have settled in nicely over the last few days, haven't they?'

'I'll say.'

A loud bark came from the back of the car. They both turned around and laughed as they reached over and patted Olive on the head.

'Good girl!' said Gayle, in a soppy voice. 'You're such a good girl.'

Robyn rubbed her ear, thinking that perhaps they shouldn't encourage her to bark in the car. Olive had been dozing on the back seat the whole way there, enjoying the car ride. She always fell asleep in the car. But she must have heard her name – either that, or the engine being switched off had jolted her awake.

Gayle had told Nick the plan, that she'd take Robyn to work later that morning, so there was no need for him to drop Olive off at Rose and George's for doggy day care; they'd do that too.

Nick normally took Olive to work with him, and dropped her off at Rose and George's – Robyn had broached the idea with them, and unsurprisingly, like everyone else, as soon as they met Olive, they'd fallen in love. But Olive wouldn't be going to work with Nick every day, enjoying doggy dare care at Rose and George's house.

Nick and Olive had only moved into Lark Lodge a little under a week earlier, on New Year's Eve, but in that short space of time, Gayle had grown quite attached to the Old English Sheepdog puppy. When she didn't have any mobile hairdressing clients to visit, and she was home most of the day, Olive stayed home with her. But that morning, Gayle had a client in town. Her neighbour had already popped round to keep an eye on her mum before they left. But asking her to look after a boisterous young dog too wasn't fair. Besides, her old neighbour had a little dog of her own, and it wouldn't be fair on her dog either. Robyn could just imagine Olive thinking she had a playmate, and wanting to play with the elderly dog.

Fortunately, Rose and George had no pets of their own. She expected they spoiled her rotten. They had a lovely garden where

Olive could frolic in the snow. Robyn could just imagine that come spring, Olive would enjoy lying in the sunshine in their garden. Nick had told her that he'd be working as a site manager on the estate for a good few months more, up to the summer and most likely beyond.

Like Gayle, Robyn would be sad to see him and Olive go. But she didn't want to think about people leaving; least of all herself.

She knew that the spring term would be starting at St Andrews University soon. She imagined her room was still waiting for her after the Christmas break. Robyn knew she would have to do something about that – contact the university and see if she could defer. Not that she intended to return, but at the back of her mind was what her mum might think when she found out she'd dropped out. She'd have to let her know.

'Robyn – are you okay?'

She'd been lost in her own thoughts. 'Yeah.' She told Gayle what was on her mind.

'Ah, yes. I forgot about that,' said Gayle.

Robyn explained that it felt as though that part of her life, being a student, wasn't actually her life. Gayle touched her arm. 'It's because you can't remember. You know, perhaps you should go back, just make the trip, go to your room, speak to your roommate, if you have one, or a lecturer on your course before you defer. Someone is bound to know you, tell you about yourself. And if you don't meet anyone you know, then at least being in familiar surroundings might help you remember.'

But that was the point – she didn't want to remember. Not now. Not ever. She liked things the way they were now, with her new friends.

Robyn looked at Gayle. 'Is that what you think I should do?'

'Yes, I think so. Going back to your old life is probably the most likely way you'll remember.'

Robyn eyed her. She knew what she was saying made sense, but she was telling her what she didn't want to hear.

'But that doesn't mean it's something I *want* you to do. I don't want you to leave, Robyn.'

'Well, neither do I. And I don't want my memories back, either.'

Gayle breathed a heavy sigh.

'What?'

'Sweetheart, you might not have a choice. If you think hiding out here will protect you from whatever it is you were running away from, at some point your past is going to catch up with you. It always does.'

Robyn stared at her. She did not want to hear that.

'But right now you're here, and that's all that matters – to me, at any rate. Sorry, that's very selfish of me.'

Robyn grinned. 'Not at all. I feel the same way.' She opened the car door, then turned to Gayle once more. 'You'll let me know if David gets in touch?'

'I'll do one better,' said Gayle. 'I'll give him Rose's phone number. Then he can speak to you himself.'

'Oh Gayle. You're so thoughtful.' Robyn leaned over and gave Gayle a hug.

Robyn got out of the car reluctantly, even though she knew that Gayle was right: she should be there today, because she wouldn't be there to work the next day or over the weekend. As the front door opened, she turned and gave Gayle a wave goodbye.

'Ah, Robyn. I wasn't sure whether you'd come today.'

Robyn fixed a smile on her face and told a fib. 'Of course I was going to come.'

'I'm so sorry to hear that David is in hospital again. How is he?' Rose asked as she closed the front door behind Robyn.

'He had knee replacement surgery last night. He was having physio this morning. Apparently, they are keen to get knee op patients up and about as soon as possible.'

'Already?

'Yes.'

Rose nodded. 'Good,' she said. 'So, what happens next?'

'Huh?'

'I chose the fabric, and you've ordered my made-to-measure curtains, cushions, and blinds. Now, how do we proceed from here?'

Robyn looked around her lounge. 'Today, we choose colour schemes and wallpaper.'

'Wallpaper?' said George, walking into the lounge to join his wife.

Rose said, 'Remember, George? We discussed this and agreed with Robyn's suggestion that wallpapering one wall in each room would add some depth, and colour, to the rooms. I still love the idea. Don't you?'

'Of course, of course,' he mumbled, looking around the room.

Rose noticed. So did Robyn.

Rose asked, 'What's the matter? Have you lost something?'

George looked across the room at Robyn. 'Where's Olive?'

Robyn looked at George, and Rose. 'Oh, god! Gayle has driven off with Olive in the back! Can I use your phone to call her mobile phone please?'

'But she will be driving,' said Rose.

'Yes, but perhaps she will pull over and answer it.' Robyn imagined Gayle would pull over all right if Olive barked at the sound of her mobile.

Rose didn't point in the direction of the house phone in the hall. Instead she opened a drawer in the sideboard in the lounge, reached inside and handed Robyn her mobile phone. She said, 'You know it's very unusual for a person of your generation not to have one.'

'I lost mine.' Robyn took the phone and rang Gayle's number. Gayle didn't pull over and answer it. Rose was right: she was driving.

Robyn was just leaving a message when she heard a car pulling up outside.

Rose walked over to the window and moved the net curtains to one side. 'It's Gayle.'

'Did she bring Olive?' George asked keenly, joining his wife at the window.

Robyn heard Olive barking. 'Oh, yes.' She went to answer the door and grinned at Gayle, who was heading down the front path with Olive pulling on her lead. Robyn said, 'I rang your mobile.'

'I know. I was driving, and I couldn't pull over. Guess who I forgot was in the back?'

'Well, you weren't the only one who forgot about her! She must have fallen asleep again in the back while we were chatting.'

'Well, here you are.' Gayle handed Robyn Olive's lead, but the lead slipped through her fingers as Olive barged past, into the house, straight into George's arms. He'd been crouching in the hallway, waiting for her.

Gayle heaved a sigh. 'Right, well, I'll be off again.'

'You will let me know if you hear from David?'

'Like I said, I'll pass him Rose's home phone number.'

Robyn looked at the mobile in her hand. 'Actually, perhaps you wouldn't mind passing him this number? I'm sure Rose won't mind if I keep this close to hand while I'm here this afternoon.'

When Robyn closed the front door on Gayle, she turned around to find Rose standing there.

Robyn still had her mobile. 'Oh, yes. Of course. Here.' She attempted to hand it over, explaining that she hoped to hear from David, and she'd asked Gayle to let him have this mobile number. Robyn winced, thinking that Rose and George have been so understanding, but perhaps this was a step too far. 'You're right, Rose. I should get my own mobile phone.' She looked at her sheepishly as she held out the mobile. 'Sorry.'

Rose didn't make a move to take the phone. Instead, she said, 'Keep it.'

'I'm sorry – what?'

Rose shrugged. 'I don't know why I need it anyway. My daughter gave it to me for Christmas, oh, years back, but it's not like my family get in touch. No one texts. Besides, I've got a phone.' She pointed at the house phone in the hall. 'They know my phone number.'

Robyn looked at the phone.

'So, I want you to have it. It's a pay-as-you-go. You can text or phone to top it up. I'm sure a top-up card came with it too. You can just top it up in a shop.'

'Oh, Rose that's really kind of you, but let me give you some money for it.'

'Don't talk nonsense. It's old, probably pack up soon.'

Robyn looked at the phone. It did not look old. It looked brand new.

Two hours later, after Rose had decided on some wallpaper and paint samples she'd like Robyn to send off for, the mobile phone rang. Robyn immediately got it out of her pocket to take it to Rose.

Rose was in the kitchen, making a pot of tea. There were homemade scones and jam on the kitchen counter. Rose turned around at the sound of the phone, looking as surprised as Robyn. She shook her head. 'Nobody rings me on that thing. It must be for you.'

Robyn looked at the phone.

'Aren't you going to answer that?' Rose said.

14

Robyn answered the phone, watching Rose pick up a tea tray with a pot of tea, two cups and saucers, milk, sugar and scones, and head out of the kitchen to the lounge.

'Gayle?' Robyn said into the phone.

'Try again.'

'David!' Robyn exclaimed. She was so happy to hear his voice. 'How did the physio go?'

'They're very pushy, but I get it. I've been down this road before.'

Robyn presumed he was referring to his last injury.

'Now seriously,' said Robyn, 'how did it go?'

Rose began to speak in a loud voice from the kitchen so that Robyn couldn't hear David's answer. 'Why don't you ask him ...' she began.

'Gayle said you're working today, so I won't keep you,' David continued. I'm just glad to know you are out and not moping about the house because of me.'

'Because of you?' Robyn shook her head. She walked over to the kitchen door and closed it. 'You know it's because of me that you were on the ice in the first place.'

'Uh-huh. That's right,' David agreed.

'But you *were* being a bit of a show-off,' Robyn joked. David was a really good skater, and from what she'd seen when he'd skated with the puck, and hit it into the net, it was no surprise he had been almost at the top of his game, on the cusp of joining the ice hockey big leagues.

'Steady!' David groaned.

'Sorry, David, I didn't mean ...' Had she gone too far?

'Don't be silly. I lost my balance, not my sense of humour. Besides,' he added, 'everything has worked out just fine. Great, actually. I've had the op, and my dad actually apologised. Not sure for what, exactly, but it's a start. That was a bit surreal.'

The start of what? Robyn thought. She recalled that his father's visit had ended in a row over David's mum. It sounded as though she'd wanted to take David with her when she'd left.

Robyn pursed her lips. He hadn't brought that up when the two of them had talked about his mum, so he obviously didn't want her to know.

She promised to visit him again soon. 'As long as it's OK with Gayle – you see, I seem to have lost my ride,' she said playfully.

'Oh, don't you worry about that. Gayle and I have it all worked out.'

Robyn put the receiver down, wondering exactly what David and Gayle had been saying. She assumed he was talking about Gayle giving her a lift into work while he was getting back on his feet.

'Everything alright?'

Robyn turned around. George had popped his head around the kitchen door.

Robyn nodded.

'Rose sent me to fetch you for a cuppa and a scone.'

The door suddenly flew open, and an exuberant Olive came lolloping into the kitchen.

'Ah, there you are.' Robyn hadn't seen the dog since Gayle had brought her back. She guessed George was keeping the playful dog out of the lounge, leaving Robyn and Rose in peace to go over the colour schemes for the house. She knelt to give Olive a fuss. 'Oh, you're all wet.'

George stepped into the kitchen with a towel. 'She's been outside in the garden, frolicking in the snow. It's not that deep, but she does love to roll around in it.'

Robyn could tell.

'Here.' George handed her the towel. 'Would you give her a rub down for me? My old knees, and my back, don't take kindly to getting down on the ground.'

'Of course.' Robyn took the towel and started to dry Olive's wet fur.

Olive thought it was a game and grabbed a corner of the towel.

'No, Robyn is not playing tug-o-war with you, Olive,' said George, smiling affectionately at the dog.

Robyn laughed, and prised the towel out of Olive's jaws, giving her a gentle tap on the nose. 'No, Olive.'

Olive clamped her jaws shut, and then sneezed.

'God, you're so cute,' said Robyn as she towelled Olive down. Olive rolled onto her back, big paws in the air, as Robyn dried her and gave her a belly rub.

Robyn sat back on her knees. 'There – you're all done.'

George was watching from the doorway.

Robyn looked up. 'Do we leave her in the kitchen while we have tea?'

'I think so. Otherwise she might get into mischief. I'm sure she'd thinking nothing of stealing a freshly baked scone or two in the lounge.'

Robyn thought so too. From her experience over the last few days, living with Olive at Lark Lodge, the dog did love her food. Like most dogs, she thought nothing of stealing food, even bacon and sausages, straight from your breakfast plate on the table, if you weren't paying attention.

'I have something for Olive that will keep her occupied.' George walked over to a kitchen cupboard.

Olive suddenly got to her feet and hurried after George.

'You know where the treat cupboard is, don't you, girl?' George patted her on the head, opened the cupboard, and turned around with a treat.

Olive settled herself in the middle of the kitchen floor, paws holding the bone-shaped dog treat as she chewed.

'Right, let's go and have that tea,' said George.

In the lounge, Robyn wandered over to the bay window and looked outside. 'They're certainly getting a move on with the houses opposite.' The last time Robyn had been there, the houses opposite had just been footings. Now, the property was up to the first floor and was starting to look like a house. 'I bet you're looking forward to having neighbours.' Robyn knew it was lonely for them, being the first occupants on the development. The show home next door would probably be the last property to be sold.

'I've met some of my new neighbours already.'

Robyn turned from the window, surprised. 'You have?' She

caught George nodding his head.

'Yes, when they came round to view the show home. I saw them with the estate agent, standing on the pavement outside, so I nipped out to introduce myself. They're lovely people – aren't they, George?'

George picked up a scone. 'Oh, yes.'

'They're local,' said Rose. 'Just like us, they're downsizing from large, old properties to something brand new where they don't have to worry about whether their old boiler will pack up, or what the next maintenance issue will be.'

Rose poured three cups of tea. Robyn walked over and took a seat on the sofa next to Rose.

'I told them all about you.'

'Pardon?' Robyn spluttered into her teacup.

'Oh Robyn,' she laughed, 'don't be alarmed. With all this wonderful work you're doing, I couldn't say a bad word against you. Unless there's some big bad secret you're keeping.' She wiggled a questioning finger at Robyn.

'Of course there isn't.' Even though she was aware by Rose's expression that it was meant as a joke, she was suddenly feeling uncomfortable. Of course they didn't know about her memory issues – perhaps it was that secret that was making her feel nervous. Or the fact that she had no formal qualifications in interior design. Rose knew that – but did her new neighbours?

'I suspect you'll be around for a long while yet.'

Robyn opened her mouth to ask what she meant by that, when Rose added, 'You'll pop in and see us, won't you, dear? Better still, perhaps our new neighbours will invite us over for tea, and we can see what you're doing.'

'Huh?' Robyn really had no clue what she was talking about.

Rose looked at her strangely. 'You must promise that we can pop in and see you, and see how you're doing at our neighbours' houses.'

'Oh, I see. The thing is, Rose, I'm not sure if they'll want me to—'

'My, my, we are slow on the uptake today,' Rose interrupted. 'That business with David has really got to you, hasn't it, dear?' She reached for the teapot. 'Now, drink up. I've got plenty more tea.'

Robyn obliged.

'Remember I said that I told my neighbours all about you …'

Robyn nodded.

'It's all arranged,' added George.

'What is?'

'You're being hired by Number 2 and Number 3,' said Rose impatiently, pointing at the window. 'I told them they could come here, while their properties are being built, to discuss with you what they'd like to be done in terms of wall and floor coverings, curtains – that sort of thing. I get the impression they're keen to see how ours has turned out when you've finished work. That way, they'll get to see your work first hand. I know they won't be disappointed.'

Robyn gaped at her. She hoped not. 'It sounds as though I might have two more commissions.'

'You certainly have.'

'I hope they like what I'm going to do here.'

'Don't you worry about that, Robyn. We've got faith in you – isn't that right, George?'

George leaned forward in his chair and helped himself to another scone. He pointed it at Robyn before he took a bite.

'Our place is going to knock spots off the show home next door when you're finished, Robyn. They'll wish they hired you for the interior design of the show home instead.'

'Oh, I can't imagine that,' she replied modestly.

'I can,' Rose quipped. 'Now, would you like another scone, Robyn, before there's none left?' Rose eyed her husband disapprovingly.

Robyn had just helped herself to a scone when she heard the sound of a car drawing up outside.

Rose glanced over at the window. 'Oh. That's Gayle come to pick you up.'

'So soon?' Robyn asked. She looked at her watch, wondering where the afternoon had gone.

'I hope she's got time for tea and a scone before she leaves, unless you are going straight to the hospital to visit David.'

'I was hoping to, yes.'

'Well, in that case, I'll wrap up some scones that you can take for David, and some for Gayle to take home too. I hear you're not the only new arrival at Lark Lodge. Nick tells me he's moved in there with Olive.'

'Yes, that's right. It was my idea. I kind of sprung it on Gayle when I found out he'd been kicked out of his bed-and-breakfast. The said they were pet-friendly, but apparently not Olive-friendly.'

George laughed. 'Yes, that doesn't surprise me. She can be a bit of a handful, seeing as she's so big but still a puppy.'

As if on cue, there was a woof, then a whine, and finally a howl from the kitchen.

George cast his gaze at the door, and sighed. 'I think someone has just finished her dog treat and has finally realised she's been shut in the kitchen. I'd better go and fetch her.'

'Will you fetch me a Tupperware pot from the kitchen, George? I'm going to send these scones back with Robyn.'

George frowned.

Rose sighed. 'Don't worry, there's another batch cooking in the oven.'

George grinned. He left the room to fetch Olive.

Rose looked at Robyn. 'Now, where were we?'

'I'm not going to ask Gayle to take me to the hospital. I'll phone David this evening instead.' Robyn held up her new mobile phone.

'It won't be the same,' said Rose.

'I know. I do want to see him, but I'm not going to ask Gayle to take me back to the hospital. Then she'll have to hang around, or come to collect me later. And that isn't fair. She's got a lot on, what with the funeral tomorrow.'

Rose slowly nodded. 'Oh, yes. That's right. We'll be there. I expect half the town will be too.'

'And her relatives,' Robyn added. She frowned.

Rose noticed. 'Don't you want to meet them?'

'Yes, of course. She's got three older siblings, and I'd love to meet them. I'm just worried they might not like me, or Nick and Olive, staying at Lark Lodge.'

'I don't see what the problem is. In fact, Lark Lodge would make a lovely little guesthouse.'

Robyn managed a smile. 'Those are my sentiments exactly.' Robyn lowered her voice. 'Can I tell you a secret?'

Rose's eyes went wide. 'Oooh, yes – please do.'

The doorbell rang.

'I'll get it!' George called out.

Rose looked expectantly at Robyn. 'The secret?'

Robyn moved along the sofa, closer to Rose. 'I think Lark Lodge would make a wonderful guesthouse. I'm going to redecorate the place, restore it, get it ready for more guests. I haven't told Gayle yet. I want to surprise her when I've finalised my plans.'

Rose clapped her hands. 'How wonderful.'

'The problem is that Lark Lodge is Gayle's family home, but it doesn't belong to Gayle.' Robyn told Rose what she'd found in the basement – the boxes full of items that the three older siblings had already chosen to keep for themselves before their mother passed on.

'Well, that's just awful.'

'I know. That's what I thought. They'd obviously taken things from around the house that they wanted, and of course their mum has dementia, so she wouldn't even notice.'

She looked around at the door to the lounge. It was still closed. They could hear George talking to Gayle as she stepped in the house.

Robyn whispered, 'I think her siblings might have something to say about me and Nick staying at their mum's house. And, of course, my idea of Gayle running a guesthouse. I think it's a wonderful idea on paper. She needs the money. She can't return to nursing *and* look after her mum, so all she has coming in at the moment is the money from her mobile hairdressing, and her mum's pension, I guess. Nick is paying money. He told Gayle that he'll stay there as her lodger – that way I believe she can earn at least some money tax-free. Gayle won't take any money from me, so that's why I want to redecorate for her instead.'

Rose nodded.

Robyn didn't know why she was telling her all this. But she

continued, keeping an ear out for Gayle. 'The thing is, it's not her house, so realistically, turning it into a bona fide guesthouse …' Robyn trailed off. She didn't have to state the obvious, but she said it anyway. 'The house would eventually be split between all four siblings.'

'Is that a fact?' said Rose.

'Oh, yes. I expect so. At least, that's what Gayle has said.'

Rose turned to Robyn. 'Now *I've* got a secret to share. Actually, it's not mine, it's Dr Belafonte's secret – Gayle's dad.'

Robyn knitted her eyebrows. 'What do you mean?'

'Well, this was something Dr Belafonte just happened to mention to George during an appointment not long before he finally retired.'

Robyn thought that by the sound of it, he had worked well past his retirement age, but as soon as he'd stopped, he'd unfortunately suffered ill health, and had never recovered.

'Go on,' Robyn prompted.

They both looked towards the lounge door before Rose continued. 'I don't know why, but during his last GP appointment with Dr Belafonte, George happened to mention that we were struggling with whether to make amendments to our wills. You see, the children and grandchildren have nothing to do with us. We understand they lead busy lives, but … well sometimes we just feel like cash cows, and that they're waiting in the wings to cash in when we go.'

Robyn pursed her lips. 'Oh, I'm sure that's not—'

Rose held up her hand, stopping Robyn in her tracks. 'It's how we feel. And I can't escape the fact that although they send us expensive gifts at Christmas – the phone is a case in point – it feels like they are just going through the motions. It would be nice if they visited once in a while. But no. So, I broached it with George whether we should leave our money to a worthy cause. My children and grandchildren are comfortable, settled in their lives.'

Robyn didn't quite see what this had to do with Gayle's father.

'So, to get to my point,' continued Rose. 'George happened to mention what he was thinking to Dr Belafonte. He has grown-up children, and grandchildren too. George wanted to know what, if the good doctor were to find himself in our shoes, he might do.'

'What did he say?'

'That he had a similar dilemma. His older children, who had been born in Trinidad and who had come over to live in England with him and his wife, were all financially secure. The twin brothers had done very well for themselves in their chosen professions – I think one of them is a lawyer, and the other followed his father into the medical profession. I believe he qualified as a surgeon.'

Robyn nodded. 'Gayle told me that Xavier is a surgeon, and Jerome became a lawyer. Her older sister, Dinah, has her own estate agency selling upmarket property.'

'Well, anyway, to cut a long story short, like George, Dr Belafonte was struggling with what to do about his will. He happened to be contemplating changing it at that time. I believe that, like us, he and Doris had originally had wills that stipulated the house was left to the surviving spouse, and thereafter on both their deaths, the estate was to be shared equally between Gayle and her siblings. However, back when Doris was first diagnosed with dementia but still had mental capacity, she had decided to sign her share of the property over to her husband to keep things simple once she was unable to manage her own affairs.'

'And did he change it?'

'I don't know.'

'So, what was he thinking of changing, do you think?'

'George told me that Dr Belafonte was worried about his youngest. He regretted not pushing her like the others. By the time she had come along, they had been settled in their house, he had a job he adored, and life had fallen into place. But she hadn't married well, like the others, and with no children, or responsibilities, he could envisage she would be left taking on the caring responsibilities for them when they got older.'

'Well, he was right,' commented Robyn.

'Yes, he was. From what George has said, he got the gist that Dr Belafonte was considering changing his will in her favour.'

'What does that mean?'

Rose raised her eyebrows. 'I would imagine it means he might have left Gayle the house, with a caveat regarding his wife still living in the house until she passed on.'

'Oh my god – really?'

Rose nodded solemnly.

'And Gayle doesn't know? Her siblings don't know?'

Rose nodded again. 'I don't know whether Dr Belafonte went ahead and changed his will. But you must keep this a secret. The truth will out soon enough when they read the will. But until then …'

'My lips are sealed,' Robyn said. 'Oh my god. I'd be so happy for her if—'

'You'd be so happy for who?' Gayle asked. She'd just opened

the lounge door and caught the last thing Robyn had said. Fortunately, Olive came bounding in at that moment, creating havoc.

Robyn stood. She looked at Olive, who was running circles around the coffee table. She tried to grab her.

So did Gayle.

George said, 'I think she needs a walk.'

'It's all right, George.' Gayle grabbed Olive by the collar. 'I'll take her out when we get home.' She clipped the lead to the dog's collar. 'Good girl. Come on.'

As Robyn followed Gayle and Olive out of the lounge door, Rose said, 'Ah, Robyn. Just one more thing. Shall I arrange for you to meet your new clients? This is turning out to be such fun – I am so pleased we moved here after all. I can bake some more scones, and we can have tea and scones, and we can all get to know one another.'

Get to know on another? Robyn wanted the work, but she wasn't looking forward to meeting her new clients. What if they asked her searching questions? What if they found out she'd dropped out of university? Robyn plastered a smile on her face as she waved goodbye to Rose and George.

'I overhead Rose. What's this about new clients?' Gayle asked as they walked out of the house.

Robyn explained about Rose's new neighbours, who would be moving in once their properties completed. 'They're interested in my interior design services.'

'Well that's great news – isn't it?'

Robyn offered up a tentative smile, trying to be positive and not to think about what she imagined would be a job interview over tea and scones.

'You know, you're going to have to start thinking of a name for your interior design business. And have you thought that you might need premises?'

'Premises – what do you mean?'

'A shop. It's taken you time to source materials, and you've had to take a lot of materials, swatches, that sort of thing over to Rose's house. Well, what if your clients could come to you? If you had a place, a shop where people could come in, browse materials, fabrics, catalogues. You could still visit clients in their homes, measure up, fit their curtains and blinds, redecorate. But wouldn't it be handy if you had a shop to run your business from?'

Robyn brightened. 'Yes, that makes perfect sense.' Her face dropped.

'Ah, you're wondering where you'd get the money. You could set some of your earnings aside to invest back into the business. I know it will take time …'

Robyn knew it didn't have to; the wads of cash in the bottom of her bag back at Lark Lodge and the money in her savings account came to mind.

'But where would I find a suitable shop?'

Gayle opened the car door, and Olive jumped on to the back seat. As they settled in the front, and Gayle started the car, she said, 'I'm sure something will come up. I believe things happen for a reason. And sometimes life can surprise us – in a good way.'

Robyn smiled at her best friend. It sounded like another line from one of those self-help books Gayle loved to read. She happened to glance at Rose's house and saw Rose and George standing at their front door, waving. She waved back, thinking of what Rose had said about Gayle's father considering changing his will in Gayle's favour. Robyn had a feeling he had gone ahead and done just that. She looked at Gayle as they set off.

'What?'

'I was just wondering when will you find out about your father's will? Sorry, I know it's an odd question.'

'No, not at all. After the funeral tomorrow, and the wake, the local solicitor is going to stay on at the house where me, mum and my siblings will gather for the reading of the will.'

Robyn suppressed a smile, thinking of what Gayle had said: *things happen for a reason.* Gayle was there, looking after her mum, just as her father had predicted. And along the way, Lark Lodge was now home to three more occupants – herself, Nick, and Olive. Lark Lodge, the guesthouse, was only an idea just then. It would never happen – but for one thing – what was in that will.

Gayle said, 'But I already know what's in it – we all do.'

Robyn hoped that the next evening, life was going to surprise Gayle in a positive way.

15

Robyn was looking out of the window, focusing on nothing in particular as they were passing through town, when they were caught in traffic as they approached Gillespie's general store. 'Pull over!' Robyn said urgently.

'What?' Gayle sounded distracted.

'I want to get out. Stop the car!'

'Alright, calm down.' Gayle pulled the car into a parking bay a short distance along the road before they reached the store. She switched the engine off and turned to Robyn. 'What's going on?'

Robyn could feel herself sweating despite the cool breeze coming from the open window. 'I'll just be a minute.' She opened the car door. If she didn't go straight away, she knew she'd lose her nerve.

'Where are you going?'

'Gillespie's General Store.'

'That place is pricey. Why don't you go into a supermarket instead?'

Robyn shook her head.

'Want some company?' Gayle said, unbuckling her seat belt.

'No. It will just take a minute.'

'What will?' Robyn heard Gayle ask as she jumped out and strode at pace down the street.

As she stood in front of the store, Robyn's urge to give David's father a piece of her mind was now shrinking at an alarming rate. It didn't help that she could see Mr Gillespie through the window, standing at a counter. He was serving a customer.

She nervously tucked a wisp of hair behind her ear as she glanced back at the car. Gayle had turned in her seat and was staring at her through the back window.

Robyn took one more look through the window before she considered venturing inside. Mr Gillespie was packing some groceries in plastic bags for the lady at the till.

From the outside, it looked like one of those old-fashioned stores that Robyn thought only existed in movies. Double-fronted, it had old, leaded windows and a display in each window on either side of the entrance. On the left were tins of food – spaghetti, beans and soup – stacked in a neat pyramid. There were packets of rice, flour, sugar, and a lot more besides, in baskets and on shelves.

Through the other window, Robyn noticed all sorts of bread – wholemeal, white, sliced and unsliced, along with bread rolls, croissants, and some cakes, packaged in packs of six, from a local bakery.

After Rose's delicious scone, it's just as well I'm not hungry, thought Robyn, *otherwise I'd be tempted to buy a croissant.* But she wasn't there to buy anything.

She opened the door. A bell tinkled, announcing her presence. Robyn frowned. Inside the shop, long, bright strip lights glowed above a very modern interior that belied its old-fashioned store front. There were several aisles piled with modern convenience food, just like a regular supermarket, and Robyn noticed a clothing and accessory corner at the back, with walking gear and some fishing rods and nets.

She stood to one side, holding open the door for the lady with the shopping bags. Now it looked as though she was the only one in the store besides Mr Gillespie. She closed the door, and the bell tinkled again. She picked up a basket, just in case there was someone else in the shop who thought she was acting suspiciously.

Robyn stood on her tiptoes and looked over the shelving, spying on Mr Gillespie. He didn't appear to have seen her come in. As she spied on him, she had the strongest sense of déjà vu, as though she had done it before, pretending to peruse the aisle of a shop while keeping an eye out for a shop assistant.

Her hand involuntarily moved to a packet on the shelf. She whipped it off the shelf, and stuffed it in the pocket of her jacket without a second thought.

'What the hell am I doing?' Robyn exclaimed under her breath, shocked that she'd do such a thing. She took it out of her pocket and was putting it back on the shelf, her hand shaking in case anyone had noticed, when she dropped it.

'Here, let me.' A teenage boy crouched down and picked up the packet of noodles.

'Oh, thanks.' Robyn didn't know why, but she put them in her basket. Perhaps she was feeling guilty that a moment earlier, she'd been shoplifting. That was still bothering her – that and the déjà vu moment. She really felt like she'd done this before.

But I'm a student, with a healthy savings balance. Why would I steal?

'Where are you, lad?' a booming voice shouted out.

Robyn jumped.

The teenager sighed, rolled his eyes, and said under his breath, 'I hate this job.'

With a boss like Mr Gillespie, Robyn could understand. 'Thanks,' she whispered, 'about the noodles.' She threw him a sympathetic glance, watching him disappear down another aisle towards the clothing and outdoor gear area at the back of the shop.

Robyn walked down the aisle, carrying her shopping basket and absently scanning the shelves. As she walked down the next aisle, she heard voices coming from the clothing area.

'I told you I wanted it done this way!'

She stopped dead. Robyn couldn't mistake Mr Gillespie's voice. She'd heard enough of it while she was hiding behind the bathroom door.

'Can't you get anything right? Honestly, I don't know why I employed you, Alec.'

'Because my mum asked you to. We need the money.'

Robyn raised her eyebrows. That was a surprise, hearing that Mr Gillespie had done a good deed.

Looking up, she noticed a large round mirror high on the wall opposite her. There were others too, she noticed. She expected they'd been put there so Mr Gillespie could prevent shoplifting. Of course, it also meant he could see what his shop assistants were up to when they were down the aisles stacking shelves, or helping out customers. You couldn't get away with pocketing anything if the shopkeeper caught you in the mirror.

Robyn could feel the colour rising in her cheeks at the thought of Mr Gillespie catching her pocketing noodles.

In the mirror, Mr Gillespie and his young shop assistant –

the tall, lanky teen who'd just picked up the noodles from the floor – were standing next to a shop mannequin dressed in ski wear. The shop assistant was rearranging the clothing.

'Yes, that's the way I want it done. Have you got it this time?' Mr Gillespie said in a patronising tone. 'Or do I need to spell it out one … more … time?'

'Yes, Mr Gillespie. I mean, no, Mr Gillespie.'

'Are you having fun with me, young man?'

'Of course not, Mr Gillespie. Perish the thought.'

Robyn put her hand to her mouth to stifle a giggle as she saw Mr Gillespie do a double-take. He stared at the young man for a moment as he carried on dressing the mannequin.

'Well, um … that's good. Carry on.'

Robyn saw the teenager pull a face at Mr Gillespie's back as he walked away. She smiled.

Mr Gillespie disappeared from view, but didn't pass her in her aisle. Robyn breathed a sigh of relief. David's father was in a bad mood. Mind you, he always seemed to be in a foul temper. Even so, she decided that today wouldn't be a good time to speak to David's father about what she had on her mind.

She looked at her basket and wandered down the aisle to the far end, scanning the shelves. There wasn't anything she really needed, but she wanted to put the noodles back. Staring at the basket, wishing she didn't have to return down the aisle, she rounded the corner.

'Watch it!' a familiar voice growled.

Robyn stopped abruptly, staring into familiar, piercing blue eyes. Mr Gillespie, holding a large open box, stared back, not moving aside to let her pass.

'Sorry.' Robyn apologised.

He studied her for a moment before moving aside.

Robyn scooted past, relieved he hadn't appeared to recognise her. The first and last time they'd met had been during Hogmanay, when she'd been wrapped up in a hat and scarf and was wearing different clothing. He'd barely said a word to her. *Probably barely looked at me*, thought Robyn.

Then she thought, *why did I apologise? What happened to the adage that the customer is always right?*

Despite her first inclination to walk out, depositing her empty basket at the door, Robyn turned around. 'You don't recognise me, do you?'

Mr Gillespie was kneeling on the floor, depositing the contents of the box onto the lower shelves. He carried on unpacking the box.

Robyn was just thinking that he hadn't heard her, when he looked up. With his eyes firmly fixed on her, his face expressionless, he stood up with the empty box in hand. Feeling unnerved, Robyn couldn't think of what to say next, so she held out her hand, thinking she'd introduce herself. 'I'm Robyn,' she said. 'Robyn Parker.'

He looked at her hand.

'I'm a friend of your son, David.'

'Is that right?' He dropped the empty box.

'Yes, it is.'

Robyn wondered what he was going to do next. To her surprise, he grasped her hand.

'So, David's friend. What can I do for you?'

What Robyn wanted him to do was let go of her hand. A horrible thought flashed through her mind – *Customer murdered in aisle three for disturbing shopkeeper who was busy unpacking* … Robyn looked at the shelf where he had been kneeling, unpacking … *jammie dodgers*. Robyn imagined the headline.

He looked at her quizzically. 'What did you say?'

'Oh, er … nothing.'

He let go of her hand. 'What are you doing here?'

To her amazement, he abruptly turned his back on her and disappeared down the next aisle before she had a chance to answer. Robyn was just shaking her head at his total disregard for any manners when he returned carrying a second identical box of what she now knew contained jammie dodgers.

He stopped dead, as though she had just appeared from nowhere and hadn't been standing there the whole time. 'Didn't you hear my question?' He dropped the box, which made a dull thud on the floor. Robyn imagined all those customers who were going to buy packets of broken biscuits.

He regarded her for a moment, as if he were challenging her to say something about the biscuits, then bent down and proceeded to pile them on the shelves.

Robyn knew that the question meant, *what are you doing in Aviemore?* When David had introduced her to his father during the New Year's Eve celebrations, Mr Gillespie had made it abundantly clear that he wasn't the least bit interested in meeting her. She decided it was none of his damn business what she was doing in that part of the world – the fact that she didn't really know was none of his business either – but she *was* going to tell him what she was doing in his shop. 'The reason I'm here,' Robyn took a deep breath, 'is that I wanted to talk to you about David.'

She watched him stop what he was doing and turn to look up at her, one hand in the box and the other on the shelf. 'Is that right?' he said again.

'Yes, it is,' Robyn said boldly, looking him in the eye.

'Well, are you going to say what you want to say, or aren't you?' He turned his attention back to unpacking the box.

For some reason, Robyn hadn't expected him to be interested at all in what she had to say. She'd thought he'd just tell her that she wasn't welcome in his shop, and to leave right away.

Robyn decided that the direct approach would be best. 'David wants to go to college to study history.'

He had finished unpacking his box, but he was still on his knees, and he seemed to be staring vacantly at the shelves. 'His mother liked history.'

Robyn was taken aback that he'd brought up David's mother. 'Yes, David told me.'

He got up. 'And what does he think he's going to do with a qualification in history?'

Robyn recalled David's scepticism when she'd suggested he could apply to study history at college. 'He could teach history,' she said quickly. She knew that David had been sceptical about that idea too. But after his accident on the ice, Robyn wished she hadn't encouraged him to think about coaching ice hockey. History was a much better idea; safer.

Mr Gillespie's expression told Robyn he wasn't exactly enthralled with the idea.

'Perhaps a lecturer,' Robyn added. 'At college. Perhaps even a university, a top university like … like St Andrews.' Robyn frowned, wishing she hadn't mentioned that one in particular. 'You know, those top red-brick universities where posh people go.'

'Posh people?'

Robyn didn't know why she'd said that. After all, she was meant to be a student there, and she wouldn't call herself posh.

'I know what a red-brick university is,' he continued, his eyes narrowing. 'I may live in a small town and run a small store, but that doesn't mean I haven't had a university education, does it?'

'You've been to university, got a degree?' Robyn said, astounded.

'Does that surprise you?'

She avoided the question. 'Where did you go? What did you study?'

He eyed her. 'I was in the army. Then I left, decided I wanted an education.'

Robyn stared at him. David had never mentioned that.

Mr Gillespie looked at the floor. He toed the empty box.

'David doesn't know, does he?' Robyn couldn't hide her surprise.

'Look, it's not common knowledge.'

'But …' *He's your son*, Robyn wanted to say.

'Listen.' Mr Gillespie pointed a finger at her. 'I've got friends in this town.'

Robyn didn't understand. Was he threatening her?

'They're ordinary folks, you know, we went to school together. We dropped out of school together.' He chuckled to himself, and Robyn realised she had never seen him smile before.

'We all joined the forces, to leave this place, get away, have an adventure. Except I did night classes, unlike my mates. I wanted to better myself. I was young and foolish, but I grew up fast in the army, although I knew I didn't want to stay in the forces. Education was my way out.' He continued in a small voice. 'At least, I thought it was.'

Something dawned on Robyn. 'You're afraid they might look at you differently if they knew you'd been to college?' Robyn ventured. She wondered how he'd wound up back in his hometown, and ventured the question.

'A girl – what do you think?'

'David's mother?'

'I should never have come back. It was only meant to be a short visit, picking my parents up to take them to my graduation. That's when I met her. I popped into the general store, and there she was. Moved into the area with her parents. She was the most beautiful thing I'd ever seen in my life.'

Robyn stared at him.

'Her parents ran the general store.'

'This place?'

'And before I knew it, we were married. Her parents were older, needed help running their store. And … well the rest is history, as they say.'

He sighed and picked up the empty box. He paused in front of Robyn, frowning. 'Forget what I just said. I don't know why I told you all that.' He promptly disappeared down another aisle.

Robyn stood there, staring after him. She heard the door to the shop open and the bell tinkle as another customer walked in.

Robyn walked around the corner into the next aisle, expecting to find Mr Gillespie unpacking another box. The aisle was empty. She walked down the aisle and turned the next corner. The shop assistant glanced up from dressing the dummy, then returned to his work. Robyn heard Mr Gillespie talking to someone. She headed towards the checkout and saw him packing the customer's purchases into a plastic bag. The bell tinkled again as the customer left the shop. She walked up to the counter, where Mr Gillespie was putting some notes into the till.

'It's nearly closing time,' he said, without looking up.

'Is it?' Robyn looked at her watch. It was only mid-afternoon. 'I don't think so.'

Mr Gillespie shut the till and folded his arms. 'If I say it's nearly closing time, then that's what it is. You'd better pay for that.'

'Oh.' Robyn looked down at the shopping basket containing the packet of noodles.

He clicked his fingers impatiently, holding out his hand for the basket.

Robyn reluctantly handed it over. She happened to glance around the counter, and saw sweets, and some dog toys and chews. Robyn took a packet of doggy treats, a ball and a chew toy and put them on the counter, along with a box of chocolates. She had a thought. 'Do you sell wine?'

Mr Gillespie cocked his head to the left.

Robyn walked over and chose a bottle of red wine – just the sort she thought Gayle would like. She looked at the bottle in her hands as she returned to the counter.

'Having a little celebration – are we?'

'Not exactly.' Robyn knew she was being presumptuous, but she hoped there was a surprise in store for Gayle at the reading of the will. Even so, her father had died, so there really wasn't anything to celebrate. But she still wanted to buy Gayle a bottle of wine and a box of chocolates, hoping she'd appreciate a small gesture that might cheer her up a little.

Thinking of lifting her spirits, Robyn intended to tell Gayle her idea about restoring Lark Lodge and setting it up as a guesthouse.

Mr Gillespie eyed her. 'Have you got the money for all this?'

'Yes – of course I have.'

'Is it David's money?'

Robyn looked at him a long moment. 'Of course not.' It was, in actual fact, his brother Joe's. He'd handed her far too much money for a sandwich and a drink at the hospital the previous night before he'd left. She hadn't realised it was a fifty-pound note until she'd got it out of her purse. Perhaps Joe hadn't realised either. Luckily she'd had some loose change for a drink from the vending machine. She'd pay him back – of course she would. But she wasn't about to tell Mr Gillespie any of that.

She did say, 'I'm not after David's money. I'm not like his previous girlfriend, if that's what you're thinking. I know he's got a nice house, and some investments …'

'He has investments?'

Robyn pursed her lips. She shouldn't have said that. It sounded like news to him. 'They're tied up, apparently, so he can't touch them.'

'I see.'

'I don't think it's much. Just some savings.' Robyn wished she'd shut her mouth. She had no idea how much David had put by from his earnings in professional ice hockey. 'Anyway, I was about to say I have my own income.' Robyn didn't know why she cared what he thought, but she did. 'I'm an interior designer,' she said proudly.

'Are you now?'

Robyn stared at him. She did not like his tone. 'I want a carrier bag. And I can pay for that, too,' she said sarcastically.

He plucked a carrier bag from below the counter, took his time opening it, and rang up the items on his till.

He handed her the bag.

She frowned at him. She'd seen him packing for his other customers. Robyn packed her own carrier bag and handed over the fifty-pound note.

He took the note. 'Fresh off the press?'

Robyn looked at him. 'What do you mean?'

'It was a joke. You know … like it was just printed. As in counterfeit.'

Robyn stared at the note and suddenly had a peculiar thought. Were the wads of cash in her bag fresh off the press? The cash was bothering her enough without the idea that they might be counterfeit. Where had she got it from? And how could she check whether it was real or not?

She expected him to put the note in the till and give her the change. Instead he picked up a pen and held the note on the counter.

'What are you doing?'

'Checking it's not counterfeit.'

Robyn had it on the tip of her tongue to say, *It can't be. Your son, Joe, a police officer, gave it to me.* Instead she watched him scribble on the note with the pen. She didn't see any marks on the note afterwards. 'Is that it? Is that how you check?'

'Yep.'

'Can I borrow that pen?' Robyn blurted.

'Why?'

Robyn wished she hadn't asked. 'Um, er … it's just for a practical joke,' she said off the top of her head.

'Here.'

Robyn was taken aback. She cautiously took the pen.

'I will need it back, mind. I don't get many fifty-pound notes, but you never know.'

'Of course. I'll bring it back tomorrow.' Robyn slipped the pen in her pocket.

Robyn gathered up the carrier bag and paused. 'I just want one more thing.'

'You don't want much, do you?' he said sarcastically. 'You know I've got a store to run, and other customers?'

Robyn cocked her head to one side. She hadn't heard another tinkle of the bell. 'Aren't you closing now?'

'Oh, yes, right. So, what is it you want now?'

'I want to ask you a question.'

16

She had gone in there to ask Mr Gillespie to help David out, to pay for his tuition for college, thinking that perhaps Rose was right – Mr Gillespie had money tucked away somewhere that he hadn't told David about. But what Rose didn't know was that Mr Gillespie had a gambling problem. He'd lost his house, and was now living with his son. How could he come up with tuition money? It was a stupid idea.

But there was something he could do for his son.

'He loves ice hockey; he told me himself, whatever he's told you. I know it's his life. But he has to move on, and so do you.'

Mr Gillespie stared at her.

Robyn couldn't believe she was talking to him like this. She was sure that any minute, he was going to tell her to shut up and mind her own business. But David *was* her business. She was in love with him, and whatever Mr Gillespie said, she was going to fight his corner. 'He's lost without hockey, but he can't stay here, working in this store.'

'Do you think that's what I want for him? Do you know why I encouraged him into hockey when I realised he had a serious talent?'

So that you could get back at your ex-wife. Robyn kept her mouth shut.

'To get him out of this town.'

Robyn stared at him. That was not what she'd overhead him tell David in the hospital.

'I wouldn't even let either of them work here on a regular basis when they were growing up, apart from helping me out with Christmas deliveries. I didn't want them to get stuck in a rut like I had.'

'But you could have just left.'

Mr Gillespie shook his head. 'She wanted me to help out her parents, so I did, and then we had kids …' he shrugged.

And you became a bitter old man. Robyn didn't want to voice that thought. She imagined that this wasn't the life he'd really wanted, and that was why his marriage had failed – he'd taken out his anger and frustrations on her. It was little wonder she'd run away. *I'd run away too if I was with someone like you – not a very nice man,* she thought.

Robyn stared at Mr Gillespie. Was that what had been happening on Christmas Day – she'd been running away from a man who was not good to her?

'Are you all right?'

'Yes, I'm, er … fine.' She was still staring at Mr Gillespie, willing him to continue his story.

'Then she decides the life we'd built together, here, taking over her parents' store, wasn't what she wanted after all. But by then, this was all I'd known. This was my livelihood. And I had the boys to raise. She met someone else, skipped town.'

'Met someone else?' Robyn shook her head. 'David never said that,' she blurted.

He stopped short, and pointed a rude finger at her. 'Look, whatever he's told you – and I know he thinks I pushed him hard as a kid, and he blames me for his mother leaving, thinks I drove her away, and that she wanted to take him with her – none of it is true. Well, driving him hard to achieve big, something I hadn't achieved with my life – that's true. Who could blame me? But his mother … that's a different story. She didn't want to take them with her. I just let him believe that. Out of the two of them, David, who was older and had a close relationship with her, was hit the hardest by her leaving. Sometimes a lie is better than the truth if it saves the ones you love from heartache. And you know what? Ice hockey saved him, saved us both. It gave us something to focus on other than …' he trailed off.

Robyn wondered why he was opening up to her like this. It wasn't what she'd expected at all; certainly not from the reception she'd got when they'd first met. She had to ask, 'Why are you telling me all this?'

'Because you have given David something to focus on. At first, when we met at Hogmanay, I thought David could do without getting involved with someone right now. He'd got enough on his plate, losing his career. And you're an out-of-towner. I thought you were having a little holiday fling, whereas I could tell immediately that his feelings for you were serious. Too serious for a holiday fling. For him to want me to meet you, well, he's fallen for you – hard.'

Robyn could feel butterflies in her stomach. *He really loves me.*

'You're good for him. I see it now. And I see you're not going anywhere. And the fact that you're here, talking about his future, it means a lot. Young girls these days just seem so … so self-absorbed – it's all me, me, me. You're different. You're kind in nature. You're just what he needs. Annie told me that it was you who encouraged him onto the ice to coach those kids when the accident happened.'

'It's all my fault, I know it is. That's why I'm here. I don't want him going back on the ice. He needs to do something else.'

He shook his head vigorously. 'I disagree. I think it's a bloody good idea. So, he fell on the ice. Since visiting Davie in hospital, I've had a chance to mull things over. Despite what he says, he still needs ice hockey, and what better way to stay in the game than to coach? You're right, he'd make a great teacher – but not history. He could do it was a hobby, but hockey will always be his game.'

'So, you don't blame me for what happened?'

'Not at all. And Annie shouldn't blame you either – that's very wrong of her. But like me, she's just wary of you, Robyn, because she doesn't want David to get hurt again – and neither do I.'

'Like your ex-wife hurt you.' Robyn understood now.

'You loved her, didn't you? So much.'

'Of course I did. Why on earth would I have stayed here, helping her parents run this store? I had dreams. Big dreams. But they all ended here – with her.'

Robyn didn't know what to say. 'Is that why you started your gambling habit?' she said in a small voice.

'Pardon me?'

Robyn looked at him sheepishly. 'David told me that you're living with him.'

'Did he now?'

'Yes.'

'None of us knew you, what your intentions were. You just

appeared one day.'

Robyn looked at him. He'd abruptly changed the subject. She just shrugged, not wanting to get into that question – the elephant in the room; what was she doing there?

Mr Gillespie continued, 'You see, before you came along, Davie was falling into a deep depression. He wasn't sleeping properly, eating properly. I knew I had to do something. I wanted to move in with him, keep an eye on him. But he'd never let me do that. Unless … I had to.'

Robyn stared at him. 'Are you saying that you made up the gambling debts?'

'I'm not proud of that.'

'But you sold your house. That's a bit extreme.'

'I had to.'

'I don't understand.'

'My store, it's going under. My sons aren't aware. I'm mortgaged up to the hilt. The supermarkets that have moved into town have taken a lot of my customers – the visitors, skiers and holidaymakers. It's mostly only the old folk who shop here now. But after all these years, I'm attached to the old place. I mortgaged the house, took a gamble – so yes, I did gamble; with saving the business. And it didn't work out. The shop is haemorrhaging money.'

'Why didn't you tell David this? Ask him for help?'

'You mean ask him for money? I'd never take a penny from him. That's his money. But you see, it worked out – I got to move in with him.'

Robyn frowned, casting her gaze around the shop. 'But what about your store?'

'Well, unless I win the lottery, or some anonymous

benefactor steps in and saves my bacon, the old place will have to close, and then I'll be letting down all my loyal customers, the old folk who've shopped here for decades.'

Robyn glanced over her shoulder, thinking of the young man dressing the mannequin. 'How can you afford to keep on the shop assistant?'

'I can't. But he is one of my customers' grandsons whose mum has fallen on hard times, and they need the money.'

'But you need money too.'

'Yes – I know that!'

Robyn looked at the pen in her hand and thought of the wads of cash she'd found in her bag. She could help him out – if the money wasn't fake. She also had a load of money in her savings account – when she could work out how to access it without ID. But she knew he wouldn't take her money, although she could do it anonymously. But Robyn had a feeling that if she did that, he'd think she'd told David about his predicament, and it had come from him.

Why should I help him? she wondered. Because, despite first impressions, and what she'd overheard between David and his father in that hospital room, all he wanted was to do right by his son. He'd certainly gone about it the wrong way. He shouldn't have been so hard on David. Then maybe David wouldn't be so full of resentment towards his father. But she now understood why he'd done what he'd done – all he'd wanted was for his sons to succeed in life. *What about happiness, though?* she wondered.

Robyn shook her head, turning her thoughts to his business. She thought of the ski wear and fishing items he was stocking in a large area at the back of his store. 'I noticed all that ski and hiking gear, along with the fishing equipment.'

'Yes – do you want to buy something?'

'No, but I'm wondering what it's there for.'

'To sell – what do you think?'

Robyn ignored the sarcasm. 'Does it sell?'

He breathed a heavy sigh, and shook his head.

Robyn didn't think so. Not wanting to state the obvious, she said, 'But this is a grocery store.'

'I was trying to attract new customers – skiers, walkers. There are loads of tourists who come here. I thought if they stopped here to buy some of that stuff, they might get their groceries too.'

'But they don't even know you sell that sort of thing.' Robyn had seen the window display – it was all food. 'Perhaps if one of your windows had some ski wear, and hiking gear …' she trailed off.

'Do you think that would help?'

'Can I be brutally honest with you?'

Mr Gillespie cocked his head to one side. 'You have so far – why stop now?'

'Sorry.'

'Why are you apologising? I like it. No beating about the bush.'

They exchanged a smile. 'Well, go on …'

In the course of the conversation, Robyn had grown accustomed to his curt manner.

He cast his gaze over her head to the back of the shop. 'So, you don't think a window display would help.'

'Probably not. There's lots of shops in the town selling hiking and skiing equipment, specialising in that sort of thing. Why would they come in here to browse your small selection when they can get so much more choice at one of several shops just down the road?'

He sighed heavily. 'You're right. I just had all that free space, and took a punt. But it's not working out. I need some way of saving my store.'

She had a feeling that Mr Gillespie would be lost without his shop. It was more than a job, a livelihood – it was his life. And perhaps a little part of him was hanging on to the place because it was all he had left of the woman he loved.

Robyn actually felt sorry for him. Behind that gruff, abrupt exterior was a man who deeply cared; about his old, loyal customers – his community – and about his sons. In a high street full of modern shops, catering mostly to tourists and visitors, this shop, with its old-fashioned store front, like the old bookshop, was probably one of the few remaining stores that had been there before Aviemore became a huge tourist destination.

Robyn wanted to help, but she couldn't just hand over money to this proud man. However, she did have the most unexpected idea that could help them both out …

Robyn grinned.

He frowned at her. 'What's so funny?'

What was funny was that she'd walked in there wanting David's father to help him out, and now she was thinking of helping out Mr Gillespie instead – and herself.

'I've got an idea that might help you, and your shop.'

'Oh, yeah?' he said sceptically. 'And why would you be at all interested in doing that?' He narrowed his eyes. 'What's in it for you?'

'Do you want to hear my idea – or not?'

He leaned on the counter. 'Have I got a choice?'

❖

She'd just finished telling Mr Gillespie her brilliant idea when she heard the tinkle of the bell above the door. When she turned around to see who had walked in, it was Gayle, her face a picture of concern.

Robyn smiled as she approached.

'Robyn – are you okay?' Gayle threw a suspicious look in Mr Gillespie's direction. 'You were such a long time, I started to worry.'

'I'm fine. More than fine.'

Mr Gillespie said, 'Shall we shake on it?'

Robyn turned to her new business partner. 'Oh, yes.' She held out her hand to shake hands with Mr Gillespie and out of the corner of her eye caught Gayle raising her eyebrows in astonishment.

Robyn accompanied Gayle out of the shop. As they walked back to the car, Gayle said, 'What was that all about?'

'Remember the conversation we were having on the way here? What you said after we'd left Rose's house – had I thought about a shop to run my business from?'

'Yes.' They stopped by the car and got in.

'Well, I've found somewhere.'

Gayle was about to switch on the car engine. She turned in her seat to look at Robyn. 'You're not talking about Mr Gillespie's shop – are you? He'll never sell that place.'

'I know. And he doesn't have to. Look, when do you think a shop is going to come up in this small town? And if one does – it's going to cost a fortune to buy the lease in such a popular tourist destination in the Cairngorms.'

'Yes, I suppose you're right.'

'But there's space in his store to set up my business.'

'How is that going to work? I don't think you've thought this through, Robyn. It's a grocery store.'

'Yes, I know. But it's a double-fronted property, which means …'

'You can display your business in one of the windows.'

'Exactly! And I don't have to buy or lease a whole shop, which I won't be able to afford.' She didn't add that she'd be helping David's father out too, by sharing the costs of running the whole store because he desperately needed the money.

Robyn had thought Gayle would be pleased that she'd taken her advice to find premises for her business, but Gayle's expression told her otherwise. 'What is it?' she asked. 'I thought you'd be happy for me.'

Gayle scratched her forehead. 'Are you sure about this? You do know you'll be in a shop all day with that horrible, curmudgeonly old man.'

Robyn breathed a sigh of relief. For a moment, she'd thought Gayle was going to tell her something she didn't know. She grinned. 'Yes.'

'But I thought you didn't like him.'

Robyn considered her reply, thinking of what Gayle had also said to her on the way there. 'Let's just say that like you, I believe things happen for a reason.' She was thinking of David and his accident on the ice. Now she didn't feel bad about that at all. If that hadn't happened, she'd have never found the gumption to walk into Mr Gillespie's store to talk about David's future. As it had turned out, she'd talked about her future instead, with a man who was not at all what she'd first thought. She wondered what David would think when he found out.

As they passed by Mr Gillespie's store on their return journey to Lark Lodge, Robyn said, 'People can surprise us – in a good way.'

17

Robyn sat down at the kitchen table. It was Saturday, the morning after the funeral. She should have been looking forward to the weekend – David was going to be discharged from hospital at some point – but she'd had a restless night over her plan for David not to go home but to go to Lark Lodge instead to recuperate. She hadn't run it past Gayle. She had been planning to do so at some point after the funeral, but then she'd talked to Mr Gillespie at his store on Thursday. Now she thought the best thing for David was to go home to his father, and hopefully over time they could repair their relationship.

Gayle walked into the kitchen, still in her nightgown.

'Morning, Gayle.' Robyn wondered how she was feeling after the funeral. Robyn hadn't had a chance to really talk to Gayle the previous day. The wake had gone on long into the evening, which wasn't surprising, considering the number of people who'd turned up from the local community to pay their respects. For some families, Dr Belafonte had been their GP for three generations.

By the time everyone had left, and they'd cleared away the food and washed up all the dishes, they'd both been way too tired to talk – especially Gayle. All she'd said was that she was glad the day was over. Her three siblings hadn't planned to stay the night at the house – they'd booked into a fancy hotel in Aviemore. After the reading of the will, she doubted they'd be back to see Gayle before they left. Perhaps she wasn't surprised, after the revelation that their father had left the whole house, and some savings, to Gayle.

'Morning.' Gayle stifled a yawn.

Robyn noticed she had a pile of letters in her hand. Robyn had thought she'd heard the postman. She watched Gayle sifting through them, turning one over, studying it for a moment, sighing and tucking it back like a pack of cards.

Robyn rubbed the sleep out of her eyes. 'Would you like a cup of tea?' She looked at the mug on the table in front of her. 'I've just made myself one.'

'Huh?' Gayle looked up from her letters. 'Oh, um … yes please.' She seemed preoccupied as she sat at the table with the letters. She was still looking through the pile. So far she hadn't opened any. Robyn put a mug of tea on the table in front of her.

Gayle absently picked up the cup and took a sip while discarding another letter on the ever-growing pile. 'Well, that's the last of those.'

Robyn sat down opposite her.

'That pile are all bills,' Gayle said, eyeing the offending stack of letters. 'I don't think mother and father were keeping on top of things.'

'They all look like reminders.' Robyn hoped Gayle didn't mind her making that observation.

'That's because they are.' She sorted through some other letters. Robyn expected they were cards of condolence from people who had been unable to come to the funeral. There were lots of sympathy cards on the mantelpiece in the lounge already.

Robyn put her teacup down and folded her arms on the table in front of her. She looked at Gayle. 'Let me pay some rent.' She paused. 'It would help with ...' Robyn trailed off, glancing at the bills.

'That's not your problem.' Gayle stretched, letting out another yawn.

'I know that,' Robyn said quickly, not wanting to interfere. 'But I live here, and I would like to pay my way.' She sighed. *How many times have we had this conversation?* she wondered. 'I've got a job now.'

'Yes, and you've also got the expense of running a shop – remember.'

'I'm not running a shop. I told you. I'm renting a bit of shop space.'

'Yeah, and I bet Mr Gillespie is charging you an arm and a leg for the privilege of a tiny space in his store.'

Robyn bit her lip. That wasn't far off the truth, even though she was the one who'd suggested meeting him halfway with the running costs of the entire shop, and paying for his shop assistant, Alec.

'I do get a window display.'

'Pah!' Gayle dismissed that comment with a flick of the hand. 'I don't care if you've got a window display in Harrods. Robyn, you're my friend, and besides, this is not a guesthouse.'

'It could be.' Robyn had intended to broach the idea with Gayle after the funeral. Now here was her chance.

Gayle let out a heavy sigh. 'Have you seen the state of the place? Of course you have – you live here!'

Robyn grinned at Gayle's sarcasm.

Gayle continued, 'The wallpaper is peeling.'

'Yep.'

'The carpets are threadbare.'

Robyn nodded, still smiling. 'Uh-huh.'

'The furniture's old.'

But nice, Robyn thought.

'The plumbing is a nightmare.'

Robyn nodded again.

'Tell me the last time you had a hot bath.' Gayle held up her hand. 'No, not a luke-warm bath – a really hot bath. The sort that wrinkles up your skin and makes it all red and blotchy.' She glared at Robyn. 'Shall I go on?'

Robyn nodded in good spirits. 'Yes please.'

Gayle put the letters down and threw her a look as she lifted her hands in despair. 'I can't see what there is to smile about. I find it all rather depressing.'

Gayle's gaze fell on the pile of bills. 'I really wish you wouldn't waste your time with unrealistic ideas that are going to come to nothing.'

'What if ...' Robyn chose her words carefully, 'the house could be restored to its former glory?'

'And how do you propose to do that?' Gayle said stiffly. But Robyn noticed her demeanour had subtly changed and her eyes had brightened. 'You know how I love interior design. I could redecorate …'

'You've already got a job, and besides, I couldn't pay you.'

'I wouldn't want you to. I could do up the rooms and then photograph them to add them to my portfolio of work, along with Rose and George's house, to show to potential clients, and display photos in my shop. You'd be doing me a favour.' Robyn eyed Gayle. She could tell she was considering it.

'Let me think on it.'

Robyn smiled to herself. She had an idea of how she'd convince Gayle to let her go ahead with the plan.

'Anyway, when it comes to turning this place into a guesthouse, you've forgotten one little factor in the equation.'

'What's that?'

'My mother.'

'What about her?'

'Even if by some miracle this place was done up to an acceptable standard to run as a guesthouse – and believe me, I don't know how we'd pull it off, but let's just daydream a minute …' She paused. 'My mother wouldn't want strangers staying here.'

Robyn thought of Nick. He had been a stranger – in the beginning. She hadn't minded him staying.

Gayle shook her head. 'And she's confused enough as it is. She needs some peace and quiet in her own home.'

'What I see,' Robyn started throwing diplomacy to the wind, 'is that she might end up spending her final years in the company of strangers, but at least here she will be in her own home.'

'What do you mean?'

'What do you think will happen if you lose this house?' Robyn said, aware that Gayle just wasn't facing facts. 'The house your father left you is gorgeous, but it's a money pit. The bills are piling up …'

Gayle looked at the bills on the table and said miserably, 'Tell me something I don't know.'

Robyn had assumed that Gayle being left the house would be

a cause for celebration. Of course it was, but a big reality check had almost immediately set in with the arrival of the post.

'I never want to see her in a care home, if I can help it!' Gayle stood up abruptly.

'I know. That's why we're going to sort this.' Robyn gestured at the bills on the table. She thought of the cash in her rucksack and the money in her savings account. All those bills would go away in an instant if Gayle would just accept some financial help. But she still wouldn't hear of it. The next best thing was to turn the house around and set it up as a business, earning Gayle money. Robyn realised that it was the best plan. And as much as she wanted to give Gayle some money, she realised that even her savings account wasn't a bottomless pit. At some point, Gayle couldn't rely on her to keep bailing her out with the bills – Robyn realised that Gayle already had the foresight to see that.

'I want your mother to stay here too.' Robyn frowned when she remembered what she'd overheard the previous day at the wake, something she hadn't shared with Gayle; it had turned out that her brothers and sister had been more than happy to send their mother packing – sooner rather than later. They were talking about putting their mum in a home, reasoning that it was the best place for her.

Of course, in a lot of instances it was definitely the right decision for families to make on their loved one's behalf. But what rankled with Robyn was that it appeared Gayle had not been included in conversations surrounding this. Furthermore, it didn't appear to be about a concern for Doris's welfare, and what would be best for her, but rather just getting one problem sorted, and out of the way, leaving them free to get their hands on their inheritance. It turned out that they'd already looked into care homes. They'd even had one lined up for her, the plan being that once the funeral was behind them, they'd book their mother in and then sell the house, setting some money aside for her care home fees. The rest of the proceeds would be divided between the four of them.

Robyn only knew this because she'd heard the three of them discussing the plan after the funeral. Robyn had gone to the kitchen for a glass of water during the wake and had passed by their father's study. She'd heard voices and had realised that it was where the three of them had disappeared to. Of course, they hadn't included Gayle in the conversation. She hadn't meant to eavesdrop, but had found that she couldn't help herself. They had been nice enough to her face, although she had overheard Gayle's sister, Dinah, make some comment about Gayle inviting people to stay in their house.

She could tell what they were planning; ensuring Gayle did not stay on at the house. They'd assumed that they would all inherit a share, and that they'd be able to pressure Gayle into agreeing for it to be sold. The last thing they'd expected was that he'd changed his will.

Robyn would have loved to have been a fly on the wall during the reading of the will in their father's study shortly afterwards.

She imagined it was going to take some time for it to sink in for Gayle that her father had left her the house, with the caveat that her mum would live there as long as was medically possible; a condition he'd known his youngest daughter would respect. Gayle also now had sole power of attorney over Doris's affairs, which she'd previously shared with her father.

Gayle could not afford to lose the house because of some

unpaid bills. She still needed an income to support it and ensure her father's wishes were fulfilled. And Robyn had every intention of helping her achieve that. Now that she owned the house outright, there would nothing, and nobody to stand in their way.

'I need to go into Aviemore to do some shopping,' said Gayle. 'So, what are your plans today?'

'Ah, that's what I wanted to talk to you about. I need a lift into town.'

18

'Are you alright?'

Robyn brushed her hair out of her eyes to see a Good Samaritan offering her a hand.

The stranger hauled her off the pavement.

'Thank you,' she said lamely, brushing her clothes and giving an embarrassed nod to the lanky young man towering above her.

'You took quite a tumble,' he said cheerfully.

'I tripped.' Robyn had been standing outside Mr Gillespie's shop, admiring her window display. She'd worked hard all Saturday to get it just right, hoping that it did the trick and would entice customers to come who might want some haberdashery, or interior design work, once her outlet opened. She wouldn't find that out for at least a couple of weeks. The shop wasn't stocked – that would take a week or two if she was lucky with the suppliers – but she'd made a start by clearing out the ski, fishing and hiking gear. Mr Gillespie had sold it all to a nearby shop, and had surprised himself by making a reasonable profit into the bargain.

As his assistant was also spending time helping her, Robyn had suggested she should pay the assistant's salary.

'I'll accept no charity,' he'd said.

'And I'm not dishing out any,' Robyn had replied, knowing full well he wouldn't. But she had twisted his arm to let her pay Alec's wages. Mr Gillespie really didn't need too much help on the shop floor, whereas Robyn realised that if she was out at a client's home, she couldn't be in two places at once – and that was where Alec came in. She'd anticipated that Alec would not be that happy, and would be extremely bored, at the prospect of working in her little outlet, but it had turned out to be quite the opposite. He hated skiing, hiking and fishing, so he was quite keen to see the back of all that stuff, along with the creepy mannequin. They'd had a private little joke about how the old mannequin had creeped Robyn out too, but had kept that to themselves when Mr Gillespie had heard their laughter and had asked them to share the joke.

It turned out that Alec defied stereotypes, and enjoyed joining his mother at her knitting group in the local library, so the thought of spending the majority of his time working for Robyn in her business, rather than stacking shelves, was right up his street. He'd told Robyn, while they were busy prepping the shop, that his mum, and all her friends, had to travel to another town, miles away, to a haberdashery shop that sold small items for their sewing and dressmaking.

Robyn knew exactly where they meant; it was where David had taken her to source the fabric for Rose's curtains and cushions, about an hour's journey from Aviemore. Whilst she'd enjoyed the trip, she'd noticed that in addition to the distance, the shops had seemed to sell what she needed at an inflated price. Robyn knew she could source the items and sell to locals cheaper.

Alec had said that he knew it was a bit of a cheek, but

wondered if she'd consider setting aside a small part of her shop as a haberdashery supplying buttons, ribbons, knitting needles, thread – things for needlework, knitting and sewing.

Open to a new business opportunity, Robyn had readily agreed. It made sense to locate that counter over by the fabrics and materials in Robyn's little shop. However, as it was Alec's idea, Robyn made sure he would take the profits from the haberdasher.

Robyn had asked Alec to order some materials online – he knew what he was looking for – to display in the shop window. Now that the window displays were sorted, all she and Alec were waiting on was the delivery of the stock to fill the new outlet in Mr Gillespie's store.

Robyn had handed back Mr Gillespie's pen that day, aware that she'd shaken his hand and agreed to be business partners while forgetting that the cash she was intending to use might be fake. Luckily for her, it wasn't. Otherwise she'd have had to make a trip to a bank, probably miles away, to try and access the funds in her savings account. Although she was nervous about using the cash, she didn't have time to sort out a trip to a bank either.

David was leaving hospital the next day. It was a day later than anticipated, but it had turned out he'd been in a lot of pain, which meant less physio, and because of that he was unable to manage stairs; they'd decided he wasn't leaving until Sunday, which had also given the clinicians more time to get the dosage for his pain meds correct.

She had been intending to ask Gayle if she'd take David in so that he could recuperate at Lark Lodge instead of going home to his mean old dad, but that had been before she'd got to know Mr Gillespie, who was now looking forward to collecting his son from hospital and having him home. It was all he'd talked about that day while they'd been busy in the shop.

She'd spoken to David over the phone that morning, and he hadn't been at all happy with the idea of being stuck at home recuperating. Robyn had had that on her mind, standing outside the window display, when she'd taken a step back to get a better view, had forgotten about the kerb, and had taken a tumble. Luckily for her, there hadn't been a car driving along as she fell into the road. Instead, a passerby had helped her up.

'Are you sure you're okay?'

'Apart from a bruised ego.' Robyn was feeling embarrassed.

The young man peered in the window. 'What were you looking at?'

'My window display.'

'*Your* window display?'

Robyn nodded.

He read the banner in the window, and then turned to her. 'You're Robyn Parker – Interior Designer?'

Robyn nodded proudly. 'That's me. Do you like it?'

'Of course I like it.' He turned to look at her. 'What's not to like?'

There followed an awkward moment when their eyes locked. Was he flirting with her? She thought, *how old are you?* He looked no more than seventeen, eighteen. That was the problem with being so small in stature. She looked younger than her years.

He seemed familiar. They didn't know each other, did they? Robyn couldn't imagine so. She wasn't from the area. But that was the problem with her memory loss – it put her at a big disadvantage. What if someone from her past *did* recognise her? She would not recognise them.

'You know, there's no other place in town like it.'

Robyn wasn't sure whether he was referring to Mr Gillespie's general store, or her little outlet inside.

'I'm Marty. Here, I think this is yours.'

He was holding a handbag.

'It went flying out of your hand when you fell.'

'Oh, right. Thanks.' She was about to take her handbag when the shop door opened, and Mr Gillespie came rushing out. 'What's going on here? I saw you fall. Are you okay, Robyn?'

She was about to reply when Mr Gillespie spotted Marty. 'Hey, give that back!'

Robyn immediately guessed what he was thinking. 'Oh, Marty didn't push me over. He helped me up. I'm so clumsy. I was so busy admiring my handiwork in the shop window, and I stepped back and forgot there was a kerb.' She looked at her handbag. 'He was just handing that back.'

'Marty?' Mr Gillespie stepped forward and eyed the young man closely. 'Hey, I know you. Your father is a gardener at The Lake House.'

'The Lake House?' Robyn thought, *that name rings a bell.* She was just wracking her brain, trying to think why the name sounded familiar, when Marty said, 'Surely, you've heard of the Rosses. The Lake House is their holiday home.'

'One of Scotland's richest families,' Mr Gillespie clarified.

And Gayle's neighbour. She remembered now; Gayle had mentioned that they were her neighbours, kind of – their property backed on to hers. They'd owned it for years, but it was their holiday home. They lived mainly in London when they weren't abroad, by the sound of it. Then she recalled something else. After her car accident, when she'd watched the news on TV in her hospital room, she'd discovered there had been another accident on Christmas Day in the Cairngorms. The young woman in the other accident hadn't been so fortunate.

Robyn said, 'Didn't someone from that family have an accident skiing on Christmas Day?'

Mr Gillespie shook his head. 'Terrible business. They're good people. So sad for a tragedy to befall a loved one on Christmas Day.'

Robyn thought how lucky she'd been to survive her accident on Christmas Day. She turned to Marty. 'Did you know her?'

'No. Hardly saw her when I was growing up. Sometimes I'd accompany my father when he was working there, but they came to use the house mostly in the winter for skiing, and my father didn't work there during the Christmas break.'

'How is the old boy? I haven't seen your father around lately, Marty.'

Old? It sounded to Robyn as though Marty's parents had had him later in life.

'He's okay,' replied Marty. 'He's retired now. They've recently moved house, downsized. He didn't want to retire, but he couldn't keep it going any longer with his bad back. I've taken over his gardening work.'

'I see. Is that what you want to do with your life? You don't have to, you know. You can be anything you want to be.'

Robyn wasn't surprised by Mr Gillespie's remarks. He wouldn't want his sons to take over his business.

Marty, on the other hand, did seem taken aback by the question. 'Of course I want to. I wouldn't be doing it otherwise, would I?'

Mr Gillespie nodded. He turned to Robyn. 'I'm locking up.'

Robyn had been on her way out.

'Is there anything you need before I lock the shop up?'

'That spare set of keys?' The shop would be closed the next day. It was Sunday. Unlike the large supermarkets which appeared to be open seven days a week, from early morning until late at night, Mr Gillespie would not open all hours. That probably put a dent in his profit margin, but Robyn could understand. If he opened all hours, he'd have no life.

Besides, Mr Gillespie had said, 'Call me old-fashioned, but if you desperately need something at stupid o'clock in the morning, or late at night, then you should take some lessons in time-management, and learn to be organised. Honestly, I don't know where this notion came from that everything has to be open twenty-four seven. Shopkeepers need time off work too.'

Robyn agreed. However, it meant that Robyn's little shop, located in his store, was only open during *his* opening hours. That wasn't something she'd considered when she'd thought up the idea to set her business up in his store. But that didn't mean she could only work when the shop was open. She could still arrange home visits for fittings, and decorating, during evenings and weekends.

She still wanted a key, though, in case she wanted to arrive early, or leave late, on the understanding that the shop's opening and closing hours would remain the same. She also wanted to show David her new business premises, just the two of them, out of hours. She hoped he liked it.

She watched Mr Gillespie lock the door. He deposited the keys in her hand.

'Oh, but these are your keys.'

'I'm betting you're going to be here before me, and leave

after me. I see your dedication. I'll get myself a key cut at some point.'

Robyn deposited the keys in her handbag.

He said, 'Just don't go tripping up on any more kerbs and losing your bag.'

Robyn smiled. 'I'll try not to.'

'Now, before I go, do you need a lift?' he asked.

'No, thank you. Gayle is doing some shopping in Aviemore …' she winced. She'd tried to encourage her to shop in Mr Gillespie's, but she didn't want to pay his prices. 'I'm going home with her.'

'Well, I'll see you on Monday then.'

'Yes, see you Monday.' She watched him walk to his car. He was using that to make his deliveries while the van was in the garage being repaired after it had broken down the night David had been taken into hospital – another expense he could ill afford.

Robyn stared after Mr Gillespie. *I might see you sooner than Monday*, she thought. She wanted to see David the next day, when he was being discharged from hospital. She hadn't seen him since Wednesday, the day he'd been admitted and had surgery, although she'd spoken to him on the phone every day since. It had only been two days, but it seemed like an age. She was used to his company. She missed him coming up with excuses when he turned up in the van, taking her wherever she wanted to go, like her own private chauffeur.

Robyn sighed. She'd relied on those lifts – relied on him. If only she had her own car, then she could visit David at home. She thought of all that cash. She could go out and buy one tomorrow, something second-hand, a reasonably priced runaround. She'd need one once she had more clients – she was thinking of Rose's neighbours – and when her new business premises officially opened in a couple of weeks' time. But there was a problem – after her car accident, she'd lost her confidence in getting behind the wheel of a car.

Marty fell in step with Robyn as she headed in the other direction. She looked at him. 'Are you walking this way?'

He smiled at her. 'I am now.'

Robyn felt awkward. Should she tell him about David? Perhaps she was just reading too much into things. She'd feel pretty stupid if she told him there was a guy, and he'd shrugged, and asked what she was telling him that for – did she think he fancied her? She kept her mouth shut. She did not want to embarrass herself further. She did have another thought. 'How would you like to see what you could do with a really wild and overgrown garden?' she asked him.

He stared at her intently.

'Can you take on some extra gardening work?'

'Oh, yes. Just point me in the right direction.'

'Come with me.' She grabbed his arm. 'There's somebody I'd like you to meet.'

19

'Gayle, I'd like you to meet Marty.'

Gayle was back from shopping. She'd parked the car a little way down the street from Mr Gillespie's store. She was standing at the back of her car with the boot open.

'Here, let me help you.' Marty picked up a carrier bag and put it into the boot.

'Wow, what a car!' Marty exclaimed, admiring the old Bentley.

'It was Gayle's father's car.'

'It's a beauty.'

'Do you like old cars?' Robyn asked.

'Yeah, grew up with my dad tinkering with vintage cars. It's his hobby. Now he's retired, he can restore them to his heart's content. So, if you ever need a spare part, or if something goes wrong …'

'Thank you, Marty.' Gayle shut the boot. 'I haven't had any problems yet – fingers crossed.' She loaded the last bag of shopping into the car and shut the boot. Gayle turned around and eyed them both. 'So, is this the young man you were talking about who you're going to be working with in the shop?'

'Oh, no. That's Alec. Marty is a gardener.'

Gayle looked from Robyn to Marty, clearly perplexed. 'Okay. Do you mind me asking why you've introduced me to your, er, new friend?'

Robyn decided not to tell her the embarrassing story of how she'd met Marty.

'Marty is going to come along and take a look at your garden.'

Gayle was just opening the car door. 'Pardon me?'

Marty said, 'As it's winter, there's only so much I can do. But I can start clearing the garden in preparation for planting in the spring, and we can talk about landscaping.'

'Landscaping? I thought you said gardening?'

'I landscape too. I'm at college part-time, studying horticulture and landscaping.'

Robyn turned to him and grinned. 'Fantastic. I bet Gayle's garden is going to look amazing when it's finished.'

Gayle frowned. 'Robyn, get in the car.'

'Why? I don't want to leave just yet.'

Gayle glanced at Marty. 'I need a private word, please.'

Robyn turned to Marty. 'Will you just wait a moment?'

He shrugged. 'Sure.'

Robyn got in the car next to Gayle, leaving Marty on the pavement, admiring the Bentley.

They both slammed their doors shut.

Gayle turned to Robyn. She said in a hushed voice, 'What are you doing? I can't afford a gardener, and certainly not a load of new plants and landscaping.'

'Yes, I know. But I can. Here's the deal. As you won't take any rent from me for staying in your house, I've decided to spend that rent money on a gardener – Marty.' Robyn folded her arms. 'And I won't take no for an answer.' Robyn sighed. Gayle could easily say no, whatever Robyn said.

'Look, Gayle, if you're going to turn Lark Lodge into a bona fide guesthouse, like we talked about, you need a good first impression when people turn up to the house. The front garden's a mess.'

'Don't sugar-coat it, will you?' Gayle said sarcastically.

Robyn didn't add that the back garden was a mess too, and that she'd like to hire Marty to work on that next.

Marty tapped on the front passenger window.

Robyn wound her window down.

'Look, I can provide references,' Marty said to Gayle.

Robyn glanced at Gayle.

'Well, don't look at me,' she said. 'I'm not hiring you.'

Robyn threw her arms around Gayle and gave her a hug. 'Thank you.'

Marty grinned too. 'Great.' He shifted his attention to Robyn. 'I'm sure I can contact the Rosses and get that reference.'

'You work for them?' Gayle said, surprised. 'Lark Lodge backs on to their place – The Lake House. In fact, the whole street does. Not that we can see much of it from ours, as they have a walled garden, and extensive grounds. Their garden must keep you busy, Marty.'

'Yes, that's true, it's a lot of land – so your garden is going to take no time at all.'

Robyn pursed her lips. He hadn't seen the state of it. She could just imagine that wealthy family's manicured lawns and perfectly neat borders.

'My garden,' repeated Gayle.

Robyn glanced at Gayle and smiled. She looked at Marty. 'So, when you can pop round to look at the garden?'

'Whenever suits you.'

Robyn grinned. 'I'll be in touch.' She got out her mobile phone. 'Can I have your number?'

20

'Thanks for taking me to see David this morning,' Robyn said as they set off in the car.

'Don't thank me – he's my friend too. Although not as close a friend as with you.' She nudged Robyn playfully with an elbow and a wicked twinkle appeared in her eyes.

Robyn grinned. The bills were forgotten, and the carefree Gayle was back. She wondered which self-help book Gayle had read yesterday evening to put her back on track. Robyn decided against asking, lest she found herself with a bit of bedtime reading courtesy of Gayle's personal self-help library, collected over the years.

They swung into the hospital car park and got out of the car. Walking towards the entrance, Robyn happened to glance up at the windows on the second floor. She spotted David sitting at the window. She was sure it was him, looking right at her, so she stopped and waved.

He turned away from the window.

That's odd. Perhaps he didn't see me, thought Robyn as she slowly lowered her hand.

She caught up with Gayle at the entrance. They made their

way down the now familiar maze of corridors to David's room.

'Just stay away from her!'

Stopping outside the door to David's room, Robyn and Gayle exchanged confused glances at David's angry outburst.

'*She* came to *me*!' an angry voice shouted back.

Robyn recognised that voice. It was David's father. Robyn could feel the colour rising in her cheeks. They were talking, or rather arguing, about her. Perhaps David's father had told him that they were business partners. She didn't see why that should cause a row. She was free to do what she wanted. Although she did wonder if he was afraid that his father would drive her away, just as David still believed he'd driven away David's mother. That wasn't true, but David didn't know that.

Robyn and Gayle stood awkwardly on the other side of the door, both unsure as to whether they should announce their presence. Gayle motioned at the door handle. Robyn pointed down the corridor, mouthing, *we should leave.*

Robyn could hear muffled voices now from inside the room.

Gayle reached for the door handle.

Robyn moved away from the door, shaking her head and looking longingly down the corridor.

'Just go to hell!' David yelled, making them both jump.

'Alright!' The door suddenly swung open, and Gayle found herself face to face with David's father. She stepped aside. He left the room, slammed the door behind him and growled at her, 'What do *you* want?'

Gayle seemed to have lost her voice. She swallowed.

Robyn stepped forward. 'We're visiting David.'

'Well, enjoy your visit. He's in a foul mood.'

'I'm not surprised,' Gayle said, finding her voice, giving him a cold, hard stare.

Robyn grabbed Mr Gillespie's arm and pulled him to one side. She whispered, 'I heard you two arguing behind the door. I know what it's about. You have to tell him what you told me – about his mother.' Robyn didn't feel she had any choice, but to add, 'If you don't – I will.'

Now Mr Gillespie grabbed her arm. 'Don't! I mean it. You'll break his heart.'

'Ow! You're hurting me,' Robyn wailed.

Gayle rushed over. 'Let go of her!'

The door was suddenly flung open. David, in a wheelchair, dressed in casual clothes, stared at all three of them. 'What the hell …?'

Mr Gillespie let go of Robyn's arm in an instant.

Robyn quickly said, 'I slipped. Your dad caught me before I fell.'

Robyn saw Gayle staring at her.

'Right, I'm off.'

Robyn watched Mr Gillespie heading off at a pace down the corridor. She turned to David and caught him frowning at his father's back.

'Hi. How are you? And what are you doing in the wheelchair?' Robyn intentionally didn't mention the argument they'd overheard or the altercation she'd just had with his father.

'It's the nurse. I've got to leave hospital in this.'

It immediately brought to mind Robyn's discharge from hospital after the accident on Christmas Day. 'Hey, remember *my* discharge? We had such fun wheeling me down the corridor on my way out.' Robyn was trying to lighten the atmosphere. She glanced at Gayle and thought *why are you frowning at me?*

'This is kind of ironic,' said David, slapping the arm of the wheelchair, 'when the physio has been on my case these past few days, badgering me to get me up and about.'

Robyn laughed. She glanced at Gayle. She wasn't smiling. *What is her problem*, thought Robyn.

'Look, guys. I'm just going to use the bathroom, collect my washbag.' He glanced over at the bed. 'Can someone pass me those?'

Robyn followed his gaze to a pair of crutches in the corner of the room. 'Oh, I didn't realise—'

'Yep, me neither. I don't know what I was thinking – that the physios could work miracles and I'd be running out of this place. It takes about six weeks to fully recover – give or take. Until then, I'm stuck with those, then it's a walking stick for a bit thereafter, I guess.' He looked at Gayle.

'Yes, that's how it works, I'm afraid.'

Robyn realised she'd stupidly assumed that he'd just get out of that wheelchair and walk unaided out of the hospital.

As soon as the bathroom door closed, Gayle appeared by her side. 'Why are you defending him?' Gayle said in a whisper, out of earshot of David. 'I don't get it.'

Robyn didn't understand the question. 'Defending who?'

Gayle glared at her.

'Oh, right – you mean David's father. You're still thinking about that?'

'Well, of course. He was hurting you, and you covered for him.'

Robyn pulled her over to the window, about as far as they could get from the bathroom without leaving the room.

Gayle folded her arms. 'Well?'

Robyn cast a glance over at the bathroom door before she said in a hushed voice, 'He told me something, well, a lot of things – secrets that he's kept from his son, that David should know. I just can't tell him.'

'Can't tell him what?'

'Him – who? Me?' David had emerged from the bathroom to find the two women staring at him, wide-eyed.

They realised he'd caught the tail-end of their conversation.

'Are you talking about me?' he said light-heartedly, looking from one to the other expectantly.

'Yeah, of course – who else?' Gayle replied. 'We were talking about you coming home with us to Lark Lodge.'

'We were?' Robyn furrowed her brow. She knew they hadn't been talking about that just then, but also that at no point had Gayle mentioned the idea. Robyn certainly hadn't brought it up herself. She still wanted David to go home to his father.

Gayle turned around to look at her, eyes wide, as if to say, *are you serious? You need to play along.*

Robyn resisted the urge to smile. Gayle was telling a fib. 'Oh, yeah, right. Of course.'

Gayle turned back to David, and added, 'It was meant to be a surprise.'

David returned to the wheelchair and stood beside it. 'What was?'

'I had this brilliant idea that you could come home with us to recuperate at Lark Lodge.'

Robyn turned to Gayle. She didn't know how she didn't blurt, *That was my idea – in the beginning. I just haven't brought it up.* Was Gayle some kind of mind-reader?

'Actually, I have a confession to make,' said Gayle.

I want to hear this, thought Robyn, wondering what on earth she was about to say. Please don't bring up the fact that his father and I are business partners. She did not want that to start another argument.

Robyn closed her eyes, hoping that wasn't it.

'I only came here this morning to see you, expecting a family member would come and pick you up. Well, now I see who that family member is, I want to invite you to stay at Lark Lodge. I don't think your father is one of those people who is going to be conducive to your recovery. I really don't.'

Robyn's eyes shot open. 'I disagree.'

David and Gayle turned to her. She caught their surprised expressions. Robyn wanted to tell David that he needed to go home to his father, and talk. But neither of them were in the right place to do that. She wanted to tell David the secrets his father had been keeping from him, about his life with their mother, about the reasons she'd walked out. But Mr Gillespie was right – it wasn't her story, her secret to tell.

'You don't want me to come and stay at Lark Lodge?'

'Of course she wants you to come home with us,' Gayle butted in. 'If you want to – that is.'

'Yeah, of course I do. We'll need to swing by my house to collect some things.'

'No problem at all.'

Robyn stood in the room, listening to them making plans.

'What are we waiting for?' Gayle said light-heartedly. 'Let's go!'

David was stopped at the door by a nurse. 'Where do you think you're going?' he said to David.

'I've been discharged.'

'That's not what I meant – and you know it.' The nurse walked into the room and stood behind the wheelchair. 'David, you know the drill.'

David sighed, rolled his eyes at the nurse, and handed Gayle his crutches. He sat down in the wheelchair.

The nurse pushed the wheelchair down the corridor to the lift. Gayle walked alongside. 'I don't know where you live, and I don't have SatNav, so you'll have to direct me.'

David nodded.

Robyn joined them all in the lift. 'What about your dad?'

David looked up at her. 'What about him?'

'He's going to expect you home.'

'If he's not there, we'll leave him a note,' said Gayle.

Robyn shot her a look.

She shot one back, lifting her hands and shrugging as if to say, *what's the problem?*

Robyn faced the front of the lift. Now she wished she hadn't asked Gayle to take her there that morning to see David before he left the hospital. She expected Mr Gillespie was going to think it was her idea when he found out David was not going home just yet but was staying at Lark Lodge instead.

Robyn hoped he wasn't home, although there would be no getting away from him on Monday when she started organising the space for her outlet in the shop.

The nurse wheeled David out of the lift and along to the entrance.

On the way, a physio caught up with them and handed David a couple of leaflets, encouraging him to keep up with the daily exercises.

Robyn could tell he was pleased to leave the wheelchair at

the door. They headed out across the road to the car park, David on crutches.

Robyn and Gayle walked ahead.

Gayle glanced over her shoulder at David before saying in a hushed voice, 'What is up with you? I thought you'd be pleased to have David living under the same roof. I've seen the way you look at him, undressing him with your eyes.' There was a mischievous twinkle in her eye.

Robyn ignored her suggestive remark, although she could feel her cheeks flush in embarrassment.

They reached the car, and Gayle put her hand on her hips.

'I don't get it. You invite any Tom, Dick or Harry to stay and it's fine. I invite someone to stay in my own house and you disagree.'

'How well do you really know him?' Robyn said defensively, trying to talk her out of it. David still wouldn't tell her about the accident that had ended his ice hockey career. Something had happened, but it hadn't happened during a game. David refused to share the details. She wondered what the big secret was.

Gayle threw an exasperated hand up in the air. 'Honey, what did you know about Nick when you invited him to stay? Come to think of it,' she stared at Robyn, 'what do I know about you?'

'Oh, Gayle,' Robyn giggled nervously, 'you know me.'

Gayle raised her eyebrows. 'Do I?'

Robyn's smiled slipped. 'Sure, you do.'

She folded her arms. 'Really? Because I was under the impression you'd lost your memory. If you can't remember who you are, how can I possibly know the real you?'

Robyn frowned. This wasn't the conversation she'd expected with Gayle. She was about to say, *Well, ask me anything*. But of course, she couldn't do that – she didn't have the answers, not with her memory issues.

'Why don't you ask David about the accident that ended his career? That would be a start.'

'All right, I might just do that. I don't see how it will change my mind. I still want him to stay.'

They'd arrived at the car.

'What about me?' Robyn asked.

'What about you?'

'Will you still be happy for me to stay when you find out all about me?'

Gayle dropped her hands from her hips. 'Look, I'm sorry about what I said. I like David, and I feel sorry for him having a mean old man like that for a father.'

'But he's not—'

'My father was a lovely man,' continued Gayle, 'and sometimes I forget how lucky I've been to have had him in my life for all those years. So, forgive me if I want to do a good deed. And for getting shirty with you. That was uncalled for. Do you forgive me?'

Robyn glanced back at David, who was still making his way to the car.

She turned to Gayle. 'Of course I do.'

'What's going on?' David said breathlessly as he caught up with them.

'Nothing,' they said in unison. Robyn cringed at the outright lie. She still wasn't happy with this new arrangement.

Gayle smiled at David and opened the car door. 'I think we'd better seat you up front.' She opened the door. 'There's more space.'

David looked from the open door to Robyn. 'Is that all right with you, Robyn?' he said in a soft voice, and she knew very well he wasn't asking about the seating arrangements in the car.

'Why wouldn't it be?' she said, stealing a glance at Gayle.

'Good. That's settled then.' Gayle said before anyone could change their minds.

They were all about to get in the car when Gayle said, 'Who is that?' She pointed.

Mr Gillespie was standing by his car, waving at them across the car park. 'I'm over here!' he shouted.

Robyn rolled her eyes. Of course he would have waited for his son. Despite having a row, he wouldn't have just driven off and left David to make his own way home. 'I suppose you'll be going home with your dad now,' Robyn said, smiling to herself.

'Why?' David looked over at his father. He didn't wave back.

'What do you mean – why? He's right there, waiting for you.'

'Well, it's going to be a long wait. I'm coming home with you guys.'

'Aren't you going to go over and tell him what's going on?'

'Nope.'

'But if he follows you home, he's going to think that Gayle is just giving you a lift.'

'I don't care.'

'But you'll have to tell him.'

'I don't have to do a goddamn thing!'

Robyn shot him a black look. 'I'll go and tell him myself.'

'I want you to stay away from him.'

Robyn caught Gayle's expression. She knew what Gayle was thinking – David was still annoyed at the fact that Robyn had gone into business with his father. She expected they were both thinking about the row they'd overheard them having in the hospital room..

Robyn wasn't going to think about that right now. What was on her mind was setting the record straight with Mr Gillespie that this was not her idea. She had been wavering as to whether to do that until David had said, *I want you to stay away from him.*

'David, don't tell me what to do!' Robyn stalked off. She walked straight over to Mr Gillespie, who was still standing by the open door of his car, waiting for David.

Robyn looked over at them getting into Gayle's car. 'He's not coming.'

'I see. He's still angry with me.' Mr Gillespie got in his car too. 'He'll cool off by the time he gets home.'

'But you don't—'

He slammed the driver's side door shut before Robyn could finish her sentence.

She ran around to the passenger side, opened the car door, and got in next to him.

Mr Gillespie had been about to start the car engine, he paused, fingers on the key in the ignition, and turned to look at her. 'What are you doing?'

'I was about to tell you that you don't understand. He's not going home.'

'He's not?'

'Well, he is, but—'

'He is. He's not. For goodness' sake, what are you prattling on about, woman?'

Robyn ignored his belittling tone. 'Look, he's only going home to collect some clothes and other stuff, and then he's going to stay with us at Lark Lodge.'

'He's staying at Lark Lodge tonight – why?'

Tonight? Robyn got the impression he was moving in for a while. She didn't exactly know how to tell Mr Gillespie that.

Robyn nervously chewed her bottom lip. 'It's not my fault, honestly. It wasn't my idea. Gayle asked him to stay after she overheard you both arguing. I tried to talk him out of it.'

'Well, you clearly didn't do a very good job of it.' He eyed her. 'You said he's collecting some clothes. He's not coming back tomorrow, is he?'

It wasn't a question. Robyn nodded all the same, expecting Mr Gillespie to give her an earful.

'Shut the door!'

Robyn looked at him. 'What?'

'The car door. We've got to get moving. I don't want him arriving at the house before me and leaving before I have a chance to stop him.'

He started the car, and looked at her. 'Or go with them.'

'I don't want to.' Robyn shut the car door.

He put the car in gear, and they drove off, passing Gayle and David standing by their car, looking surprised to see her in Mr Gillespie's car.

She caught Gayle's expression as they drove past – *what are you doing?*

And David's, looking shocked.

'Why don't you stop the car and try and convince David to come home with you?'

'I'd rather he was home. Then he'll probably cool off.'

Robyn turned around in her seat to see them getting into Gayle's car. 'But what if they go straight to Lark Lodge?

'Oh, he'll follow.'

'How can you be so sure?'

'How do you think?'

At first she had no idea. Then she turned around in her seat and remembered what she'd overheard them arguing about – her. David had said, *Just stay away from her.*

She'd heard Mr Gillespie's angry voice shout back, *She* came to *me*!

'He'll probably think I kidnapped you – silly boy.'

Robyn pursed her lips, and admitted, 'I heard you arguing when we approached David's hospital room. You were arguing about *me*.' She wanted to know what exactly had been said. She asked him as they drove out of the hospital car park, Gayle's car in hot pursuit, Robyn noticed, when she glanced over her shoulder.

She heard Mr Gillespie sigh heavily before he answered her question. 'I made the mistake of mentioning that I'd met you, and we'd talked, and it was decided that you could set up your business in my store. He was not happy. He thinks I'm taking advantage of your kind, generous nature.'

Robyn said, 'Silly boy.'

They exchanged a smile. Robyn had wanted to tell David herself, but she hadn't factored in his relationship with his dad and what that might mean in terms of his reaction when he found out.

'I'm sure he believes I'll drive you away, just like I did his mother – which you know is only part of the story. It takes two to tango, as they say. I know I was unhappy, and a bit disillusioned with life, but I never wanted her to leave me, to leave our boys. I would have done anything for her to stay.'

Robyn hoped that Mr Gillespie had told her the truth.

'So, now you know what caused his outburst that you overheard. You're not going to change your mind – are you?

'About working in your shop?'

He nodded. 'We did shake on it, you know.'

'I have no intention of backing out. If David thinks he's going to persuade me otherwise, he can think again.'

Mr Gillespie grinned at her. 'By god, you remind me of my Catherine.'

'Your Catherine?'

He frowned. 'Well, she isn't mine anymore. Hasn't been for so long. You just bring it all back, the memories, when we were young and in love.'

'I'm sorry she left you.'

'So am I.'

They travelled on in silence until Robyn glanced over her shoulder. 'Gayle is tailgating you.'

'I know. I told you they'd follow.'

Robyn turned in her seat. 'I've never been to David's house before.'

'You haven't?'

She shook her head.

'It's a bit out of the way.'

'What do you mean?'

He grinned. 'You'll see.'

21

A short distance outside Aviemore, they joined a winding road, travelling in the opposite direction to Lark Lodge. It wasn't far along the road, and they turned off. Robyn turned to look at him. 'Mr Gillespie, I thought you said—'

'You can call me by my Christian name, you know.'

'I don't know what that is.'

'Ah, right. It's Duncan. You were asking me a question?'

'Yes, I noticed we've turned off the main road already. I thought you said it was a bit out of the way.'

'Yes, it is. There's a way to go along here.'

Robyn had noticed a brown tourist sign pointing to a loch. 'Is David's house by a loch?'

'Oh, aye.'

They drove along the bumpy single-track road through a forest of pines. Robyn glanced over her shoulder at Gayle's car, which was following. It had slowed down to travel along the bumpy road and was now some distance behind. Robyn wasn't surprised. Gayle wouldn't want to damage her dad's old car, and the suspension on the old Bentley wasn't that great. She bet it was a very uncomfortable ride, especially for poor David. He was going to feel every jolt along the poorly maintained road.

'It's not a very good road, is it?'

'That's the Forestry Commission. I expect they'll come and repair it one of these days. People come here to walk around the loch, and fish. I used to bring the boys here, take a boat out fishing.'

'When they were kids?'

'Oh, yes. Highlight of the weekend.'

Robyn had thought that all he'd done was to take David to hockey practice. She said as much.

He glanced at her. 'Who told you that?'

'Who do you think?' She had a thought. 'How did you get a boat to the loch when you took them fishing?'

'I didn't have to bring one with me. There was a boat at the boathouse.'

'The boathouse?'

Robyn noticed Duncan take his eyes off the road for a second to look at her. 'David didn't mention the boathouse to you?' he said.

She shook her head. 'No. Not at all. He didn't even mention that you took your sons fishing.'

'David clearly loved those trips so much that he went and bought the place – well, that's what he tells me. I don't know where he got the money from. I guess he's been a saver, unlike his old man.'

'What place?'

'The boathouse I used to rent for the summer. We'd have to sleep upstairs in the little room in the eaves. We had a cooking stove, sleeping bags, and I'd tell them stories around the fire.'

Robyn stared at him. This was not the childhood that she

had pictured from what David had told her. He had never mentioned any of this.

'What do you mean – you don't know where he got the money from?' Robyn didn't think an old boathouse would cost that much money. Besides, he had money from playing professional hockey. She told Duncan her thoughts.

Duncan shook his head, and smiled. 'What sort of money did you think he earned in professional ice hockey?'

'I have no idea. A lot?'

'You're thinking of professional footballers.'

Robyn shrugged. 'I guess.'

'Look, most players probably earn an average wage, if they're lucky. However, salaries can really vary. David was reaching the top of his game, the peak in his sporting career. He could have earned ten times that – six figures.'

Robyn recalled what David had told her; he'd just transferred to one of the teams that played in the Elite Ice Hockey League, the top tier of ice hockey in the UK. 'He said that two Scottish teams compete in the league, and he was going to play for one of them.'

'Aye, that he was.'

They continued along the single-track lane in silence. Robyn was about to ask him how the accident had happened that had ended David's career, when he said, 'You'll see what I mean when we arrive. It's quite a place.'

'He had it renovated, then?' Somehow she didn't imagine David in an old wooden boathouse, even if he had renovated it and enlarged it to live in. She'd pictured him in a modern, architecturally designed property. She didn't know why.

Duncan chuckled. 'Renovated? He had the old boathouse

torn down and built something in its place.'

Robyn smiled. That was just what she'd pictured – something newly built. Robyn cast her gaze around the beautiful scenery. She imagined it would be amazing.

Her smile at the thought of finally seeing where he lived was tempered by the circumstances surrounding her first visit. She should be travelling with him to see his house, not with his father.

'What's the matter?' Duncan asked, catching her expression.

'It's nothing.'

'You two have had a lovers' tiff, I take it?'

Robyn frowned at him and didn't reply. They were not lovers – not yet, anyway. She didn't appreciate his choice of words, even though she knew it was just an expression.

They travelled on in silence, passing a detached cottage, then a couple of bungalows, also detached, and finally a farmhouse.

'Just a couple more miles, then we arrive at the loch.'

Robyn didn't think it was as remote as he made out. Other people lived along this stretch of country road, and it wasn't too far from the main road. Although if you wanted to nip out in the morning for a latte and a croissant, this certainly would not be the place.

She thought how a house by the loch would be right up Nick's street. Nick would love it there – as would Olive. She could just imagine the two of them going for a bracing run around a loch first thing in the morning. She smiled. Sometimes Nick did just that. He had to take Olive in the car, though.

'Not far now.'

They'd turned into a wide drive, the road surface so smooth compared to the bumpy, pot-holed single-track road they'd just travelled along that she felt they were floating along.

Gayle and David were some way behind. They'd lost them around a gentle bend.

Up ahead, through the trees, Robyn could see a pitched, tiled roof with a chimney. Nothing else just yet. But she said, 'It looks like a house.'

'That's because to all intents and purposes it is. You'd only know it was a boathouse from the loch. That's where you'll see the boat on the water underneath.'

'He has a boat too?'

'Oh, aye. Above is a wooden balcony overlooking the loch. I like to call it a veranda. It leads off the reception room on the first floor which has exposed brick walls, a log burner and a beamed ceiling. It's got a real cabin-in-the woods vibe. The veranda looks over the loch, obviously, and you get stunning views. I enjoy sitting out there, watching the sun set over the mountains.'

Robyn turned her gaze on him. By the sound of it, Duncan was feeling quite settled in his son's home.

'The kitchen is pretty impressive too. I've got a soft spot for the big American fridge.'

Robyn got the picture. 'It sounds wonderful. I think David should recuperate at home, not go and stay at Lark Lodge.'

'I concur. But then I would say that, wouldn't I? I'm biased. I love the place. It's just going to be a bit lonely out here without him around. Although to be fair, I spend a lot of my time in the shop, and he spends a lot of his time running around after you, like he's your personal taxi service.'

Robyn looked aghast. 'No he doesn't!'

'In my van.'

Robyn was still shaking her head. 'No, he's been out on

deliveries for you.'

'Oh, aye. He seems to spend a lot of time making just a handful of deliveries.'

Robyn pursed her lips. Of course, he was quite right: David had been her personal taxi service. And now he wasn't. It occurred to her that if he was way out here, in his boathouse, recuperating, she would hardly get to see him over the next six weeks, or however long it took for him to get back on his feet properly, and back in the van.

They rounded a bend in the drive and there it was – David's boathouse.

Robyn drew in a deep breath.

Duncan pulled the car to a stop outside the three-storey property. It looked like a stone-built house under a pantile pitched roof. There was no evidence that it was a boathouse from where they were; as Duncan had explained, that part could only be seen from the loch.

Duncan turned in his seat to look at her shocked expression. He chuckled. 'I knew you'd be surprised.'

Robyn was surprised all right. She remembered the place.

'Come on, let's go inside before they arrive. I'll get the kettle on, and we can sit down and persuade David to see sense.' Duncan got out of the car and marched up a garden path through an open, grassed garden area next to the house.

Robyn saw him turn around when he realised she wasn't following. He marched back to the car and opened the door. 'Come on. They'll be here any minute!'

Robyn reluctantly got out of the car. She slowly shut the car door and turned around to face the house. She didn't remember the drive because it had been dark when she'd been there before

– she was sure of it. But who could forget this boathouse? She couldn't explain it away by convincing herself that she must have seen something similar in a magazine. This house was individually architecturally designed.

Robyn was reluctantly walking towards the house when an alarm went off.

'Oh, hell's bells!' Duncan shouted over the din.

Robyn instinctively turned around and ran to the car.

'Where are you going?' Duncan called after her. 'Come back here and give me a hand with this darned thing. I need to shut it off.'

Robyn already had the car door open, about to jump in, and she had no idea why. She slammed the car door shut and joined Duncan at the front door. He was furiously punching some numbers into a keypad. 'God, why does this always happen to me? Any suggestions?'

'Do you know the key code?' As soon as the words were out of her mouth, she thought he'd tell her off for asking a stupid question.

'I did. But he keeps changing it, and I keeping forgetting what it is. I swear he's doing it on purpose. Urggh! This infernal thing! I told him not to have an alarm installed, but of course he went ahead anyway.' Duncan stopped stabbing his finger on the keypad for a moment, and turned to Robyn. 'What's your birthdate?'

'I'm sorry – what?'

'Your birthday?'

Robyn thought about her details that had been found by the police through the DVLA because her driving licence was missing in the car accident. 'Why do you want to know?'

He rolled his eyes at her. 'Why do you think?' he shouted above the din, pointing at the keypad.

'You think he'd use *my* birthday? I don't think I told him what that was.'

He tried the six digits anyway. They didn't work.

Robyn rolled her eyes. 'See. I told you.'

'When did you two first meet?'

That was easy. Robyn looked at the keypad. 'Christmas Day – when we literally bumped into each other on the road.'

'Oh, yes – the date of the accident.' He shrugged, shouting in her ear, 'Worth a try.'

Six digits entered into the keypad later, there was blessed silence.

'Oh, thank god!' Duncan shook his head as he unlocked the door.

22

Robyn followed Duncan inside. He'd already disappeared into the kitchen. She stood in the entrance hallway, staring at a large stuffed fish in a glass case on the wall. A glass-panelled staircase rose to the next floor, with a very modern open-tread staircase, where she imagined was the lounge with the balcony that Duncan had described. She could see through a couple of open doorways that there was an impressive modern kitchen on the ground floor, along with a study. She stood in the hall and exhaled in relief. None of this was familiar at all. She'd never been inside this property in her life.

Yeah, that's because I was the getaway driver.

Robyn's heart skipped a beat. *Why would I think that?* she wondered. *How strange.*

Duncan was already in the kitchen, putting on the kettle and arranging some mugs, preparing to make tea. He joined her in the hall. 'Come on, let's go upstairs,' he said. As they walked up the stairs, he added, 'Thanks for helping me with that blasted alarm.'

'I don't get it,' said Robyn, thinking of the keypad. 'Why does he need a house alarm all the way out here?'

'That's what I said to him. I thought he'd had it installed just to make my life difficult while I'm living here. Then he told me he'd been burgled.'

Robyn stared at him. 'What?'

'Yeah – on Christmas Day, when he was out. Unfortunately at this time of year, when people have spent money on presents, you hear about it all the time, people getting burgled. And out here, when your house has no neighbours to spot someone breaking in …' he trailed off.

'That's awful.'

'Yes.'

'But all the way out here? How would they even know this house was here?'

'I think they got lost down this country road and happened upon the house, unoccupied.'

'Did they take all his Christmas presents?'

'No, they didn't touch those, even though they were right there, in plain sight – right under a beautiful spruce Christmas tree by the fire.'

Robyn stared at the space where the Christmas tree would have been. She cast her gaze around the spacious room. It was just as Duncan had described.

She followed Duncan over to the double doors that led out onto a balcony with glorious views of the loch and the tree-covered hills beyond.

'The view of the loch is spectacular – isn't it?'

Robyn could see it was, but she barely gave it a glance. The burglary was still on her mind. She turned around to face Duncan. 'So, if they didn't steal the presents under the tree, what did they take?'

'David wouldn't tell me what they stole, initially. But I got it out of him.'

Robyn looked at him expectantly.

'Cash.'

'Cash?'

'I'm afraid so.' Duncan nodded his head. 'And now I know where he got it from.'

Robyn caught him staring at her intently. 'You mean – me?'

'You mentioned he has investments. Sounds to me as though he must have cashed one in.'

'Why do you say that? He could have withdrawn some cash from the bank to spend on Christmas shopping.'

'Not that amount.'

'What amount?'

'Thousands of pounds.'

'What?' Robyn looked at him wide-eyed. 'Why?'

'Yep. That was what I said when I found out. Why leave a heap of cash lying around? I mean, not that you'd expect to be burgled all the way out here, in the middle of nowhere. That was just bad luck. But even so, why risk it?'

'What did he need the cash for?' Robyn asked, even though she assumed he hadn't told his father that.

'How do I know? After I had a go at him for leaving that sort of cash lying around, and said whatever he needed to pay for, why not pay by cheque, for goodness' sake, or do a bank transfer – he got cheesed off, and wouldn't tell me.'

'How much cash was it?'

When Duncan gave her the figure, Robyn could feel the room spinning. 'I need to sit down.' She'd come over faint.

'Are you all right? Do you need a glass of water?'

'Yes, please.'

Robyn heard Duncan clomping down the wooden stairs. She also heard something else – the sound of a car turning up outside the house. 'Oh, god! It's David,' she said under her breath.

'They're here!' Duncan called up the stairs.

Robyn was thinking about the cash she'd discovered in the bottom of that rucksack. It had been in her car when she'd been speeding out of town on Christmas Day. *It wasn't me – surely,* she thought. *I'm a student at university – at least I was until I dropped out. And it's not as though I needed the money.* She was thinking of the money her mother kept sending her via cheque, and the amount in her savings account. *Surely, it must be a coincidence.*

The problem was that she knew how much cash was in that bag – she'd counted it to the last note, and the amount matched the cash that had been stolen. And she knew how much would be left after she'd paid for her outlet in Duncan's shop; she'd counted out six months upfront. It was sitting in an envelope, waiting to be handed to Duncan on the first day that her outlet officially opened. He wouldn't accept the money any sooner. But she couldn't back out now. She'd committed herself to loads of expenses.

Alec had suggested she could hire a company to set up a website for her business too. That sounded like a fantastic idea – but it would cost money.

The income from her first interior design job for Rose and Goerge would not cover any of her expenses. She hadn't charged Rose and George that much. She was lucky if she'd make a few hundred pounds of profit. Although they were fairly well off after downsizing from their larger property, they were retired on a fixed income, so she hadn't felt inclined to charge them too much. In fact, she didn't know what to charge. It was something she'd have to look into before she opened her outlet and found any new customers.

She had also committed to paying Marty for gardening and landscaping – he'd already turned up bright and early that morning, before they'd left for the hospital, and had made a start clearing the front garden. The garden would turn out to be a few months' work, according to Marty, and would cost a lot of money for plants and materials. But she'd said yes to his estimate on the spot, and he'd surprised her by getting stuck in straight away.

She could mentally calculate that she'd already burned through half of the money.

'Here we are.' Duncan handed her a glass of water. 'I'm just going to nip back downstairs and make that tea.'

Robyn wished he wouldn't. She wanted to leave straight away. Never mind persuading David to stay there; she was going to help him pack if it meant she could leave the scene of the crime.

Robyn suddenly relaxed when she realised she didn't remember setting foot in the place. 'I did not steal anything,' she mumbled to herself as she gulped down the water, trying not to think about the fact that her memory hadn't returned – so how could she know for sure? But she *had* remembered the outside of the place. And the amount in the rucksack was exactly the amount that had been burgled. How could that be a coincidence?

Robyn heard voices downstairs and the dull thud of what she imagined was the sound of David walking into his house on crutches on the wooden floor. She wasn't looking forward to an argument with him over the fact that she'd made the trip there with his father.

'She's upstairs,' Robyn heard Duncan say.

Gayle came up the stairs first. 'Hey! There you are.' She lowered her voice, 'Why did you take off like that in Mr Gillespie's car? I thought you'd been kidnapped or something.' Gayle was only half-joking. 'Are you all right?'

Robyn risked standing up. Fortunately, the room didn't spin around. She stood there, holding the empty glass. 'I'm fine.'

Gayle might be her best friend, but she was not going to bring up the stolen money. Not until she'd found out what had really happened that night – not until her memory came back and she was sure why she'd been travelling alone on Christmas Day with a rucksack full of money.

Robyn knew she'd been lucky that the money was well hidden at the bottom of the bag beneath a lot of clothes. If the bag had been opened by the police, they hadn't had a good rummage, otherwise they would have found the wads of cash.

'So, what was that all about?' Gayle asked.

Robyn looked at her. 'What are you talking about?' she said defensively.

'You going in the car with Mr Gillespie instead of coming with us.'

'Oh, right,' Robyn said in relief. For a moment, she had irrationally thought that Gayle could read her mind.

Gayle lowered her voice. 'David wasn't happy.' She glanced over her shoulder. 'He is on his way up.'

Robyn frowned. 'On crutches?'

'No, he's got to use a walking stick. He wasn't happy about that either, when I reminded him. One hand on the rail, the other on the stick. The physio shows you how to do it. And so will I if he doesn't do as he's told.'

The thought occurred to Robyn that David might change his mind about going to stay at Lark Lodge if the thought that Gayle was going to boss him about the whole time.

Robyn smiled. She would be quite happy with that. Then she could leave even quicker. She looked at Gayle, and spoke her thoughts – well some of them. 'I think we should leave.'

'But we've only just got here, and David has some clothes and things to pack.' Gayle looked at her askance. 'What's the rush? Did something happen before we arrived?'

Robyn laughed nervously. 'No, not at all. Why do you ask such a silly question?'

'I don't know. You seem a bit …'

'A bit what?'

'Out of sorts.'

'Robyn had a funny turn,' said Duncan, appearing in the lounge with David's crutches. 'David's preparing to climb Mount Everest.'

'That's not funny, Dad,' David shouted up the stairs.

Duncan laughed at his own joke before he turned to Robyn. 'Are you feeling better now you've had some water?' He left the crutches propped up by the stairs and took Robyn's empty glass.

'It was nothing, really.'

'Nothing? You looked as though you were going to pass out.'

'Who was going to pass out?' David asked, reaching the top of the stairs. He leaned heavily on the walking stick for a moment..

She looked from Gayle to David. 'I said it was nothing.'

Gayle folded her arms. 'Did you have a memory? Is that what it was?'

Robyn wished Gayle wasn't so perceptive. 'No. Why would I have one here?'

Gayle knitted her brow. 'That's true. You've never been here before.'

'Exactly!' Robyn tried to sound convincing.

Duncan butted into their conversation. 'I'm sorry, but I'm a bit lost. Why did you ask Robyn if she had a memory? A memory of what?'

Robyn sighed heavily and rolled her eyes at Gayle, watching her mouth forming into a great big, *Oh.*

'Oh, Gayle. Why did you have to go and say that!' Robyn plopped down on the sofa behind her.

'I'm sorry. I assumed they knew.'

'Did I tell you that they knew?'

'Well, no. But as you're on really friendly terms with them, I thought … well … that you had … would.'

David slipped a crutch under one armpit, and stepped closer. 'Knew what?'

'Anything.' Robyn closed her eyes, shook her head, and said, 'I lost my memory in the car accident on Christmas Day and … and I'm still waiting for it to come back.'

David moved a bit closer. 'What are you talking about? You told me your name, where you go to college, how old you are.'

'Only because it was on the police report. They found my car reg on the DVLA and traced the registered address back to my university accommodation. There are letters from my mum that I found in my things. She's travelling at the moment. She sends the letters to my university address. Dr Jamieson calls it selective amnesia. Obviously I can remember how to read, write, walk, talk, you know, I just can't remember … me.'

The room fell silent.

David said, 'So what were you doing on that road on Christmas Day?'

Robyn could feel the colour rising in her cheeks as she glanced around the room.

Duncan answered the question for her. 'How do you expect her to know that? She just told you. She lost her memory.'

David ignored Duncan. 'Why didn't you tell me?'

Robyn didn't know what to say. But she wasn't the only one keeping secrets. She folded her arms, and looked at him askance, throwing the question back at him. 'What were *you* doing on that road on Christmas Day?'

Duncan weighed in on the question too, surprising Robyn. 'Yes, what were you doing all the way out there on Christmas Day? I know you said you were on your way to see Annie and Joe, but that's going in the wrong direction.'

'You know what? I'm not having this conversation,' David growled at his father.

'Well, you started it,' Duncan replied.

'No,' David shook his head, 'Robyn started it.'

Gayle shook her head. 'Will everyone please stop behaving like children. Now, David, get some things together if you're coming home with us,' said Gayle, taking charge.

'I need to go up another flight of stairs,' he complained.

Robyn saw him walk to the end of the room, and look up a spiral staircase.

Gayle said, 'You're not going up those any time soon. Tell me what you need.'

David did as he was told.

Robyn noticed that Duncan wasn't exactly trying to persuade

him to stay. She sidled up to him as David was telling Gayle what he wanted to take with him and said, 'I thought you didn't want him to go?'

He whispered back, 'Looking at that sour expression, I'm thinking perhaps he is better off with Gayle. I'm no nurse. I've been down that road before, after his first accident, and he gave me hell.'

Gayle came down the stairs carrying a bag. 'Robyn, why don't you go and wait in the car? I've just got a few more things to fetch, then we'll be right on out.'

Robyn took one look at David, who was throwing her a black look, and blurted, 'I'm not coming.'

Gayle had one foot on the stair, about to make her way up the spiral staircase again. 'What do you mean, you're not coming?'

'There's a spare bedroom,' said Duncan.

David rounded on his father. 'You are joking.'

'No. I'm not. I don't see what the problem is. She's working in my shop. I could give her a lift to work in the morning. Then we'll take it from there.' He added, 'Give you two lovebirds a chance to cool off.'

Robyn rolled her eyes at Duncan.

He caught the look and shrugged. 'Sounds like a plan to me.'

David said, 'Whatever. I'm too tired to argue.'

Gayle stood there for a moment. 'Is that what you want, Robyn?'

Robyn stole another glance at David. She walked over to Duncan and stood beside him, arms folded defiantly. 'Yes.'

Gayle sighed and returned to the top floor to collect a few more things.

As she watched Gayle reappear with another bag, she

realised that it looked as though David was taking Gayle up on her offer to recuperate there properly; he was taking enough with him for a few weeks. Robyn realised she didn't have an overnight bag – just some spare knickers, in case she got her period, but nothing to sleep in. But another look at David convinced her she was staying put – at least for the night.

Robyn watched David make his way down the stairs with the aid of his walking stick. Gayle followed, carrying two bags. Duncan brought up the rear, carrying the crutches.

Robyn hung back at the top of the stairs. She heard Gayle's voice. 'I'll take your things out and wait for you in the car.'

'Thanks, Gayle.'

A moment later, Robyn heard David's voice again, speaking to Duncan. 'You're not going to convince me to stay then?'

'Nope,' Duncan replied.

'I thought that was why you were rushing back here, to get the kettle on and try and make me see sense over a cup of tea?'

'Yeah, that was the plan. I've changed my mind. I much prefer my new house guest.'

Robyn heard David's grumpy voice. 'It's not *your* house.'

Duncan said, 'Do you want me to carry the walking stick to the car?'

Robyn leaned over the banister and caught of glimpse of David leaning on his crutches. He reached out a hand. 'Give me that!' He shifted his attention to the stairs.

Robyn moved away from the banister, out of sight.

'Well, I'll be seeing you then.' Duncan sounded in surprisingly high spirits. 'Now, I'm going to make myself a nice cuppa.' He paused. 'Robyn would you like one?'

'Um, yes – I guess so,' she called down the stairs.

There was a moment's silence. She knew David was still standing in the hall – alone. She hadn't heard the tell-tale dull thud of his crutches on the wooden floor that she anticipated as he walked out the door.

She stood there, waiting for him to ask her, plead with her, to change her mind and return to Lark Lodge with them.

He did not.

The next thing Robyn heard was David shuffling out of the door.

She walked over to the window of the double-fronted room and watched David make it to the car. He didn't look back.

Gayle turned the car around. Then they were gone.

Robyn stared out of the window. *What just happened?* she wondered.

23

'Do you need some help?' A young woman with a pile of books in her hands passed Robyn by, paused mid-stride, turned around and peered at her. Robyn realised that she was the librarian, who must have noticed her standing in the entrance to Aviemore Library, looking a bit lost.

Robyn was there on her lunch break. Not that she had an official lunch break yet. She was in Aviemore that morning, sorting out her area in Duncan's shop while she waited for the paint and materials she'd ordered to finish redecorating Rose and George's house. She'd had an unexpectedly lovely evening getting to know David's father a little better while they played a board game in front of the log burner. Then they'd watched the sun go down and chatted while sitting wrapped up in blankets on the balcony overlooking the loch. The one thing he wouldn't talk about, Robyn noticed, was the accident that had ended David's ice hockey career. What was the big secret?

Robyn had still been thinking about secrets that morning when they'd left David's house together to go to work. It was Monday. Although Duncan had to be in his shop all day, Robyn did not. She could be gone as long as she liked. She'd had an idea, and it involved a trip to the local library.

Aviemore Library was part of the Aviemore Primary School and Community Centre, so it was housed in a spacious modern building and was open all week. Robyn wasn't sure where to start in her quest to discover the truth about what had happened to end David's career, but if nobody was going to tell her, then she planned to find out for herself. Then perhaps when she saw David next there would be no elephant in the room, at least from her perspective. When it came to her memory loss, though, a fact which understandably David had been surprised to learn the previous day, she still wasn't ready to talk.

Robyn didn't want to think about her feeling that she had been to his house before. There had to be a logical explanation as to why she seemed to remember turning up in a car outside the house. She tried to explain away the money. *Just a huge coincidence*, she thought, trying to convince herself.

'I need to see some of your local newspapers,' Robyn said to the librarian, reading the identity badge swinging on a chain from the young woman's neck.

'You'll find the papers in racks in the alcove over there,' she pointed ahead and then started to walk.

'No – wait,' Robyn said darting after her. She caught up with her just as she was about to put the pile of books on a trolley. 'I'm looking for papers from some time ago.'

'You'll be wanting the microfiche, then.' She put the books on the trolley and pushed it along. Robyn assumed she was going to show her where that was. In a small corner two machines looking like they were out of the ark stood gathering dust.

'Not much call for them now,' the young woman said. 'Most people come here to use the free internet.'

Robyn thanked her and then pulled out a chair and sat at one of machines. She fumbled for the switch, realising she probably hadn't used one of these things before.

'What year?' The librarian asked, watching her.

'Huh?'

'I'll need some idea of the year you want to research so that I can get the right film, and even check if it is available as a microfiche.'

'Oh, right.' Robyn thought quickly and asked for the last two years.

The librarian raised her eyebrows. 'The last two years?'

'Yes, I think so.' Robyn realised she didn't know. She furrowed her brow trying to remember if David had mentioned when he stopped playing professional ice hockey. She couldn't remember. Robyn looked at the librarian, and said, 'Perhaps three years.'

'You won't be needing microfilm, then.'

Robyn turned in her seat to look at her. 'How come?'

'Because you'll find most newspaper content online going back even to the 2000s. Some even have articles online from the 1990s, would you believe.'

Robyn felt stupid. Why hadn't she thought of looking online?

'Come with me.'

Robyn followed the librarian and her trolley down another aisle into a cosy corner behind some bookshelves, where there was a row of computer terminals along a desk. 'There's one free. I'll log you on.'

A moment later, the librarian got up. Robyn took a seat in front of the screen. She stared at the keyboard, then at the screen.

'Are you computer literate?' the librarian asked.

Robyn turned in the chair. 'Am I computer literate?' She didn't understand the question. 'What does that mean?'

'Okay,' the young woman said slowly. 'I guess not.'

During her quick lesson in surfing the web, Robyn had made a discovery before she even did her first Google search. 'I'm obviously computer illiterate,' she said.

She glanced at two teenagers who were sitting at computer terminals. They had been busy tapping at their keyboards, most likely surfing the internet too, but had stopped what they were doing and had stared at her in disbelief.

Robyn pursed her lips and raised her eyebrows at them, as if to say, *mind your own business*, and did her first Google search. *But I must know how to use a computer, surely. I was at university, studying for a degree.* She stared at the screen for a moment, thinking that it didn't make any sense; selective amnesia meant that she could remember how to do things like dress, read, write, even use a mobile phone – she still had the one that Rose had kindly given her; she was waiting to see if David called or texted. So far, she'd heard nothing. So, why couldn't she remember how to use a computer and get on the internet? How could she forget how to do something that most people did every single day, and that she imagined was second nature?

Robyn tried to put this mystery to one side and concentrate on the one in hand – what exactly had happened to David that had ended his ice hockey career? And why didn't anyone want to talk about it?

She glanced at the teenagers, who had lost interest in their weird neighbour two computers down.

Robyn looked at her watch, yawned, and stretched in her chair. Surfing the web had taken her down all sorts of rabbit holes in the last hour. She'd read so many news stories that her head was spinning from so much information.

Giving her eyes a break from the screen for a moment, she noticed the two teenage boys at the computer terminal had gone and had been replaced by another teenager, a girl this time, with a very bad case of acne.

Robyn looked back at the screen, resolving not to get drawn into reading any more current news articles. She did a search instead for David's name, along with professional ice hockey teams in Scotland, and the word *accident*. A lot of different articles came up, but nothing about one hockey player in particular.

Robyn was on to reading yet another article, about ice hockey in general, not about David or an accident, when the sound of a voice right behind her made her jump. 'How's it going?'

Robyn turned in her seat. The librarian was back with another trolley full of books. She'd stopped beside Robyn's chair while she placed a couple of books on the shelves just to her left.

Robyn sighed heavily.

'That good – huh?'

Robyn looked at her, surprised to find that the bespectacled young lady had a dry sense of humour. 'Is there a knack to this? I just can't find what I'm looking for.'

Robyn rubbed her bleary eyes; she had no idea how people worked at computer screens all day. She'd only been here an hour.

The librarian leaned over Robyn and peered at the screen. 'What are you looking for?'

'I want to find out—' Robyn stopped abruptly. Perhaps it was not a good idea to tell her exactly what, or rather who, she was researching. This was a small town. What if it got back to David, or his father, what she'd been doing there?

'I was researching news stories about ice hockey players who originally came from this area.'

'Sounds interesting.'

Robyn wondered if she was just being polite. Unless you were a huge ice hockey fan, then this was about as interesting as watching paint dry.

'So, what you want is the sports pages, if it's a local sports personality …'

Robyn wouldn't exactly call David that, but he had been on the cusp of joining the Elite Ice Hockey League, which probably explained why he was quite well paid at that time, and why he was well known in Aviemore. In a small town where most people live out their lives in obscurity – Robyn thought of Duncan still working in the shop he'd stepped foot in decades ago, all because he'd fallen in love – making it in something like sport, or film, or anything that took you out of your comfort zone and everything familiar, would seem like quite an achievement, she imagined.

Robyn stepped to one side so the young woman could type something into the keyboard.

'There you go.' The sports page loomed large as life.

'There's more where that came from. They're in date order. Just click there to view them.'

'Wow – how did you do that?'

'It's magic,' she whispered.

Robyn swivelled her head to look at her over her shoulder.

Her expression gave way to a smile. 'You'll get the hang of it after a while.'

Robyn nodded and returned the very helpful librarian's smile.

She turned her attention back to the computer. When the sports section flashed up, she stopped and scanned the page; nothing. She repeated this exercise for half an hour.

Her initial enthusiasm for her fact-finding mission had waned. She glanced at her watch. Although she didn't have to return to the shop at any particular time, she imagined Duncan would be worried and wondering where she'd got to. It would not surprise her if he sent Alec to fetch her. She had said she was popping to the library. Perhaps he'd think she was choosing a novel. *Perhaps I will*, she thought, although there was no shortage of old paperbacks she could borrow at Lark Lodge.

Robyn contemplated where she would stay that night. Duncan was doing his best to persuade her to return with him to David's place that evening, and spend another night there, although the plan was to take her to Gayle's after work – she had yet to decide whether she was collecting some clothes, and returning with Duncan, or not. That depended on David. She checked her phone, still expecting him to text and ask her to head home to Lark Lodge. She sighed. There was still nothing.

She saw the teenager putting her notepad and pen away in her bag. She'd finished on the computer. All the computer terminals were now free, the desks deserted; Robyn was alone.

She randomly clicked on another webpage, her concentration waning. She scrolled half-heartedly to an article in a local paper wondering if she should ask Duncan again. Or David. This was such a waste of time when she knew the very people who could tell her all about the accident. She wasn't just being nosy. Something told her they were keeping a secret for a reason, and she desperately wanted to know what that was.

She imagined if the librarian knew what she was doing, she

might ask her why it really mattered that she found out David's secret. She knew that she would most likely find out in time. But as someone who obviously had secrets of her own, which even she wouldn't know about until her memory returned, she couldn't bear the thought that David was keeping things from her. Before she got too involved, she had to know everything.

'It's happened to me before,' she said under her breath. She was sure of it. Was it the father of the child that she had lost who had kept secrets from her? Who was he? The question resurfaced that played on her mind from time to time – had she been running away from him on Christmas Day? She shuddered at the thought. That was why she didn't want any nasty surprises with David. She even wanted to know what had made him cash in his investments, and then leave all that cash in his house.

Robyn turned her attention to the computer screen once more. She was about to click on the sports section in another local paper when a headline on the front page immediately caught her eye – *Ice Hockey Star's Fall From Grace.*

Robyn's heart skipped a beat at the mention of David's name straight after the attention-grabbing headline. She took a deep breath and proceeded to read the article.

24

Robyn re-read the first sentence of the online newspaper article, dated two years earlier, before she continued.

He had a bright future ahead of him, but now rising ice hockey star David Gillespie's hopes for glory in the Elite Ice Hockey League have been dashed after an altercation inside a grocery store in Aviemore.

Witnesses have described the moment when the young, talented player, who was on a night out with friends, confronted a suspected burglar in his father's shop. The suspect, who had appeared to be raiding the cash register, was arrested at the scene.

Robyn paused for a moment. David was a hero. She shook her head. She didn't get it. Why hadn't he told her this? Why hadn't his dad? What was the big secret?

She read on.

The suspect's accomplice was taken away by ambulance, and died later in hospital.

Robyn frowned. So there had been *two* burglars. She wondered how the second had died. She kept reading, hoping she'd find out.

The police recovered a gun at the scene which had been in the possession of one of the suspects. Sources say that Mr Gillespie got into an altercation with the suspect who was holding the gun. It discharged twice, injuring the suspect, who later died, and injuring Mr Gillespie, whose injuries are described as not life-threatening.

Robyn sat back in her chair and stared at the screen. Was that why David wouldn't talk about the so-called accident that had ended his career – because he'd been involved in the shooting and wounding of a man who had later died? Even though it wasn't malicious, or his fault. He wouldn't have known the burglars had brought a gun when he'd entered the shop and confronted them.

The article went on to summarise David's life, stating that he'd always dreamed as a boy of becoming an ice hockey star, despite his father's deep misgivings about his early abilities.

Robyn wondered where the reporter who had written the article had got that information, because she knew for a fact that it wasn't true.

She continued reading about his triumphs in ice hockey, and how he'd been talent-spotted to join the EIHL, but that sources close to the family had confirmed that the injury would unfortunately spell the end of his career.

Robyn moved her face nearer the screen to look at the black-and-white group photo of the ice hockey team, all standing together and smiling for the cameras; one of the faces was circled. Robyn looked more closely and recognised David. The players were all wearing their ice hockey uniforms, including shoulder pads, elbow pads, shin guards and gloves, along with their jerseys in the team colours and logo. They'd removed their helmets for the photo.

The next picture was just of David. He looked very young, a teenager posing in his hockey uniform on the ice, but there was something different about him. Robyn realised what it was – he looked so happy. She got a lump in her throat, staring at David's younger self, who had no idea that in a few short years one altercation in his father's shop would change the trajectory of his life forever.

But if it hadn't been for that, Robyn realised that she would most likely never have met David – let alone fallen in love with him. He would have stayed with his previous girlfriend, flying high in his sports career, and their paths would never have crossed.

There were no photos of the two burglars who had changed his life forever. Robyn was thankful for that. She didn't want to look into the faces of the two men who had taken away David's promising future. The news story focused on David. She imagined this was because it was a local newspaper. Perhaps they saw little point in releasing the photos of the two men; they weren't at large. One had already been caught and apprehended. The other was dead.

The article concluded with the words:

It is not yet known whether criminal charges will be brought against Mr Gillespie.

'Oh, my god. That can't be right. How could they charge him when all he was doing was trying to protect his father's business?' Robyn said out loud.

'I'm afraid that's the law,' a voice said behind her, making her jump.

Robyn turned around to find the young librarian standing behind her.

'I heard what you said. I saw you engrossed in an article, so I was very nosy, and stopped to see what you were reading.'

Robyn frowned at her. 'Yes, that's very nosy.'

'That's me!' The librarian pushed her large glasses further up the bridge of her nose and smiled unapologetically. 'Mind you, it kind of comes with the territory with the profession I want to work in.'

'You mean being a librarian?' Robyn guessed perhaps she was a trainee.

'A librarian?' She looked at the books in her hand. 'Oh, I can see how I've confused you. This is a holiday job. No, I meant law.'

'You're a lawyer?'

'Not yet. I'm a law student. I'm in my final year of a law degree at Edinburgh University.'

Robyn decided not to mention that she was a university student too. She hadn't exactly dropped out, just deferred this year, but she knew in her heart that it was where it was leading.

'I hope your final year is going well.'

'Yes, thank you.'

Robyn glanced back at the screen. 'So, what did you mean, I'm afraid it's the law? You can be arrested when it was the burglar's fault for breaking into the store? And when they brought the gun?'

The young woman nodded solemnly. 'This isn't America, with the right to bear arms and all that. If someone breaks into your property, and you hurt them, or worse, then you can be arrested, I'm afraid. Obviously, you can plead self-defence, but that won't stop the police charging you with a crime.'

Robyn shook her head. 'That's awful.'

'I agree. But as I said before, it's the law.'

Robyn glanced at her computer screen. She wanted to find out what had happened after David had been taken to hospital, along with the man who had later died, but she couldn't find any further articles. Perhaps it was time to call it a day with her search and return to the shop.

Robyn got out of her seat. 'I think I've had enough of searching the world wide web for one day.'

The young woman choked back a laugh.

Robyn looked at her thoughtfully. 'What's so funny?'

'You're weird – do you know that?'

'Why do you say that?' Robyn asked defensively. She felt a little insulted. If anything, the young librarian was a bit weird herself, with her old-fashioned dress style – woollen pleated skirt, high-necked jumper in an awful green, and flat shoes with buckles, which looked like children's school shoes. Added to that, her hair was tied up in a bun, when a lot of young people seemed to wear their hair down. But Robyn wouldn't say what she thought out loud.

'Sorry, I've offended you. It's just that no one calls it the world wide web anymore. Well, that's not strictly true. She lowered her voice and looked about her. 'Not to sound ageist, and don't get me wrong, a lot of older people are really tech-savvy – they're sometimes called Silver Surfers – but then again there are some older people who just don't go online at all.'

'So, you think I'm weird because I've never surfed the world … er, I mean … the web.'

'Actually, it's your age, more than anything. I would say unless you've led a very, very cosseted life, with everything done for you, and have no need of online banking or stuff like that …'

Robyn thought of those cheques she'd kept getting from her mother, who was travelling abroad. It was possible that she didn't have a bank account herself – she'd only found a savings book. So maybe she had no need to bank online.

'It's just really unusual for someone of our generation to have never used the internet. It's second nature for most people.'

'Not for me,' remarked Robyn.

Perhaps she had used the internet in the past, but then why would she forget how? The young woman was right – it was weird.

Outside the library, Robyn turned to the young woman, who had been on her way out for her break as Robyn was leaving.

'I'm Robyn, by the way.'

'Melissa.'

'So, where do you go on your lunch break, Melissa?'

'I eat a homemade sandwich at my desk. I can't afford to buy lunch every day, but I do know a lovely place for a cup of coffee.'

'Can I come too?' Robyn hadn't had lunch yet – Duncan had insisted on making sandwiches for both of them for lunch. He'd also made a large thermos flask of tea. Robyn fancied an excuse not to return to the shop quite yet, although she knew that when she returned, Duncan was going to ask what had taken her so long.

She had considered asking Duncan about the burglary and

about what had happened to David; whether he'd been arrested for shooting that man. She'd changed her mind. Now she knew the circumstances – that his so-called accident had actually happened there in his shop, and wasn't an accident at all – she could understand why Duncan didn't want to talk about it.

Robyn fell in step with Melissa as they left the library. 'Where are we going?'

'You'll see – it's one of my favourite places.'

'In that case, I'm sure I'll love it.'

'Oh, you will.'

25

Ten minutes later, they arrived at Melissa's favourite spot for a cup of coffee.

Robyn halted.

Melissa noticed. 'Ah – you're wondering why I've brought you to a bookshop.'

The sign read *Open*. The last time Robyn had been there, the bookshop had been closed. Gayle had taken her to Wilbur's Bookstore, hoping it would jog her memory because she'd told Gayle that she had a sketch of the bookshop in the diary she'd found in her suitcase. The shop hadn't brought back a single recollection about being there, and she still had no idea why she'd drawn the bookshop. There might have been no significance to the sketch at all; maybe she had just liked the appearance of the old shop.

In her sketch, there were two women sitting at the table in the window. Gayle had asked her if she thought perhaps it showed her and a friend, although nobody had visited her in hospital after her car accident on Christmas Day apart from David and Gayle.

Gayle had then suggested that perhaps it was just two

strangers she'd seen sitting in the window.

Standing outside the bookshop, Robyn was still none the wiser as to why she'd sketched the bookshop and who the two people sitting in the window had been. Perhaps she'd find out now the shop was open.

'Are you all right?' Melissa had opened the bookshop door and had noticed that Robyn was hanging back, hesitant to step inside. 'Would you rather go somewhere else?'

'No, it's fine.' Robyn took a deep breath and followed Melissa inside the bookshop.

'Why don't you take a seat at the table, and I'll go grab a couple of coffees?'

Robyn stepped up to the little table in the window and stared at it. She had a strong sensation that she'd been in the shop before and had sat at this table with someone. She lowered herself into a chair and sat staring at the empty seat opposite, thinking *who was I with, and why didn't they come and visit me in hospital?* Her car accident had been in the local paper.

'Wilbur not here today?'

Robyn turned in her seat at the sound of Melissa's voice. She saw a young, good-looking man, around her age, stacking some books on to a bookshelf. Robyn couldn't help but smile. Now she had an idea as to why it was Melissa's favourite place for coffee.

Melissa came over with two cups of coffee. 'I love the little old bookshop. It's been here ever since I can remember.'

Robyn nodded knowingly, casting her gaze over at the young man. 'Who's the guy?'

'That's Wilbur's grandson. He's at uni too. We're not at the same university, though.'

Robyn caught her frown. She guessed that Melissa wished they were.

'So, you only see him during the holidays?'

'Yeah, when he's working in here. He wasn't around at Christmas – he was away with his family, including his grandparents. Someone else was minding the bookshop, apparently. They were meant to be here until New Year, but they disappeared on Christmas Day, and never came back.'

'That's not good. Who were they?'

Melissa shrugged. 'I don't know. I didn't visit the shop over Christmas.'

'But I thought this was one of your favourite places?'

'Um, yes … well, it is.'

'When Wilbur's grandson is around.'

Melissa looked at her, wide-eyed, and cast a furtive glance over her shoulder.

Robyn lowered her voice. 'Your secret is safe with me.'

'I don't know what you're talking about.'

'I think you do.' Robyn picked up her coffee. 'When are you going to tell him?'

'Tell who?'

'Wilbur's grandson …'

Melissa shook her head. 'I still don't know what you're—'

'That you're in love with him.'

Melissa stared at her. She didn't deny it.

'How long has it been?' Robyn asked.

Melissa furtively glanced over her shoulder once more, then put her coffee to one side, and leaned forward in her seat. She whispered, 'Like, forever.'

'Have you asked him out?'

She shook her head furiously. 'No, of course not.'

'Why? Does he have a girlfriend?'

'Well, no. But look at me. Why would he go out with such a dork?'

'A … dork?' Robyn didn't understand. She looked at Melissaa for a moment, at her green jumper and her dark hair tied up in a bun.

Melissa moved her large glasses up the bridge of her nose. 'He's just so cool. And I'm … well, I'm not.'

'Who says?'

'I do,' Melissa said glumly, reaching for her coffee.

'Oh, right.' Robyn drank some coffee, and put her cup down. She studied Melissa intently.

'What are you thinking?' Melissa asked.

Robyn was thinking that Melissa was a very pretty girl, and that she shouldn't put herself down just because she was bookish. What was wrong with that? But perhaps changing her clothes and her hairstyle would make her feel more confident to approach the young man in the bookshop. 'What is his name?'

'Brodie.'

'Okay. I've got an idea. How about a makeover?'

'Like those TV shows?'

Robyn wasn't sure what she was referring to. 'Uh, yeah – I guess.' She looked at Melissa's hair. 'When was the last time you had a haircut?'

'It's hard, being a student …' Melissa trailed off.

Not in the recent past, then, thought Robyn. 'My best friend is a hairdresser …'

'I can't afford to go to a salon.'

'You won't have to. She doesn't work at a salon. She's a

mobile hairdresser. She could come to you.' Robyn had an idea. 'Or, better still, come over to her house.' Robyn had a lot of clothes she didn't wear, and Melissa was her height and build. And there was a whole trunk full of clothes in the attic. There might be some clothes she could choose that would make a nice outfit.

Melissa shook her head. 'I don't think the fact that she's a mobile hairdresser will make a difference. It's still going to be costly.'

Robyn had no idea. She said, 'It will be my treat.'

'Really? But you barely know me. Why would you pay for me?'

'Call it paying it forward.'

'Huh? Oh, you mean like someone helped you out, so you're going to help someone else out in return.'

'Exactly.'

'Then I'd like to pay it forward too. What can I do for you?'

'I don't think that's the idea.'

'Well, it is for me.'

'All right,' Robyn said slowly, wondering what she could ask of Melissa. Her attention was drawn to the railway station opposite. She mumbled, 'I've always wanted to go on the steam train that leaves Platform 3.' That's what she'd told Gayle when they'd visited previously and the bookshop had been closed. As Gayle had pointed out, she'd actually had a memory – of sorts. How had she known there was a steam train that left from Platform 3?

'That's expensive, even without the afternoon tea,' Melissa said apologetically. 'I don't think I could afford the ticket for you.'

'Oh, I wasn't expecting you to pay for a ticket for me to do that.' Robyn shifted her gaze to Melissa. 'I've got another idea.' When she looked back at Melissa, she had taken her glasses off to reveal striking green eyes set in a delicate porcelain face.

Melissa caught her surprised expression. 'Yes, these glasses really are dreadful, aren't they?' she said, using a cloth in her handbag to clean the lenses. 'I'm as blind as a bat without them.'

Robyn looked at the glasses in her hands.

'I know what you're thinking. Why on earth don't I get some contact lenses?'

Robyn sipped her coffee, staring at Melissa and guessing that it was because money was tight. She wouldn't find contact lenses among her clothes, or the one in the trunk in the attic.

Melissa said, 'Were you saying you had a better idea?'

'Pardon?'

'You know, because I can't help you out with a ticket for the steam train.'

'Oh yes – right.' Robyn put her coffee cup down and moved it to her left. Putting both forearms on the table and leaning forward, Robyn asked Melissa if she would like to do some research for her.

'You want me to do some research? What sort of research?'

For a split second, she imagined telling Melissa about her memory loss, and asking her to find out all she could about her life. But the wads of cash in her possession that may or may not have been stolen from David immediately came to mind and stopped her in her tracks.

'What is it?' Melissa asked.

The realisation that she should be cautious about how much she revealed didn't stop her asking Melissa to find out what had happened to David after his arrest. She checked her watch. She didn't have time to return to the library and start searching the web again.

Robyn looked at her. 'I'm sort of involved with some guy. We haven't long known each other, and I like him, I really do.' *That's an understatement*, she thought. 'He's keeping secrets from me, I know it.' She winced, knowing she was doing the same.

'That's who you were looking for in the news articles?'

'Yes. His name is David Gillespie.' She paused, expecting Melissa to say she recognised the former ice hockey player's name. But there was no sign that she was familiar with it.

'He was an ice hockey player. Quite well known around here.'

Melissa apologised. 'Sorry – never been into the game.'

Robyn went on to explain the circumstances surrounding his injury that ended his sports career – what she knew so far from the article. 'The thing I want to find out is what happened after the confrontation in his father's store, when he was taken to hospital.'

Melissa knitted her brows. 'I don't get it. Why don't you just ask him, or his dad?'

'Well, that's the thing. They won't talk about it.' Something occurred to Robyn. She voiced her thoughts. 'Now, if I bring up the fact that I know about the burglary, they'll think I've been trying to find out things behind his back.'

'Which you have.'

Robyn sighed. 'Why won't they just tell me?'

'So, you want me to find out instead.'

Robyn nodded.

'It seems to me that he's got something to hide, otherwise he would have just told you. I think they're all in on it. That's why his dad won't talk about it either.'

Robyn hadn't thought of that. 'You think there's some sort of conspiracy?' Even as she was saying this, she thought that it sounded ridiculous. *Maybe it's just the fact that it was a painful episode that they'd rather forget*, she thought.

'Could be,' said Melissa, nodding her head. 'So, what did that article say?'

Robyn went over the details.

'So that's what they told the police had happened in that shop. That doesn't mean it's true.'

'Why would David lie?'

'Good question.'

Robyn rubbed her forehead. This conversation was going to unexpected places. 'I just wanted to know what had happened after the burglary, whether he'd been arrested.'

'Oh, I'll get to the bottom of it. When I've finished, you'll know everything there is to know about David Gillespie. I'm really good at research.'

Robyn was relieved she hadn't mentioned her own predicament. She would not want Melissa digging into her own past. Who knew where that would lead, or where she might end up – like being arrested as an accomplice for stealing a lot of money. Unfortunately, she couldn't get the memory out of her mind of sitting in a car outside David's house, waiting for someone. No matter what she told herself, or how she tried to explain it away, she knew she'd been there before.

'Are you all right?' Melissa asked, reaching across the table to rest a comforting hand on her arm.

Robyn suddenly had a flashback. She had been sitting right there, in the same seat, and a young lady – not Melissa, but another young woman – had asked her that same question.

Robyn snatched her arm away, looking at Melissa wide-eyed.

'What is it? What's wrong?'

'I need to go.' What she meant was, *I need to get out of here*. She had a strong sensation that when she'd been there before, that had been what she was thinking. But it had not been to do with leaving Wilbur's bookshop. It had been about getting out of Aviemore.

Melissa stood up. 'All right,' she said slowly, peering at Robyn. 'I've got to get back to the library.'

Robyn was relieved that Melissa didn't question her further over her sudden strange behaviour.

They stepped outside the shop. Melissa closed the shop door and lingered for a moment, staring in through the shop window.

Robyn stared through the window too, although she wasn't looking at the cute guy. She was looking at the table where they'd just been sitting. She had been there on Christmas Day – she was sure of it. But how could that be? The bookshop would have been closed. She turned to look at Melissa, thinking, *I must have arranged to meet someone here – but who?*

Melissa turned from the window and caught her staring. 'Don't worry. I'll get to the bottom of what happened.'

For a split second, Robyn wondered what she was talking about. 'Oh, you mean David?'

Melissa looked at her a moment. 'Well, of course. What else would I be talking about?'

Robyn shrugged, avoiding eye contact.

'And if there's been a miscarriage of justice, I *will* find out.'

'What do you mean – *a miscarriage of justice*?' All Robyn wanted Melissa to do was look for some more newspaper articles online, reporting what had happened – had David been arrested?

That might explain why he didn't want to talk about it. Perhaps he thought she'd look at him differently if she found out he'd shot a man. What if he'd had to spend some time in prison? She told Melissa her thoughts as they walked along the street together. Duncan's shop and the library were in the same direction.

'Yes, I get that, but here's another scenario …'

Robyn pursed her lips, wondering if she was going to regret getting Melissa involved.

'Whatever happened in that shop when David and his friends came across those burglars, the story they told the police—'

'Story?'

'Whatever went down in there that left one of the burglars dead, well, someone had to potentially take the fall for that, once it was reported to the police. What if …'

Robyn had an idea what she was going to say. 'David was protecting someone?'

'Yes, from going to prison if they were charged.'

Robyn stared at her. 'Why would he do that?'

'I'm not saying he did. I'm just looking at it from all angles. Until I know the facts …'

Robyn hoped David wasn't protecting someone, because if Melissa found out …

'Can you imagine if I solved a miscarriage of justice as a student?'

'You mean if he didn't shoot that burglar, and someone else did?'

'Yes.'

Robyn didn't like where this was going. That meant David would have lied – didn't they call that perjury? He'd get into trouble.

'But it still would have been self-defence.'

'I know. But if David was charged with something he didn't do, wouldn't you want to clear his name? I mean, I would if it was Brodie. If that did happen – and I'm not saying it did – but just for a moment suppose something like that had happened, what sort of friend would have let David take the rap for it?'

Robyn eyed her. She had a point.

They'd reached the library. Up ahead was the grocery store. They stopped in front of the library. 'How can I get in touch with you?' Melissa asked.

Robyn wasn't sure she wanted her to. A saying came to mind – *let sleeping dogs lie*. She really hoped she wasn't going to stir things up. She reluctantly gave Melissa her mobile phone number. Then she had a thought. 'Look, I'm setting up an interior design outlet in Mr Gillespie's general store—'

Melissa raised her eyebrows. 'Where the burglary took place?'

'Yes. I'd rather you didn't visit me in the shop and talk about … you know, the research.'

'Oh, of course not. I'll text if I find out anything.'

Robyn breathed a sigh of relief.

Melissa turned to go. 'Oh, wait. What about that makeover?'

Robyn had forgotten all about that. Her idea had been that Melissa came over to Gayle's house, where she could have her hair done, and together they could find an outfit or two that might make her feel more confident. She frowned at the thought that David would be there. Gayle could go to Melissa's house but then there would be no opportunity to have a rummage through some clothes and choose an outfit too.

Robyn sighed. 'Have you got a car?'

'Yes. It's old but it gets me back and forward to uni.'

'Okay. I'll speak to my friend and arrange for you to come over.'

'Will you be there?'

Robyn knew she couldn't stay with Duncan indefinitely, although he would love her to stay. But David would be back at some point. And besides, she missed Gayle, and her mum, and Nick, not to mention sweet Olive.

'When? I'll be going back to university soon.'

If she was going to stay on with Duncan at his son's house for a few more days, she'd need to pick up some clothes. Robyn had an idea. 'Are you free this evening?'

Melissa nodded enthusiastically. 'Oh, yes.'

'What time do you finish work?'

Melissa told her.

'If I come by the library after I finish in the shop today, we could go back to Gayle's together.' And on the way, Robyn would have to tell her that David was there, and not to get into a conversation with him about the burglary.

'Great. I'll see you after work!'

Robyn hoped Gayle wouldn't mind cutting Melissa's hair. She thought she'd better call Gayle. Robyn checked her phone. She still hadn't got a text – nothing from David asking her what she was doing that evening or whether she was going back to Lark Lodge, or telling her he missed her. Robyn frowned as she texted Gayle. She was not looking forward to seeing David when she got back.

26

Robyn stretched under the duvet and opened her eyes. For a moment she was confused, expecting to wake up in David's house – but she was back in her familiar room at Lark Lodge. She stretched again, then snuggled under the duvet, happy to be home.

She lay there smiling. She'd had a wonderful evening. It had been such fun to watch Melissa's transformation. She'd met Melissa at the library after work, as arranged, and had introduced her to Gayle as soon as they'd arrived at Lark Lodge. Then she'd whisked her new friend upstairs to her room to have a look for an outfit before she had her haircut. Robyn would have been happy if Melissa had found something among her own things that she liked, but in the end it had been the old trunk in the attic containing clothes from another era that had captivated her.

She'd settled on a tailored grey wool two-piece suit that came with a jacket nipped in at the waist, shoulder pads, and large buttons. She'd had a choice of either generous, wide-fitted trousers or an A-line skirt to complete the look, along with a plain white blouse. It was simple, yet chic, and suited Melissa perfectly. She'd found shoes in the trunk that didn't fit, but had said she had some suitable shoes at home that would work with the outfit. And the accessories she'd found in the trunk – a silk scarf, a handbag, and even a hat that looked a bit like a French beret – worked so well on her.

The outfit was exactly what she had been looking for – something she could wear to work, but more importantly that she wouldn't feel embarrassed wearing when she visited the bookshop at lunchtime and saw Brodie.

Robyn had told Melissa that Brodie would love her outfit. *He's not going to be able to resist you*, she'd thought. And that was before Gayle had completed her transformation with a new hairstyle.

Afterwards, Robyn had planned to show her how to apply some makeup. Not too much; she needed hardly any with her complexion – but a little bit of blush, some mascara and lipstick wouldn't go amiss.

After finding her outfit, and trying to get Gayle to accept some money for it, which she would not, Gayle had cut her hair. She hadn't cut too much off the length – it fell just below her shoulders – but had just taken off the split ends. She'd added some long, graduated layers, accentuating her high cheekbones, and had then used heated tongs to create textured waves which softened and added body to her hair.

She'd insisted on giving Melissa a spare pair of tongs she didn't need, or so she said, which meant Melissa could create the look at home too.

Robyn had been impressed with the hairstyle and had thought that it was probably time for her to have a makeover herself. She'd said as much to Gayle, who had reminded her that not long after she'd left hospital and moved in with Gayle and her mum at Lark Lodge, she'd mentioned the idea of dyeing her hair blonde. It had been during a conversation when she'd accompanied Gayle on her mobile hairdressing round and had met Rose for the first time. Gayle had offered to cut her hair, to give her a new hairstyle. Robyn winced when she remembered what she'd blurted in response. *Can you make me blonde too?*

The question had come out of nowhere, along with a thought she wished had never entered her head and which she'd chosen not to share with Gayle; she'd had the sudden urge to change her appearance to protect herself. Even more disturbingly, the question remained – from whom?

She lay there in bed, frowning when she remembered the rest of the conversation the previous evening. She wished Gayle hadn't remembered what she'd blurted. Melissa, whose hair colour was mousy brown, had said, *That would be extreme. I love your dark, glossy hair. Don't dye it.* Robyn had assured her, and Gayle, that she wouldn't be changing her hair colour any time soon. Whoever she was running away from, if indeed that's what she was doing, hadn't caught up with her yet. As time marched on, with no sign of anyone from her past, she was beginning to feel that they never would.

There were just two things that were tempering her happy mood that morning. One was the phone call she'd made the previous evening, letting Duncan know that she was staying on at Lark Lodge, so she wouldn't be returning to spend the night at David's house. She knew he'd miss her company, as she would his, but he'd said it hadn't come as a big surprise. She had told him at lunchtime that she would be returning to Lark Lodge after work with a friend to collect some things. She hadn't been intending to stay, but as soon as she'd returned to Lark Lodge, that had been it – she hadn't wanted to leave.

The second thing that was really dampening her mood was David. After the haircut, Gayle had insisted that Melissa join them all for dinner. She had met Nick, and of course Olive, who had taken her by surprise, and with whom she'd instantly fallen in love, joking that Brodie had some competition. But dinner had been an awkward affair – and it had all been David's fault.

Despite the presence of Gayle, Nick, Melissa and Olive (who had been naughty and had constantly tried to get attention when she was meant to stay in her dog bed by the Aga while people were eating), nobody had failed to notice the atmosphere at the far end of the table, from where David had refused to join in the conversation.

Robyn had forewarned Melissa that David might be at dinner, and that they'd had a little falling-out, so things might be a little strained. But she hadn't expected him to be so rude, barely acknowledging her friend and sitting away from the group as though he was on the only one in the room.

She wished Gayle hadn't invited him to stay and that he'd just go home. Duncan would be coming round later in the morning to pick her up for work, and he was planning to use it as an excuse to see David and try to persuade him to come home – he'd been honest enough to tell her that.

Robyn planned to give David a piece of her mind before Duncan arrived. And if he wouldn't leave, then she'd pack a bag and return to David's house with his father that night after work. She couldn't face another awkward dinner with him at Lark Lodge.

It wasn't just dinner time that was the problem; she'd know he was there in the house, limping around on his crutches, and she didn't fancy the thought of bumping into him whenever she went downstairs.

Robyn checked the time on her phone. Duncan would be picking her up at eight-thirty. She was glad she would be working in the shop that day; it was Tuesday, and preparations were still underway to get her outlet ready for opening, so she didn't have to figure out how to get to Rose's house just yet. She'd just have to cross that bridge when Rose's materials arrived.

Robyn gathered her clothes and shower bag. She opened her bedroom door a crack, checking the hallway for any sign of David. She didn't feel like a confrontation while in her pyjamas. She could hear Gayle's voice in the kitchen downstairs; she was remonstrating with Olive for stealing a sausage off her plate when she wasn't looking.

Her frown at the thought of confronting David turned into a smile. Olive was up to her little tricks again – appearing all sweet and innocent, getting lots of fusses, but with an eye out for her chance to steal some food.

'Is that you, Robyn?' Gayle called out.

Robyn winced. She'd only just stepped outside the bedroom door. 'Yes!' she called over the stair banister, still keeping an eye out for David.

'Are you joining us for breakfast?'

Us? Robyn sighed. 'I'll be down soon. I'm just using the bathroom.'

She couldn't very well shout downstairs, *I'll join you for breakfast only if David isn't there too.*

27

David wasn't there for breakfast. Gayle told her he was still asleep in the lounge, where he was using the sofa as a makeshift bed because he was finding the trek to the bedroom upstairs bothersome. It turned out that Gayle and David had had a falling-out too, of sorts, because she wasn't happy with his sleeping arrangements. This was partly because it meant she had to clear off out of her own lounge when David became tired, but it was mostly because avoiding stairs wasn't going to do his rehabilitation any good – she'd told him this in no uncertain terms.

Robyn had found this out over breakfast, and pointed out that if David went home he'd have no choice but to do stairs – unless he wanted to sleep in his kitchen on the ground floor. His lounge was on the first floor, and the bedrooms were on the second, up a spiral staircase, which meant plenty of stairs.

Gayle put her cup of tea down on the kitchen table. 'You want him to go home – don't you?'

Robyn sighed, picked up her empty breakfast plate, and navigated her way around Olive, who sniffed the air and followed her and her empty plate over to the sink. Robyn put it in the washing-up water and turned around to face Gayle. 'I know he was cheesed off that I went home with his dad, but Duncan is not the terrible person that David makes out.' She sighed. 'David didn't even speak to me when you both turned up at his house to collect some things. He didn't text to see how I am when you both left without me.'

'But you're back now.'

'Yeah, and he's still not exactly making any effort to speak to me.'

'Perhaps *you* should speak to *him*.'

Robyn narrowed her eyes. 'Oh, so you're on *his* side.'

'Really, Robyn. It's not about taking sides. You're being childish.'

'*I'm* being childish?' Robyn couldn't believe what she was hearing. 'It's David that's being childish!'

Olive whined and retreated to her dog bed.

'Yep, I'm going to talk to him all right.' Robyn stormed over to the kitchen door and nearly ploughed into Nick, who was back from his early morning run.

'Whoa! Where's the fire?' Nick exclaimed.

Robyn frowned at him. He was in her way. 'Sorry, but I need to get past right now.'

Nick held his hands up and stepped aside.

Robyn heard Nick say to Gayle, 'What's got into her?'

Robyn flew into the lounge and walked straight up to David. Hands on hips, she stared at him. 'Unbelievable!' He was fast asleep. She looked at him, all cosy under a duvet. It was cold in the lounge, and she rubbed her bare arms. It had been so warm and toasty in the kitchen that she'd taken off her cardigan and left it on a chair.

Feeling cold and angry, she reached down and grabbed a corner of his duvet that was dangling over the side of the settee and casually walked down the length of the settee with the corner of the duvet still tucked between her thumb and forefinger, peeling it away from David. As she went, she watched the duvet disappear from where it was lodged just under David's chin, travel down his chest and finally expose his legs and bare feet.

She was relieved to see him wearing cotton pyjamas for it only just occurred to her that he might sleep in the nude; although whilst it would have been embarrassing for them both, it occurred to her that she wouldn't have minded at all. She brushed that thought aside as she dropped the duvet in a heap on the floor at the end of the settee. Her teeth began to chatter. She looked at the duvet, shrugged and picked it up, throwing it around her shoulders. She trudged to the armchair opposite David, sat down on the duvet and wrapped it around her, holding it tightly under her chin. She waited for the chill morning air to wake him up.

Her eyes moved to his crutches, which were lying on the floor beneath him. As quick as she could, she dashed out of the cosy warm confines of the duvet and moved them out of his reach. She sat back down, huddled into the duvet and waited. She didn't have to wait long. He stirred within a few minutes. His eyes were still closed at first, but his right hand moved down to his knee and a distinct look of discomfort crept across his face as he opened his eyes. The damp cold must have seeped into his knee joint, and a pang of guilt ran through her.

She fought the urge to run over and cover him with the duvet. It was too late, anyhow – his eyes were wide open, and he was looking down at his body, obviously wondering what on earth had happened to his duvet. Despite her bad temper, Robyn found it quite comical. She watched him lift his head from the pillow to look at the floor turning his body in her direction and throwing an arm over the side, assuming the duvet had fallen to the floor. Robyn watched his hand stop patting the floor as his eyes fell on her. She tucked the duvet tighter under her chin for effect.

He didn't say anything as he sat up, which surprised her. It was as though it was the most natural thing in the world to wake up and find someone had stolen your bed covers.

Robyn was about to tell him that his father would be round soon, and it was time he went home, when Gayle walked into the room carrying a mug, taking her by surprise. Gayle threw Robyn a sideways glance as she said to David, 'I thought you'd be awake, so I brought you in your morning cuppa.'

Morning cuppa? Robyn stared at David, who was nodding and smiling sweetly at Gayle as he took the mug. *I thought they'd had a falling-out*, Robyn thought.

'Now, how about we try those stairs today?' Gayle suggested. 'Then you can use one of the spare bedrooms.'

David nodded at Gayle. 'All right. I'll try.' Robyn thought he'd timed his pained expression very well.

Gayle immediately said, 'Is your knee playing up? Shall I fetch you a cushion so you can put your leg up?'

'That's very kind of you, Gayle.'

Robyn narrowed her eyes. It seemed unlikely that David would go home. She could tell he was enjoying Gayle's tea and sympathy. She imagined he'd get none of that from Duncan – not overtly, anyway. That didn't mean Duncan didn't care for his son deeply. But for David, after years of having no mother to fuss over him, she guessed this was quite a novelty.

She sat staring at him, thinking, *don't expect any tea and sympathy from me!*

'You're going to catch your death, sitting there like that,' said Doris. She had appeared in the doorway behind Gayle. 'What happened to your duvet?'

Gayle passed David a cushion and looked at her mother. 'That's a good question.'

All eyes were suddenly on Robyn, who was sitting there with the cosy duvet wrapped around her.

Robyn saw Gayle's expression. She imagined what she was thinking – *you're still being childish.*

Well, maybe I am, thought Robyn. But just then, she didn't care.

When Gayle realised that Robyn wasn't going to relinquish the duvet, she turned to David. 'Shall I pass you a throw?'

David made a show of trying to reach for the throw on the arm of the sofa.

Robyn rolled her eyes.

Gayle tucked the throw around his legs before crossing the room to her mother. She took her mother's hand. 'I didn't know you were awake. Come on, let's make you some breakfast.' She paused in the doorway. 'David, do you want me to hand you in some toast – or some cooked breakfast?'

'Just some toast, please, Gayle.'

'Why isn't he joining us for breakfast?' Gayle's mother asked as they walked out of the room.

Robyn heard Gayle's reply. 'David and Robyn have some things to discuss.'

'What things? Have they had a lovers' tiff?'

Robyn grimaced. *Not again*, she thought. Duncan had said the exact same thing to her on the way back to David's house from the hospital.

A moment later, Gayle was back with a plate of toast. 'I did the toast just as you like it, lightly toasted with plenty of butter and strawberry jam.'

'Thank you, Gayle. That's so kind of you.'

'Not at all.'

Robyn got the impression that Gayle was enjoying running around after her new house guest. As Gayle left the room, Robyn looked at the toast, done just the way David liked it, It reinforced her view that trying to persuade David to go home would be futile. She stood up.

'Where are you going?'

'To pack.'

'Pack? What do you mean? Are you leaving? But you've only just got back. Where are you going?'

Robyn was a bit taken aback by all the sudden questions. 'Why do *you* care?'

'Why do I care?'

Robyn looked at her watch. She didn't have time for an argument. She didn't have long before Duncan arrived to collect her for work. At least someone would be pleased to see her. He was going to be even more pleased when he found out she was going home with him afterwards.

David put his plate of toast to one side and tried to get up. 'Damn – where are my crutches?'

Robyn walked out of the room.

'Wait!'

Robyn paused outside the door. She was feeling guilty for moving them. Still, it meant that David couldn't follow her – or at least, if he tried, she'd be packed and ready to leave before he caught up with her.

Robyn bounded up the stairs. She was just packing when she heard Gayle call out, 'Oh, good, you're taking my advice and walking up some stairs. Good for you.'

Robyn glanced over at her door as she got her old suitcase out from under the bed. She could hear the creak of the stairs. David was on his way up.

She filled the case with the contents of her wardrobe, and was just clicking the case shut when she remembered the rucksack full of money. She fetched it from the back of the wardrobe. She put it on the bed, opened it and stared at the wads of cash. The bag was heavy, but she'd have to take it with her. She thought about what Duncan had told her; David had been burgled, and a load of cash had been stolen. Why had he withdrawn all that money and kept it in cash at his house?

A knock on the door startled her. David couldn't have made it up the stairs that quickly. Robyn walked over and opened the door. She was wrong. She went to slam the door shut, but David's walking stick was wedged in the crack between the door and the doorframe. Robyn realised her mistake; she'd assumed David would be walking up the stairs on crutches – she'd forgotten he'd switched to a stick, which would make his progress a lot quicker. She said, 'What do you want?'

'To talk.'

'There's nothing to talk about.' *You're staying, and I'm leaving,* thought Robyn.

She held on to the door, waiting for him to remove his stick.

'Look, Robyn, I don't know why you got into the car with my dad and decided to stay the night.'

'I did not decide. You wouldn't talk to me.' She waited, but David did not respond. 'Can you remove your stick, please?'

David did as he was asked.

Robyn slammed the door shut.

28

She'd just hoisted her case off the bed when there was another knock on the door.

'Please let me in.'

Robyn rolled her eyes. She couldn't believe he was still standing outside her door. *I really don't have time for this*, she thought. 'No!'

'I've got something for you.'

Robyn looked at the door. 'What is it?'

'Let me in, and I'll show you.'

She walked over and deposited her case by the door. She was leaving, so whatever he had to give her, this would be his only chance. She supposed she ought to open the door.

As soon as she did, he let go of the walking stick. It fell to the floor. He cupped her face gently in his hands and kissed her.

Robyn pulled away. 'What do you think you're doing?'

'I'm apologising. I am *so* sorry for being such an idiot. Wherever you're going, please don't.' His eyes flickered to the suitcase by the door. 'Please, please stay. If it's because I'm here, I'll leave.'

Robyn stared at him.

David eyed her anxiously. 'Please say something.'

Robyn touched her lips with her fingers. 'I don't think one apology is going to work.'

'Huh?'

Robyn stepped closer, took his hands in hers, and placed them on her face.

It took David a moment to realise what was going on. 'Oh … right. Of course.' He kissed her again.

This time, Robyn kissed him back.

She took a step back. He limped forward, walking through the doorway. They were still kissing.

Robyn reached out and pushed the door shut behind him.

She took his hand, leading him over to the bed.

He said, 'Here, let me move this.'

Robyn caught him reaching for the bag. 'No, no don't do that, it's …'

He went to pick it up, not realising how heavy it was, and instantly dropped it.

The bag fell to the floor.

Oh god! Robyn froze. She'd forgotten to buckle up the bag. She stared at the contents strewn over the floor.

David stared at the wads of cash too. He turned to Robyn. 'What's all this?'

A lie popped straight out of her mouth. 'I cashed in all my savings to pay for setting up the shop.'

The money was for setting up the shop – that part wasn't a lie. She quickly got on her hands and knees, scooping the cash back into the bag.

'What do you think you're doing? For god's sake, Robyn, take the money back.'

Robyn's face flushed bright red. She looked up at him. 'What?'

'Deposit the money back in your bank. You shouldn't have this sort of cash lying around. Trust me.'

Robyn let out the biggest sigh of relief. For a moment she had thought he was talking about taking the money back to his house – that he thought it was the cash that had been stolen.

But I still don't know if this is his money, she thought. She didn't want to think about the coincidences that added up to the possibility that it might be. Right then, she was just relieved he didn't think the cash was his, and was just giving her advice.

'All right.'

'Promise me?'

'Yes – I will.' She knew she could put it in her savings account, but she'd have to make a trip to another town to find a branch of the bank to do that, and she still didn't have any other ID in case she then wanted to make a withdrawal.

Despite what she'd just said, she knew the cash would be staying right there, in the rucksack. She picked up the bag and stashed it back in the wardrobe. Out of sight, but most definitely not out of mind.

'Oh, my god.'

Robyn whirled around. 'What is it?' Had David just put two and two together? Had the thought crossed his mind that the money might be his?

'This room is amazing. It looks so different to the rest of the house.'

Robyn had to sit down. She sat at the end of the bed.

David limped over and sat next to her, shoulder to shoulder, casting a gaze around the room. 'I can see why Gayle put you in this room. She did give me a little tour of the house, but we didn't look in here. She said it was your room. Besides, she said she couldn't show me the room anyway because you keep your door locked.'

Robyn managed a smile. 'There's a reason for that. This is Gayle's surprise.'

'What is?'

'The room.'

'You did this? You redecorated?'

'Yes. I want to redecorate the whole place, in readiness for Lark Lodge becoming a guesthouse.'

'Does she know about your plans?'

'Not about the redecorating. You know what she's like. She'll want to pay me, and I know she can't afford it. So I'll have to twist her arm to let me do it for free – although I am getting free board and lodging, so I think it's only fair I do something for her in return.'

David reached out and tucked a wisp of hair that had fallen in front of her face, behind her ear.

He was just moving in for another kiss when Robyn's phone buzzed with a text.

David whispered in her ear, 'Just ignore it.'

She was about to do just that when she remembered. 'That's my ride to work!' She scrambled along the bed and reached for her mobile phone on the side cabinet. She checked the time and the text. Duncan was outside. 'I've got to go.'

'What – right now?'

'Yes, right now.'

David looked at her phone. She knew he was going to ask her who was giving her a lift. She really didn't want to get into that right now. She did not have time. She knew his attitude towards her working in his father's shop.

'Robyn.' He held out his hand. 'Can you help me up?'

Robyn helped him to stand up. He limped over to the window while she was answering Duncan's text to say she'd be right out.

'Is that my father's car?' David turned from the window to look at her.

'You need your walking stick. Where is it?'

Robyn looked about her, and remembered he'd dropped it outside the bedroom door when they were busy kissing.

'Is he taking you into work?'

She stopped with her hand on the door handle. 'Yes, we arranged for him to pick me up this morning. I am working in the shop today, so it made sense.'

Robyn moved the suitcase out of her way.

David looked at it. 'Is that where you were intending to go – back to my house?'

'Yes – what of it?'

'Why would you want to stay with *him*?'

Robyn sighed. She really did not have time to get into all that. But she did say, 'Look, you need to talk to your dad.' She wanted to tell him that Duncan had been keeping secrets from his son, but knew it was not her place. She hesitated. 'Things are not … what they seem.'

'What's he been saying? You know he'll twist things to suit him.'

Robyn pursed her lips. 'Will you be here when I get back?' Robyn asked, afraid he was going to leave now he'd found out where she was intending to go once she'd packed this morning.

'Yes. I'm not going anywhere.'

Robyn was so relieved to hear it. She quickly walked over and gave him a kiss. 'I'll see you later – after work.'

'All right.'

Robyn glanced out of the window before walking to the door. 'I'll just grab your walking stick.'

Robyn opened the door to find Gayle outside, bending over. Robyn quickly stepped outside and closed her bedroom door while Gayle picked up the walking stick.

'I was just walking by when I noticed this.' She held it up in surprise.

'I can explain …' Robyn began.

Gayle grinned as she looked at the bedroom door. 'You are allowed visitors, you know.'

Robyn pursed her lips. 'I was just showing David my room.' Robyn had whipped the door closed because she didn't want Gayle to see the room too – not just yet. It was meant to be a surprise. She hadn't really wanted Gayle to see David in her room either, but the stick had given him away.

Gayle folded her arms. 'Ah, I like the euphemism.'

'The – what?'

'Showing David your room, indeed.' Gayle nudged her, and winked, offering up naughty grin.

Robyn couldn't help but grin too, even though things hadn't quite got that far. She wished she hadn't arranged for Duncan to pick her up. If she hadn't, Robyn would have taken the day off work to spend with David.

There will be plenty of time for that, she reminded herself, smiling.

Gayle said, 'I take it that David is moving upstairs.'

Robyn blushed. She looked at the door and whispered, 'Yes,

I think so.'

There was no mention of David moving into his own bedroom.

Gayle clapped her hands. 'Wonderful – just wonderful.'

'There's a stranger outside!' Gayle's mother shouted up the stairs.

'Oh, that will be my lift into work.' Robyn looked at the walking stick in her hand.

'Shall I give that to David, if you're in a hurry?'

'No, it's fine.'

'Ah, you two lovebirds will want to say goodbye. I get it.' Gayle nudged her, and grinned again. She handed Robyn the walking stick and made her way along the hall.

When Robyn was sure Gayle was out of sight, she opened the bedroom door.

David said, 'I heard that.'

'About moving upstairs?'

He nodded.

'Are you okay with that?' Robyn asked, handing him the stick, wondering if she'd been presumptuous.

'Of course I am – are you?'

'I've never been so sure of anything in my life.' She might not remember her past, but standing in front of her was her future – and nothing, and nobody, was going to get in the way of her future happiness.

For some reason, Melissa came to mind. She knew why; Robyn was still having second thoughts about giving Melissa the go-ahead to look into David's past. She didn't want to think that she'd opened a Pandora's box.

29

'Is he still out there working?' Gayle's voice carried from the lounge.

Robyn was washing up the dinner plates. She glanced out of the kitchen window into the front garden. Marty, with his shirt sleeves rolled up, was busy digging over some earth in a flower border. 'He said he wanted to finish planting the border before he went home.'

Gayle walked into the kitchen with a book in her hand. She joined Robyn at the window. 'Just as well we've got lighter evenings now. I love the spring.'

Robyn smiled. 'Me too. And I love your garden. I can't believe it's April already. Look what Marty has achieved in just three months.'

Easter was just around the corner, and the plan was for Marty to finish landscaping and planting up the front so that he could start on the back garden for the summer.

'It looks amazing,' commented Robyn. With the high hedge that marked the boundary between Gayle's house and the neighbouring land, and also provided privacy from the road, the front garden was a lovely spot to sit out on the lawn before the back garden was landscaped. Marty had planted an assortment of heathers adding a rich tapestry of purples and pinks to the borders, creating a stunning contrast with the lush green foliage of hardy pines that thrived in the cool Highland air.

David had taken Robyn to the farm shop and shopping centre they'd visited before. Robyn loved visiting the place at weekends. Normally, she'd just browse the shops and drink coffee with David, or have lunch. But on the last trip, she'd spent a bit of money on a small cream cast iron table, and matching chairs, along with some seat cushions in a cream and delicate green leaf pattern.

Gayle had loved the purchases, although she had been annoyed that Robyn had not let her pay for the new garden furniture. But that didn't stop Gayle and her mum wandering outside on a beautiful spring morning with a cup of tea, sitting at the table, enjoying the sunshine, and admiring the beautiful garden and the amazing work that Marty had done.

Marty planted the last plant into the border and stood up, surveying his handiwork. Robyn saw him cast his gaze down the border in the direction of the house. She waved from the window.

Gayle waved too. 'I think he's finished the front garden – don't you?'

'Oh, yes.'

'Well, this calls for a celebration.'

Robyn nodded enthusiastically. It would have been nice if it had been a double celebration – officially opening the guesthouse to new guests – but the work on the inside of the house was still underway.

Robyn was so pleased at how the front garden had turned

out. It would give an amazing first impression for the guests. 'I bet this garden rivals the neighbouring garden now.'

'Are you talking about The Lake House?'

Robyn nodded as she washed up the last dinner plate and left it on the draining board. She wiped her hands dry on the dish cloth.

'What's the house like?' she asked, not expecting that Gayle would know. It was in extensive grounds, so couldn't be seen from the road. She said as much.

'I've seen photos of their house in the press.' Gayle flicked the kettle on. She got two mugs out of the kitchen cupboard. 'Why don't you go and see it for yourself?'

'Oh, I couldn't possibly wander up some stranger's driveway to gawp at their house.'

Gayle made them each a cup of tea. Doris had fallen asleep in a chair in the lounge, so there was no point making her a cuppa. Nor did she offer Marty a brew – he didn't like tea or coffee.

'I expect you'd get a good look at it from the loch, if you hired a motorboat, or went fishing.'

Neither of those options appealed to Robyn. She followed Gayle into the lounge. Marty was still clearing up; he had his tools still lying around the garden, and they'd need to go back into his van.

'You could go with Marty when he goes to do some gardening at The Lake House. I'm sure he wouldn't mind if you tagged along.'

Robyn sat down in the lounge and watched Gayle put the cups of tea down on the coffee table in front of them. Gayle cast a glance at her mum and then put on her reading glasses. She picked up the book she was reading. A moment later, she sighed, took off her reading glasses, and cast the novel to one side. She leaned forward in her chair. 'What's the matter?'

Gayle had caught Robyn staring into space. Robyn sighed. 'Oh, nothing.' But it wasn't *nothing*. She had a strange feeling in the pit of her stomach at the thought of seeing their holiday home, even though she wanted to. Perhaps it was the thought that she only wanted to visit out of morbid curiosity, knowing that the Ross heiress, Eleanor, who was not that much older than her, had a serious accident on the mountain during their traditional Christmas Day ski.

'Ah, I know what it is,' Gayle said, getting up from her chair, and leaving the room.

'Gayle – where are you going? Your tea will get cold.'

'Marty!' she called out.

Robyn was out of her seat like a shot. She joined Gayle at the front door. 'What are you doing?'

'Yes, Gayle?' Marty appeared so fast it was as though he had been standing right the other side of the door, but for the fact that he was breathing hard. He must have raced down the garden.

'Robyn would like to see The Lake House.'

'We both would,' Robyn interjected quickly, looking at Gayle.

'Oh no, you don't,' Gayle said in mock indignation. 'I wasn't the one who brought up wanting to see it.' Gayle winked at Robyn. 'You go and look. Perhaps it will give you some ideas and inspiration for planning the back garden here at Lark Lodge. Marty will show you around – won't you Marty?'

'Yes of course. The grounds are beautiful.'

'Well, you would say that.' Gayle winked affectionately at Marty.

'Actually, it wasn't me. I'm just really the caretaker now, keeping the weeds at bay, the flowers in bloom, and the lawns mowed and tended to. I can't take credit for it – that was my father. He was the one who planned and designed the gardens.

'Sounds like he had a real talent.'

'Yes, he's going to be a hard act to follow. I've discovered it's quite a job keeping on top of it just by myself. My father used to employ some other gardeners who also worked in the grounds, but they'd been working years and retired too when he passed over his gardening business to me. I'm doing the best I can at the moment, but I expect I'm going to have to get in touch with the Rosses, tell them that things have changed, and I can't do all the work myself.'

Robyn nodded as she leaned to one side, taking in the beautiful garden that had taken shape in the last three months. Spring meant planting season, and although it would take some years for the garden to feel established as the border plants and trees grew and spread, Marty had done an amazing job.

Gayle was also looking at the garden when she said, 'It looks to me as though you should have no worries on that score. Your father would be very proud if he saw the work you've done here,' she added. 'You are welcome to bring him along any time if you want to show it off. There'll be a brew waiting.'

Marty smiled. 'That's very kind of you.'

'Gayle! Where are you?' Doris's insistent voice came from the lounge. It wasn't so much that she was being demanding; she had just woken up from her snooze and found herself alone. Robyn could hear it in her voice – fear.

Over the last three months, everything had been moving inexorably on for Robyn – redecorating Lark Lodge, finishing

Rose and George's house, and working for her new customers who had moved in opposite Rose and George. Her business, operating out of Duncan's shop, was starting to flourish, which had turned Duncan's fortunes around – and what had helped tremendously, in the beginning, was the money, now dwindling, in the bottom of her rucksack. Even the garden had come on in leaps and bounds. But unfortunately, what had also moved inexorably on was Doris's condition. The dementia was getting worse, and Robyn could see that her decline was gaining momentum.

Gayle couldn't have popped down the street and round the corner to The Lake House anymore, even if she'd wanted to. Someone had to be with her mum pretty much all the time. Before, as long as the neighbour popped in just to keep an eye, Gayle was free to nip out to her clients, or go shopping, or take Olive for a walk. But now she couldn't call on her neighbour – it was too much of a responsibility.

Increasingly, Gayle's hairdressing clients were coming to her. But they wouldn't all do that. She was losing clients – and money. Robyn was aware that she had a dwindling client base. She needed more paying guests besides Nick and Olive. They'd had words – Robyn still wanted to pay for her room. If she didn't, then it would be one less room that Gayle could make money from. But Gayle insisted that while Robyn was paying for the garden work, that she was not going to pay for a room in her house too. She'd insisted that Robyn was her friend, and that she couldn't charge her rent.

Well, maybe we'll need to have a falling-out,' Robyn had joked.

They'd both smiled at that. They were best friends. That was never going to happen. But what *was* going to happen was that as soon as the gardening work finished, and Gayle could no longer hold that over her head, she was going to start paying for her room. *Otherwise I'll move out* – that was her last bargaining chip; she knew Gayle would not want that.

'You could come now, if you like, and I'll show you around,' Marty said.

Robyn peered past Marty into the gathering gloom.

'Perhaps when it's lighter,' Gayle said, reading her mind.

'Yes – after all, I want to be able to see it, don't I?' Robyn laughed.

Marty glanced about him. 'I suppose it is getting a bit late.'

'Anybody would think you didn't have a home to go to,' Gayle said to Marty. 'But listen – I want to have a little celebratory meal, cook us all a special dinner, now you've finished the front garden.'

Marty's face lit up. 'Oh, that would be fantastic.'

'Gayle!' Doris shouted from the lounge.

'All right, Mum! I'm coming! Don't get your knickers in a twist.' She turned to Marty. 'Sorry that it can't be tonight, but I will arrange something.'

Marty's face dropped. 'Well, I guess I'd better be going then.'

'Do you need to wash up again?' Gayle asked.

Robyn took at his grass-stained jeans and soiled shirt, along with his grimy fingers.

Looking past them into the house, he shook his head and turned to go. 'Oh, thanks for lunch. It was lovely joining you all.'

'It was lovely to have you, Marty.' Gayle had invited him in for lunch, which he'd readily accepted. She'd said it was the least she could do. He had volunteered to work on Saturday, after all.

Gayle was just closing the front door when she looked at Robyn, cocked her head in Marty's direction, and said, 'Something's not right.'

Robyn nodded. She'd noticed it too. They both stood there and watched Marty dragging his heels and walking awfully slowly back to his van, which was parked a little way down the drive.

Robyn looked at Gayle, and whispered. 'Do you get the impression that for some reason he'd rather not go home this evening?'

Gayle cast her eyes heavenward. 'You know, if I keep inviting people to stay here, there will be no room left for paying guests!'

Robyn smiled. She knew Gayle wouldn't turn anyone away. 'Perhaps he's had a falling-out with his mum and dad?'

Gayle nodded. 'It's possible. But I thought they got on really well?'

'Yes, so did I.'

Gayle said, 'I'll go and talk to him. Will you sit with my mum?'

'Of course.'

Robyn heard Gayle call out Marty's name as she walked over to Doris in the lounge, taking her hand and giving it a reassuring squeeze. 'I'm just walking over to the window.'

'All right, dear.'

Robyn stood by the window. Through the old single-glazed glass panes, she could see and hear everything outside.

'Yes?' Marty called back, moving a few steps towards the house.

'It's getting late,' Gayle said, which wasn't strictly true, although it was starting to get dark. 'I was wondering if you would you like to stay the night?'

'Here?'

'Yes, I've got the room. I haven't got any paying guests at the moment.' Marty knew that the gardens at Lark Lodge were being landscaped because the place was going to be turned into a guesthouse.

Robyn heard Marty reply, 'It would mean I could make an early start in the morning, on your back garden.'

'You don't have to do that. It's Sunday tomorrow, Marty. I hope you stay for Sunday lunch.'

Robyn smiled. It was really kind of Gayle to offer him to Sunday dinner.

'Are you sure?'

'Of course. Come inside. There's a bedroom with a sink so you can get cleaned up.'

'All right.' Marty followed her into the house. Robyn heard the creak of the stairs as Gayle showed him to a bedroom on the next floor. She overheard Gayle chatting on the way up the stairs. 'You could take Robyn to see The Lake House after breakfast tomorrow morning – she'd love that.'

A funny feeling in the pit of Robyn's stomach told her she wasn't so sure.

30

Gayle wandered into the kitchen wearing a silk dressing gown over her pyjamas. She gave a wide yawn and acknowledged Robyn, but her attention was on a pile of letters in her hand. There was no post on a Sunday. Robyn had collected them from the doormat the previous day and had left them on the sideboard in the hall, but Gayle hadn't bothered to pick them up or open them straight away. She sifted through them, turning one over, studying it for a moment, then sighing and tucking it back into the pile as if into a pack of cards.

Robyn had a strong sensation of déjà vu. 'More bills?' she asked.

'Oh, yes.'

Robyn imagined that this explained Gayle's reluctance to look at them when they'd arrived the previous day.

'They're all addressed to me,' commented Gayle. 'But I'm not complaining.'

Robyn smiled as she picked up her cup of tea. Of course she wouldn't complain. The family home she'd grown up in was now hers, so she didn't have to worry where she would live when her mother was no longer around – all thanks to her father changing his will. It meant that all the bills were in Gayle's name now.

Robyn had wondered why Gayle's father hadn't told Gayle and her siblings that he'd changed his will. But she had seen how angry and upset Gayle's siblings had been after the reading of the will. Perhaps, towards the end of his life, their father had not wanted his older children haranguing him to change it back.

Previously, Gayle had rented all her life. Her father had given her the security of a home – something her brothers and sister already had. Robyn glanced at the letters in Gayle's hand. All Gayle had to do was pay the bills. Her father had left her his savings, which had given Gayle a financial cushion to pay the bills. And she had the rent money from Nick, her lodger. But very soon, come the summer, Lark Lodge, the guesthouse, would be open for business, and Gayle would hopefully earn a decent income.

'You're up early,' Gayle observed as she flicked the kettle on.

Robyn had already washed and dressed. She'd woken early, and had tried to get back to sleep, but she had been unable to. The planned visit to The Lake House with Marty that day had been on her mind. She'd quietly slid out of bed so as not to wake David, and had crept downstairs, trying to avoid the creaky stairs, which was a bit difficult when every single one creaked.

She had thought that Nick, who liked an early morning run with Olive, might have gone out already, but she had soon discovered that it was too early even for him on a Sunday morning. When she'd walked into the kitchen to put the kettle on, Olive had still been there, on her cushion, and had been unable to get out of her bed fast enough, excited to see Robyn, as though she'd been gone for months, not just one night.

After lots of cuddles and licks from the energetic dog,

Robyn had filled Olive's bowl with dog biscuits and had then made herself a cuppa. No sooner had she sat down at the kitchen table than Gayle had appeared. She was still sorting through the letters while she waited for the kettle to boil.

'Oh, there's a letter for you, Robyn.'

'A letter – for me?'

Gayle handed her the envelope.

'Who's it from?'

Robyn didn't want a letter if it was from someone in her past, especially if she couldn't remember them.

I don't want to remember my past life, thought Robyn. *And I don't want anything or anybody turning up to take me away from the life I love here, or the people I love too.*

Gayle was still holding out the letter. 'It looks as though it's been redirected from the university.'

Robyn looked at Gayle, and thought *why did I let her persuade me to give the university a forwarding address when I told them I wasn't coming back?* Gayle had persuaded her not to drop out completely but to defer instead, just in case. Who knew what would happen when her memory came back? Robyn did not feel very reassured when Gayle had said that.

Robyn took the letter. She already had an idea who it was from. She recognised the expensive stationary and the neat handwriting.

'Is it from your mother?' Gayle asked.

'Yes.' Robyn had discovered letters in her suitcase from her mother that she'd kept hold of. She'd discovered from the dated letters that her mother contacted her just before any major holiday, sending her a cheque to cover flights, hoping she'd join her for a holiday in whatever destination she happened to be travelling to. *Why didn't she just text me, and then deposit the money straight into my bank account,* thought Robyn. Perhaps it was just the way she preferred to communicate, Robyn reasoned, in case she was in a place with poor mobile phone reception, and no bank.

Robyn had lost her phone, and her purse, in the car accident on Christmas Day, so apart from the savings book in her suitcase, she would have no clue whether her mother had called or texted her mobile, or put money in a bank account.

Perhaps she thought she'd send letters because I wasn't answering her texts or returning her calls. Robyn had no way of knowing unless she regained her memories at some point.

She'd been putting off writing to her mother to tell her she'd dropped out of university. She could go back in the new academic year, in six months' time, if she wanted to, but she had a life, a business, friends, David. Robyn couldn't imagine changing her mind. She hadn't told her mother that yet. She hadn't told her anything – about the accident, her memory loss, or the life she was building.

She stared at the letter.

Gayle turned around with a cup of tea. 'Aren't you going to open it?'

'I haven't written to her and told her I've dropped out.'

'Deferred.' Gayle took a sip of tea, sat at the kitchen table, and stroked Olive, who was sitting on the floor by her chair. Gayle put her mug down. 'Do you want to leave the course permanently?'

'Yes, of course I do. I can't imagine leaving this place.'

'You can't stay here forever.'

Robyn's face dropped.

'I meant at the guesthouse.'

That did not make her feel any better, especially when she realised that by coming up with the guesthouse idea, she might just have done herself out of a room. 'I said I'd pay rent.' Robyn didn't know how many times she'd told Gayle this.

'It's not the money, sweetheart.'

'Then what is it? I don't understand.'

'You and David.'

'What about us?'

'*Us* – that's the operative word. One day, possibly quite soon, you will want to move in together – properly, I mean, in your own home.'

'Oh, I see.' Robyn breathed a huge sigh of relief. She didn't know when or if that was going to happen. But she did ask, 'Can I stay here until—?'

'Robyn, I wouldn't mind if you stayed forever. For my own selfish reasons, I wish you'd never met David. Perhaps you two could have a huge falling-out. Then you wouldn't leave.'

'All right. I'll try.' Robyn laughed. 'I thought for a moment there that you were showing me the door.'

'Nonsense. I wouldn't dream of it.'

'Wouldn't dream of what?'

Robyn swung round in her chair to see Marty standing at the kitchen doorway. He looked at them both sheepishly. 'Sorry, couldn't help overhearing.'

Robyn stared at him, wondering how much he'd overheard.

Gayle said, 'Morning! Did you sleep well? Would you like a cup of tea?'

'I'd prefer orange juice.'

'Oh, yes, of course. I forgot you don't like tea.'

He joined them at the kitchen table.

Gayle poured him a glass of orange juice as she said, 'We were just discussing Robyn moving out.'

'Really? That's a shame.' Those words were barely out of his mouth, Robyn noticed, when he asked, 'Does that mean there's a spare room going for rent?'

'Why – do you want one?'

'I'm not moving out,' Robyn said quickly.

Gayle sighed. 'I know, Robyn. There are other rooms.'

'Yes, but they're in a bit of a state,' Robyn blurted.

'I don't mind,' said Marty. 'Anything will do. Honestly, I'm not fussed.'

Robyn and Gayle's eyes met across the table. She wondered if Gayle was thinking the same thing – what had precipitated Marty suddenly wanting to move out of his parents' house?

Gayle smiled. 'You're welcome to use that room for as long as you like, but …'

Robyn looked at Gayle, realising the words had caught in her throat. She wasn't surprised. Gayle was a lovely lady, and was just too nice to ask people for money, even if she was meant to be running a business. Robyn had tried to think of the possible obstacles to turning Lark Lodge into a bona fide guesthouse – this was not one of them she'd considered.

Robyn was going to help her out. She turned to Marty. 'What Gayle is trying to say is that she needs to charge you rent money.'

'Of course. I pay my way at home. I'll just pay to live here instead until I figure something else out. I'll go and pack my things after breakfast.'

Gayle handed him a cup of tea. 'But won't your parents miss you? And, um … what about the money you pay them?'

'Yeah, they'll miss me. They're okay for money, though. More than okay. It was me who insisted on paying them for my keep once I took over the gardening business and started earning. I would never want them to think I'd take advantage.'

Gayle smiled. 'Of course not.'

There was a long silence. Robyn and Gayle exchanged another glance, realising that Marty wasn't going to tell them what was going on at home.

Everyone sat watching Olive hoovering up the dog biscuits that she'd managed to spread all over the kitchen floor and under the table. As soon as she finished, she pounced on Marty, cheering him up no end when she offered him her paw and then put her huge head on his lap.

Gayle pointed at Robyn. 'Aren't you going to read that?'

Robyn had forgotten all about the letter in her hand. She waved it in the air. 'This can wait.'

Olive suddenly jumped up and snatched the letter.

'Hey!'

There ensued a frantic chase around the kitchen table, and then Olive ran out of the door into the lounge, followed by Robyn, Marty, and Gayle in quick succession. Olive was having great fun.

This game was nothing new. Stealing was her favourite past-time. Everyone had learnt the hard way not to leave things lying around, especially shoes by the front door.

They were trying to corner her, but she managed to get past them.

She ran out of the lounge, just as Nick called out, 'Walkies!'

Olive skidded to a halt at the bottom of the stairs.

At the top of the stairs, Nick had appeared in his jogging gear. 'There you are,' he said, smiling at his dog.

The three of them appeared behind Olive. Robyn saw Nick's smile fade. 'What's she done now?' he said, resignation in his voice.

Robyn shook her head. 'Oh, nothing.'

'Really,' Nick replied, walking down the stairs. He was used to everyone covering for his naughty dog.

'I just need to get this…' Robyn prized her jaws open and retrieved her letter, which had two rather large holes where Olive's teeth had been.

Nick looked at the letter. He turned to his dog. 'Olive!'

'It's fine, really. It's nothing important.' Robyn stuffed the letter in the back pocket of her jeans. She turned to Marty. 'Shall we go and visit The Lake House now?' David was still asleep, and she rather fancied having breakfast with him, and spending the day together. It suited her to do the visit early.

'All right. Let's go.' Marty opened the front door.

Olive took that as her cue to follow them.

'No, no – not you.' Nick jogged down the stairs. 'Olive – here, girl.'

Olive stood beside Marty, ignoring Nick.

Although Marty had only been there one night, Olive had taken rather a shine to the new house guest, Robyn noticed. Olive wasn't the only one. Nick had made friends with Marty too, chatting amiably to him at the dinner table the previous night. She realised that Marty was going to fit right in at Lark Lodge.

Robyn was still smiling at the thought as she walked down the drive with Marty, on their way to The Lake House.

31

They left the house along with Nick, who followed them with Olive pulling on her lead. Robyn could hear Olive panting.

Nick set off, jogging. He waved as he passed by. Robyn waved back. She glanced at Marty. He suddenly stopped. 'Do you think Gayle would like to come too? I forgot to ask her.'

Robyn shook her head. It was kind of him to ask, but she knew that Gayle had a few more things on her mind than their beautifully manicured lawn and their flower borders – like a pile of bills, and her poor mum. Robyn said, 'I think she's busy. Perhaps another time.'

'All right.'

They fell in step again.

'Oh – we're not taking the car?' Robyn asked as they passed by his small van parked outside.

'No. I'm not gardening today, so I won't need my stuff in the van. I thought it would be nice to walk.'

Robyn looked back at the house. So much for having breakfast with David. She knew how long Gayle's road was. Once they got to the end, then presumably they'd have a bit of a walk up the drive to The Lake House.

'I know a little shortcut,' he said. 'But mum's the word.' He tapped his nose.

Robyn thought that the old-fashioned phrase was rather funny coming from one so young. Which reminded Robyn – she had a question. 'How old are you? If you don't mind me asking.'

'Twenty.'

'Are you enjoying your part-time course at college?'

'I am, yes. I'm just a bit worried that there won't be the gardening work around when I'm finished and want to go full-time.'

'But I thought you took over your father's business?'

They'd got to the end of the drive and turned down the street.

'I did – yes. But the people on his round are all getting on in years, and some don't have the money from their pensions to pay me, so I've ended up doing their gardens and getting paid in apple pies and strawberry jam.'

'Pardon? They pay you in pies and jam?'

'Yeah – I suppose you'd call it bartering, just like what you're doing with Gayle.'

'You mean the redecorating in exchange for staying there.' That wasn't by choice, Robyn wanted to add. She frowned.

Marty halted when he caught her expression. 'I can pay my way at Lark Lodge. I have some savings.'

After hearing he was doing people's gardening work for almost nothing, she felt bad for making Marty pay for his room when she knew Gayle would have let him stay there for nothing; although she reminded herself she was paying Marty very generously for the gardening work – in cash. She resolved to increase his rate.

'I'm sure you'll land some new clients,' Robyn said. 'But in the meantime, you won't have to use your savings, Marty, to pay for your room. After what I saw you've done to the front garden at Lark Lodge, I decided that you're worth a lot more than your current rate.'

'Really?'

'Oh, yes.'

Robyn was factoring in his room and board, and adding that to his final bill for the garden work – she just wouldn't tell him. She'd already sat in her room last night and counted out the cash she'd be giving him. She'd just have to count out some more.

Robyn tried not to think about where the cash had come from. There had to be a simple explanation. Vacation work – that was it. Perhaps she had been paid in cash. But who would have paid a student that much cash for a temporary job?

Robyn really didn't want to think about the other possibility – that the cash wasn't hers.

Nothing will make sense until I remember, she thought. Whilst part of her didn't want to remember, it had now been four months since the accident, and her memory wasn't coming back. If there wasn't a physical reason for it, as her doctor at the hospital had intimated, then what was her subconscious protecting her from? She now wondered if it was something she'd done rather than someone she was running from.

'I'm so pleased to have Gayle's gardening work. It will tide me over until some more work rolls in,' said Marty.

Robyn nodded, thankful for the distraction from her thoughts. She had an idea. 'Have you seen the new estate going up on the outskirts of Aviemore?' She knew it was a silly question. Nobody could miss the flags outside the entrance to the development just off the main road.

'Yes – Nick was telling me all about it at dinner yesterday evening. That's where he works as a site manager. He said that I should come along, and he'd introduce me to some of the residents, and see if they are interested in any gardening and landscaping work.'

'That's really kind of him.'

'I know.'

Robyn was aware that Rose and George's garden had been landscaped by the developer, but only because they were next door to the show home, and anybody viewing the show home could look out of the window into their garden. It would not make a good impression for potential buyers if the adjoining property's garden was not looking its best.

However, for the rest of the properties on the estate, apart from the front gardens, which were laid to lawn, the back gardens were not, leaving lots of potential gardening and landscape work for Marty if homeowners were interested. Then there was the maintenance of the gardens – mowing lawns, trimming hedges. There would be all sorts of gardening jobs that needed doing.

Marty said, 'I hope I can pick up some more work. I'm not complaining about some of my father's old clients – the pies and homemade jam are lovely, but I can't exactly live on those.'

Robyn eyed him as they walked down the street. It was a beautiful spring morning, quite different from the winter in the Scottish Highlands. She loved waking up to the dawn chorus and the sunshine. Spring had brought with it warmer weather, even though it was only April.

They cut through a lane between houses, which led to the

shores of a loch. And there, in a beautifully serene setting on the bank of the loch, was a large, detached residence. They'd emerged from the lane at the back of a property that she guessed fronted the loch. 'Is that The Lake House?'

'Yes, that's it.'

She looked at the high garden wall and imagined they'd have to circle the wall and then walk up a long drive to the house. Robyn looked at her watch. She sighed.

'We won't be long. Look, I've got a key.'

'A key?'

He stopped at an iron gate in the wall. 'We can get straight into the gardens from here. Saves a long walk round to the front of the house.'

As he unlocked the gate, Robyn whispered, 'Are the family here, do you think?' She didn't know why she was whispering. It occurred to her that the family might not take too kindly to a nosy stranger wandering around the grounds of their house.

'No, they're not here.'

The house was huge. 'How can you be so sure?' Robyn asked, her voice hushed as they walked into the grounds.

'The family haven't been back here since the accident on Christmas Day. I don't know if they'll ever return.'

'But they keep paying you to look after the grounds in their absence?'

'Oh, yes. It's their holiday home, and they are rarely here, so it's normal to be working here when they're not around.'

Robyn followed Marty down a winding, cobbled pathway between trees. They emerged from the trees. 'Oh, wow!' was all Robyn could say when she saw the beautifully manicured lawn and the huge variety of established plants and flowers. The flower border that ran along the garden wall was much deeper than the one Marty had planted at Gayle's house. It looked like the garden of a stately home that would be featured in a magazine, or like a National Trust property that people paid to visit.

'So, this is the back garden,' said Marty.

Robyn had already guessed as much when she saw the house, which had a large conservatory and a flagstone patio with cast iron garden furniture.

'Come on.'

Robyn stood and stared at the house.

Marty turned around when he noticed she wasn't following. 'What's the matter?'

Robyn didn't know. She just felt peculiar being there.

'Look, I can assure you there's nobody home. Come on.'

Robyn stepped out from the shade of the trees and followed Marty across the lawn. She spied a cream-coloured wooden structure with a door and windows either side. It looked like a summerhouse.

'The gardens are beautiful,' Robyn gushed as she followed Marty across the lawn, her eyes drawn back to the house. As they walked around, she continued to compliment the grounds, but her mind was elsewhere. There was a familiarity about the place that she couldn't put her finger on.

'It really is enchanting.' Robyn wasn't talking about the garden, but the house. She found herself staring vacantly at a pile of dead leaves. She looked up at Marty, who had crossed his arms over his chest and was looking rather peeved.

'So, you think this pile of rotting leaves is enchanting?'

'Well, it has got a kind of ...' Robyn gesticulated with her hands, 'nice shapeliness to it.' She cringed.

'You're not really here to see the garden, are you?'

Marty unfolded his arms and took her hand. 'Come on.'

'Where are we going?'

They headed towards the house. 'You've been fascinated by it since we walked into the garden.'

They stepped onto the patio outside the French doors next to the conservatory, whereupon Marty knelt and lifted a worn door mat. Robyn saw him pick up a key.

She looked at him, surprised. 'They leave a key under a mat?'

'Yeah – I discovered it once, when I'd mowed the grass and was sweeping up the patio. I dislodged the mat, and that's when I'd found the rusting key. I reckon it's been there years, and they've forgotten about it.

'And it still works?'

'Yes. I cleaned it up, and put it back under the mat.' He unlocked one of the French doors and motioned her inside. 'There's really not much to see, just a lot of white dust sheets.'

Robyn stood motionless on the mat, peering inside.

'Aren't you coming in?'

Her stomach was churning, and she had no idea why. It felt like something bad was going to happen. 'But we're trespassing.'

Marty's expression clouded over. 'Do you want to see the place or not? There might not be another opportunity.'

She took a deep breath and stepped into the house.

She cast her gaze around a small study.

'This is William Ross's study.'

Books lined one wall. There was an old oak desk, a chair, and a couple of wing-backed chairs on either side of the French doors. It reminded her of Gayle's father's study. Robyn had been working her way through Gayle's house, redecorating one bedroom at a time. At some point, she'd start on the rooms downstairs. But the study was not to be touched. Gayle wanted it to remain as it was.

'There's no computer,' Robyn observed, thinking, *talk about old-fashioned.*

'They don't come here to work. Mr Ross told me that once. It is purely a holiday home.'

'What's he like?'

'Who – Mr Ross?'

Robyn nodded as she followed Marty out of the study into the hallway. The décor, along with the house, was not unlike that of Gayle's home – it was just on a much grander scale.

'William Ross is a very nice guy. I met him just a handful of times when I was a little kid accompanying my father here, helping out with gardening during the school holidays. I remember a good-humoured man who always had time to stop for a chat and ask after my mum. He always gives a generous Christmas bonus. They were nice, down-to-earth people, from what I remember, but I rarely saw them. They mostly only spent Christmas here.'

'That's a shame. I think they're missing out. I love spring here.' Robyn suspected she'd love the Highlands in any season.

Marty smiled, echoing her thoughts. 'I love this place any time of year. But then I'm biased. I'm from here.'

As they chatted, Marty opened several doors off the hallway. Robyn popped her head around the kitchen door, then the lounge. She could see the outline of a huge flat-screen television beneath a dust sheet. There was a TV in the dining room as well. She paused, staring at the long dining room table, imagining them all seated around it on Christmas Day, eating their final meal together before the accident on the ski slopes changed their lives forever.

Marty stood in the doorway too. He sighed. 'It's so sad, what happened to his daughter. I just don't get it.'

She turned to look at him. 'What do you mean?'

'There was an avalanche. There's normally an avalanche risk forecast between about the middle of December to mid-April from the SAIS.'

Robyn looked at him blankly. She didn't recall hearing about the avalanche on the news when she was in hospital, but then she had been faffing about, trying to locate the television controls. She had missed part of the news story.

'Oh, right. You don't know what that is. It's The Scottish Avalanche Information Service, who assess the potential for them in six areas – the Cairngorms is one of them, but the winters have been so mild lately with not the same level of snowfall there used to be, so I'm thinking it came as a bit of a surprise.'

Robyn shrugged. 'Perhaps it's something to do with climate change.'

She stepped back into the hall as Marty closed the door. She'd been admiring the décor in each room, and it was giving her ideas for the rooms downstairs in Lark Lodge. Marty was right: there wasn't that much to see – white dust sheets abounded everywhere.

'How long has it been like this?' Robyn's voice carried down the wide expanse of hallway like an echo. Then she remembered. Nobody had returned since Christmas. 'What's in here?' she asked. They'd walked straight past a door.

'No – don't open that one.'

'Why?' Robyn said ignoring his protestations. She opened the door. There were just more dustsheets.

Marty came striding down the hallway as she was just shutting the door. Then something caught her eye. In the sea of white shapes, something stood out that caught Robyn's attention. One of the pieces of furniture was uncovered. Robyn was just opening the door wider when Marty slapped his hand over hers and pulled the door shut. 'I think you've seen enough down here. Why don't we go and look upstairs?'

She looked at him in bewilderment. He gestured in the direction of the stairs. She turned as if to follow but as soon as his back was turned, she opened the door again and stepped inside the room.

As she expected, Marty was right on her tail; his head appeared around the door in an instant. 'What are you doing? I thought we were going upstairs?'

'I just wanted to see this room – what's the problem? This room is just like all the others.' She threw her hand in a wide arc around the room.

'That's my point exactly.' Marty sighed heavily. 'So why don't we go up—'

'What's that?' Robyn's gaze wandered back to the uncovered sofa that had caught her attention in the first place. Her attention lingered there as she moved towards it to take a closer look.

'There's nothing to see, honestly. Let's go upstairs.'

Robyn glanced at Marty, who was holding out a pleading hand.

On the floor next to the sofa was an empty plate with crumbs on it and what looked like the remnants of a sandwich.

There was an open carton of orange juice. She walked around the back of the sofa to discover a sleeping bag laid out along the sofa, with a cushion placed at one end as a pillow. Moving along the sofa to the end, she felt something underfoot. Looking down, she saw that she was standing on a strap of some kind. Bending down, she pulled a large rucksack from under the sofa. Robyn hoisted it up in front of her and held it up.

Marty looked at her sheepishly– it belonged to him.

'I thought you said you were going *home* to collect your stuff after breakfast?'

'I didn't actually say I was going home, did I?'

Robyn let the heavy rucksack drop out of her fingers, making a dull thud on the carpet. 'I suppose you're going to tell me that you can explain?'

32

'So, do you want to tell me what's going on?'

Marty rolled up his sleeping bag, avoiding eye contact. 'You weren't meant to come in this room.'

She put her hands on her hips, watching him.

When he'd finished, he slumped down heavily on the sofa. He picked up the cushion and held it over his chest.

Robyn stood watching him pluck at the corner of the sleeping bag, where there appeared to be a worn hole, and dislodge one of the tiny white feathers. It came free and floated to the floor. They both watched this in silence.

Robyn frowned. 'Gayle asked you to stay at the guesthouse because it appeared that you didn't want to go home. We thought you were living at your parents' house, and that you got on well with them.'

'I did. I do.' He stared at the floor.

She sat down next to him, and said softly, 'Do you want to tell me what's going on?'

'Both my parents are retired.'

Robyn knew that. She didn't see what that had to do with Marty leaving home and squatting at The Lake House.

'I needed to leave home, but I had nowhere else to go, not immediately. It's not like I could walk into an estate agent and rent a place on my salary at the moment, and all the B&Bs and hotels are fully booked with tourists.'

Robyn nodded. She recalled the trouble Nick had had in trying to find a place when he'd had to leave the B&B where he was staying before he came to Lark Lodge.

She glanced at the sleeping bag. 'Couldn't you have waited until something came up to move into before you left home?'

He shook his head adamantly. 'No. They sold their house and moved out of Aviemore.'

'Couldn't you move with them until you found a place?'

'No. My mum always wanted to move back to Edinburgh, to live near her sister. They've bought a flat. Moved in a couple of weeks ago. It's too far from Aviemore where my work is.'

'But didn't you tell them you had nowhere to live?'

'I had a friend who was going to let me sofa-surf for a bit, but his new girlfriend put her foot down at the last minute and said no. By that time, my parents had exchanged contracts, and the sale was going through. But even if that wasn't the case, I wouldn't have told them and stood in the way of something they were looking forward to.'

Marty turned to look at her, smiling. 'You should have seen them, so excited about moving back to the city. It's where they met, and had their first home together in a little flat in the old quarter, apparently. I couldn't ask them to back out of their sale and give up their dream.'

'What – even if you were made homeless?'

Marty sighed and shook his head.

'Why didn't you tell us what was going on?'

Marty studied his fingernails and shook his head. 'I couldn't tell you or Gayle. I was afraid you'd look at me differently and that Gayle would ask me to leave Lark Lodge if she found out I'd broken into someone else's house and started squatting.'

'But you didn't break in. You used a key.'

Marty rolled his eyes at Robyn. 'That's not the point, is it?'

Robyn sat back on the sofa. 'You don't have to lie to me – or Gayle, like you've been doing with your parents.'

Marty started to cry. 'I really didn't know what I was going to do before Gayle invited me to stay. I was scared every night that they might come back, even though I knew it was unlikely.'

'Why didn't you ask if there was a room available at Lark Lodge? You know how big the house is. Only Nick and I are staying there.'

'But the guesthouse hasn't opened officially yet, and you and Nick are Gayle's friends.'

Robyn smiled. 'Well, you are Gayle's friend too – and mine, and Nick's. Oh, and of course, Olive's too.'

Marty laughed, wiping the tears from his cheeks with the sleeve of his jumper.

Poor Marty, thought Robyn. It sounded as though he was such a good son, letting his parents think that he was okay so they could enjoy their new life in Edinburgh with no clue their son had been left homeless.

'Nobody is going to tell you to leave Lark Lodge, I can assure you.' She squeezed his hand, and stood up. 'Come on, let's finish the tour of the house.' Robyn wasn't sure she needed to see the rest of the house. She didn't tell Marty, but as soon as she'd walked into the house, she'd had a strong feeling she'd been there before. But she had no idea how that could be.

'Then what are we going to do?' Marty asked.

'After breakfast, you can take your van and come back and collect your things.'

'What are you going to tell Gayle?'

'Nothing. When you're ready, you can tell Gayle yourself.'

❖

'Do you suffer from vertigo?'

'Vertigo?' Marty paused in the hall.

Robyn had answered the door when he'd returned from The Lake House with his belongings after breakfast. She'd suggested he leave his sleeping bag in the car unless he wanted to explain to Gayle straight away where he'd been sleeping for the past few nights. He did not.

'Heights.' Robyn said. 'Are you afraid of heights?'

'I know what vertigo means,' he said, slipping the rucksack off his shoulder in the hallway. 'This thing is heavy.'

Robyn shut the door and followed him down the hall. 'Well, are you?'

He paused at the foot of the stairs, and looked at her. 'I wouldn't really be much use as a gardener if I couldn't get up a ladder and trim hedges and creepers, now would I?'

Robyn realised he had a point. She watched Marty pick up the rucksack again and haul it over his shoulder. 'I tried to pack all my belongings in here. Perhaps it's just as well I let my parents look after some of my things, because I wouldn't have been able to fit all my stuff in.'

Robyn could empathise. She'd obviously done the same, packing her old suitcase and her overnight bag full of her stuff, before leaving university to head to Aviemore.

'Are you any good with a paintbrush?'

'Maybe … I guess.' He asked, 'Why all the questions? What's this about?'

Robyn cast her gaze around the hallway. 'How would you like to work with me on a little project?'

'What have you got in mind?'

Having established he could be trusted up a ladder, she said, 'Have you done any painting before?'

'Landscape painting?'

For a moment, Robyn didn't understand. 'Oh, you mean a painting on a canvas.' She shook her head. 'Not that kind of painting. I'm redecorating Gayle's house, but I could do with a hand. Want to earn some extra money?'

'Absolutely. Just point me in the direction of the paint pot!'

'Perfect.' Robyn left Marty to take his bag upstairs. She walked into the kitchen to find David making a cup of tea, waiting for her. 'I can help redecorate too.'

Robyn realised he must have overheard their conversation. She looked at him, and thought *there's no way you're climbing up a ladder*. It had taken three months of rehabilitation on his knee to get to where he was. The walking stick had gone. He hadn't thrown it away yet – he had said it might be bad karma – but it hadn't seen the light of day for some weeks. Robyn knew she couldn't wrap him up in cotton wool, as much as she'd like to, but he was certainly not climbing ladders. Not on her watch.

However she wasn't about to refuse his offer to help. The more people pitched in, the quicker the place would get done. Now all she had to do was twist Nick's arm too. And she knew just the person who could do that – Marty.

She looked at David. 'You could paint below the dado rails.'

'Of course. I'm guessing you don't want me climbing up ladders.'

'Nope.' It was bad enough that he'd returned to ice hockey. David was now a volunteer coach for a local youth sports programme that organised the team he'd been playing with when he'd had his accident on the ice. He was also working towards a certification and further training, which hopefully would lead to a paid coaching position. David was also applying to do a part-time history degree at the university locally, just as an interest – a hobby, he'd said. Robyn had wondered if perhaps history would become his new career, and coaching ice hockey would become his hobby. Who knew what the future held?

David's life was really coming together. The only fly in the ointment, as far as he was concerned, was his father.

Robyn had asked both of them, separately, to just sit down and talk, but they were both just as proud and stubborn as each other.

David wouldn't move back home until his old man had left – that's what he'd said. The problem was that poor Duncan had nowhere to go.

Robyn heard the creak of the floorboards as Marty made his way up to his room. She suddenly had a thought. Duncan might not be able to buy a house unless he sold his shop – but he wouldn't hear of it. But he could afford to take a room there, at Lark Lodge.

She looked at David. There was a problem with that idea – it meant David would leave Lark Lodge. Robyn didn't want that.

'You've gone quiet. What are you thinking?'

Robyn was thinking that if he left, he'd want her to go with him, to live at his place. But she didn't want to leave Lark Lodge.

She decided she'd rather things stayed as they were.

33

Seated at the kitchen table, Robyn idly stabbed at the food on her plate with her fork.

'Not hungry?' Gayle said. She was sitting opposite, finishing her bowl of muesli. 'That's not like you.'

Robyn looked down at her plate and nodded. She felt bad that Gayle had gone to all the trouble of cooking her breakfast, but she'd lost her appetite. Reluctantly, she put her fork down and pushed the plate away. David was outside, *helping* Marty with the garden – although for the life of her, she couldn't see what help David could be. He didn't know the first thing about landscape gardening. She knew that he was avoiding her.

'So, you and David had a fight.' Gayle said matter-of-factly, pointing the spoon at her. 'Well, that's how you know.'

Robyn looked back at her curiously. 'Know what?'

'You aren't really serious about each other until you've had your first fight.'

They'd already fallen out, on New Year's Eve, and again when David had left hospital after his knee op. They'd patched things up fairly quickly. But this felt different.

'And which self-help guru said that little gem?' Robyn asked sarcastically, not feeling in the mood to talk about it.

Gayle hadn't asked her what their argument had been about, but Robyn decided that maybe she did want to talk about it after all, and get it off her chest.

She lowered her voice, even though they were the only ones in the house. Nick was out on his early morning run with Olive. Marty and David were in the back garden, and Doris had been picked up and taken to the community centre for a coffee morning with her old friends.

She leaned across the table. 'Something happened …'

'Yes, I realise that. That's why you two have fallen out.'

Robyn shook her head. 'No, I meant something happened in David's past that he won't talk about.'

Gayle sighed, and sat back in her chair. 'Ah, I know what this is about.'

Robyn looked at her I surprise. 'You do?'

'Of course. He won't talk about his accident – the one that ended his career.'

Robyn nodded. 'It's true – he won't. How do you know? Have you asked him?'

'No, I haven't. It was a good guess, though, obviously. I'm sure he'll talk about it, when he's ready.'

'You're wondering why I'm making a big deal about it.'

'I didn't say that.'

'But you were thinking it.'

'What I don't understand, is why, after all this time, are you bringing it up now?' Gayle reached for her dish and finished her cereal. 'You know he doesn't want to talk about it.'

Robyn had got a text from Melissa to apologise and say that she'd been so busy at university after the Christmas break that she hadn't had a chance to look into David's past. She would be back for the Easter break and had said she was looking forward to researching the case. For some reason, Robyn hadn't appreciated her calling it a *case*. It was her boyfriend that Melissa was talking about.

Robyn grimaced at the thought. She didn't want to wait for her to come back and start digging around. Gayle was probably right: David would tell her … in time. But there wasn't time to wait. After the makeover three months earlier, Melissa had boldly asked Brodie from Wilbur's bookshop out, and not surprisingly, he'd accepted. Melissa had insisted on following through with her side of the bargain; to do the favour for Robyn that she'd promised, despite Robyn trying to ask her to leave things be.

She'd almost forgotten about Melissa's mission to delve into David's past until the text out of the blue had reminded her. The Easter holiday was nearly upon them. Melissa would be returning to Aviemore soon. The text had prompted Robyn to come right out with it and ask David bluntly about his so-called accident.

Not surprisingly, David still wouldn't talk about it. She'd had it on the tip of her tongue to bring up the newspaper article she'd found about the incident in his father's shop, but before she'd had a chance to mention it, he'd stormed out into the garden, refusing to join her for breakfast.

Gayle put her spoon down and moved her cereal bowl to one side. Her arms stretched out across the table and her soft hands enveloped Robyn's. She looked up at her.

'People deal with loss in different ways. Perhaps he still isn't ready to talk about what happened. I'm sure that in time …'

Robyn stared at Gayle, not listening to the self-help psychobabble that was spilling out of her lips. It wasn't her thing at the best of times, but Gayle was her friend, and she respected her even though she didn't have time for such thinking herself.

Robyn lowered her voice. 'Did you know that there was an attempted robbery in Mr Gillespie's store?'

'Oh, my god! When? Are you okay? Is Duncan?'

'Oh, sorry. I didn't mean recently.'

Gayle put a hand to her chest and exhaled in relief. 'Has this got something to do with David? Is that what you're saying?'

'Yes, I am. It turns out that when David was on a night out with his friends two years ago …' Robyn told her all about the burglary. Robyn watched intently for Gayle's reaction as what she said slowly and deliberately cut across Gayle's self-help monologue. 'He didn't want to tell me because it turned out that he killed someone.'

Gayle stopped talking. 'What did you just say?'

Robyn had her attention. She repeated herself word for word slowly and deliberately.

'What on earth makes you say a thing like that?' Gayle was clearly shocked. She released her hands from Robyn and sat back in her chair.

Robyn reached into the pocket of her dungarees and withdrew a folded piece of white paper.

Unfolding it, Robyn lay it flat on the table and smoothed out the creases before slipping it across the table to Gayle. She sat back as Gayle picked it up.

'What's this?' Gayle looked at Robyn.

Robyn nodded her head at the piece of paper, motioning for Gayle to read it. Robyn watched Gayle's eyes move over the page.

'Where did you get this?' she said, slowly putting the piece of paper on the kitchen table.

'The library,' Robyn said, certain that Gayle would believe her now. 'From the newspaper archives. It's a printout.' She decided not to tell her about Melissa and the research project she was doing – or would be when she got home from university for the Easter break.

'Aren't you forgetting something? If David did this,' Gayle tapped the piece of paper with her finger, 'like you said, killing a man, even if he was a burglar, wouldn't he have been arrested for murder or manslaughter? Even if he pleaded self-defence and was let off?' Gayle looked at the article. 'That's what it says in the article.' Gayle read out loud, *It is not yet known whether criminal charges will be brought against Mr Gillespie.*

'I know.' Melissa had told her that if someone breaks into your property, and you hurt them – or worse – then it's you that could be arrested. She'd said that you can plead self-defence, but that won't stop the police charging you with a crime.

'I couldn't find out what happened next.'

'Why is it so important? He's not in prison now – if he ever was.' Gayle eyed her. 'Is it because you found out he killed someone?'

'Yes … no. I don't know. I just have a feeling that it's important somehow.' That memory of turning up at David's house with Duncan, and recognising the place, kept playing on her mind. That didn't mean it had anything to do with the burglary at Duncan's store. Why would it? But still, something was nagging away at her that she couldn't put her finger on. Perhaps if her memories returned, then there would be nothing to worry about.

Worry about? Even that thought had Robyn over-thinking, wondering why that notion had just popped into her head.

She looked at Gayle sheepishly and decided not to share what was on her mind in case Gayle came out with some self-help tosh and gave her a book to read from her extensive library.

'I think you're over-thinking things.'

Robyn sighed. Trust Gayle to realise that.

'Next, you'll be telling me that there's some conspiracy, and Joe was in on it, keeping his brother out of gaol.

'Do you think that's a possibility?' If that came to light, Joe would lose his job. Maybe that *was* it. David was protecting his little brother. That would explain a lot – why he wouldn't bring up the burglary, let alone tell her what happened.

Gayle shook her head and tutted. She got up from the table, scooped up both plates and gave Robyn a quizzical look before she walked over to the sink.

'What?' Robyn held up her arms questioningly as Gayle returned to the table with a cloth.

Gayle picked up the article Robyn had given her to read. 'You know what I think of this?' Gayle tore the piece of paper into four pieces, then casually walk over to the rubbish bin. She tapped the lever with her foot, held the pieces of paper theatrically in the air, then dropped them into the bin. She let her foot off the pedal, and the lid clanged shut. Gayle turned around. 'You need to let this go – whatever this really is.'

'What do you mean?'

'I think there's something you're not telling me.'

Robyn didn't know why the dwindling cash in the rucksack suddenly came to mind. A lot of it was now gone – spent on Gayle's garden, and doing up her house, along with the money to set up her little interior design outlet.

Robyn rose from the table. 'I'm going to find David.'

'Robyn?' Gayle called out as she was about to step out the room.

She turned around. Robyn could tell by Gayle's expression that she had something on her mind. 'What is it?'

'This memory thing. I know you still can't remember. I don't think it helps, you know. I think your imagination might be running away with you or …'

'Or?'

Gayle said in a small voice. 'You're starting to get paranoid.'

Shaking her head, Robyn opened her mouth to deny this, but no words came out. Instead, an uncomfortable truth had struck her. *Could Gayle be right?* Perhaps David wasn't the problem. Perhaps she was.

Gayle shook her head solemnly. 'You want David to tell you the truth about his past. Have you considered the possibility that he'd like the same consideration from you?'

Robyn stared at Gayle.

'After all these months, David doesn't really know a blessed thing about you, does he?'

'That's just not true. You've talked to him about me. You must have when David stayed here that one night when I was staying with Duncan the night he got out of hospital.'

Gayle didn't deny it. She shrugged. 'We've just assumed that you're a nice ordinary, sane person. For all we know, you could have some crazed, gun-toting, knife-wielding jealous husband or boyfriend on your trail. Or, heaven forbid, I could be hiding a fugitive who has escaped from prison and is in all kinds of trouble, having committed some heinous crime.'

Robyn was completely taken aback, surprised that she could think such horrible things about her.

'But you don't believe that – do you?'

'Well, honey, anything's possible.'

'But … we're friends.' Robyn protested.

Gayle walked around the table, and reached for two more breakfast plates – Nick's and her mum's. She stood in front of Robyn with one in each hand. 'Well, there's the rub. I *do* know you, and I wouldn't believe a word of it if someone told me those things about you.'

She walked to the sink and deposited the dirty dishes into the sink. She turned around. 'And I know David, and I don't believe a word of that article either. I don't think he could bring himself to shoot a man – even if it was in self-defence.' Gayle started washing up. Then Robyn could see that something had occurred to her. She put a dish on the draining board and turned around, soap suds dripping down her sleeve. 'Your memory really hasn't improved any?'

'No,' Robyn said crossly. She steered the conversation back to David. 'If that newspaper article wasn't true about David shooting the burglar, then what *did* happen?'

'What did I just tell you? Let it go, Robyn,' she nodded her head wisely. 'I think you're losing some perspective on things.' She turned back to the sink. 'Why, just the other afternoon I was watching Dr Phil on Oprah Winfrey, and he said …'

Robyn closed her eyes. She obviously wasn't going to get through to Gayle. Robyn thought of Melissa; despite her reservations, she was now very happy indeed that Melissa was still on the case. *Thank goodness someone believes me*, she thought.

Gayle washed the dishes as she poured forth her self-help sermon, but to Robyn's relief, her monologue was promptly drowned out by the sound of an approaching car on the gravel outside the kitchen window. Gayle lifted a soapy hand and waved.

Curious, Robyn got up from the table and stood beside Gayle to look out of the window.

A police car came to a stop at an angle, centred in the driveway 'What's a police car doing here?' Robyn said suspiciously.

'Maybe he's come to arrest his brother for murder.'

Robyn shot Gayle a look. 'That's not very funny.'

'I know. Maybe they're here for you.'

Robyn's heart leapt to her throat. That wasn't funny either.

34

Robyn watched the car door open.

'It's only Joe!' she said, relieved. And he wasn't in uniform. Joe was wearing a casual outfit, looking relaxed in faded jeans, a sweatshirt and trainers. He waved, but he hadn't seen them at the kitchen window. Joe was waving at someone in the garden – David.

'See, what did I tell you?' Gayle said in a sing-song voice. 'The cuffs will be coming out any minute now.'

'Oh, do shut up.' Robyn said, staring out of the window as David went over to greet his brother.

'What's this?' Robyn looked down at the tea towel that Gayle had placed in her hand.

'If you're going to stand here, you might as well be useful.'

Robyn reached for a plate and slowly wiped the rim, her attention riveted outside the window. Joe was patting David on the shoulder and said something, pointing at David's knee. David nodded and smiled.

Joe slapped David on the back as though he was happy with what he'd been told. Then David leaned close and started to talk animatedly. Joe's smile faded. When David had finished, they both turned in an instant and looked toward the house.

Gayle raised a soapy hand and waved.

Robyn backed away from the window. Were they talking about her – about what she'd asked David that morning?

'Where are you going?' Gayle grabbed her arm, making her sleeve wet. 'That plate is dry. You'll be rubbing the motif off.' Robyn looked down at the plate that she hadn't realised was still in her hand as Gayle lifted it from her grasp and deposited a wet one in its place.

Robyn moved back to the sink and looked again out of the window. Joe had returned to his car. The car door was open on the passenger side. He was casually resting a hand on the car roof, talking to somebody inside.

David had disappeared.

Robyn exhaled in relief. Gayle was right: she was being paranoid. Joe's visit had nothing to do with her, and the conversation with his brother had nothing to do with her either. She smiled at Gayle as she took another soapy plate off the draining board and dried it.

She stared at Joe, wondering who he was talking to. Was Annie in the passenger seat? Why hadn't she spotted her in the car when Joe had arrived?

David reappeared with Marty. They joined Joe, briefly chatting to the person in the car before Marty crossed the driveway, returning to the garden.

Robyn paused as Joe and David stepped away from the car, continuing their conversation. Joe had left the car door open. Sitting inside was a small child.

Robyn smiled when she realised who it was. Small for her age, Evie – Joe and Annie's daughter – was six years old. Robyn had met her several times over the course of the last three months while David had been living at Lark Lodge. She and David had babysat Evie together at Joe and Annie's house, and Evie had visited Lark Lodge often to see her favourite uncle and play in Gayle's large garden with Olive.

Evie adored the dog. She'd been badgering her parents for a puppy, and now she was badgering her parents for an Olive – which was out of the question in their small, two-bedroomed house with its through lounge and kitchen. They just didn't have the room for an Old English Sheepdog.

Evie loved bringing along ribbons and hair clips, making everybody smile when she made the long fur on Olive's head stand up in little tufts. It didn't seem to bother Olive. She just loved all the attention. Of course, all the ribbons came out as soon as Evie left.

Robyn picked up a mug from the draining board. As she wiped up the remaining plates and mugs, her attention wandered back to Evie, who was still sitting in the front seat, her head just above the dashboard. A little hand darted up and waved furiously. She'd spotted them at the kitchen window.

Robyn waved too.

'Is that Evie?' Gayle spotted her and waved.

Evie took that as her cue to get out of the car. She paused, looking in the direction of her dad and uncle. They had their backs to her, deep in conversation.

Robyn watched as she crept towards the house, realising that she'd probably been told to wait in the car.

A moment later, Evie came running into the kitchen. 'Robyn! Gayle!' She ran up to them.

Gayle said, 'Hello, petal,' and gave her a hug.

Robyn was next – little arms were thrown around her waist as Evie gave her a hug too. Evie tilted her head up at Robyn, showing her a gummy smile – she had lost her front baby teeth.

Robyn smiled down at the little girl, who was Joe's mini-me. There was no mistaking her for anyone other than Joe's daughter; she had his features and colouring, and his build. A round little girl, with a large round face, Evie loved playing with her dolls, plaiting their hair, and plaiting Olive's fur. Robyn remembered that David had told her about the time that Joe and Annie had bought her some ice-skates and had tried to get her on the ice. Evie had had none of it. That was why she hadn't been there when Joe and Annie had been skating on the frozen-over pond; a friend had been babysitting.

She let go of Robyn and saw Olive's empty dog bed by the Aga. 'Where's Olive?'

Gayle said, 'Ah, Olive is out at the moment, going for a run with Uncle Nick.'

Robyn glanced at Gayle. They exchanged a smile. Nick had become Uncle Nick, Gayle and Robyn had become aunties. It was a kid thing. Little Evie clearly loved her new grown-up friends so much that she now considered them pseudo-family.

'Oh!' Evie frowned. 'When are they coming back?'

Gayle cast her gaze at the clock on the wall. 'Soon, I expect.'

Evie ran over and sat cross-legged in Olive's dog bed, elbows on her knees, face planted in her hands, looking cross.

Robyn glanced out of the window. Joe had turned around and discovered his daughter was not in the car. He turned to the house. So did David.

Robyn walked over to Evie. 'I think your dad is looking for you.'

'I don't care. I want to see Olive.' She sat there, picking at the hem of her pretty floral dress.

'If you wait outside, you'll see her coming up the drive with Uncle Nick.'

Her face lit up. She scurried out of the dog bed and raced out of the kitchen.

Robyn felt a bit guilty for saying that. While it was true, Robyn's ulterior motive was to get her out of the house before David and Joe came inside to look for her. Even though Robyn had convinced herself that they weren't talking about her, Robyn could still feel the colour rising in her cheeks at the thought that David had told Joe about her outburst that morning. Cross with him for keeping secrets, she'd shouted, 'Don't tell me, then!' and had stormed out of their bedroom and down the stairs. She'd felt embarrassed at her childish outburst.

Robyn popped her head out of the kitchen and saw Evie standing in the open doorway of the house, her hands thrust inside the pockets of her dress. She turned around, spotted Robyn and ran up to her. Robyn stepped out into the hall, keeping an eye out for Joe and David appearing at the front door. 'What are you doing? I thought you were keeping an eye out for Olive?'

'It's my birthday,' she announced, her eyes dancing beneath thick black lashes. 'I'm six, and you're coming to my party.'

'Party?' Robyn had completely forgotten about that. She glanced at Gayle, who had appeared in the kitchen doorway. 'Well, happy birthday, Evie. That reminds me …' Gayle disappeared up the stairs. Robyn knew where she was going – to fetch the present she'd bought her.

Robyn looked back at the child standing right in front of her.

She didn't know how to say it, but she just had to tell her she couldn't go. She opened her mouth. 'Evie, look. I can't go to—' she stalled.

'Robyn can't go to the party, Evie.'

Evie turned around at the sound of her father's voice. He was standing in the doorway, his large frame squeezing out the daylight and dimming the hall. Robyn guessed the conversation outside had been about her after all. Joe had guessed that she'd decided not to come to the party. It was because of the argument she'd had with David that morning when she'd asked him to tell her about the incident in his father's shop.

She hadn't brought up the newspaper article she'd found. She hadn't had a chance before he'd stormed out in the garden.

She imagined that David felt, as she did, that it would be better if she didn't come along to the birthday party. They might spread an atmosphere because they weren't talking to one another – or, heaven forbid, have another argument in front of the children, and spoil Evie's birthday. She imagined that David had told Joe his feelings on the matter, and that Joe agreed.

'Why not?' Evie raised her voice and stamped one foot.

She turned back to Robyn, her voice a whisper. 'Please come to my party.' Her eyes wide, she leaned towards Robyn as if she were trying to hypnotise her with wide, saucer-like eyes into saying yes.

Robyn glanced over at Joe, who was still standing in the doorway.

'Don't you like me anymore?' Evie asked Robyn.

Robyn swallowed. 'Oh, that's not it at all.' She couldn't get the words out fast enough.

'Evie.' Joe said with a slight warning in his voice. He was

used to his daughter's endearing methods of getting her own way.

Evie turned around. 'She's *my* friend.' Evie stamped her foot. 'And it's *my* party. So I can have who I want.'

Robyn stared at Evie. She did have a point.

Evie turned around, chubby arms reaching up, angling for Robyn to pick her up.

Robyn picked her up. She was surprisingly heavy for one so small. She gave her a cuddle.

Evie wrapped her legs around Robyn's waist and rested her cheek against Robyn's. Suddenly Robyn felt determined that she wasn't going to let Evie down.

She whispered, 'I'll be there. I promise.' How could she refuse?

A little voice whispered in her ear, 'I knew you'd come.'

Robyn had absolutely no idea why Evie seemed to have formed such an attachment to her. And the amazing thing was that Robyn felt the same way.

'I agree with Evie,' said Gayle. She was still standing in the kitchen doorway. She eyed Joe crossly. 'It *is* her birthday.' Gayle put her hands on her hips. 'Surely she can choose who she wants to come to her party.'

Joe looked at Gayle. Then his eyes travelled to Robyn and Evie. He was outnumbered. Joe backed down.

Evie smiled at Gayle, then scowled at her dad, her grip tightening around Robyn's neck.

Robyn didn't know how she was going to show her face at the party, knowing that David had been having words with Joe about the argument between them that morning.

35

'Robyn and David can take my car,' said Gayle, as if it had all been amicably settled.

Robyn put Evie down and turned to Gayle. 'Now, hold on just one minute …' she said. *Why do I have to go with him?* she thought. Because he was going to the party too, obviously. Gayle couldn't go. She was looking after her mother.

Robyn had an idea. 'Joe, does Annie need some help preparing for the party? I'm not a great cook, but decorations I can do.'

'Ooh.' Evie cooed. 'Can you make pretty butterfly decorations? I like butterflies.'

'I'll try,' said Robyn softly.

Joe considered. 'Annie has been a bit …' he seemed to be searching for the right word, 'peaky lately.'

'Is she coming down with something?' Gayle asked.

Joe glanced at her and then turned to Robyn. 'I know she won't admit it, but I think she could do with some help.' He seemed to make up his mind. 'Yes, I'm sure she could.'

'Good, I'll come now then, shall I?'

Evie stood there, looking up at the adults. 'Does that mean

Robyn's coming to my party now?'

Joe rested an affectionate hand on the top of Evie's head. 'Yes, I guess it does, sweetheart.'

'But do we have to leave right now? I'm waiting to see Olive.'

Gayle stepped forward. 'Perhaps David can bring Olive to your party, if Nick doesn't mind.'

'Oh, can he?' Evie jumped up and down, clapping her hands. 'Then I can show all my friends how I put ribbons in her hair.'

Joe rolled his eyes, ready to put his boot in. 'It's fur, Evie. Dogs don't have hair. I really don't think that's a good—'

'Olive likes having ribbons in her hair.'

'I'm not talking about the ribbons. I'm talking about a dog coming to your party.'

Robyn could just imagine all those little six-year-olds dressing Olive with ribbons. With all that attention, Olive would be in her element. She'd seen Olive sitting there, still as a statue, while Evie dressed her fur like she was a dolly. She knew the dog would be so good. Even so, she could understand Joe's reluctance, having a big dog around small children.

'I'll keep an eye on Olive and make sure she behaves. If she doesn't, I'll take her outside. I promise.'

Robyn got another big hug from Evie. She wanted another cuddle again. Robyn picked her up.

Evie bounced up and down in her arms, so excited that Robyn thought she might drop her, or that her own neck was going to snap clean off.

Joe sighed. 'Come on, then. We'd better get going.' He walked out of the house.

It was Saturday morning. Robyn had things to do, but then again, she didn't fancy hanging around Lark Lodge, trying to avoid David. The house and grounds were big – but not that big. At some point, they'd run into each other. At least this way, she could get out of the house, do something productive and helpful for Evie and her mum, and then fade into the background when David arrived at the party later. If he borrowed Gayle's car to get there – he'd have to, because he hadn't bought himself another car yet – then Robyn intended to go home in that, leaving the party early, on her own. David could make his own way back to Gayle's. She hoped he stayed over at Joe's – or returned and slept on the sofa in the lounge.

'Wait just one minute.' Gayle held up a finger at Robyn, who was walking slowly to the front door with Evie still in her arms.

Robyn watched Gayle dart upstairs.

'What's this?' Robyn said when Gayle returned, carrying a large fabric bag. Robyn tried to put Evie down, but the little girl objected.

'Here.' Gayle took one of her arms and looped the bag over Robyn's arm.

'What is it?' She was half afraid the weight of the bag would send her and Evie toppling over, but it was unexpectedly light.

'Just take it and use it, will you?'

Robyn wondered what was in the bag, but she nodded anyway.

Gayle stood back, arms folded again, and eyed her up and down. 'I'm so glad you let me cut your hair.'

Gayle had cut it the previous night for the party which, this morning, after the row with David, Robyn had forgotten all about. Gayle had even put some highlights in her hair, and created subtle waves, giving it body, just like she'd done for Melissa. Last night, when they were still on good terms, David had looked at her, stunned, and said, 'Wow!'

'Your hair looks amazing, even though I do say so myself.' Gayle grinned.

'But I slept on it, and now I've lost the lovely wavy look. My hair is flat.'

'Hold on.' Gayle disappeared again, this time into the study, which had now been transformed into a zen space with self-help books, soft lighting, easy chairs, and a stereo system that played whale calls. It wasn't a room that Robyn ventured into much. Although in hindsight, she was wondering whether she should.

Gayle was back like a shot with another bag.

'What's this?'

Gayle handed it to Evie. 'They're tongs. I showed you how to create the look – remember? There's a makeup bag in there too. It's some samples I got free – blusher, mascara, lipstick, that sort of thing. You're welcome to give them a try. Otherwise, do you want me to pop upstairs to your bedroom to fetch some of yours?'

'No!'

Gayle took a step back and held up her hands. 'Okay – I was only trying to be helpful.'

'Sorry.' Robyn hadn't meant to be rude, but all this time, she'd managed to hide what she'd done to the bedroom. It was meant to be a surprise for Gayle. The last thing she wanted was the surprise to be spoiled just because Gayle went to fetch her makeup bag.

Gayle breathed a sigh. 'You've still got that argument on your mind, haven't you?'

Robyn looked at Evie. She didn't want to get into that in front of her little friend, who was getting very heavy in her arms.

'I'm going to put you down now, sweetheart.'

'All right.'

Robyn put Evie down. She didn't know what was in the large, sealed bag that Gayle had given her, but she thanked her all the same.

'It's for the party.'

'I know.'

Gayle leaned in and gave her a hug. 'Forget about David, and just go enjoy yourself.'

Evie took her hand. 'Come on.'

'Wait!'

Robyn turned around at the front door. She looked at Gayle quizzically. 'Have I forgotten something?'

'Yes. How are you going to get home?'

Robyn told Gayle the plan. 'If you don't mind David still borrowing your car to get to the party.' Robyn left out the part where she was going to ditch David and come back in Gayle's car alone.

'Not at all.' She walked up to the front door with them and happened to glance outside first. 'I think there's been a change of plan.'

Robyn stepped outside with Evie and turned around to look at Gayle. 'What?'

Gayle pointed.

Robyn followed her gaze to find that David was climbing into the car. 'Oh, no.' She had not considered the possibility that he was heading back with Joe and Evie straight away. But she should have. After all, what had Joe and Evie turned up at Lark Lodge for? He was collecting his brother.

Robyn immediately changed her mind about accompanying

Joe back to his house to help out Annie. She turned back to Gayle.

Gayle wagged her finger in Robyn's face. She beckoned at Evie. 'Don't even think about changing your mind. Now, have a good time. I will see you later.'

Gayle shut the door.

Robyn reluctantly turned to the car. Evie held her hand, pulling her forward.

As she walked over to the car, Joe opened the passenger door.

Robyn heard David exclaim, 'She's not coming with us, is she?'

Everyone knew who he was talking about – even Evie. 'She's my friend and she's coming to *my* party.'

Joe said, 'Well, I'm not going to argue with that.'

Robyn wasn't either.

David got out of the car.

Joe looked at his brother. 'Oh, for goodness' sake! Don't tell me you've decided you're not coming now.'

Evie looked at her uncle. 'You're not coming to my party?' she said, her voice rising several octaves.

After depositing the bag that Gayle had given her in the boot, Robyn stood up, throwing her arms wide, stretching. She felt her forearm connect with something hard that shouldn't have been there. Robyn turned in time to see the surprised look on David's face as he lost his balance and fell onto his rump, scattering stones of gravel in his wake. Joe rushed to his side and bent down, grasping his forearm. 'What happened – did you lose your balance?'

Joe's quick movement seemed to galvanise Robyn's body into

action. She had been rooted to the spot, mortified. After David had got out of the car, sending a clear message that he wasn't going to Evie's party, all because of her, she bet he thought she'd done it on purpose. She inwardly groaned, thinking, *could I make things any worse?*

Robyn darted from her spot and bent down, reaching for his other arm.

'Will you get off me!' David shook off Robyn and Joe's help, Obviously, neither of them were in his good books; Robyn for agreeing to go to the party and Joe for letting her.

Joe and Robyn sat back on their haunches on either side of David, and exchanged a smile, which turned into a fit of giggles, and then laughter.

David looked up at Robyn, then Joe. 'What's so funny?'

Evie giggled too. 'Uncle Davey, you're funny.'

Joe agreed. 'You did look, um, rather taken aback by the forearm to the face. It was kind of funny.'

'I guess you found the perfect clown for Evie's birthday.'

'You're going to be a clown at my party!' Evie took the comment literally, and clapped her hands. 'I like clowns.'

'Let's get you up, shall we?' Joe was trying to look anywhere but at David when his eyes roved over to Robyn. By the time David was on his feet, Joe was grinning again, and so was Robyn, both trying to contain another fit of giggles.

'Thank you,' said David with as much dignity as he could muster.

'Oh, don't thank us,' Joe said in an uncharacteristically high-pitched voice which made Robyn slap her hand over her mouth, trying to control the laughter.

David turned around and glared at them both.

Robyn gained her composure and avoided looking at Joe, who would just set her off again.

Joe scratched his head and tucked in his shirt. 'Ahem, right – let's get going, shall we?' He gestured toward the car. Joe avoided eye contact with David. Robyn did the same, skirting around him on the other side.

Joe opened the front passenger door. 'There you go, honey.' he said to Evie as Robyn sat down in the back seat.

'No. I want to ride in the back.'

'But you always want to ride in the front.' Joe paused and glanced at Robyn. 'Oh, I see.'

Robyn sighed in relief. She would much rather Evie joined her in the back. Joe unbuckled the booster seat in the front and fastened it in the back instead, next to Robyn.

Evie sat in the seat while Joe buckled her in. She waved her hand for Robyn to sit closer. Evie snuggled in and rested her head on Robyn's shoulder. She tilted her head and offered Robyn a sweet grin. Robyn shifted her arm off the back seat and wrapped it around Evie's shoulders. Satisfied by the show of affection, Evie faced the front, and so did Robyn. She caught David, who was now sitting in the front seat, staring at her over his shoulder. 'Sorry,' she mouthed silently at him.

He turned around and faced the front.

Robyn stuck her tongue out, wondering why she was bothering to apologise.

Evie giggled and stuck her tongue out at David too.

David whipped around and looked at them both, but he hadn't caught them. They were too quick. Both Robyn and Evie were innocently looking out of the side windows as Joe manoeuvred the car down the drive.

Joe turned into the street, and exclaimed, 'It's party time!'

Evie did a little happy jiggle in her seat.

Robyn exchanged a smile with Joe in the rearview mirror. Whatever David had told him about her, Joe had clearly forgotten about it – for the time being.

Unfortunately, the same couldn't be said for David. The falling-out earlier that morning was still fresh in Robyn's mind, and obviously wouldn't be forgotten by either of them any time soon.

36

Robyn sat at the table by the window in Joe and Annie's lounge-diner, which overlooked the small patch of grass they called a back garden. She thought of Marty and how he could transform their sorry excuse for a garden into a little oasis, with decking, and a patio, perhaps some artificial grass they didn't have to take care of, along with a little water feature, and maybe some pretty potted plants and some hanging baskets along their fencing.

'She's pretty,' Evie said, holding the angel that they had just decorated to go on her cake. Evie liked angels, Robyn had discovered. She didn't just like angels; she believed in them. Robyn turned her attention from the garden and smiled at her. Robyn started filling the small party bags – one for each of Evie's little friends who were coming to her party.

Joe stood on a ladder by the bay window in their lounge area, securing a string of letters along the curtain pole which spelt out the words *Happy Birthday* in bright colours. Annie was in the kitchen, preparing the party food.

Robyn looked across the room at David, who was sitting in an easy chair by the window, half-heartedly blowing up party balloons. He could at least make an effort, she thought crossly.

Everyone else was mucking in. Why had he even bothered to come? She watched him staring out of the window until Evie tugged on her arm to start decorating another angel for her cake.

'That's very good, Evie. Do you think you can do this all by yourself while I go and talk to Uncle David?' Evie wanted to make more angels, so Robyn drew an outline of one on a piece of coloured card and handed her a pair of child-friendly scissors, making sure Evie was holding the scissors correctly. There were crayons, glue and white crepe paper screwed up into little balls for her to draw the angel's faces and decorate the angel wings.

Joe got down from the ladder and took it out of the room.

Her eyes fixed on David, Robyn walked up to him and stood next to his chair with her arms folded. David was still looking out of the window. He turned his head towards her. She crouched in front of the chair, lowering her voice so Evie wouldn't hear.

'I know you don't want to be here. Well, neither do I.' Robyn paused to look over at Evie, who was still studiously cutting the coloured card, a look of stern concentration etched on her face.

'Actually, that's not true. I *do* want to be here. So … so stop being an ass, get those balloons blown up, and stop spreading an atmosphere.' She made to get up, but David caught her forearm, holding it gently.

She looked into his gorgeous brown eyes. He opened his mouth to say something.

Was he about to apologise?

'Auntie Robyn – look at my angel!'

David looked over at his niece. He shut his mouth. The moment was lost.

Robyn looked over at Evie too. 'That's wonderful, sweetie.'

'Come and help me decorate the angel.'

'Hold on, I'll be over in a minute.' Robyn had one final thing to say to David. 'You are not,' she whispered vehemently, 'going to spoil your niece's party. Do you understand?' She wagged her finger.

David stared at her.

Robyn stood up. 'Now, are you going to get busy like everybody else and make this a party to remember?' She folded her arms and tapped her foot impatiently, waiting for a response.

'What do you expect me to do?' David said helplessly. 'Just blow up these balloons?'

'That would be a start.'

Robyn picked up the bag of balloons on the side table by the window. 'Here.'

David picked out a red balloon and put it to his lips. He looked up at her. 'Are you going to stand there and watch me?'

Robyn cocked her head to one side. 'Maybe.'

He frowned at her.

'I want to see you put some enthusiasm into it.'

David made a show of blowing up the balloon as hard as he could, before tying the end. 'There – satisfied?'

'Now the rest.'

'All of them?'

'Oh, yes.'

When Robyn turned around, she caught Joe and Annie standing in the doorway with plates of party food, smiling at her.

She walked over, and shrugged. 'What?'

Annie handed her plate of party food over to Joe and took Robyn's hand. 'Come help me in the kitchen.'

Evie heard that. 'But I want Robyn to help me with my

angels.'

Joe said, 'Uncle David will help you when he's finished blowing up the balloons.'

There was a groan from the chair in the window.

Annie led her down the little hallway into their small kitchen, where Robyn asked her, 'What were you two smiling about?'

'I think David needs a kick up the backside. I'm afraid that after his accident—'

'Are you talking about the accident when his career ended?'

'I am. We all pussy-footed around him. It's about time someone came along and gave him what for.' Annie smiled at her as she slipped on a pair of oven gloves. 'Now, are you any good at icing fairy cakes?'

Robyn stared at her as she turned to the cooker and took out a tray of freshly baked little cakes. She hadn't thought to ask Annie about the burglary at the shop. Annie had brought it up – David's so-called accident. Now would be the perfect time to ask her what exactly had happened.

Annie said, 'We'll have to wait for them to cool a little, but it shouldn't take long. In fact, I could slip them in the fridge for a bit – what do you think?' She did it anyway before Robyn had a chance to reply.

'I'm probably overdoing it,' said Annie, as she reached in the cupboard for a box of icing sugar. 'She's already got a birthday cake, I know.' She shrugged. 'Well … it is her birthday.' Annie turned around with the icing sugar and had obviously noticed that Robyn was very quiet.

She put the box on the kitchen counter. 'What is it, Robyn? I noticed an atmosphere around you and David. Is something going on with you two?'

'Yeah, you could say that.'

'What happened? If you don't mind me asking?'

Robyn didn't mind at all. 'I asked David about his accident, the one that wrecked his career.'

'Ah, well, um …' Annie let out a nervous laugh. 'What did he say?'

'Nothing – that's the point. He won't talk about it at all.'

'Well, it's all water under the bridge now. I expect he just wants to move on.' Annie turned around and put the kettle on, busying herself with preparing the icing sugar. 'As do we all.'

Robyn stared at her back, thinking that it was a peculiar thing to say – *as do we all.*

Robyn wasn't going to drop it. 'Can you tell me what happened?'

Annie was just spooning some icing sugar into a glass bowl on the kitchen counter. She stopped what she was doing and turned around. 'Look, Robyn, that's all in the past.'

Robyn blurted, 'I know about the burglary at his father's shop.'

'What?' Annie nearly dropped the bag of icing sugar in her hand. 'Did Duncan tell you?'

Joe walked into the kitchen at that moment. He stopped in the doorway and looked from Robyn to Annie. 'What's going on?'

Annie said, 'Nothing. We were just icing some fairy cakes.'

'I thought I heard you talking about my dad …'

Robyn looked at him. He must have overheard a snippet of the conversation behind the door before he walked in. 'He is still coming to the party – isn't he?'

Annie laughed nervously again. 'Of course he is.'

'Then what were you two girls talking about?'

'Honestly, Joe. You know better than to ask that – just girl talk, that's all.'

Robyn stood there, staring at Annie.

Annie avoided eye contact with her as she scooted her husband out of the kitchen. 'Unless you want to help us ice some cakes, you'd better skedaddle.'

'Um, no thanks.' Joe backed out of the kitchen but not before Annie passed him a plate of sausage rolls. 'You can put those on the coffee table. Can you start clearing the dining table of Evie's arts and crafts bits and bobs? She'll have to stop making angels now. I've got a tablecloth I want to put on the table for the rest of the party food.'

'Evie is going to play up when I tell her it's all going away.'

'Well, read her a story, or something, keep her occupied until her friends arrive.'

Joe left them alone in the kitchen again.

Robyn turned from the door to look at Annie. She narrowed her eyes. What was she hiding?

'What really happened the night of the burglary, Annie?'

37

The doorbell rang. Robyn had already heard the sound of excited children's chatter as they ran up to the front door; the party guests had arrived.

Evie clambered off David's lap and shouted out, 'I'll answer the door!' The book he was reading to her was instantly forgotten. David looked up and caught Robyn's gaze. 'What is it?'

She'd been wrong about David – that was what was on her mind after she'd spoken to Annie, who had told her what had really happened on the night he'd come across the burglars.

Robyn opened her mouth to say something when Annie and Joe appeared in the room.

'Where's Evie?'

David looked over at them. 'Her friends have arrived. She's gone to answer the door.'

Joe smoothed down his hair and tucked in his shirt. He'd changed into beige chinos and a light blue shirt for the party.

Annie hastily removed her apron. She looked down at her dress, presumably checking for any signs of flour, icing sugar or other ingredients she might have spilled down herself while preparing for the party.

She turned to Joe. 'Do I look okay?'

Robyn noticed she'd even slipped on some heels.

Joe smiled at his wife. 'You look gorgeous, as ever. But …'

'What is it?' Annie asked, studying his face.

'You've got a little bit of flour right here.' He licked a finger, and gently wiped it away from her cheek.

'Oh, Joe – now I'll have to go and reapply some foundation.'

'Sorry.'

David stood up as Annie left the room. He'd also dressed for the occasion. Robyn hadn't realised that he must have nipped up to their room and changed out of the clothes he'd been gardening in while she was eating breakfast with Gayle, just before Joe had arrived that morning.

Robyn found it faintly amusing and quite sweet that all the adults were acting as though they were at a job interview. Even David was standing to attention, ready to greet Evie's friends.

Robyn looked down at her dirty, faded dungarees. She had glue on the trousers and icing sugar down her top. And her fingers were covered in yellow crayon where she'd been helping Evie colour in the angels. *I'm a mess*, thought Robyn.

Just to make her feel even more self-conscious over what she was wearing, Annie reappeared; she'd put on some jewellery – a nice set of beads and a matching bracelet. Robyn sighed. Why hadn't she thought to bring anything with her to change into?

She glared at David. It was all his fault. If they hadn't rowed that morning …

She caught Annie looking anxiously at her.

Robyn threw her a reassuring smile. She'd promised that she wouldn't repeat what Annie had told her in the kitchen. It was their secret. Hers, Annie's and David's. There was just one adult in the room who had no clue what had really happened during that burglary. No wonder Annie had scooted her husband out of the kitchen before Robyn said anything more. Joe was the only person in the dark about that night.

Robyn stole a glance at David. The question on her mind was whether or not to tell David that she knew.

She'd be telling Melissa – but not what she'd found out; she couldn't do that. She'd get David and Annie in huge trouble. Annie had no clue that Robyn had a friend, a budding lawyer, keen to look into *the case*. But now Melissa didn't have to. There was just one thing bothering Robyn – David had good reason to keep his past to himself, but she had a feeling that Melissa wasn't the sort of person to back down once she had her claws into something. *I'll just have to persuade her to let it go*, thought Robyn. She knew Melissa wanted to return the favour after her makeover, which had done the trick, getting her a date with the man of her dreams. Perhaps something else would crop up where she'd need a lawyer and some legal advice in the future. Robyn hoped not.

Evie ran into the lounge, followed by several small children from her class at school, all carrying presents for Evie.

Robyn realised something with a jolt. *Oh, god! I forgot to bring Evie's present.*

She looked around in dismay and spotted the large fabric bag, which had been all but forgotten on the chair in the corner. She grabbed it, along with the small bag containing the tongs – perhaps she could at least do something with her hair. She sidled out of the room. She doubted, with all the commotion of girls running around, and adults trying to calm them down, and parents – looking equally well turned out – walking in, that she'd be missed. She ran up the stairs, praying that Gayle had miraculously provided some unexpected gift for Evie.

Opening the first door she came to, Robyn stepped into what was the main bedroom. Robyn flung the bag on the bed and prised it open. At first, the plastic bag appeared to be empty. When she looked inside, all she could see was black nothingness. Robyn sunk her arm inside and fished around the bag. She touched something soft. Pulling it out, she breathed a sigh of relief. Gayle had somehow found something for her to give to Evie as a present in lieu of the doll she'd already bought but had forgotten in the rush to leave.

Robyn pulled out the soft, silky item. 'What the ...?' She held it up. 'This can't be right.' It was a dress, and it wouldn't fit Evie, surely. It was too grown-up. Robyn frowned. What was Gayle thinking?

Robyn clutched the dress to her chest and turned around to see herself reflected in a long mirror standing in the corner of the room. 'Oh, I get it.' she said aloud, realising that it wasn't for Evie at all, and thinking back to Gayle eyeing her up and down, taking in her dungarees and oversized t-shirt before she left.

Still holding the dress over her dungarees, Robyn turned sideways, not taking her eyes off the mirror, wondering what it would look like on. 'It kind of suits me.'

Robyn took off her dungarees and t-shirt and slipped on the dress. It wasn't a perfect fit; it was perhaps more suited to someone with a fuller bosom, but it was the colour that made it special – it was a deep purple satin material that gave off a different hue depending on the light. It was very flattering, hugging her figure in all the right places, apart from her chest, but she could do something about that.

Robyn scooped up her clothes and scooted out of the

bedroom and into the bathroom next door. She tore off some handfuls of loo paper and stuck them down the dress. Popping her dirty clothes in the bag to take home, she returned to the bedroom and did some adjustments so that the unseen filler was even on both sides.

She did a twirl in the mirror. The dress fell just above the knee, and one strap hung off the shoulder, which she imagined was the style.

Is it too much for a children's birthday party? That was the question. Robyn glanced at the other bag. If she was quick, she could do her hair too and apply a little bit of makeup.

She raced over and took the other bag with her back into the bathroom. She laid out the tongs and makeup samples. And there, in the bottom of the bag, she discovered a small package wrapped up in children's wrapping paper. Robyn didn't recognise the package, but the tag said it was from her. 'Oh, Gayle. You are amazing!'

Robyn applied the makeup, and used the tongs to create soft waves. Back in the bedroom, she did another quick twirl in front of the mirror, turned left, then right, and finally looking over her shoulder at her outline. 'Not bad.' She grinned at her reflection. 'Even if I do say so myself.' Then her eye caught something in the mirror that did look bad. She looked at her feet. On the floor, where she'd slipped them off to try on the dress, were her dirty old trainers.

'Ah well.' Robyn said, resigned to wearing her dungarees at the party. She couldn't possibly wear such an amazing dress with those. *It was a nice thought while it lasted.* She started to unzip the dress, feeling disappointed that she couldn't wear it after all. Then her eyes roved to the bag. It was a big bag, but surely there wouldn't be a pair of shoes inside. Once again, she felt inside, and to her surprise withdrew a pair of strappy, heeled black shoes. 'I don't bloody believe it.'

But they won't fit, will they? Robyn held them up in front of her. Tentatively, she put one on. It was a little tight, but they would do. 'Gayle, I could kiss you,' Robyn said as she put the other shoe on. She stood in front of the mirror and did the zip of the dress back up. She fiddled with her hair a little, running her fingers through it, and leaned in towards the mirror, taking in her barely-there makeup. At least she had good skin.

She took one last look in the long mirror. The dress was still a little big on top, the shoes a little small. But despite that, she felt sexy. She felt like a real woman. She laughed at that thought. It made it sound like she had just been pretending to be one all this time.

Robyn flicked her hair again, and pouted her lips. The bright red lipstick was rather nice. At least she would look as though she had made an effort for Evie – that was what was important.

Robyn left the room, carrying Evie's present, and closed the door behind her. Then she lost her nerve. She was about to rush back into the bedroom when she heard young children singing *Happy Birthday*, accompanied by some adults. She hurried along the upstairs hall. She did not want to miss Evie blowing out her birthday candles and making a wish.

She kicked off the shoes and picked them up, holding them in one hand with the present tucked under her arm and holding the stair rail with her other hand, just in case she tripped over her own feet. She walked briskly down the stairs, hoping that in the furore of the party, no one would notice her slipping back into the room.

Robyn slipped on the strappy black sandals, straightened her dress and ran her fingers through her hair – checking her appearance just in case someone did see her slip back into the room – and then pushed open the door.

38

When Robyn reappeared wearing that dress, there were now only three adults in the room – the parents must have dropped off their kids, taken one look at the chaos of too many children running around a very small space, quickly made their excuses, and left. All the children were gathered around the cake. Joe had a lighter. He was about to light the candles.

Standing tall in her heels, she suddenly felt self-conscious. Joe, Annie and David were rooted to the spot and were staring at her across the room.

Robyn quickly checked her dress. Nothing was hanging out, like a long piece of bog roll that had escaped her cleavage. Everything was in order. She tugged the dress a bit further down her hips and looked up, wondering why they were staring.

'Oh, thank god. I haven't missed it.' She realised the *Happy Birthday* she'd heard them all singing must have been a practice run while someone carried out the birthday cake and set it on the table in the dining area.

Robyn looked at the lighter in Joe's hand. 'Please don't let me interrupt you.'

Annie stepped forward. 'Oh, but you already have.' Annie

walked over. 'You look …'

Robyn felt suddenly embarrassed. It was just as she had thought. 'The outfit is a bit too … grown-up for the party, isn't it?' Robyn didn't know how else to express what she was thinking.

'... stunning.' Annie breathed. 'I was going to say that you look absolutely stunning. You need to wear this sort of thing more often, do you know that?'

'I do?' said Robyn feeling flustered by all the attention. She glanced over Annie's shoulder first at Joe, then at David.

'Uh-huh.' Annie said, linking her arm as though Robyn had just joined a secret club and was now a fully-fledged member.

'Shall we join them?' Robyn said, looking at the children seated around the table and longing to sit down so that she didn't have to walk too far in the shoes and really embarrass herself.

'What, in that dress?' Annie turned serious. 'With this lot?' Annie shot a look at the table. 'That dress needs to stay away from sticky fingers, snotty noses and the like. Let's watch from afar.'

As soon as Joe lit the candles, Evie wasted no time blowing them out, scrunching up her eyes while she presumably made a wish.

Robyn was led away, giving the table full of excited, hungry children a wide berth. 'I think I know someone who would like a closer look,' said Annie, grinning.

'What do you mean?' Robyn asked, tottering along on the heels. She couldn't wait to slip them off before she fell over and made a prat of herself. Robyn was feeling embarrassed and awkward, especially when she realised that some parents were, in fact, still there.

She hadn't noticed them at first when she'd walked into the

room. She caught a couple of the dads staring at her, one with his hand suspended in mid-air, about to take a bite out of a sausage role. The woman standing next to him slapped him on the arm, trying to get his attention and presumably to stop him staring.

Annie steered her right up to where David was standing by the window. He was staring at her too. Annie planted her opposite him and whispered in Robyn's ear before leaving them alone, 'I think I'm right in saying you've blown him away.'

Robyn didn't care for her choice of words. Her eyes followed Annie back to the throng at the party table. If she had known that wearing the dress meant she'd have to steer clear of Evie and her adorable little friends, she wouldn't have put the stupid thing on.

Robyn raised her eyebrows and turned around to find David still speechless. Why wasn't he saying anything? She asked, 'Is there something the matter?'

'That dress …'

Robyn pulled the hem of the skin-tight dress down a little. It was riding up her thighs. 'Urrgh. It looked lovely in the mirror. Then I tried to walk in it.' She looked down at her feet. 'And as for these!' Robyn sat down in the chair by the window, slipping off the sandals. She looked up. David was still standing in front of her, still staring.

'Oh for goodness' sake, why don't you sit down?' She motioned at the other chair, almost touching hers in the little bay window.

David slowly took a seat. 'You look …'

'Stunning – I know.' Robyn rubbed her sore foot. 'I need a drink.' Robyn stood up.

David caught her hand.

She turned to him, surprised.

'Robyn, I'm so sor—'

'Uncle Davey! Uncle Davey!' Evie squealed, nudging past Robyn and grasping David's other hand, trying to pull him out of his seat. 'I'm opening my presents now.'

Helped by Evie, David shot out of his seat and nearly lost his balance. Robyn instinctively reached for his arm to steady him. The knee was healed, but she still worried he'd have another fall, which she realised was pretty silly; they were in a carpeted room, and most evenings he was out on an ice rink, teaching. That was when she should be worried.

David took her hand in his and smiled at his niece. 'We'll be right there.'

'Wait – Evie. I have something for you.' Robyn still had the little box with the children's wrapping paper and pretty bow. 'Here you are, sweetheart. Happy birthday.'

Evie tore off the wrapping paper. Inside was a pale cream square box. It looked like a jewellery box. Evie squealed in delight.

'It's an angel necklace!'

Robyn said, 'What?'

'It's the best present ever!'

Robyn smiled at the little silver angel hanging from the chain. 'So it is,' she said, trying to hide her surprise.

Robyn didn't know how she managed to kneel down for a kiss in the dress. But she did, feeling guilty that she hadn't actually picked out the present.

Evie ran over to her mum and dad to show them the necklace. 'Can I put it on?'

'Of course you can, sweetheart,' said Annie, throwing Robyn an appreciative smile for being so thoughtful.

Robyn thought of the doll, the biggest one she could find in Aviemore, which was still on her bed, waiting to be wrapped.

David took her hand again. 'I thought you bought her a doll?'

Robyn shrugged. 'We girls have our secrets, you know.'

David turned to look at her. 'Don't I know it.'

Robyn shot him a look. 'It's not my fault I still can't remember.'

'If you say so.'

Robyn frowned at him. 'I told you. I don't remember anything before the accident on Christmas Day.'

'All right, Robyn.' David sighed. 'Perhaps one day you'll trust me with your secrets.'

He still didn't believe her. She shot back, 'Perhaps one day you'll trust me with yours.'

'What does that mean?'

She glanced at Annie and shut her mouth. She'd promised not to speak about it; not unless David brought it up – and certainly not there, at a party, with lots of other people who might overhear. Annie had told her she had to be careful not to repeat what she'd said. Of course, she understood why. It wasn't David who had picked up the gun and fired it in the botched burglary. Melissa had been right – he'd been protecting someone; someone he was prepared to take the fall for, and go to prison for if he had to. But it wasn't his brother, as Robyn had first thought. Although in a roundabout way, it was him he was protecting.

It was David's sister-in-law, Annie. She had been there on a rare night out with her friends and had passed by the Gillespie store in her car when she too had noticed something going on inside. Her protective instincts had kicked in, and she'd rushed inside, catching the burglar who'd shot at David by surprise. Startled, he'd backed up right into a shelving unit, knocking the gun out of his hand. The gun had skidded along the floor to Annie's feet. She'd picked it up, and just like Joe had taught her, she'd aimed. After she'd discharged the gun once, felling the burglar, she'd dropped it.

David, despite lying there in agony, had picked up the gun and fired off a shot. He'd watched CSI enough times to realise he needed gun residue on his hands if he was going to make it look believable. There was no way he'd let his sister-in-law be charged, or go to prison. Annie had a child. Annie had Joe. His reasoning was that his life was over – his career was gone. He had known that the minute the bullet hit. But his brother and sister-in-law's life together wasn't going to be over that night too.

Robyn suddenly put her arms around David, and squeezed him tight. He was a hero in her eyes. She whispered, 'Let's just start over, from today. What does the past really matter? I can't remember, and I don't want to. I just want to be here, with you, and nothing is going to get in the way of that.'

When David didn't answer, she dropped her hands from his neck, and stepped back.

He said, 'What about what you said – *perhaps one day you'll trust me with your secrets*?'

Robyn's eyes drifted over to Annie. 'Forget I said that.'

David followed her gaze. He raised his eyebrows. 'Did Annie … say something?'

Robyn debated whether to tell him or not. She nodded. 'Yes, everything. Sorry.'

David surprised her by smiling. 'Don't be sorry.'

'I don't want any more secrets between us.'

There was something Annie hadn't had a chance to tell her – what exactly had happened in the aftermath. She whispered, 'Did you … go to prison?' She looked about her, aware she really shouldn't be having this conversation right now. However everybody was gathered around the table on the other side of the room, watching Evie eagerly unwrapping the rest of her presents. Nobody could overhear them.

David shook his head. 'I was charged with manslaughter, but a very, very good lawyer got me off – self-defence.'

'Oh, I'm so relieved.'

'Yes, so was I.'

'And that was the end of it?' Robyn asked.

David hesitated. 'Oh, er … yeah. Yeah, of course.'

There was a noticeable inflection in his voice as he said that.

Robyn also noticed he was avoiding eye contact. She studied him for a long moment. He was looking uncomfortable under her gaze. She'd said she didn't want any more secrets between them. She had a feeling there was more to the story than he was letting on; something even Annie didn't know about.

'I'm going to get a slice of birthday cake. Do you want some?'

Robyn eyed him. 'Yes, all right.'

'Great!'

Robyn turned to look out of the window, thinking, *How well can anybody really know another person?* How well did David know her? He might have his secrets, but she knew she was guilty of keeping secrets too; it wasn't true when she'd said to him, *I can't remember*. That made it sound as though her memories hadn't come back at all. It had been true when she'd told him that she didn't want to remember; she just wanted to be there, in the moment, with him. The trouble was that her memories were seeping through the seams of her protective armour against the past.

She'd had some memories, more like flashbacks; things she hadn't shared with David. She couldn't tell him what had happened during her visit to the bookshop with Melissa. The last thing she wanted him to find out was what she'd asked Melissa to do – look into his past. Thankfully, that little spying episode was over. She just had to convince Melissa of that.

Robyn didn't want to think about the past anymore – his or hers. She turned from the window as he approached, carrying two paper party plates, each with a generous slice of chocolate birthday cake.

'You're looking very pensive. What are you thinking?'

Robyn cast her gaze around Annie and Joe's lounge-diner, which was filled with mementos of their lives together – framed photos of their family, and prints they'd bought, and nick-nacks they'd chosen together. And of course the most important thing of all – the memories they were making together.

Robyn looked at David, and said, 'I want this.'

'This?' He cast his gaze around the room. 'A two-up, two-down terraced property in a village?'

'No, not *this*, silly.' Robyn playfully slapped his arm. 'Although it is a lovely little home. But what I meant was that I'm thinking about the future – our future, you and me.' They couldn't keep living together in one room in Lark Lodge. She loved the place, and Gayle, Nick, Marty and Olive, but looking around Annie and Joe's home, she realised what was missing – a home of her own – of *their* own – to make their own memories together as a couple.

David smiled knowingly. 'Come live with me at the boathouse.'

Robyn turned her attention back to David. 'What?'

'Don't get me wrong; I love Lark Lodge almost as much as you do, and all the guys who live there – even Olive, who steals my fried bacon in the morning.'

Robyn laughed. It was true.

'But I want to go back to my own house.'

'Why haven't you?'

'Oh, my god. Why do you think? I was waiting for you.'

'For me?'

'Of course. For you to be ready to leave. I think that time has come.'

Robyn smiled. 'I think so too.'

'So – is that a yes?'

Robyn hesitated, wishing she hadn't had a feeling of déjà vu – no, it was more than that, a *memory* of sitting in a car outside the boathouse. She'd been there before the trip with Duncan in his car.

David frowned. 'I know what you're thinking – what about my dad?'

Robyn had been thinking no such thing. She asked, 'What about your dad?'

'Well, he's obviously got to move out before we move in.'

Robyn was about to ask why, but that was a conversation for another time. She wasn't going to move anywhere if it meant Duncan had to leave the boathouse – leave his home, his son.

Unfortunately, David still hadn't mended bridges with his

dad. Duncan needed to tell him just what had transpired – his mother having an affair and choosing to leave her boys.

Evie came running over and stood between them, taking Robyn's hand, then David's. 'Uncle Davey, Auntie Robyn, you have to come see my presents.'

As she propelled them forward, Robyn caught David smiling affectionately at his niece. Robyn smiled too, as in that moment she suddenly had a strong sensation that she was glimpsing her future. She looked at Evie, and thought of the baby she'd lost. She was hoping for a second chance at motherhood. Perhaps this time, it would be with the right person.

39

Gayle's birthday came and went, soon after Evie's, as adult birthdays tend to do with very little fanfare – along with the birthday surprise that Robyn couldn't wait to show her. Gayle loved the redecorated bedroom, of course, and laughed when she'd discovered why Robyn had been keeping her bedroom door locked – it wasn't because the young couple were afraid someone would walk in on them, as Gayle had assumed, or would see how messy they'd left their love nest when they were both out.

Gayle declared that she didn't mind in the least when Robyn confessed that she'd borrowed the old family photographs to try and recreate the décor of the room from days gone by. Although Gayle had no clue what had been going on behind Robyn's bedroom door, the fact that she had already started redecorating the rest of the house made her wonder if that might have given it away.

But it was the reaction of Gayle's mother to the restored bedroom that really made Gayle's birthday something special, for the memories had enlivened Gayle's mother to the point where she had her most lucid day in a long, long time, and even remembered Gayle's birthday. This was probably the best gift of all, for it turned out that the bedroom Robyn had redecorated had been Gayle's childhood bedroom.

The one thing Robyn was not going to tell Gayle about on her birthday was their plan to move out. They had decided to tell her soon after. Robyn hadn't had the heart to mention it before, and now another month had passed, and the redecoration of the rest of the house was in full swing, so their move had been pushed back even further.

'You're going to have to tell her some time,' David had said, offering to tell her himself.

She'd promised she would find the right time. In the meantime, with everyone's help – David's, Nick's, Marty's – the redecorating was progressing well. Even little Evie helped when she came round to visit; she always brought with her a spare set of painting clothes so she could join in too, slapping paint on the walls, her dungarees, her trainers, and everyone else in close proximity. Even Olive ended up with paint on her fur.

Gayle's objections to all the work, and the cost, fell entirely on deaf ears, and she knew she would not change Robyn's mind.

As the house renovation progressed, and Gayle could see the pleasure it gave Doris to witness the house being restored to its former glory, Gayle's objections lessened – although she never stopped voicing her concern over where all the money was coming from to do the place up or how she would ever repay everybody.

Robyn and David had started paying rent for their room, feeling it was unfair that Marty and Nick were paying guests without them paying too. Still, there was the matter of back rent that Robyn insisted she owed.

Gayle knew it was costing Robyn far more in materials to do the place up than the amount she owed in rent money. *I should be paying you to do all this*, Gayle had insisted. Robyn knew she didn't have the money, and besides, even if she had, Robyn had told her she wouldn't take a penny.

Gayle then said that she had a business proposition instead, and that before Robyn objected she wanted her to seriously think about it. She wanted Robyn to be her business partner when Lark Lodge became a fully-fledged guesthouse. Gayle told her that Robyn wouldn't have to do a thing – she intended to run it herself. But her mum wasn't going to be around forever, and neither was Gayle. And after what she'd found out about her brothers and sister, she did not want the family home to fall into their hands if something were to happen to her.

Robyn suddenly understood where she was coming from. She'd shaken her head, reminding Gayle that she had nieces and nephews.

'They are more than taken care of by their parents. They don't need this house, and they won't want it. They'll just sell it. But you, Robyn – you love this house.'

'I know, it's true.' Robyn had stared at her wide-eyed, amazed that she would even consider passing the guesthouse to her. She didn't know what to say, although she had expressed her gratitude at such a lovely idea. 'The thing is, Gayle, I couldn't possibly accept, and besides …' Robyn hadn't known quite how to say what was on her mind without sounding ungrateful, but she'd just had to be honest, and had told her. 'Gayle, I haven't got time to run a guesthouse.'

'Not right now. But who knows what the future holds …' Gayle had let the sentence hang, giving Robyn the impression that it was already decided.

Robyn stood with a paintbrush in hand, staring at the wall in the hallway and thinking about that conversation with Gayle. For once, she was the only one in the house, so no one would catch her lost in thought. Of course, Robyn wouldn't want the house to fall into Gayle's siblings' hands. Gayle had also been thinking about how she'd protect her mum. It was something Gayle's father obviously hadn't considered when he'd left the house to Gayle, with a view that her mother, his dear wife, would be able to live out her days there. But what if, heaven forbid, something were to happen to Gayle first?

Robyn couldn't take care of Doris, but round the clock carers could come and look after her.

And Gayle was right: Robyn did love the house. Robyn didn't want to become business partners with Gayle, because that would mean Gayle would hand over a percentage of the guesthouse profits to her. Robyn wasn't having any of that. She had plenty of work, and income, from Rose's lovely new neighbours on the housing estate, and her shop in Duncan's grocery store was proving quite the hit – her window display was attracting people inside to look at blinds and curtains, and to consider interior redesign ideas that didn't have to cost a fortune, such as re-covering old sofas with new fabric, or just buying some colourful scatter cushions to brighten up a room.

Robyn smiled. It wasn't just her outlet that was doing well; Alec's idea for a haberdashery corner for needlework, sewing, and mending – selling everything from buttons, ribbons and thread to knitting needles, scissors and iron-on tape – was also going down a treat with local people, and even with tourists who needed a needle and thread or a spare button. It wouldn't earn

Alec millions, but it was a good, steady income while he was a student.

The only reason that Robyn was at Lark Lodge that day, decorating on her own while everyone else was at work, and Doris was at her weekly community session, was that Robyn now had help in the shop. It meant she actually got a day or two off each week.

Annie worked as a part-time teaching assistant two days a week in Evie's school, but she had the rest of the week free, and the school holidays, so she worked with Robyn too.

Evie enjoyed helping her mum and Auntie Robyn in the cushion shop, as Evie called it. When Evie was there, she spent her time either playing with her dolls or reading a book on a large cushion. Sometimes she rang up purchases on the till and entertained customers with her cute impression of a shop assistant. She took her role very seriously. She knew how to operate the card machine, and always said, 'Have a nice day!' when people left. It was something she'd seen on American television programmes.

That day, Annie was minding the shop. It wasn't like Robyn to take a day off mid-week, when no one else was home, but she wanted a day to herself to think things through.

Something belted out of the kitchen, giving Robyn a fright.

'Oh, Olive! You scared me.' Robyn had forgotten she wasn't actually all alone in the house. She knelt down. 'I'm going to miss you so much – do you know that?'

Robyn put the paintbrush down. 'I suppose I might as well tell you first.' She sat cross-legged on the floor, giving Olive lots of fusses. Olive tried to climb in her lap, circling around, flicking Robyn's nose with her tail. 'Hey, you're too big for that now. You won't fit.' She had just about fitted a few months earlier, when she had first moved into Lark Lodge with Nick. But now she was almost fully grown.

Olive stopped and stood in front of her.

Robyn reached out and smoothed her fur down around her eyes. 'David and I will be moving out soon.'

Olive whined, as if she knew exactly what Robyn was saying.

'I know. I don't want to leave either, but you know, life moves on. You'll find that out one day. The estate where Rose lives will be finished at some point, and … well I expect you and Nick will be moving on to. Nothing lasts forever.' Robyn choked back a sob, surprised at how emotional she was feeling about telling Olive all this. She didn't know how she would tell Gayle.

David had sat down with her last night, taking her hands in his. She'd known the conversation would come up sooner or later. Every time he'd attempted to bring it up since Evie's birthday party, Robyn had found a way to avoid it – the conversation about when exactly they would be leaving.

The previous night, she hadn't been able to avoid it any longer. They'd made a decision. Things had come to a head because Duncan was moving out of the boathouse, helped in no small part by Robyn. It hadn't been her idea. She'd wanted Duncan to stay, but he wouldn't hear of it. As soon as he'd heard the plan for Robyn and David to move in together, he'd decided to move into the flat.

Robyn recalled her and David's reaction – *what flat?*

It turned out that the loft Duncan used for storage in the eaves of the shop wasn't a loft at all, but a large apartment with skylights, unused for decades. His ex-wife had lived there with her parents before Duncan and she had married and they had taken over the shop. By the time they had their two boys, they had bought the house where the boys grew up.

Robyn wasn't surprised by the row that ensued when David found this out, shouting at Duncan that he could have moved into the flat or rented it out for an income. In fact, he still could rent it out and live somewhere else if he didn't want to live above his work. The crux of the matter was the fact that Duncan hadn't had to move in with his son at all.

But David didn't understand. Duncan had wanted to be with his son. And she suspected Duncan hadn't wanted to move into the flat where he'd courted the love of his life. All it would do was remind him of her and bring back painful memories.

But now Duncan was doing just that. Since finding out about the flat, Robyn, Alec and Annie had been going after work to help Duncan sort it out ready to move into. The last of the dwindling cash in Robyn's rucksack had been used to redecorate the place, which was stuck in a seventies time warp, and to reupholster the old furniture. It was now a bright, airy open plan living area, painted in white. The old-fashioned kitchen, with very seventies beige kitchen units, was in a surprisingly good condition. All Duncan had needed were new white goods. Even the old green bathroom with orange wall tiles in a large, vibrant psychedelic pattern had grown on Robyn.

Robyn had ordered some blinds for the skylights, and some plain curtains to hang at the kitchen and bathroom windows. As she'd told Duncan while she polished the old G-plan furniture, seventies kitsch was back in fashion. She could tell he really didn't care about what was fashionable, as long as it was functional. But he was obviously rather taken with his new abode.

She'd suggested a little get-together, a house party among

family and friends, to celebrate him moving into his new home, but Duncan really didn't want any fanfare. He'd packed his suitcase a few days earlier and had moved out of the boathouse – just like that. The only reason Robyn knew about it was when she'd turned up to work in the shop and Duncan had arrived with his suitcase.

Now the boathouse was standing empty – something David wasn't happy about. He'd wanted his dad to move out, but now there was no one living there. Robyn understood his concerns. David still hadn't mentioned the burglary at his house, when all that cash had been stolen. She'd reassured him that it would be okay with the burglar alarm, but she couldn't avoid the conversation any longer. And so their moving date had been decided. Robyn had started to pack to leave Lark Lodge.

She looked at Olive and stroked her long fur. 'I'll come back and visit, I promise. You can visit us too. You'll love the boathouse, you and Nick, and Marty. You can all come. And Gayle, and her mum. We won't be far, just down the road. The thing is, Olive, I'm going to miss you. All of you.'

Robyn thought she heard a click. When she turned around, Gayle was standing in the hallway, a bag of shopping in her hands. She dropped the shopping bag. 'You're leaving?'

40

Robyn twiddled the pen in her hand, trying to concentrate on the form she was filling in for a customer's curtain order. She was standing at the counter, a large book of swatches open in front of her along with the measurements she'd taken at her customer's house. The paperwork normally didn't take her so long, but she was finding that she just couldn't concentrate.

Robyn sighed. 'It's no use,' she said to herself, lifting the cover of the swatch book and slamming it closed.

She heard the familiar jangle of the shop bell. She saw Annie walking towards her and smiled as she approached. 'Thanks for minding my shop yesterday, Annie, while I had the day off.' Robyn had finished the last of the painting in the hall. Apart from some fabric that was on order to re-cover the sofas in the lounge, and some new curtains and blinds, Lark Lodge was almost ready to open as a guesthouse.

'Not at all, Robyn.'

Robyn glanced at the clock on the wall. 'You're early.'

Annie nodded. 'I didn't stop to chat to any of the parents this morning after I dropped Evie off at school.'

Duncan walked by, carrying a box of produce to put in the

shop window. 'Good morning, Annie.'

'Hi Duncan. How's things?'

Robyn caught Annie's eyes roving up to the ceiling and guessed she was thinking about Duncan's move upstairs.

Duncan replied, 'I'm fine. I wish everyone would stop asking me that question!'

Annie turned to Robyn, wide-eyed, and whispered, 'Someone got out of the wrong side of the bed this morning.'

Robyn sighed. 'He's like that every morning since he moved upstairs.'

Annie didn't look surprised.

Robyn wasn't either.

'What about if he had some company up there?'

'What do you mean … like a pet?'

They both turned to look at Olive, who was fast asleep on the large cushion that Evie liked to sit on and read. After collecting Evie from school, Annie normally brought her back to the shop for a bit before they went home.

For a while, Olive had been going to work with Nick, who would drop her off at Rose and George's house, but now they'd made new friends who'd moved into their development, they were often out and about with them. The last Robyn had heard, they led quite the social life and were hardly ever home. Robyn found it quite amusing, considering she'd done up their home just the way Rose liked it, for her to enjoy – and now they were hardly ever there.

Doggy daycare for Olive switched between the shop and Lark Lodge – the latter when Gayle wasn't out doing her mobile hairdressing; she rarely visited clients at their homes anymore.

Robyn rubbed her temples and put her pen down, casting

the paperwork to one side.

'Anything I can help with?' asked Annie, taking her coat off.

'Perhaps you could fill out this order for me. I just can't concentrate this morning.'

Annie joined her at the counter. 'You told her – didn't you?'

'What?'

'Gayle – about you and David moving out.'

'Oh, that.'

'What did you think I was talking about?'

Robyn was thinking of Melissa. Her friend still kept in touch. She'd had a text that morning to say she was sitting her final exams soon and returning home. Part of her finals was a dissertation she'd researched based on an idea Robyn had given her. It was to do with someone falsely admitting to a crime to protect someone, and what would happen if the truth came out.

Robyn really hoped that Melissa was not still looking into the burglary and had done as she'd asked and dropped it. Not just for Annie's sake; there was still something David wasn't telling her about that night – she was sure of it. That was playing on her mind too. Whatever it was, she didn't want Melissa to find out.

Annie said, 'Are you okay?'

Robyn had more than one thing on her mind. 'No, not really. You're right, I told Gayle.' Strictly speaking, she hadn't told Gayle. Robyn eyed Olive. 'How did you know I told her?'

'David mentioned to Joe the good news, that you guys are moving into the boathouse together, and he mentioned it to me. Honestly, I thought you'd never leave, even though we'd done up the flat upstairs, ready for Duncan to move into.'

'Well, things sort of came to a head when Duncan moved out. The boathouse is now standing empty, and David was worried about that. I mean I don't see as there's anything to be concerned about. He has got a burglar alarm.' She looked at Annie, wondering if she was aware of that.

'Yeah, I heard he had one fitted. I didn't see the point. His house is really off the beaten track, and he left the place standing empty loads of times when he was playing away in hockey tournaments with no problems. Then he goes and has one installed when he's living there all the time, and his dad was even there too. Doesn't make sense.'

Robyn eyed her and pursed her lips. He'd had one fitted because he'd been burgled. What she had gleaned was that no one else knew about the burglary at David's house.

Annie lowered her voice. 'I think it has something to do with the burglary here at the shop, even though it was a couple of years ago.'

'What do you mean?'

'It shocked us, the community. I'd like to think that everyone knows everybody else, but I know that isn't true; there are a lot of tourists who come and stay in Aviemore, but even so, they're here for skiing and sight-seeing holidays, not going around robbing shops. That sort of thing just doesn't happen round here.'

But it didn't just happen at the shop, thought Robyn. How had they found David's boathouse? Annie was right: it was in the middle of nowhere. Worse still, David had been so unlucky to have all that cash around when it had happened.

She eyed Annie but kept her thoughts to herself.

'But anyway, I'm so happy for you. You're going to love setting up home together. I think it's about time.'

Robyn sighed. 'I know.'

'Lark Lodge is not that far. You can pop in and catch up with Gayle, Nick and Marty any time. I expect you told Gayle that.'

'I did. She admitted she wasn't surprised and had thought we'd have moved out sooner.'

'You were redecorating her place, though. It was easier to come home after work in the evenings, and weekends, being on site, so to speak, to get it done.'

'Yeah, I guess.' Although it was true that it was easier being there to finish the decorating, it was also an excuse to hang on as long as possible. It wasn't that she didn't want to move into the boathouse with David. Of course she wanted them to have their own home together. It was what she'd realised she was longing for when she'd gone to Evie's birthday party.

'Well, now it's all finished, you've got no excuses,' said Annie, smiling.

Robyn nodded. 'That's what David said.' She glanced over at Duncan, who was standing at the shop counter serving a customer.

Annie followed her gaze. 'Duncan is going to be okay.'

'I know.' Her reluctance to leave hadn't just been about Duncan having to leave the boathouse. It was that her reluctance to leave Lark Lodge ran deeper than she'd thought. It was more than missing the wonderful house, and its inhabitants – much more. They'd become her family. She thought of Melissa leaving home, making that break, and going to university, and imagined this was exactly how it felt – moving out of your family home.

Robyn wondered if that was how she'd felt when her mum had gone off travelling. She guessed her father had passed away. She'd seen the drawing of a funeral in her old diary. Had she rented out the family home – or sold it? Robyn didn't know. She still couldn't remember. It was June next month, which would mean the end of the summer term at St Andrews, where her mum still thought she was. That meant her deferment would be coming to an end too. The university would be contacting her to find out whether she was returning in September. That wouldn't be happening. Robyn had decided that when she moved into the boathouse, it would be time to stop avoiding her mum's letters, along with the redirection she'd put in place for mail from her mum, which was still being sent to the university.

Robyn thought of the letter with a cheque enclosed she'd received just before Easter. She'd been right: it was another invitation for her to join her mother on holiday in a country abroad – Sicily, this time. Her mother was getting ever closer – she was now in Europe, a short flight away. Robyn hadn't responded to the letter.

If her mum hadn't been out of the country for so long, Robyn knew that she would not have got away with the deceit. She imagined her mum would have taken a trip to the university after her letters went unanswered. Of course, she could have flown back home anyway to check on her. But the fact that all those cheques she'd sent had been cashed, even though Robyn had clearly never bothered to take her up on the offer to visit her abroad – not once – said that things couldn't have been exactly hunky-dory between them.

If that were the case, Robyn had resolved to change that. It was one thing in her past she wished she'd remembered – her mum, and what might have gone wrong in their relationship. How could she put it right if she didn't know what had happened between them?

She imagined that her mum would write to her again, once

the summer term ended next month, probably sending her another cheque and inviting her abroad again for a holiday. Robyn intended to reply to the last letter and tell her mum all about her new life, where she was, and that she'd dropped out of her university course. Perhaps her mum wouldn't care, as long as she was leading the life that made her happy. Robyn hoped so.

'So, are you all packed?' Annie asked, giving Olive a stroke. Olive had woken up and run over to Annie, happy to see another person who would give her lots of fusses.

Robyn nodded. 'Almost.'

'When is the big day?'

'Big day?'

'You know … moving day.'

'Oh, yes. Right.' For a moment, Robyn had thought she was referring to a wedding day. David hadn't proposed. The thought probably hadn't even crossed his mind – although it had crossed hers.

'You know, for a moment there, I thought you meant a wedding day.'

'Oh, ha ha! That is funny. Why would I say that? I wouldn't say that. No, not me.'

Robyn stared at her.

Annie had become flustered, looking anywhere but in her direction. Robyn's mouth dropped open. 'Oh, my god, he's going to propose – isn't he?'

Annie looked up sharply. 'Who? What? I really have absolutely no clue what you're talking about, I swear. I really don't. I did not say a word.'

She was getting flustered again, Robyn could tell.

Annie's shoulders sagged. 'Oh, god, I've ruined the surprise.

I really wish David had never told me. I was so excited about it, I knew I couldn't keep my mouth shut.'

'It's true, then?'

'Yes. That's why I expect he's been badgering you to move into the boathouse. It's where he wants to propose, on the little balcony overlooking the loch.'

Robyn stared off into space. She could just imagine it.

'I am so sorry for ruining the surprise.'

'Don't be.' Robyn ran over and gave her a hug. 'I don't like surprises.'

'But I think you would have liked that one.'

'I know. Oh, I am so excited.'

When she stood back, Annie said in earnest, 'You're going to have to practise looking surprised.'

'Huh?'

'When he pops the question.'

Robyn grinned. 'Oh, I can do that.' She suddenly thought about the letter she was going to write to her mum. *Just wait until she finds out her daughter is getting married*, she thought. *Then she'll have to come home from abroad for the wedding.*

Robyn had to ask, 'Do you know if David has planned the big day too?'

Annie slowly shook her head. 'No, thank god. I wouldn't want to spoil that surprise either.'

Robyn laughed.

'I get the idea that he thought you'd enjoy planning it.'

'I would. Oh, but I would.'

Annie laughed. 'I felt the same way when I got engaged to Joe.'

'We're going to be sisters – well, you'll be my sister-in-law, but sisters all the same!' Robyn never felt so happy. 'I don't think I've ever had a sister.'

'You don't think …?'

Robyn came back down to earth immediately. She shouldn't have said that, although it just occurred to her that she may, or may not, have siblings. For some reason, she'd assumed she hadn't. She looked sheepishly at Annie. David knew she'd lost her memory, but he clearly hadn't shared that fact with anybody else. And Robyn didn't want him to.

'Um, just a figure of speech,' Robyn said, quickly changing the subject. 'I've been thinking about Gayle. It was her birthday last month, soon after Evie's, and we didn't have a party. Even though she said she didn't want one, I feel bad that the day just came and went without doing anything special.'

They'd all had some wine and nibbles in the evening to celebrate while Gayle unwrapped some presents they'd bought her. Nick had been really thoughtful and had even bought a present for Gayle from Olive, which had been a nice touch. But it still bothered Robyn that she hadn't done anything really special for her best friend. She said as much.

Annie disagreed. 'You showed her the bedroom you'd redecorated, didn't you?'

'Yes, but I didn't make an occasion out of her special day.' Robyn sighed. 'I'd like to make up for it.'

Annie patted Olive on the head and sent her back to her cushion in the corner. 'What did you have in mind?'

Robyn grinned. 'I was thinking I could organise a party to celebrate the opening of Lark Lodge as a guesthouse. I've got some curtains and blinds still on order, but the interior décor is finished. And Marty has just finished landscaping the back garden. It looks stunning.'

Robyn thoughts turned to the garden. She told Annie it was now full of colourful flowers. The borders were overflowing with bright clusters of hardy lupins. Tall foxgloves stood proudly along the edges, their purple and white spires attracting bees to the garden. 'Marty also planted Scottish bluebells filling the gaps in the borders with their gentle blue hues.'

Annie said, 'The garden sounds wonderful. What about a garden party? It's nearly June. The weather is warmer, and we've had some lovely sunny days.'

'A garden party.' Robyn's eyes lit up. 'Oh, what a fantastic idea!'

'You could invite all her friends and family. Make it quite the event.'

Robyn doubted Gayle's brothers and sister would come, even if they were invited. Especially as the party would be a celebration of the new guesthouse in their former childhood home.

Annie said, 'Everyone will love the garden. The little wooden summerhouse at the end of the garden is a lovely touch.'

That had been Robyn's idea. It was painted sky blue, and looked a bit like a beach house, with double doors that opened on to a small veranda. Inside were some rattan chairs with flower print cushions and some throws. It was just perfect for sitting inside to read a book, or a chair could be taken outside to the little veranda to while away some time admiring the pretty garden.

Annie said, 'I just love the neat lawn and deep borders full of colourful shrubs and plants. It reminds me of some National Trust houses I've visited, with their beautiful formal gardens.'

The garden reminded Robyn of one house in particular.

Marty had got his inspiration and ideas for the back garden from the Rosses' holiday home. Gayle's back garden was nowhere near as big, but it still had the same look and feel, just on a smaller scale.

Annie said, 'It's like something out of a period drama. I can just imagine ladies from another era in their long dresses, strolling through the gardens or having high tea.'

Robyn smiled. 'Yes, I can just imagine that too.'

'I love period dramas. I think that was me in a past life,' Annie said, smiling ruefully, 'a lady living in a huge house, walking around a manicured garden and taking tea on the lawn.'

The thought of huge houses reminded Robyn that she had to be somewhere. She looked at her watch.

'What do you think you were in a previous life?' Annie asked.

Robyn found her handbag. 'Oh, some rich, beautiful heiress to a fortune,' she said off-handedly, putting her handbag over her shoulder and picking up her large notepad in case she needed to make some notes.

Annie giggled, 'You wish!'

Robyn stopped at the front door. She turned to Annie, looking at her quizzically. 'I wish what?'

'It's a figure of speech – as in, you should be so lucky.'

Robyn stared at her. 'Why would I want to be an heiress when I've got everything I've ever wanted right here?'

'But you just said ... oh, never mind.' Annie looked at her. 'Where are you going?'

Robyn opened the door to the shop. 'I don't know how long I'll be. I've got a new commission.'

'Sounds interesting, where is it?'

'It's at The Lake House.'

'The Lake House? Why does that sound familiar?'

'You've heard of the Rosses?'

'Oh, who hasn't? They've got a holiday home in the area—' Annie stopped. 'Oh, yes, I remember – that's its name.'

Robyn nodded. She decided not to tell Annie that she'd been to the house before, because of the circumstances – Marty's secret squatting.

Annie looked at her, wide-eyed. Robyn understood her surprise. The family were so wealthy that they were like celebrities in Aviemore, even though they weren't models or film stars, or anything remotely like that.

'You know, I think you're right,' said Annie.

'About what?'

'About being an heiress. It didn't do Eleanor Campbell-Ross any good. Look where it got her. She came to stay for Christmas in their amazing holiday home, then went skiing and had an accident.'

Robyn stared at her. She remembered watching the news about Eleanor Campbell-Ross from her hospital bed and thinking, *there but for the grace of god go I.*

Annie said, 'I heard the family haven't been back to The Lake House since the tragedy.'

Robyn wasn't surprised. She'd heard that too from Marty.

'How did the family know about you? Have they returned to The Lake House? Did they visit you here in the shop?'

Robyn shook her head. 'No. It was Marty, the gardener. He's still employed by them to look after the gardens. He must have put in a good word for me, if ever they need some interior design. And I guess they do.'

'So, is one of the Rosses meeting you at the house?'

'I presume so.' For some reason, Robyn felt nervous about the meeting, most likely because they were very rich – which was so silly. Rich people weren't any different to everybody else. But even so, she had butterflies in her stomach about finally coming face to face with one of them.

Robyn walked over to the shop door.

Annie called out, 'Good luck.'

Robyn reached for the door handle and hesitated.

Annie noticed. 'Everything all right?'

'I feel nervous.'

'Whatever for?' Annie sighed. 'They're only people, albeit rich people. Don't be intimidated.'

For a split second, she had a bizarre thought – that it wasn't a good idea. She should send Annie instead. She dismissed the thought and left.

41

Annie appeared by Robyn's side. 'You did it. It's everything I imagined it would be.'

'It was your idea.'

'Yes, but you organised the garden party.' Annie lifted a china cup to her lips. She paused. 'Everyone is having a wonderful time, aren't they? And we all dressed for the occasion.'

Robyn smiled as she looked about her. Annie was right: everyone was having a wonderful time, and they had definitely dressed for the occasion.

Gayle's mum was wearing her poshest frock, as she called it. Robyn could see her sitting on a wicker chair outside the summerhouse with a plate of finger sandwiches and a cup of tea. Duncan had joined her, looking very suave in a brown linen suit, pressed cream shirt, and trilby hat. He sat in the other wicker chair, chatting amiably to Doris. She had known him for years, but the bemused look on her face showed that she didn't remember. Robyn could empathise – not that she had dementia herself, but her memories hadn't come back as she'd expected.

She spotted Gayle walking across the lawn, welcoming the guests to her party. She stopped briefly to chat to Melissa. They were both wearing pretty summer dresses, strappy sandals, and gorgeous hats – or in Gayle's case, a lace fascinator.

Robyn had told Gayle it was her party, and she should invite her own friends, but Gayle had insisted that Melissa should be invited. She liked Melissa, and besides, she was now Gayle's friend too.

Robyn smiled as Brodie re-joined Melissa, handing her a glass of wine; they stood together, eyes only for each other. They'd both sat their finals and had vowed to attend each other's graduation ceremonies. Brodie had studied English at university. Books were the second love of his life – after Melissa, of course. He hoped to take over his grandfather's bookshop and write a novel in his spare time.

Melissa had told Robyn all about the little flat above the bookshop that Brodie's grandfather, Wilbur, had said they could move into if they wished.

They'd jumped at the offer. As young graduates just starting out, getting a mortgage, or even securing a rental property so they could live together would not be easy – and they knew it.

Robyn wanted to help do up the flat for them, at no charge, of course. They were her friends. Melissa and Brodie had thanked her for the offer, but they had decided they would do it themselves, spending their weekends redecorating. Robyn understood – it was something they wanted to do just the two of them, setting up their first home together.

Robyn hadn't ventured back to the bookshop since Melissa had taken her there after work one day to get a cup of coffee and ogle her favourite guy – young Brodie, the man she'd already decided she was going to marry.

Robyn had steered away from the bookshop – a place that

she knew had some connection to her past. It was something she'd concluded after she'd had some sort of flashback. She was sure she'd sat at the table in the window of the bookshop with someone. She wanted to steer away from her past; she had a feeling that there were things in it that were not good.

'The finger sandwiches were a nice touch, and the little cakes, scones and jam,' commented Annie. 'It's like afternoon tea.'

'That was the idea.' Robyn had found a catering company to supply all the food, along with the trestle tables and the marquee they'd set up on the lawn. The marquee had been expensive, but Robyn didn't want to take the chance that a rain shower would spoil the afternoon.

'Did you order the sunshine too?'

Robyn laughed. 'I would've if I could've. I obviously didn't need the marquee after all.'

'Oh, but it was a lovely idea. Besides, you never know, it could still rain.'

They both cast their eyes heavenward. There were some fluffy white clouds in the blue sky, but nothing dark, grey and ominous on the horizon.

Robyn's eyes roved back to Melissa. She was intent on practising law, and staying in Aviemore with Brodie, where she had grown up. There were a few legal practices in the area, and one in particular where she had secured a position to complete her training to qualify as a solicitor. They specialised in family law, but apparently they had dealt with a criminal case in the past, according to Melissa – an area she was most interested in. That was why she'd chosen to apply to them.

Robyn thought of what David had told her about an excellent local lawyer who had got him off a manslaughter charge after the burglary at his father's shop. Melissa had told her that when she started at the firm, she would get access to all their past cases, for research and learning purposes.

Robyn glanced over at David, who was chatting to Joe. Melissa had mentioned the name of the local law firm who had taken her on. Robyn was still undecided about whether to ask David in conversation who had represented him.

Annie asked, 'Why the frown?'

'It's nothing – really.'

Annie sighed. 'You can't get anything past your soon-to-be sister-in-law, you know.'

Oh, but I can, thought Robyn, still gazing in David's direction.

'I know what this is about.'

Robyn doubted that, but she turned to Annie and raised her eyebrows.

'It was your last night at Lark Lodge. I get it. This party is bittersweet, isn't it? I imagine it's more like a going-away party for you, even though you'll only be moving down the road.'

Robyn hadn't thought of that. 'Yes, you're right; it is, isn't it?'

'Come, let's walk.' They put their teacups down on the trestle table and walked along the cobbled path beside the flowerbeds. Annie took her hand and affectionately patted it. 'It's a chapter closing, and a new one opening. That's the way you've got to think about it. Have you written to your mum, telling her about you and David? It's a shame she couldn't be here.'

'Not yet. But I will.'

They passed Evie, who was sitting in the middle of the lawn, plaiting Olive's fur. Robyn smiled before her eyes drifted around to take in the other people gathered on the lawn, chatting amiably. Some guests she knew; others she did not. There were far more people there than Robyn had anticipated.

'You'd think royalty was coming to tea,' commented Annie. 'Reminds me a bit of Ascot, or those royal garden parties that are held at Buckingham Palace every year and the Palace of Holyroodhouse here in Scotland. I think word got out who else Gayle had invited. Perhaps her friends and neighbours were hoping to meet them.'

Robyn knew who Annie was talking about – Gayle's very rich but rather elusive neighbours, whose property backed on to hers – the Rosses.

'Shame you didn't get to meet them when you visited The Lake House last month for your new commission.'

Robyn was actually relieved, although she didn't tell Annie that. But she had been just as surprised as Annie when no one had turned up. Although in hindsight, she imagined they had far better things to do with their time than meet an interior designer in person. They had employees for that sort of thing. They were too busy running the Ross Corporation. But no employee had turned up either, nor a friend. It was just her and Marty, visiting the house again.

Annie said, 'It's odd, though, isn't it? Why go to the bother of having an interior designer spruce up The Lake House when they're never there? I mean they haven't been down for months, have they, not since that awful Christmas Day.'

Robyn nodded. 'No, they haven't.' The reason they both knew that for a fact was because Marty had told them. He was there most days, tending to their extensive gardens, so he would have seen a car or any tell-tale sign that someone was visiting.

'Perhaps they're thinking of selling up.'

Robyn came to an abrupt halt at that comment and swivelled

her head to look at Annie. 'No, they wouldn't do that!'

Annie looked taken aback at her reaction. 'How do you know? I mean, it's just a second home.' She shrugged. 'Probably in their case a third, fourth or even tenth home. I bet they've got holiday homes all over the world. It's a wonder they haven't forgotten all about it. You hear of that sort of thing where super-wealthy people buy up property, perhaps on a whim, or as an investment, and then they never set foot in the place, and the property ends up abandoned and falling into disrepair.'

'I won't let that happen – and neither will Marty!' Robyn wondered why she felt so strongly about the place. But she did feel an affinity to the house. It was very strange. She'd only visited twice. She wondered if perhaps she felt a connection with the Ross heiress, Eleanor, because she'd had an accident on Christmas Day too.

Annie sighed. 'Forget what I said. They haven't exactly abandoned the place – they are paying you and Marty to look after it.'

'But you're right, they haven't been back.'

'Yeah, that's why I was wondering what their plan was for the house. I mean, who could blame them if they never came back?'

They both stood in silence thinking about the tragedy.

'Makes you wonder how her family, her husband, have coped since.'

Robyn nodded solemnly. 'Yes, it does.'

'Maybe when you've worked your interior design magic on the place you'll find out.'

'What do you mean?'

'I expect one of the family will visit at some point to see how it's going.'

Robyn breathed a sigh. 'I suppose so.'

'Hey, you two – why the glum faces?' Joe appeared, putting an arm around his wife. 'It's a party!'

Annie playfully punched him in the arm. 'I know that!'

'Can I borrow you for a moment? Both of you?' Joe held up his camera. 'It's nearly time.'

Robyn looked at her watch. 'Crumbs – so it is.'

David was hot on Joe's heels, bringing up the rear with two glasses of champagne.

She eyed him. The business with Melissa starting her first job at the solicitor's firm, and what she might unearth if it was the one David had used, was still on her mind.

She took the glass of champagne, determined not to put a dampener on such a wonderful afternoon by thinking about the past. She looked at David. This was about their future, and nothing was going to stand in the way of that – certainly not anything or anybody in either of their pasts.

'Everything all right?' David asked, his expression one of concern.

Robyn guessed what he was thinking – she might get cold feet about leaving Lark Lodge after the party.

She thought of all the friends she'd made over the last six months – most especially here at Lark Lodge; friends she counted on like family. Had it really been that long since the car accident on Christmas Day? The time she'd spend at Lark Lodge had flown by, and she'd loved every second of it. But Annie was right: life moves on. And it was time her life moved on too.

She offered David a reassuring smile that she wasn't going to change her mind about leaving.

David leaned in to give her a kiss.

'Oh, get a room, why don't you!' Joe joked.

'They're getting a whole house, remember?' Annie commented, laughing.

David whispered, 'We're still on for tonight – right?'

Robyn whispered back, 'Of course we are.' Their bags were packed. After the party, they were moving into the boathouse. She thought of the surprise in store that Annie had inadvertently given away, and wondered when David was going to pop the question on the balcony overlooking the loch. Robyn felt goosebumps at the thought. She couldn't wait.

42

Robyn held her glass of champagne and fell in step with David, Joe, and Annie as they crossed the lawn. They collected Evie and Olive on their way and joined the snaking line of people leaving the back garden and filing down the path along the side of the house to the front lawn. Gayle's neighbour had kindly agreed to sit with Doris in the summerhouse during their mass exodus from the back garden. They all continued down the drive, the sound of friendly chatter and laughter surrounding them as they went, the air filled with anticipation.

Robyn turned to David. 'Gayle is in for such a surprise. I hope she likes it.'

'Me too. Fortunately, I don't think she missed me, Joe, Marty and Nick as the party got underway.'

'What – in this crowd?'

'To be honest, I didn't expect so many people.'

'Yeah, me neither. But she did invite all the neighbours.' Robyn didn't mention the neighbours in particular who hadn't turned up – the Rosses.

Behind her, Robyn heard Gayle's voice. 'What's going on? Why is everyone leaving?'

Robyn glanced over her shoulder and grinned at Gayle as she caught up with them.

'Nobody is leaving, Gayle.'

'But the party is in the back garden.'

Robyn exchange glances with Joe, Annie and David. Nick and Marty had joined them too. Everybody was in the know except Gayle. That was because Robyn had insisted on sending out the party invitations, which had included a little note about a pause in the party at four o'clock – a secret ceremony that every partygoer had to keep, well, a secret.

Everyone knew where they had to be, apart from Gayle, who looked quite bemused when everybody suddenly put down their plates and appeared to be leaving – albeit with a glass of bubbly to hand.

Gayle caught her expression. 'What are you up to?'

Robyn couldn't resist a playful wind-up. 'I'm not telling.'

Gayle wagged a finger at her. 'I hope you haven't gone to any more trouble on my account.'

Robyn wouldn't answer that.

'Honestly, Robyn,' Gayle continued, 'this garden party – I've never seen the like. I think it will be the talk of the town for weeks to come.'

'Oh, you have no idea,' Robyn replied, exchanging a knowing smile with Marty, Nick, David, Joe and Annie.

Some minutes later, everybody was gathered down the drive, forming a circle around something new in Gayle's front garden so that Gayle couldn't see what the big surprise was until they were all ready.

Robyn turned to Nick, 'Is Olive in position?'

Nick grinned. 'Oh, yes.'

'Position?' Gayle repeated, looking at the crowd of people. 'What in heaven's name is going on? You know this reminds me of one of those …' she clicked her fingers. 'What are they called … those sudden gatherings of people that's organised through social media.'

Marty grinned. 'Ah, you're talking about a flash mob.'

Robyn grinned too. 'Oh, Gayle. I can assure you that our little gathering is not going to suddenly break out into some sort of song and dance routine.'

'Then what are we all doing here?'

Robyn couldn't stop smiling. 'You'll see.'

Gayle glanced at Olive. 'What's that in her mouth?'

'Evie, sweetheart, go stand over there, like we practised,' said Annie.

'Practised?' Gayle frowned. 'What on earth …?'

Robyn waited for Evie to get into position, about a hundred yards away, then she shouted out, 'Ready everybody?'

A cheer went up on the crowd. Robyn started counting down and everybody joined in, 'Ten, nine, eight …' as they did so the crowd started to move aside, revealing something new in the front garden under a tarpaulin.

'What is that?' exclaimed Gayle, although she could hardly be heard over the sound of the countdown.

'… four …. three … two … one!'

'Now, Evie!'

Evie yelled, 'Olive – come!'

With the tie in her jaws, Olive ran as fast as she could towards Evie, pulling the tie with her. And as she did so, the tarpaulin came off, revealing the newly erected guesthouse sign at the entrance to Lark Lodge. Robyn had designed it herself.

She stood with bated breath, a hushed silence enveloping the party guests as Gayle stepped forward to examine the sign.

She read it out loud. '*Lark Lodge. Welcome to Gayle's guesthouse, your home away from home.*'

The gold lettering stood out against the deep green background. And painted on the sign was a silhouette of two birds perched on a branch in front of a black-and-white sketch of Gayle's lovely home.

'Oh, Robyn,' Gayle said, staring at the sign. 'I don't know what to say.'

'Please say you like it.'

Gayle said, 'Like it? What were you thinking?' Inexplicably, Gayle started to cry.

Robyn's smile faded in an instant. She looked from Nick to Marty. It had been her idea, a parting gift before she left Lark Lodge, and they'd gone along with it, encouraging her go and get it made. It had been installed that afternoon, and Robyn had made sure that Gayle was busy in the back garden, checking everything was okay for her guests to arrive.

David and Joe had disappeared from the party to sort out covering it with the tarpaulin, preparing for the big reveal.

'Oh, my god. I've made the biggest mistake, haven't I? We can take it down.'

'No!' Gayle vehemently shook her head. 'Robyn don't do that. I love it. I adore it. I couldn't have chosen better myself. It's just—'

'Do you hear that?' someone called out, 'She loves it!'

A cheer went up.

Nick shouted out, 'A toast to the brand new guesthouse in Aviemore!'

Another cheer followed. Then everyone emptied their glasses.

'Everyone gather round!' said Joe.

Annie muttered, 'He does rather fancy himself as a professional photographer.'

Joe set up the tripod. 'Let's make it a good one. This is going to be sent off to the local paper.'

Robyn grinned. It had been David's idea to give the place a bit of free advertising and get things rolling so that hopefully Gayle would have some new guests very soon.

Everyone gathered around, laughing and smiling. Robyn looked over at Gayle. She'd been about to say something. Robyn swapped places with David so that she stood beside Gayle. 'What were you going to say?' she whispered as Joe fiddled with the camera on the tripod, waving his hand at people to move closer so that everybody was in the shot.

'I just … I just can't believe we've got here – the guesthouse is officially opened, and … and you're leaving.'

'I know. Neither can I. I think living here has been the best six months of my life. I've got a job I love, made new friends, met David.'

Gayle smiled. 'But life moves on.'

'Yes.' She had to acknowledge that a part of her wished it didn't. She suspected that Gayle felt the same way too. As Annie had rightly pointed out, the moment was bittersweet.

'You still don't remember, do you, about your past?' Gayle whispered.

'No.'

'I get the feeling that things may not have been good in your past life.'

'I get that feeling too.'

Gayle took her hand. 'I think you should count it as a blessing, then, that you can't remember.'

Robyn thought so too.

'The best thing about the past, Robyn, is that we can leave it right there and move on.'

Robyn sincerely hoped so.

A sudden gust of wind caught everyone by surprise. People grabbed at hats and hems of skirts just as Joe snapped the photo.

Gayle commented, 'That's the wind of change.' She turned to Robyn as everybody started dispersing, walking back up the front lawn towards the house. Gayle gave her a hug.

It felt like goodbye.

'Now, as they say, don't be a stranger.'

'Of course I won't. I'll be back so often, you'll think I never left.'

Gayle grinned.

'And I'll be the last to leave the party.'

Gayle looked over at David. 'I don't think you will.'

Robyn pursed her lips. She was right.

'Now, who wants a tour of the new guesthouse?' Gayle called out as she winked at Robyn.

Robyn watched her stroll up the drive to her guests.

Nick and Marty were still standing by the sign, along with David. Nick said, 'Do you need some help with your cases?'

David replied, 'No, I packed them in my Dad's car earlier.'

Robyn was aware of that. She knew why. She expected he was afraid she might bottle out and decide to spend one more night at Lark Lodge.

'So, I guess this is it,' Nick said to Robyn. He held open his arms. 'Like Gayle said, don't be a stranger.'

'I won't.'

They hugged. Then Nick shook hands with David.

Marty stepped up next. 'It's going to be weird without you. I think Gayle will still be setting two more places at breakfast and dinner for you guys, for a while.'

Robyn smiled ruefully. 'I know. But hey, maybe it won't be long, and she'll have two more guests.'

Marty said, 'I'm sure.'

Robyn asked, 'Will I see you when I'm up at The Lake House?'

Marty nodded. 'I'm there most days.'

She gave him a hug, then watched Marty heading at pace up the front lawn to join Nick and Gayle.

'Well, I guess that leaves just you and me,' said David.

A whine interrupted David.

Robyn grinned. 'Um, not quite.'

They both turned to look at Olive, who was sitting by their feet, sensing that something was up. Robyn smiled down at her. 'I guess she wants a goodbye too.'

After plenty of fusses, and a big well done for playing her part in the big reveal, they stood hand in hand, watching Olive running up to the house. Gayle had opened the front door. She turned and waved goodbye. They both waved back.

Robyn turned to look at the sign. 'I wonder who the first guests will be.'

'I imagine it won't be long and she'll get some bookings, and you'll soon find out.'

Later that evening, Nick was going to reveal another surprise for Gayle – they'd all chipped in to pay for a tech whiz to set up Gayle's very own website to advertise her guesthouse and take bookings.

Another gust of wind nearly lifted Robyn's posh hat right off her head. She took the hat off and let her hair fly.

'It's going to take a bit of getting used to.'

Robyn turned around to face him. 'I know. It's going to be strange not turning up here after work.'

'No, I meant your hair.'

'Oh, right.' Robyn smiled shyly, still feeling a bit self-conscious. Last night, she'd asked a rather surprised Gayle to dye it blonde. She knew Joe would be taking a photo at the garden party to go into the local paper – free advertising for the newly opened guesthouse in Aviemore. The trouble was that Robyn didn't want her photo in the paper, even though she wasn't sure why. There was no getting out of it, but she could change her appearance.

'So, shall we head off? Or do you want a tour of the guesthouse?' David asked. 'I have to say, the house looks amazing, but I think I'll be pleased if I don't see another paintbrush or paint tin for quite some time.'

Robyn just smiled. She thought that perhaps she shouldn't let on just yet that she already had some ideas for redecorating David's bachelor pad and turning it into a family home.

David gave her hand an affectionate squeeze. 'Come on.'

The car was waiting on the drive, all packed and ready to go. Duncan had surprised David by giving it to them as a moving-in present. He'd said he had no need of it now he lived above the shop. He'd insisted that David took it, assuring them that if he did need some wheels, he still had the old delivery van.

A moment later, they were in the car. As they turned out of the drive, Robyn glanced at the new guesthouse sign and shivered.

A thought came out of nowhere – *the winds of change are coming.* She had a feeling that things were about to change, and would never be the same again.

The Scottish Highlands Series continues in

Return to the Lake House

Paperback and Kindle eBook coming soon.

If you enjoyed *The Secrets of the Glen* I would be grateful if you would leave a review on Amazon.

For further details about the author and her novels please visit the author's website.

www.elisedarcy.com

Also by Elise Darcy

The Sunrise Coast Series

New Beginnings at the Harbour Inn

The Secret of the Summerhouse

The Cottage by the Sea

The Guest House at Shingle Cove

The Houseboat by the Quay

Return to Willow Tree Cottage

The Bookshop of Memories

The Beach House

A Summer to Remember

The Living Apart Together Series

Living Apart Together

It Takes 2 to Tango

Dear John

Love on the Rooftop

Standalone Novels

Lola & The Man

A Mallorcan Affair

We'll Meet Again

The Villa in Sicily

Printed in Dunstable, United Kingdom

80285555R00224